ARU SHAH AND THE
END OF TIME

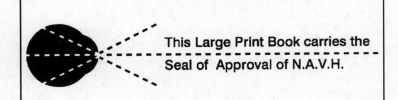

This Large Print Book carries the
Seal of Approval of N.A.V.H.

A PANDAVA NOVEL, BOOK 1

Aru Shah and the End of Time

Roshani Chokshi

THORNDIKE PRESS
A part of Gale, a Cengage Company

Farmington Hills, Mich • San Francisco • New York • Waterville, Maine
Meriden, Conn • Mason, Ohio • Chicago

Recommended for Middle Readers.
Copyright © 2018 by Roshani Chokshi.
Introduction copyright © 2018 by Rick Riordan.
Thorndike Press, a part of Gale, a Cengage Company.

ALL RIGHTS RESERVED
Thorndike Press® Large Print The Literacy Bridge.
The text of this Large Print edition is unabridged.
Other aspects of the book may vary from the original edition.
Set in 16 pt. Plantin.

LIBRARY OF CONGRESS CIP DATA ON FILE.
CATALOGUING IN PUBLICATION FOR THIS BOOK
IS AVAILABLE FROM THE LIBRARY OF CONGRESS.

ISBN-13: 978-1-4328-4981-8 (hardcover)

Published in 2018 by arrangement with Disney-Hyperion, an imprint of Disney Group

Printed in the United States of America
1 2 3 4 5 6 7 22 21 20 19 18

To my sisters:
Niv, Victoria, Bismah,
Monica, and Shraya
We really need a theme song.

CONTENTS

ARU SHAH IS ABOUT TO EXPLODE YOUR HEAD

Have you ever read a book and thought, *Wow, I wish I'd written that!*?

For me, *Aru Shah and the End of Time* is one of those books. It has everything I like: humor, action, great characters, and, of course, awesome mythology! But this is not a book I could have written. I just don't have the expertise or the insider's knowledge to tackle the huge, incredible world of Hindu mythology, much less make it so fun and reader-friendly.

Fortunately for all of us, Roshani Chokshi does.

If you are not familiar with Hindu mythology — wow, are you in for a treat! You thought Zeus, Ares, and Apollo were wild? Wait until you meet Hanuman and Urvashi. You thought Riptide was a cool weapon? Check out this fine assortment of divine *astras* — maces, swords, bows, and nets woven from lightning. Take your pick. You're

11

going to need them. You thought Medusa was scary? She's got nothing on the *nagini* and *rakshas*. Aru Shah, a salty and smart seventh-grade girl from Atlanta, is about to plunge into the midst of all this craziness, and her adventure will make your head explode in the best possible way.

If you already know Hindu mythology, you're about to have the most entertaining family reunion ever. You're going to see lots of your favorites — gods, demons, monsters, villains, and heroes. You're going to soar up to the heavens and down into the Underworld. And no matter how many of these myths you already know, I'll bet you a pack of Twizzlers you're going to learn something new.

Can you tell I'm excited to share this book with you? Yeah, I'm pretty excited.

So what are we waiting for? Aru Shah is hanging out in the Museum of Ancient Indian Art and Culture, where her mom works. Autumn break has started, and Aru is pretty sure it's going to be a boring day.

Yikes. She is SO wrong.

Rick Riordan

ONE:
IN WHICH ARU REGRETS OPENING THE DOOR

The problem with growing up around highly dangerous things is that after a while you just get used to them.

For as long as she could remember, Aru had lived in the Museum of Ancient Indian Art and Culture. And she knew full well that the lamp at the end of the Hall of the Gods was not to be touched.

She could mention "the lamp of destruction" the way a pirate who had tamed a sea monster could casually say, *Oh, you mean ole Ralph here?* But even though she was used to the lamp, she had never once lit it. That would be against the rules. The rules she went over every Saturday, when she led the afternoon visitors' tour.

Some folks may not like the idea of working on a weekend, but it never felt like work to Aru.

It felt like a ceremony.

Like a secret.

15

She would don her crisp scarlet vest with its three honeybee buttons. She would imitate her mother's museum-curator voice, and people — this was the best part of all — would *listen.* Their eyes never left her face. Especially when she talked about the cursed lamp.

Sometimes she thought it was the most fascinating thing she ever discussed. A cursed lamp is a much more interesting topic than, say, a visit to the dentist. Although one could argue that both are cursed.

Aru had lived at the museum for so long, it kept no secrets from her. She had grown up reading and doing her homework beneath the giant stone elephant at the entrance. Often she'd fall asleep in the theater and wake up just before the crackling self-guided tour recording announced that India became independent from the British in 1947. She even regularly hid a stash of candy in the mouth of a four-hundred-year-old sea dragon statue (she'd named it Steve) in the west wing. Aru knew everything about everything in the museum. Except one thing . . .

The lamp. For the most part, it remained a mystery.

"It's not quite a lamp," her mother,

16

renowned curator and archaeologist Dr. K. P. Shah, had told her the first time she showed it to Aru. "We call it a *diya*."

Aru remembered pressing her nose against the glass case, staring at the lump of clay. As far as cursed objects went, this was by far the most boring. It was shaped like a pinched hockey puck. Small markings, like bite marks, crimped the edges. And yet, for all its normal-ness, even the statues filling the Hall of the Gods seemed to lean away from the lamp, giving it a wide berth.

"Why can't we light it?" she had asked her mother.

Her mother hadn't met her gaze. "Sometimes light illuminates things that are better left in the dark. Besides, you never know who is watching."

Well, Aru had watched. She'd been watching her entire life.

Every day after school she would come home, hang her backpack from the stone elephant's trunk, and creep toward the Hall of the Gods.

It was the museum's most popular exhibit, filled with a hundred statues of various Hindu gods. Her mother had lined the walls with tall mirrors so visitors could see the artifacts from all angles. The mirrors were "vintage" (a word Aru had used when she

17

traded Burton Prater a greenish penny for a whopping two dollars and half a Twix bar). Because of the tall crape myrtles and elms standing outside the windows, the light that filtered into the Hall of the Gods always looked a little muted. Feathered, almost. As if the statues were wearing crowns of light.

Aru would stand at the entrance, her gaze resting on her favorite statues — Lord Indra, the king of the heavens, wielding a thunderbolt; Lord Krishna, playing his flutes; the Buddha, sitting with his spine straight and legs folded in meditation — before her eyes would inevitably be drawn to the diya in its glass case.

She would stand there for minutes, waiting for something . . . anything that would make the next day at school more interesting, or make people notice that she, Aru Shah, wasn't just another seventh grader slouching through middle school, but someone *extraordinary. . . .*

Aru was waiting for magic.

And every day she was disappointed.

"Do something," she whispered to the god statues. It was a Monday morning, and she was still in her pajamas. "You've got plenty of time to do something awesome, because I'm on autumn break."

The statues did nothing.

Aru shrugged and looked out the window. The trees of Atlanta, Georgia, hadn't yet realized it was October. Only their top halves had taken on a scarlet-and-golden hue, as if someone had dunked them halfway in a bucket of fire and then plopped them back on the lawn.

As Aru had expected, the day was on its way to being uneventful. That should have been her first warning. The world has a tendency to trick people. It likes to make a day feel as bright and lazy as sun-warmed honey dripping down a jar as it waits until your guard is down. . . .

And that's when it strikes.

Moments before the visitor alarm rang, Aru's mom had been gliding through the cramped two-bedroom apartment connected to the museum. She seemed to be reading three books at a time while also conversing on the phone in a language that sounded like a chorus of tiny bells. Aru, on the other hand, was lying upside down on the couch and pelting pieces of popcorn at her, trying to get her attention.

"Mom. Don't say anything if you can take me to the movies."

Her mom laughed gracefully into the

phone. Aru scowled. Why couldn't *she* laugh like that? When Aru laughed, she sounded like she was choking on air.

"Mom. Don't say anything if we can get a dog. A Great Pyrenees. We can name him Beowoof!"

Now her mother was nodding with her eyes closed, which meant that she was *sincerely* paying attention. Just not to Aru.

"Mom. Don't say anything if I —"

Breeeeep!

Breeeeep!

Breeeeep!

Her mother lifted a delicate eyebrow and stared at Aru. *You know what to do.* Aru did know what to do. She just didn't want to do it.

She rolled off the couch and Spider-Man–crawled across the floor in one last bid to get her mother's attention. This was a difficult feat considering that the floor was littered with books and half-empty chai mugs. She looked back to see her mom jotting something on a notepad. Slouching, Aru opened the door and headed to the stairs.

Monday afternoons at the museum were quiet. Even Sherrilyn, the head of museum security and Aru's long-suffering babysitter on the weekends, didn't come in on Mondays. Any other day — except Sunday, when

20

the museum was closed — Aru would help hand out visitor stickers. She would direct people to the various exhibits and point out where the bathrooms were. Once she'd even had the opportunity to yell at someone when they'd patted the stone elephant, which had a very distinct DO NOT TOUCH sign (in Aru's mind, this applied to everyone who wasn't her).

On Mondays she had come to expect occasional visitors seeking temporary shelter from bad weather. Or people who wanted to express their concern (in the gentlest way possible) that the Museum of Ancient Indian Art and Culture honored the devil. Or sometimes just the FedEx man needing a signature for a package.

What she did not expect when she opened the door to greet the new visitors was that they would be three students from Augustus Day School. Aru experienced one of those elevator-stopping-too-fast sensations. A low *whoosh* of panic hit her stomach as the three students stared down at her and her Spider-Man pajamas.

The first, Poppy Lopez, crossed her tan, freckled arms. Her brown hair was pulled back in a ballerina bun. The second, Burton Prater, held out his hand, where an ugly penny sat in his palm. Burton was short and pale, and his striped black-and-yellow shirt made him look like an unfortunate bumblebee. The third, Arielle Reddy — the prettiest girl in their class, with her dark brown skin and shiny black hair — simply glared.

"I knew it," said Poppy triumphantly. "You told everyone in math class that your mom was taking you to France for break."

That's what Mom had promised, Aru thought.

Last summer, Aru's mother had curled up on the couch, exhausted from another trip overseas. Right before she fell asleep, she had squeezed Aru's shoulder and said, *Perhaps I'll take you to Paris in the fall, Aru. There's a café along the Seine River where you can hear the stars come out before they dance in the night sky. We'll go to boulangeries and museums, sip coffee from tiny cups, and spend hours in the gardens.*

That night Aru had stayed awake dreaming of narrow winding streets and gardens so fancy that even their flowers looked haughty. With that promise in mind, Aru had cleaned her room and washed the dishes without complaint. And at school, the promise had become her armor. All the other students at Augustus Day School had vacation homes in places like the Maldives or Provence, and they complained when

22

their yachts were under repair. The promise of Paris had brought Aru one tiny step closer to belonging.

Now, Aru tried not to shrink under Poppy's blue-eyed gaze. "My mom had a top secret mission with the museum. She couldn't take me."

That was partly true. Her mom never took her on work trips.

Burton threw down the green penny. "You cheated me. I gave you two bucks!"

"And you got a *vintage* penny —" started Aru.

Arielle cut her off. "We know you're lying, Aru Shah. That's what you are: a *liar*. And when we go back to school, we're going to tell everyone —"

Aru's insides squished. When she'd started at Augustus Day School last month, she'd been hopeful. But that had been short-lived.

Unlike the other students, she didn't get driven to school in a sleek black car. She didn't have a home "offshore." She didn't have a study room or a sunroom, just *a* room, and even she knew that her room was really more like a closet with delusions of grandeur.

But what she did have was imagination. Aru had been daydreaming her whole life. Every weekend, while she waited for her mom to come home, she would concoct a story: her mother was a spy, an ousted princess, a sorceress.

Her mom claimed she never wanted to go on business trips, but they were a necessity to keep the museum running. And when she came home and forgot about things — like Aru's chess games or choir practice — it wasn't because she didn't care, but because she was too busy juggling the state of war and peace and art.

So at Augustus Day School, whenever the other kids asked, Aru told tales. Like the ones she told herself. She talked about cities she'd never visited and meals she'd never eaten. If she arrived with scuffed-up shoes, it was because her old pair had been sent to Italy for repair. She'd mastered that delicate condescending eyebrow everyone else had, and she deliberately mispronounced the names of stores where she bought her clothes, like the French *Tar-Jay,* and the German *Vahl-Mahrt.* If that failed, she'd just sniff and say, "Trust me, you wouldn't recognize the brand."

And in this way, she had fit in.

For a while, the lies had worked. She'd even been invited to spend a weekend at the lake with Poppy and Arielle. But Aru had ruined everything the day she was caught sneaking from the car-pool line. Arielle had asked which car was hers. Aru pointed at one, and Arielle's smile turned thin. "That's funny. Because that's my driver's car."

Arielle was giving Aru that same sneer now.

"You told us you have an elephant," said Poppy.

Aru pointed at the stone elephant behind her. "I do!"

"You said that you rescued it from India!"

"Well, Mom said it was *salvaged* from a temple, which is fancy talk for *rescue* —"

"And you said you have a cursed lamp," said Arielle.

Aru saw the red light on Burton's phone: steady and unblinking. He was recording her! She panicked. What if the video went online? She had two possible choices: 1) She could hope the universe might take pity on her and allow her to burst into flames before homeroom, or 2) She could change her name, grow a beard, and move away.

Or, to avoid the situation entirely . . .

She could show them something impossible.

"The cursed lamp is real," she said. "I can prove it."

Two:
Oops

It was four p.m. when Aru and her three classmates walked together into the Hall of the Gods.

Four p.m. is like a basement. Wholly innocent in theory. But if you really think about a basement, it is cement poured over restless earth. It has smelly, unfinished spaces, and wooden beams that cast too-sharp shadows. It is something that says *almost, but not quite.* Four p.m. feels that way, too. Almost, but not quite afternoon anymore. Almost, but not quite evening yet. And it is the way of magic and nightmares to choose those almost-but-not-quite moments and wait.

"Where's your mom, anyway?" asked Poppy.

"In France," said Aru, trying to hold her chin up. "I couldn't go with her because I had to take care of the museum."

"She's probably lying again," said Burton.

26

"She's *definitely* lying. That's the only thing she's good at," said Arielle.

Aru wrapped her arms around herself. She was good at lots of things, if only people would notice. She was good at memorizing facts she had heard just once. She was good at chess, too, to the point where she might have gone to the state championship if Poppy and Arielle hadn't told her *Nobody joins chess, Aru. You can't do that.* And so Aru had quit the chess team. She used to be good at tests, too. But now, every time she sat down to take a test, all she could think of was how expensive the school was (it was costing her mom a fortune), and how everyone was judging her shoes, which were popular last year but not this year. Aru *wanted* to be noticed. But she kept getting noticed for all the wrong reasons.

"I thought you said you had a condo downtown, but this dump was the address in the school directory," sniffed Arielle. "So you actually live *in* a museum?"

Yep.

"No? Look around — do you see my room?"

It's upstairs. . . .

"If you don't live here, then why are you wearing pajamas?"

"Everyone wears pj's during the daytime

in England," said Aru.

Maybe.

"It's what royalty does."

If I were royalty, I would.

"Whatever, Aru."

The four of them stood in the Hall of the Gods. Poppy wrinkled her nose. "Why do your gods have so many hands?"

The tops of Aru's ears turned red. "It's just how they are."

"Aren't there, like, a thousand gods?"

"I don't know," said Aru.

And this time she was telling the truth. Her mother had said that the Hindu gods were numerous, but they didn't stay as one person all the time. Sometimes they were reincarnated — their soul was reborn in someone else. Aru liked this idea. Sometimes she wondered who she might have been in another life. Maybe that version of Aru would have known how to vanquish the beast that was the seventh grade.

Her classmates ran through the Hall of the Gods. Poppy jutted out her hip, flicked her hands in imitation of one of the statues, then started laughing. Arielle pointed at the full-bodied curves of the goddesses and rolled her eyes. Heat crawled through Aru's stomach.

She wanted all the statues to shatter on

28

the spot. She wished they weren't so . . . naked. So different.

It reminded her of last year, when her mother had taken her to the sixth-grade honors banquet at her old school. Aru had worn what she thought was her prettiest outfit: a bright blue *salwar kameez* flecked with tiny star-shaped mirrors and embroidered with thousands of silver threads. Her mother had worn a deep red sari. Aru had felt like part of a fairy tale. At least until the moment they had entered the banquet hall, and every gaze had looked too much like pity. Or embarrassment. One of the girls had loudly whispered, *Doesn't she know it isn't Halloween?* Aru had faked a stomachache to leave early.

"Stop it!" she said now, when Burton started poking at Lord Shiva's trident.

"Why?"

"Because . . . Because there are cameras! And when my mom comes back, she'll tell the government of India and they'll come after you."

Lie, lie, lie. But it worked. Burton stepped back.

"So where's this lamp?" asked Arielle.

Aru marched to the back of the exhibit. The glass case winked in the early evening light. Beneath it, the diya looked wrapped in shadows. Dusty and dull.

"That's *it*?" said Poppy. "That looks like something my brother made in kindergarten."

"The museum acquired the Diya of Bharata after 1947, when India gained its independence from Britain," Aru said in her best impression of her mother's voice. "It is believed that the Lamp of Bharata once resided in the temple of" — *donotmispronounceKurekshetra* — "Koo-rook-shet-ra —"

"*Kooroo* what? Weird name. Why was it there?" asked Burton.

"Because that is the site of the Mahabharata War."

"The *what* war?"

Aru cleared her throat and went into museum attendant mode.

"The Mahabharata is one of two ancient poems. It was written in Sanskrit, an ancient Indic language that is no longer spoken." Aru paused for effect. "The Mahabharata tells the story of a civil war between the five Pandava brothers and their one hundred cousins —"

"One *hundred* cousins?" said Arielle. "That's impossible."

Aru ignored her.

"Legend says that lighting the Lamp of

30

Bharata awakens the Sleeper, a demon who will summon Lord Shiva, the fearsome Lord of Destruction, who will dance upon the world and bring an end to Time."

"A dance?" scoffed Burton.

"A cosmic dance," said Aru, trying to make it sound better.

When she thought of Lord Shiva dancing, she imagined someone stomping their feet on the sky. Cracks appearing in the clouds like lightning. The whole world breaking and splintering apart.

But it was clear her classmates were picturing someone doing the Cotton-Eyed Joe.

"So if you light the lamp, the world ends?" asked Burton.

Aru glanced at the lamp, as if it might consider contributing a few words. But it stayed silent, as lamps are wont to do. "Yes."

Arielle's lip curled. "So do it. If you're telling the truth, then do it."

"If I'm telling the truth — which I am, by the way — then do you have any idea what it could do?"

"Don't try to get out of this. Just light it once. I dare you."

Burton held up his phone. Its red light taunted her.

Aru swallowed. If her mom were down

31

here, she would drag her away by the ears. But she was upstairs getting ready to go away — yet again. Honestly, if the lamp was so dangerous, then why keep leaving her alone with it? Yeah, Sherrilyn was there. But Sherrilyn spent most of the time watching *Real Housewives of Atlanta.*

Maybe it wouldn't be a big deal. She could just light a small flame, then blow it out. Or, instead, maybe she could break the glass case and act like she'd been cursed. She could start zombie-walking. Or Spider-Man–crawling. They'd all be scared enough never to talk about what had happened.

Please, oh, please, I'll never lie again, I promise.

She repeated this in her head as she reached for the glass case and lifted it. As soon as the glass was removed, thin red beams of light hit the lamp. If a single strand of hair fell on any of those laser beams, a police car would come rushing to the museum.

Poppy, Arielle, and Burton inhaled sharply at the same time. Aru felt smug. *See? I told you it was important.* She wondered if she could just stop there. Maybe this would be enough. And then Poppy leaned forward.

"Get it over with," she said. "I'm bored."

Aru punched in the security code — her

birthday — and watched as the red beams disappeared. The air mingled with the scent of the clay diya. It smelled like the inside of a temple: all burnt things and spices.

"Just tell the truth, Aru," said Arielle. "If you do, all you have to do is pay us ten dollars each and we won't post the video of you getting caught in your own stupid lie."

But Aru knew that wouldn't be the end of it. Between a demon that could end the world and a seventh-grade girl, Aru (and probably most people) would choose the demon any day.

Without the red beams on it, the lamp felt dangerous. As if it had somehow sensed there was one less barrier. Cold stitched up Aru's spine, and her fingers felt numb. The small metal dish in the middle of the lamp looked a lot like an unblinking eye. Staring straight at her.

"I — I don't have a match," said Aru, taking a step back.

"I do." Poppy held out a green lighter. "I got it from my brother's car."

Aru reached for the lighter. She flicked the little metal wheel, and a tiny flame erupted. Her breath caught. *Just a quick light.* Then she could enact Plan Melodramatic Aru and get herself out of this mess and *never ever ever* lie again.

As she brought the flame closer to the lamp, the Hall of the Gods grew dark, as if a switch had turned off all the natural light. Poppy and Arielle moved closer. Burton tried to get closer, too, but Poppy shoved him away.

"Aru . . ."

A voice seemed to call out to her from *inside* the clay lamp.

She almost dropped the lighter, but her fist clenched around it just in time. She couldn't look away from the lamp. It seemed to pull her closer and closer.

"Aru, Aru, Aru —"

"Just get it over with, Shah!" screeched Arielle.

The red light on Burton's phone blinked in the corner of her vision. It promised a horrific year, cafeteria coleslaw in her locker, her mother's face crumpling in disappointment. But maybe if she did this, if by some stroke of luck she managed to trick Arielle and Poppy and Burton, maybe they'd let her sit beside them at lunch. Maybe she wouldn't have to hide behind her stories because her own life would finally be *enough*.

So she did it.

She brought the flame to the lip of the diya.

34

When her finger brushed the clay, a strange thought burst into Aru's head. She remembered watching a nature documentary about deep-sea creatures. How some of them used bait, like a glowing orb, to attract their prey. The moment a fish dared to swim toward the little light floating in the water, the sea creature would snatch it up with huge gaping jaws. That was how the lamp felt: a small halo of brightness held out by a monster crouching in the shadows. . . .

A trick.

The moment the flame caught, light exploded behind Aru's eyes. A shadow unfurled from the lamp, its spine arching and reaching. It made a horrible sound — was that laughter? She couldn't shake the noise from her head. It clung to her thoughts like an oily residue. It was as if all the silence had been scraped off and thrown somewhere else.

Aru stumbled back as the shadow thing limped out of the lamp. Panic dug into her bones. She tried to blow out the candle, but the flame didn't budge. Slowly, the shadow grew into a nightmare. It was tall and spidery, horned and fanged and furred.

"Oh, Aru, Aru, Aru . . . what have you done?"

THREE:
WAKE UP

Aru woke up on the floor. The lights flickered. Something about the room smelled off, like it was rusting. She heaved herself up on her elbows, eyes seeking the lamp. But it was *gone.* There was no sign that it had even been there except for the glass shards on the floor. Aru craned her neck to look behind her. . . .

All the statues were facing her.

Ice trickled down her spine.

"Poppy?" she called, pushing herself to a stand. "Arielle? Burton?"

That's when she saw them.

All three were still huddled together. They looked like a movie that had been paused in the middle of a fight scene. Poppy's hand was on Burton's chest. He was on his heels, tipping backward, about to fall. Arielle's eyes were screwed shut, her mouth open in a silent scream. They were suspended in time. Aru reached out and touched them.

Their skin was warm. A pulse leaped at each of their throats. But they didn't move. *Couldn't* move.

What had happened?

Her gaze snagged on the red light in Burton's pocket. The phone. Maybe she could rewind the recording. But the phone wouldn't budge from his pocket. Everything was frozen. Except her.

This was a dream. It had to be. She pinched herself.

"Ow!" she said, wincing.

She was definitely awake. In a way, so were her classmates. But then, how was everything so . . . still? A creaking sound echoed outside the Hall of the Gods. She stood up straighter. It sounded a lot like a door.

"Mom?" she whispered, running out. Her mother must have heard the noise and come downstairs. She'd know what to do.

At the entrance to the Hall of the Gods, Aru saw three things that made no sense:

1. Her mother was frozen, too, both feet off the ground as if she'd been caught in mid-jog. Her black hair hadn't even fallen against her back. Her eyes and mouth were open wide with panic.
2. The whole room looked strange and

lightless and flat. Because *nothing* had a shadow.
3. The creaking sound hadn't come from the door. It had come from the elephant.

Aru watched, stuck somewhere between awe and horror, as the stone elephant that had been standing in the museum for decades suddenly sank to the ground. It lifted its trunk — the same trunk Aru had been using as a backpack hook for years — to its forehead. In one swift, creaking movement, its jaw unhinged.

Panicked, Aru ran toward her mom. She reached for her hand, trying to yank her out of the air. "Mom! The elephant is possessed. You *really* need to wake up!"

Her mom didn't move. Aru followed her gaze. She'd been staring straight at the Hall of the Gods the moment she was frozen.

"Mom?"

A voice boomed from the hollow of the elephant. Deep and rough and wizened. Aru shrank.

"WHO HAS DARED TO LIGHT THE LAMP?" called the voice. It was as dark as a thunderstorm. Aru thought bolts of lightning might shoot out of the elephant's mouth, which, under any other circumstance, would have been very exciting. "WHO HAS DARED TO WAKE THE SLEEPER FROM HIS SLUMBER?"

Aru shuddered. "I — I did . . . but I didn't mean to!"

"YOU LIE, WARRIOR! AND FOR THAT I AM SUMMONED."

The sound of flapping wings echoed from the elephant's open mouth. Aru gulped.

This was the end, Aru was sure of it. Did birds eat people? It probably depended on the size of the bird. Or the size of the person. Not wanting to test the idea, she tried burying her face in her mother's side, but she couldn't fit under her stiff arm. The sounds from the elephant rose steadily. A shadow lengthened on the ground. Huge and winged.

Whatever had been speaking flew out of the elephant's mouth.

It was . . .

A pigeon.

"Ew!" Aru exclaimed.

Her mother had often reminded her that pigeons were "rats with wings."

"Where is he?" demanded the pigeon. "One of the ancient five warriors lit the Lamp of Bharata —"

Aru tilted her head, a question flying out of her before she could stop herself. "Why does your voice sound different?"

From inside the elephant, the bird had sounded like it could convince a mountain to turn into a volcano. Now it sounded like her math teacher that one time he had tried to perform a cappella but had stepped on a Lego piece. For the rest of the day he'd spoken in an anxious, sulky voice.

The pigeon puffed out its chest. "Is there something wrong with how I sound, human girl?"

"No, but —"

"Do I not look like a bird capable of great devastation?"

"I mean —"

"Because I shall have you know that whole cities revile me. They say my name like a curse."

"Is that a good thing?"

"It's a powerful thing," sniffed the bird. "And between good and power, I will always choose the latter."

"Is that why you're a pigeon?"

Could a bird narrow its eyes? If not, this one had certainly mastered the illusion.

"The lamp was lit. The Sleeper will start to awaken. It is my sacred duty to guide the Pandava brother who lit it."

"Pandava?" Aru repeated.

She knew that name. It was the last name

of the five brothers in the Mahabharata poem. Her mother had said that each of them held great powers and could wield fantastic weapons because they were the sons of gods. *Heroes.* But what did that have to do with the lamp? Had she hit her head without noticing? She felt around her scalp for a bump.

"Yes. Pandava," sneered the pigeon. It puffed out its chest. "Only one of the five Pandava brothers could light the lamp. Do you know where he went, human girl?"

Aru lifted her chin. "*I* lit the lamp."

The bird stared. And then stared some more.

"Well, then, we might as well let the world end."

FOUR:
IN-EP-TEE-TOOD

Aru had read somewhere that if you stare at a chimpanzee, it will stare back, smile . . . and then attack you.

She hadn't read anything about what kind of consequences might follow from staring at a pigeon.

But she did know that gazes were powerful things. Her mom used to tell her stories of Gandhari, a queen who chose to go through life blindfolded out of empathy for her blind husband. Only *once* did she take off the blindfold, to look at her eldest son. Her stare was so powerful it could have made him invincible — if he'd been naked. But no, he was too embarrassed to go without his underwear. He was still super-strong, just not as strong as he could've been. (Aru sympathized with him. That must have been a horribly awkward moment.)

And so Aru maintained eye contact with

the pigeon . . . but took one step back.

Finally, the bird relented. It hung its head. Its wings drooped.

"The last dormant Pandavas were so brilliant!" it said, shaking its head. "The last Arjuna was a senator. The last Yudhistira was a famous judge. The last Bhima was an Olympic athlete, and Nakula and Sahadeva were famous male models who wrote fabulous best-selling self-help books and started the world's first hot-yoga studios! And now look at what has become of the line: a girl child, of all things."

Aru didn't think this was particularly fair. Even famous people had been children at some point. Judges weren't born wearing wigs and carrying gavels.

And that led to another question: What was the bird going on about? All of those names — Arjuna, Yudhistira, Bhima, Nakula, and Sahadeva — were the names of the five most famous Pandava brothers. There was one more — Karna — the secret Pandava. In the stories, the other Pandavas didn't even know he was their brother until the war had begun.

And why did the bird say *dormant*? Didn't that mean sleeping?

The pigeon flopped onto its back and draped one wing dramatically over its beak.

"So this is to be my fate," it moaned. "I used to be *going* places. Top of my class, you know." It sniffed.

"Um . . . sorry?"

"Oh, that's useful!" The pigeon lifted its wing and glared at her. "You should've thought about that before you plunged us into this mess! Just look at you . . . The horror." It covered its face with both wings, muttering to itself. "Why must every generation have its heroes?"

"Wait. So there's been five Pandava brothers in every generation?" asked Aru.

"Unfortunately," said the bird, throwing off its wings.

"And I'm one of them?"

"Please don't make me say it again."

"But . . . how can you be sure?"

"Because you lit the lamp!"

Aru paused. She *had* lit the lamp. She had lowered the flame to the metal lip of the object. But it was Poppy's brother's lighter. Did that count? And she was only going to light it for a second, not *keep* it lit. Did that make her only a smidge of a hero?

"I'm fairly positive you are a Pandava," continued the bird. "Mostly positive. I am, at least, definitely not going to say no. Otherwise why would I be *here*? And on that note, *why* am I here? What does it mean

44

to wear this wretched body?" It stared at the ceiling. "Who am I?"

"I —"

"Ah, never mind," said the bird with a resigned sigh. "If you've lit that cursed lamp, the other one will know."

"Who — ?"

"We'll just have to go through the Door of Many. It always knows. Plus that's a great deal easier than putting something in Google Maps. Most confusing contraption of this century."

"You're a bird! Shouldn't you *know* which direction you're going in?"

"I'm not just any *bird,* you uppity hero. I am —" the bird spluttered, then stopped. "I guess it doesn't matter who I am. What matters is that we stop this before any true destruction takes place. For the next nine days, Time will freeze wherever the Sleeper walks. On the ninth day, the Sleeper will reach the Lord of Destruction, and Shiva will perform the dance to end all Time."

"Can't the Lord of Destruction just say *no thanks*?"

"You know nothing of the gods," sniffed the pigeon.

Aru stopped to consider that. She wasn't shocked by the idea that gods and goddesses existed, only that a person could actually get to know them. They were like the moon: distant enough not to enter her thoughts too often; bright enough to inspire wonder.

Aru looked back at her frozen mom and classmates. "So they'll just be stuck like that?"

"It's temporary," said the bird. "Provided you aren't riddled with ineptitude."

"*In-ep-tee-tood*? Is that French?"

The bird knocked its head against a wooden banister. "The universe has a cruel sense of humor," it moaned. "*You* are one of the few who can make things right again. Then again, you are also the one who started it. And so you, and the other, must be heroes."

That didn't sound very heroic to Aru. It just sounded like an epic mess that required an epic cleanup. Her shoulders drooped. "What do you mean, 'the other'?"

"Your sibling, of course! You think you can quest alone? Questing requires families," said the bird. "Your brother — or perhaps sister, although I don't think that's ever happened — will be waiting for you. When one Pandava awakens, so too does another, usually the one who is best equipped to deal with the challenge at hand. Until now, the Pandavas have always appeared as fully grown people, not squished

46

bundles of hormones and incompetence."

"Thanks."

"Come along, girl child."

"Who *are* you?"

Aru wasn't going to move a step without some kind of verification. But she doubted the bird carried a wallet.

The pigeon paused, then said, "Though such an illustrious name should not be uttered by a child, you may call me Subala." It preened. "I am — I mean, well, I *was* . . . It's a long story. Point is: I'm here to help."

"Why should I go with you?"

"Ungrateful child! Have you no sense of dharma? This is your task! The freeze will keep spreading like a disease in the Sleeper's wake. If he's not stopped by the new moon, your mother will stay that way forever. Is that what you want?"

Aru's cheeks heated. Of course she didn't want that. But she also felt as if the whole world had spun the wrong way and she was still finding her balance.

"Your name is Subala? That's way too many syllables," said Aru, fear snaking into her heart. "What if I need help and have to call for you? I could lose an arm or a leg while just trying to say the whole thing. I'm calling you Sue."

"Sue is a girl's name. I am a male."

47

Aru, who was often stuck listening to Sherrilyn's Johnny Cash playlist, did not agree with Subala.

"No it's not. There was a 'Boy Named Sue.' You know, his daddy left home when he was three —"

"Spare me the vileness of country music," huffed Subala, flying toward the elephant's mouth.

Well, if he wouldn't be called Sue, what about . . .

"Boo!" shouted Aru.

Subala turned his head, realized what he'd done, and cursed. He perched on top of the elephant's trunk.

"You may have won this, but I'd wipe that smug grin off your face fairly quickly if I were you. Serious consequences have been triggered by your actions, girl child. As this generation's Pandava, it's now your duty to answer the call to questing. The need hasn't arisen in more than eight hundred years. But I'm sure your mother told you all that." Boo peered at her. "She *did* tell you, didn't she?"

Aru fell quiet as she recalled the kinds of things her mother had told her over the years. They were small things that wouldn't help thaw the frozen people in this room: how a flock of starlings was called a *murmu-*

ration; how some tales were nested inside other tales; and how you should always leave the mint leaves for last when making chai.

But there'd been no mention of quests. No discussion of Aru being a Pandava. Or how she came to be that way.

And there'd certainly been no instructions about how she should prepare herself in case she accidentally triggered the end of the universe.

Maybe her mom didn't think Aru would be any good at it.

Maybe she hadn't wanted to get Aru's hopes up that she could do something heroic.

Aru couldn't lie this time. It wasn't a situation she could talk herself out of and magically be okay.

"No," she said, forcing herself to meet Boo's gaze.

But what she saw made her hands tighten into fists. The pigeon was doing that narrowing-his-eyes-thing. He was looking at her as if she were not much to look at . . . and that was wrong.

She had the blood — or at least the soul — of a hero. (Or something like that. She wasn't quite sure about the mechanics of reincarnation.)

"I may not know," she said. "But I can learn."

Boo cocked his head.

The lies bubbled happily to her throat. Words of self-comfort. Words of deceit that weren't necessarily bad:

"My teacher once called me a genius," she exclaimed.

She did not mention that her gym teacher had called her that in a not very nice way. Aru had established a "record" time — for her — of taking fourteen minutes to run a mile lap around the track. The next time that they ran to beat their previous records, she'd ignored the track altogether and just walked across the field to the finish line. Her teacher had scowled at her and said, *You think you're a genius, or something?*

"And I'm an *A* student," she told Boo.

In the sense that she was a student whose name started with an *A.*

The more claims she made — even if they were only half-truths at best — the better she felt. Words had their own power.

"Excellent. All my fears have been allayed," said Boo drily. "Now come on. Time is a-wasting!"

He cooed, and the elephant's mouth widened to the size of a door, its jaw hitting the ground. A breeze from some other place gusted toward her, swirling through the stuffy air of the museum.

One step forward and she'd be wandering far from Atlanta. . . . She'd be in an entirely different world. Excitement rushed through her, followed by a painful pinch of guilt. If she couldn't fix this, her mom would become like everything else in the museum: a dusty relic. Aru brushed her fingers against her mother's stiff hand.

"I'll fix this," she said. "I promise."

"You'd better!" snapped Boo from his place on the elephant's trunk.

FIVE:
THE OTHER SISTER

Grabbing one of the elephant tusks as a handrail, Aru stepped into the statue's mouth. Inside, it was cold and dry, and far larger than seemed possible. A hall appeared, carved out of stone and marble, and the ceiling soared overhead. Aru stared around her, stunned, as she remembered every time she'd leaned against the elephant, never knowing it'd been hiding a magical corridor within it.

Boo flew down the passageway, urging her forward. "Come along! Come along!"

Aru ran to keep up.

The hallway sealed itself behind her. Ahead was a closed door. Light slipped out from a gap on one side.

Boo perched on her shoulder and pecked her ear.

"What was that for?!" exclaimed Aru.

"*That* was for renaming me," said the pigeon too smugly. "Now, tell the Door of

Many that you need to go to your sibling who has awakened."

Sibling. Aru suddenly felt sick. Her mom traveled most weekends. Was she working, or was she visiting her other children? Children she'd prefer spending time with.

"How can I have a *sibling*?"

"Blood isn't the only thing that makes you related to someone," said Boo. "You have a sibling because you share divinity. You're a child of the gods because one of them helped forge your soul. That doesn't make a difference to your genetics. Genetics might say that you're never going to be taller than five feet. Your soul doesn't care about that. Souls don't have height, you know."

Aru hadn't heard anything after *You're a child of the gods.*

Up until this point, her brain had only distantly understood that she could be a Pandava. But if she *was* a Pandava, that meant that a god had helped *make* her. And claimed her as his own. As his *kid.*

Her hand flew to her heart. Aru had the strangest impulse to reach into herself as if she might pluck out her own soul. She wanted to look at the back of it, as if it had a tag, like on a T-shirt. What would it say? MADE IN THE HEAVENS. KINDA. If she couldn't hold it, it didn't seem real.

And then another thought took root, one that was even stranger than the fact that a god was her dad.

"So I'm, like, a goddess?" she asked.

That wouldn't be so bad.

"No," said Boo.

"But the Pandavas were like demigods. They could use divine weapons and stuff. So that makes me half a goddess, right?" asked Aru. She examined her hands, flexing them like Spider-Man did whenever he started shooting out webs. "Does that mean I get to do magical things, too? Do I get powers? Or a cape?"

"There shall be no capes."

"A hat?"

"No."

"Theme song?"

"Please stop."

Aru looked down at her clothes. If she was going to be meeting some long-lost sibling, she really wished she were wearing something other than Spider-Man pajamas.

"What happens after . . . after I meet them?"

Boo did that pigeon thing where he regarded her at an angle. "Well, we must go to the Otherworld, of course. Not quite what it used to be. It dwindles with humanity's imagination, so I suspect it is currently

54

the size of a closet. Or perhaps a shoe box."

"Then how will I fit?"

"It will make room," said Boo airily. "You should have seen it in its glory days. There was a Night Bazaar where you could purchase dreams on a string. If you had a good singing voice, you could use it to buy rice pudding dusted with moonlight. Finest thing I've ever eaten — well, second only to a spicy demon. Mmm." He ignored Aru's cringe. "We'll take you to the Court of the Sky. There you may formally ask the Council of Guardians for the details of your quest." Boo's feathers ruffled when he mentioned the Council. "You'll get your weapons. I shall get my place of honor back, make no mistake. And then it's up to you and your brother. Or sister, gods help us."

"Weapons?" repeated Aru. "What kind of weapons? That's not something they teach you in seventh grade. How am I supposed to stop the Sleeper from getting to the Lord of Destruction if I can't throw a bow and arrow?"

"You *shoot* a bow and arrow!"

"Right. I knew that."

Aru wasn't exactly the best at gym. Just last week she'd scratched at the inside of her nose hard enough to fake a nosebleed and get out of dodgeball.

"Perhaps you have a hidden talent some-where inside you," said Boo. He squinted at her. "Buried quite deeply, I imagine."

"But if there're all these deities, why don't *they* help? Why leave it up to, as you said, a bundle of hormones and incompetence?"

"Gods and goddesses may occasionally help, but they don't mess around with affairs that affect only humans. To them, mortal lives are but a speck of dust on the eyelash."

"You don't think the gods would be even a little upset to find out that their entire universe was stamped out?"

Boo shrugged. "Even Time has to end. The real measure of when others will get involved comes down to whether or not *you* succeed. The gods will accept the outcome either way."

Aru gulped. "Awesome. That's just the best."

Boo nipped her ear.

"Ow!" said Aru. "Could you *not*?"

"You are a child of the gods! Stand up straight!"

Aru rubbed her ear. A deity was her . . . *father.* She still couldn't quite believe it.

She had lied about many things, but she'd never invented stories about a father. She would've felt ridiculous bragging about someone who had no interest in her. Why should she go out of her way to make him sound better than he actually was? He'd never been there. The end.

Her mother didn't speak of him, either. There was only one photo of a man in the house. He was handsome and dark-haired, with skin the color of dark amber, and he had the strangest pair of eyes. One was blue, and one was brown. But Aru wasn't even sure he was her father. And he didn't look like a deity at all. At least, not like anyone in the Hall of the Gods. Then again, ancient statues weren't always a good reference. Everyone looked the same when they were cut out of granite and sandstone and their features were worn down to faded smiles and half-lidded eyes.

Apparently she herself was divine-ish, but whenever she looked in the mirror, all she noticed was that her eyebrows kept trying to join up. And it stood to reason that if you were even a little bit divine, you should not have a unibrow.

"Now," said Boo, "tell the Door of Many where you want to go."

Aru stared at the door. There were several symbols and scenes etched into its frame. Images of warriors notching their bows and letting their arrows fly.

When Aru blinked, she even saw a wooden arrow zoom across the tableau. She reached out and placed her palm against the door. The engraved wood pressed back, like a cat nuzzling her hand. As if it were trying to get to know her, too.

"Take me to . . . the other Pandava." She said the words breathlessly.

She was right. Words did have power. When she said the word *Pandava,* all the feelings that came from discovering who she really was uncoiled like a spring jumping to life.

It was not unpleasant.

It was like riding a roller coaster and relaxing enough to let the initial panic turn into something else: Exhilaration. Joy. Anticipation.

She was Aru Shah.

Suddenly the world she thought she knew had opened up, as if stage curtains had been yanked back to show her that there was so much *more* than what she'd imagined. There was magic. Secrets crouched in the dark. Characters from stories, like the ones she'd been told all her life, were taking off their masks and saying, *I was never a tale, but a truth.*

And — the thought wiped off her grin — there was also her mom . . . now frozen with a worried expression on her face. Aru's heart felt like a painful knot inside her. *I'm not letting you stay like that, Mom. I promise.*

The door opened.

Light washed over her.

Boo squawked.

Aru felt yanked forward. Gone was the mild weather of Georgia. Everything was cold and bright. When she blinked, she saw that she was standing on the large driveway of a sprawling white house. The sun had begun to set. All the trees were bare. And right in front of her was a . . . giant turtle?

Wait, no. A girl. A girl wearing an extremely unflattering backpack. She stood with her arms crossed, and what looked like black war paint smudged under her eyes. She had a thick pen in one hand and a bag of almonds in the other.

"Are there bees in the Otherworld?" asked the girl. She didn't seem very surprised to see Aru. In fact, her gaze was a little reproachful, as if Aru had arrived late. "I don't know if I'm actually allergic, but you never know. You can *die* within a minute of a bee sting. *A minute.* And I bet there are no emergency rooms. I mean, I know there's magical healing and all, but what if it isn't enough?" The girl snapped her eyes toward Aru, her gaze narrowing. "I hope you don't have a bee allergy. I only have one EpiPen. But I guess we could share? I'll stab you, you stab me?"

Aru stared at her. *This* was the other legendary Pandava sister? Descended from a god?

The girl started digging through her backpack. Boo face-planted onto the grass. Aru could hear his muffled sobs of *whyGodwhyme.*

SIX:
LOOK, BUT NOT REALLY

"Your family must've gotten frozen, too, if you came here to find me," said the girl. Her voice wobbled a bit, but she forced herself to stand straighter. "Any chance you brought cash just in case? I couldn't steal my mom's wallet. It felt wrong." She sneezed and her eyes widened. "Do you think I might be allergic to magic? Is that a thing — ?"

"Stop," groaned Boo. "Are you a Pandava?"

The girl nodded.

"Answer me!" said Boo.

Aru toed him with her shoe. "She nodded yes. . . ."

"I couldn't tell."

"Maybe that's because you're facedown in the grass?"

Boo had collapsed on the front lawn outside of what Aru could only assume was the girl's house. It was so boring here. Not

61

at all the kind of place where she thought another child of the gods would be. The grass was perfectly suburban. Neat and not so green that it would draw too much attention to itself.

With great effort, Boo rolled over onto his back. Sighing, Aru scooped him up and held him out to the girl. "This is our, um.. ."

"Enchanted assistant, sidekick, comic relief, et cetera, et cetera," said Boo. He continued to lie across her palms. "Sometimes the heroes in epics are assisted by eagle kings and clever monkey princes. But it's been quite some time. The world is rusty at being dazzling, and so . . . here I am."

"Heroes got eagle kings and we got a —" started the other girl.

Aru coughed loudly. "*We* got a being of former renown and illustriousness."

Illustriousness was a word she'd once heard in a film where people kept addressing a grand empress. Aru assumed that it meant *illustrated,* because the empress's face was certainly drawn on (*no one* had eyebrows like that). But important people didn't seem to take this as an insult. Even Boo gathered himself on her hands, shook out his feathers, and nodded.

The girl shot Aru an *are-you-sure*? look. Aru shrugged. Maybe it had been a lie to make the bird rally his energy. Maybe it was the truth. Talking this way came easily to Aru. She had done it all her life: looked at something not so great and told herself all the things that made it great.

"I'm Aru."

The other girl blinked. "Mini."

"What?"

"I'm Mini," the girl repeated.

"I mean, I guess you *are* short," said Aru. "But —"

"As in that's my name."

"Oh."

"So . . . we're siblings? But not like related-related. Like soul-related."

Mini seemed way calmer than Aru had been when she'd learned she was a Pandava.

"Something like that?" answered Aru.

"Oh."

There were so many things Aru wanted to ask. Mini's parents must have told her about her true identity, because she was — in her own way — prepared. She *knew* what was happening. She *knew* that Aru had to be some kind of relation to her because she, too, was a Pandava.

But the situation didn't sit quite right. It felt as uncomfortable as walking in shoes a size too big.

63

If Aru was being 100 percent honest with herself (she was the only person she was totally honest with), she felt a sharp pang of disappointment. But what had she expected? Often the amount of amazement she wanted to feel never quite matched reality.

Last year, when she'd heard about the middle school homecoming dance, she had imagined something from a Bollywood movie. Lights glittering. A wind — *out of nowhere* — making her hair fly, and everyone breaking into a choreographed song and dance at the exact same time. When Aru had walked in, no wind had blown her hair. But someone did sneeze in her face. All the sodas were lukewarm, and all the food was cold. Forget about choreographed dancing (aside from the Cha Cha Slide, which shouldn't count). The kids who were dancing — to bleeped-out pop hits — were weirdly . . . enthusiastic. A chaperone had to keep yelling, "Leave enough room between you for Jesus!" By the end of the night it was: "LEAVE ROOM FOR THE HOLY TRINITY!" And to crown it all, the air conditioner drew its last breath halfway through the dance. By the end of it, Aru had felt like she was wading through a steam of post-recess middle school body odor.

Which was, to put it bluntly, the worst.

Meeting Mini was better than a middle school dance. But Aru still felt cheated.

She had wanted a sisterly smile that said *I've known you all my life.* Instead, she was faced with an odd stranger and a pigeon whose sanity was slowly unraveling. Maybe it was supposed to be this way, like part of a *trial.* She was a hero (kinda?), so maybe she just had to be patient and *prove* that she was worthy of her Pandava role. Only then would the magic happen.

And so Aru fixed Mini with what she hoped was her friendliest, most blinding smile.

Mini took a step back, clutching her EpiPen tighter.

She didn't look like a reincarnated Pandava any more than Aru did. But Mini was very different from Aru. There was an upswept tilt to her eyes. Her skin was light gold, like watered-down honey. Not like Aru's chestnut brown. It made sense, though. India was a very big country with about a billion people in it. From state to state, the people were different. They didn't even speak the same languages.

Boo lifted off Aru's hands and hovered in front of the girls' faces. "You're Mini, she's Aru. I'm exasperated. Salutations done?

Okay. Off to the Otherworld now."

"Exasperated, how do we get there?" asked Mini.

Boo blinked. "Let's hope you inherited some talents, since irony evidently eluded you."

"I have an iron deficiency. Does that count?" offered Mini.

Before Boo could face-plant once more, Aru caught him.

"Don't we have somewhere to be? The Sleeper is off somewhere freezing people, and if we don't stop him by the ninth day, all of them . . ." Aru gulped. It hadn't seemed so real until she said it out loud. "They'll stay that way."

"To the Otherworld!" cried Boo.

It could've sounded really epic. Like Batman hollering, *To the Batmobile!* But it was barely intelligible, because Boo was squawking from inside Aru's cupped hands. She placed him on a nearby tree.

"I don't remember how to get there," said Mini. "I went once, but I got carsick."

Envy shot through Aru. "You've *been* to the Otherworld?"

Mini nodded. "My parents took my brother when he turned thirteen. I had to go, too, because they couldn't find a baby-sitter. I think all the parents of Pandavas are supposed to take them to the Otherworld once they show signs of being demigods. Didn't yours?"

Didn't yours?

Aru hated that question and every variation of it. She'd heard it all the time growing up.

My mom packed me a sandwich for the field trip. Didn't yours?

My parents always come to my choir practice. Don't yours?

Sorry, I can't stay long after school. My mom is picking me up. Isn't yours?

No. Hers didn't, doesn't, isn't.

Aru's expression must have been answer enough. Mini's face softened.

"I'm sure she meant to and just never got around to it. It's okay."

Aru looked at Mini: the flattened mouth and pressed-together eyebrows. Mini *pitied* her. The realization felt like a mosquito bite. Tiny and needling.

Just enough to irritate.

But it also made Aru wonder. If Mini's mom had told Mini everything, then did that mean their moms knew each other? Did they *talk*? If they did, how come Aru didn't know?

Perched on a myrtle tree, Boo began to preen himself. "Right. So, here's how to get there: You —"

"We're not driving?" asked Mini.

Aru frowned. She didn't know much about magic, but she didn't think the Otherworld should be within driving distance.

Boo shook his head. "Too dangerous. The Sleeper is looking for you."

Goose bumps prickled across Aru's arms. "Why?" she asked. "I thought he just wants to go wake up the Lord of Destruction. What does he want with us?"

"He'll want your weapons," said Boo. "The Lord of Destruction is surrounded by a celestial sphere that can only be shattered by an immortal device like those weapons."

Aru was getting a headache. "Wait, so, we need weapons to protect our weapons from becoming . . . weapons."

"But we don't have any weapons!" said Mini. "Or at least I don't." She turned pale. "Am I supposed to have a weapon? Do you have one? Is it too late for me to get one, too? Is there a specific one, like only having number two pencils for standardized tests, or —"

"SILENCE!" shouted Boo. "It is fine that you are unarmed. As for *where* you shall be retrieving these powerful weapons, I shall leave those instructions to the Council of

Guardians. They will be waiting for us in the Otherworld."

He flew down in front of them. Then he pecked at the ground while walking in a small circle. "The key to getting to the Otherworld is reaching. You must grab hold of something invisible. Imagine it's a string of hope. All you have to do is find it and tug. Simple."

"A string of hope?" said Aru. "That's impossible. . . ."

"If it wasn't, then everyone would go!" retorted Boo.

Mini pushed her glasses a little higher up her nose, and then reached in front of her. Gingerly, like the air might bite her. Nothing happened.

"It helps to look sideways," said Boo. "That's usually where you find most entrances to the Otherworld. You have to look and not look. You have to believe and not believe. It's an in-between thing."

Aru tried. She glanced sideways, feeling utterly ridiculous. But then, incredibly, she saw something that looked like a thread of light hanging down in the middle of the empty street. The world was still. All the beautiful houses were at once close and also a millennium away. Aru thought that if she were to reach out, her fingers would meet a thin sheet of glass.

"Once you've got ahold of the in-between, close your eyes."

Mini obeyed, and Aru followed her example. She reached out, not expecting anything, but *wanting* desperately.

Her fingers found nothing at first, and then . . . she felt it. Like a current of warmth.

It reminded her of summer. Those all-too-rare days when her mother took her to the lake. Sometimes there would be cold spots in the water. And sometimes there were swirling eddies of warmth, a bit of sun-drenched water ribboning around her.

Or sometimes it was just because someone had peed next to her. That was the worst.

This felt like that (the warmth, not the pee).

She grabbed the current, and something firm nosed into her hand —

A doorknob.

Not quite a doorknob. More like a bit of magic trying its best approximation of a doorknob. It was cold and metallic feeling, but it squirmed and tried to wrest itself from her hand. An indignant squeak followed when Aru gripped the knob a little tighter. All of her thoughts poured into a single command: *Let me in.*

The doorknob made a *harrumph* sound. She pulled.

And where there had once been a bit of road, a shriveled crape myrtle tree, and a slightly wonky-shaped mailbox . . . now there was a panel of light. Boo's wings rustled behind her.

The three of them walked through that entrance of light. (Well, Boo didn't walk, because he had decided to perch on Aru's head.) Her eyes adjusted slowly. All she could see at first was a cavernous ceiling arching above her. They were in a gigantic cave studded with stars. Tiny lights flew past them.

"Bees!" shrieked Mini.

Aru blinked. They weren't lights, or bees, but moths. Moths with wings of flame. Every time one darted past her, she heard a whisper of a laugh. The walls were cloaked in shadow. There were no doors leading in or out. They were in a bubble.

Aru examined the strange floor beneath her: off-white and bumpy. Each tile was a different length. In fact, the more she looked at it, the more it looked like . . .

"Bones!" said a voice in front of them. "Do you like them? Took me ages to collect. They're really quite comfy to walk on,

71

but mind the teeth. Some of those are incisors."

Aru stiffened. Mini clawed into her backpack and drew out an inhaler.

The little moths of light began to gather around a shape in the dark. One by one, they fluttered their wings and stayed still, as if they were buttoning up whoever stood in the shadows. The shape grew more distinct.

Now it resembled a crocodile that had rolled around in Christmas-tree lights. Only this crocodile was bright blue and the size of a three-story house. The crocodile was also grinning, either happily or — as Aru's growing panic was beginning to point out — *hungrily.*

Seven:
The Council of Guardians

"Pleasedonteatuspleasedonteatusplease-
donteatus," said Mini rapidly.

"Eat you?" repeated the creature, shocked.
Its eyes widened. They reminded Aru of an
insect's eyes — strangely prismed, like a
cluster of television screens. "You don't look
very edible. Sorry. I don't mean to be rude."

Aru was not in the least bit offended but
thought it wise not to point this out.

Boo flew down from her shoulder. "*Makara!* Guardian of the thresholds between
worlds!"

Aru gawked. *A real makara.* She'd seen
photos of them, but only as crocodile-like
statues that guarded temples and doors. It
was said that the goddess of the Ganges
River rode one through the water. Aru
wasn't sure whether that made them mythical boats or guard dogs. Judging from the
way the makara was excitedly wagging its
tail, she was going with the latter.

"Make way for this generation's Pandava brothers —" started Boo.

The makara frowned. "They look more like sisters —"

"That's what I meant!" snapped Boo.

"Wait . . . I recognize you," said the makara slowly, tilting its head as it considered Boo. "You don't look the same."

"Yes. Well, that happens when one has been . . ." Boo's words ended in incoherent muttering. "The heroes are here to meet the Council and receive the details of their quest."

"Ah! Another chance for the world to end! How delightful. I hope I get more visitors. I never get many visitors. Ooh! I don't think I've opened up an entrance to a Claiming in . . . well, quite a while. I don't know how many years it's been. I was never very good with numbers," said the makara sheepishly. "Every time I try to count, I get distracted. Even when I'm talking, sometimes it's like . . . it's like . . ." The makara blinked. "I'm rather hungry. Can I go now?"

"Makara," growled Boo. The makara cringed and hunkered closer to the floor. "Open the door to the Court of the Sky."

"Oh! Of course. Yes, I can do that!" said the makara. "First, I just have to see that they are who you say they are. Who are they again? Or what? You know, I've never actually seen a vole, and I read about them the other day in a book about animals. Are they voles?"

"Humans," volunteered Aru.

"Rather tiny for humans. You're certain you're not a vole?"

"We're not done growing yet," said Mini. "But my pediatrician said I probably won't get any taller than five foot two."

"Five feet, you say?" asked the makara. He rolled onto his back and raised his stubby legs. "I really think four feet are much more useful. Five might throw you off-balance. But that's just my opinion."

The makara lifted his head, as if he could see beyond them. Something flashed in his prism eyes. Aru saw an image of herself opening the museum entrance to Poppy, Arielle, and Burton. She saw the lighter flame being lowered to the lip of the lamp.

Something else shimmered in the depths of the makara's gaze. . . . Aru watched Mini discovering her parents frozen on the couch. A movie was playing on the television screen. An older boy who might have been Mini's brother was in the middle of tossing a basketball into the air.

At first Mini curled into a ball on the living room floor and cried and cried. After a few minutes she went upstairs and took out a backpack. She stared at herself in the mirror, reached for her mother's eyeliner, and made violent swipes on her cheeks. Then Mini kissed her stiff parents, hugged her immobile brother, and went outside, prepared to face down whatever evil she was destined to defeat.

Mini, for all her worries about allergies and magical bees, was brave.

Aru's face heated. Compared to Mini, she wasn't brave at all.

"Well, they are who you say they are!" said the makara. "I hope the Council trusts me."

"Me too," Boo harrumphed. "I never lie."

Aru could not say the same for herself.

Mini was staring at Aru. "You lit the lamp?"

Here comes the blame.

"I know it *had* to happen," said Mini hurriedly, as if she'd offended Aru. "My mom told me that the Sleeper was always destined to try to fight us. Don't worry, I'm not mad. There was no way you could've known what that lamp would do."

That was true, but still . . . Aru *had* known that she wasn't supposed to light it. The problem was, her mom had never told her *why.* So Aru had thought it was just one of those generic warnings parents gave to kids, like *Don't go outside without sunscreen or you'll burn!* Or, as the woman who ran the local Hindu temple's summer day camp liked to remind Aru: *Don't go outside without sunscreen or you'll get darker and won't find a husband!* Until it happened, who cared? Aru had never gotten sunburned, and she really didn't need to find a husband at age twelve.

But there wasn't any protective lotion when it came to demons. It all boiled down to one thing: she wasn't supposed to light the lamp, and yet she had. The fact that it had been "destined" to happen didn't really absolve her of blame. Aru's guilt was beginning to roil in her stomach. To the point where she thought she might throw up.

A bright moth hovered in front of Aru and Mini and Boo. Its wings grew, and light curled through the air, like calligraphy made of starlight. The wings stretched and unfurled until the girls and bird were completely enfolded.

"Good-bye, inedible tiny humans and Subala!" called the makara, no longer visible to them. "May all the doors you face in life swing open and never smack you in the butt as they close!"

The moth faded away, and they found themselves in an open-air room. No wonder it was called the Court of the Sky. Above them, the sky was marbled with clouds. The walls were ribbons of shimmering light. Delicate music laced the air. The space had that deliciously ripe aroma of the earth right after a summer thunderstorm. Aru wished the world smelled like this *all* the time. Like honey and mint and bright green growing things.

Beside her, Mini groaned, clutching her stomach. "Did I ever tell you I have acrophobia?"

"You're scared of spiders?"

"No! That's *arachno*phobia. I'm scared of heights!"

"Heights?"

Aru looked down. And then she wished she hadn't. There was a reason it seemed like they were hovering above the earth: they were.

Beneath her feet were two cloudy wisps. And beneath those . . . a *very* long fall through a lot of empty sky.

"Don't take off those cloud slippers," said Boo, flapping beside them. "That'd be quite unfortunate."

Mini whimpered. "This is where the Council meets?"

"They gather on Tuesdays and Thursdays, and during full moons and new moons, and also for the season premiere and finale of *Game of Thrones.*"

Speaking of thrones . . . Seven huge royal-looking chairs floated around them. All the thrones were made of gold. Except one, outside the circle, that was tarnished and rusty. She could only make out the letters U-A-L-A printed beneath it.

The other names were easier to read. As she sounded them out, Aru gasped. She recognized them from the stories she'd heard and the artifacts her mom had acquired for the museum.

There was Urvashi the *apsara,* the celestial singer and dancer who was said to be unmatched in beauty. Then there was monkey-faced Hanuman, the trickster who had famously helped the god Rama in his fight against the demon king. There were other names, too. Names like Uloopi and Surasa, the serpent queens; the bear king, Jambavan; and Kubera, the Lord of Wealth. These Guardians were immortal and worthy of worship, but they were often considered separate from the main league of gods and goddesses.

When Boo had mentioned a council, Aru had imagined stern summer camp counselors . . . not the very people from the myths and tales that had been crammed into her head since she was a toddler. Urvashi was, like, a heavenly nymph queen, and Hanuman, who was the son of the god of the wind, was a powerful demigod.

Now Aru *really* wished she were not wearing Spider-Man pajamas. It was like some horrible nightmare where she was walking the red carpet of a fancy movie premiere in an aluminum-foil hat and rubber-duckie rain boots, and *why was this happening to her?*

Aru turned to Mini. "On a scale of one to ten, how bad do I look? Ten being *burn your clothes.*"

"But then you wouldn't be wearing anything!" said Mini, horrified.

"So what you're saying is that I look horrible, but the alternative would be much worse?"

Mini's silence was a very clear *YUP.*

"Better pajamas than skin," said Boo. "Unless it's the skin of a demon you slayed. That would be fitting for a hero."

Wearing heavy, stinking demon skin?

"I'll stick with polyester," said Aru.

"Polly Esther? That poor child!" squawked Boo. For a pigeon, he looked thoroughly disturbed. "Middle school children are uncommonly cruel."

Perhaps sensing that the conversation was

moving from stupid to stupefying, Mini piped up. "Why are some of the thrones only half there?"

Aru peered closer at the circle of thrones. Some of them were partly transparent.

"Not every guardian of the Council is in residence at the same time," Boo said. "What would be the point of that when the world isn't in need of saving? No one believed the lamp would be lit for another ten or twenty years. They thought there was more time to prepare for the Sleeper. Until . . . *someone.*" He glared at Aru.

Aru blinked innocently. *Who, me?*

Beside her, Mini risked a look beneath her feet and started swaying. "I'm going to be sick," she moaned.

"Oh, no you don't!" said Boo. He hovered in front of her face and pecked her nose. "You two are not going to embarrass me in front of the Guardians. Spines straight! Wings preened! Beaks pointed!"

"What's going to happen?" asked Aru.

She didn't normally feel anxious about meeting people. But Urvashi and Hanuman weren't just any people. They weren't legends, either. They were *real.*

"It is the duty of the Council to deliver a quest. The Sleeper is out there right now, searching for a way to get the celestial weapons and use them to wake up the Lord of Destruction. You must get the weapons first."

"By *ourselves*?" asked Mini.

"You'll have me," said Boo primly.

"Great. Because nothing says *Come at me, demon* like a pigeon sidekick," said Aru.

"Rude!" huffed Boo.

"It's not so bad!" said Mini with false cheer. "Isn't the Council meant to help us?"

At this, Aru heard a laugh that sounded like someone tickling a chandelier.

"And why should I want to help you?" asked a silvery voice.

Before, the space had smelled like a summer thunderstorm; now it smelled as if every flower in existence had been distilled into a perfume. It wasn't pleasant. It was *overwhelming.*

Aru turned to see the most beautiful woman in the world sitting in the throne labeled URVASHI. She wore black leggings and a salwar kameez top that would have appeared as simple as white spun cotton if it didn't glimmer like woven moonlight. Around her ankles was a set of bright *gunghroo* bells. She was tall and dark-skinned and wore her hair in a messy side braid. She looked as if she'd just stepped out of dance rehearsal. Which, given the fact that she was the chief dancer of the heavens, was probably true.

"*This* is what you brought back to save us? I might as well set myself on fire and save the Lord of Destruction the trouble."

It took a moment for Aru to realize that Urvashi wasn't talking to her or Mini. She was talking to Boo.

To the left of the celestial dancer, a deep voice let out a powerful laugh.

"You really hold on to a grudge, don't you? Hasn't it been a millennium since he ruined your outfit?"

The monkey demigod Hanuman materialized in his throne. He was wearing a silk blazer and a shirt patterned with forest leaves. His tail flopped over the back of the chair, and from one of his ears dangled a jewel that looked like a small crown.

"It wasn't just any outfit, you big ape," snapped Urvashi. "It was made from the skipped heartbeats of every person who had ever laid eyes on me. It took *centuries* to sew! Subala knew that!"

"He's a bird — what did you expect?" said Hanuman.

"Not a bird!" shouted Boo. "And you know that!"

Aru was so distracted by their arguing that it took a while before she felt Mini tugging on her sleeve. She pointed at the tarnished throne bearing the letters U-A-L-A.

Now Aru could see where the other letters might have fit: *S* and *B. Subala.* Boo was one of the Guardians! But he didn't seem like the others. He wasn't glowing and powerful. And his throne had been pushed out of the circle. What had happened?

"You know why I'm here," Boo said to the Guardians. "These are the chosen heroes of the age."

Urvashi wrinkled her nose. "We've gone from training and assisting the saviors of humankind to playing nursemaid? No thank you."

Aru blushed. "We're not kids."

"Um, Aru . . ." said Mini, "we kinda are."

"We're preadolescents."

"That's the same thing, just a different word."

"Yeah, but it sounds better," muttered Aru.

"Whatever you may be, there is only one thing you are to me," said Urvashi. "You. Are. Not. Worth. My. Time." She flicked the armrest of her throne and then fixed her dark gaze on Boo. "Honestly, how did you bring two mortal children up here, anyway?"

"The usual routes," huffed Boo. "And they're not mortal children. They have the souls of Pandavas. I know it to be true."

"If they really are Pandavas, then the irony that *you* are the one who has been chosen to help them delights me." Urvashi's laugh sounded like gunghroo bells. "But I don't believe you. The Pandava souls have lain dormant since the end of the Mahabharata War. Why would they appear now?"

Aru's skin prickled with fury. "Because the Sleeper is awake," she cut in. "And we need help if we're going to save our families."

Beside her, Mini gave a grim nod.

"So you need to give us a weapon and tell us what to do," said Aru.

Hanuman regarded them solemnly. "The Sleeper?" His tail stood straight behind him. "It is as we feared, then, Urvashi. Everything we saw . . . It is him."

Under Aru's feet, the sky disappeared. Static rippled in the air, and it was like she and Mini were now standing on a giant television screen. Hanuman swept his hand over the screen, and images twisted beneath them.

The first vision was of the street outside the Museum of Ancient Indian Art and Culture. A leaf caught up in the wind hadn't fallen. The only things that moved were the clouds. It was silent, but the silence wasn't pleasant. It was like a graveyard — lonely, eerie, and undisturbed.

The second vision was on the suburban street where they had first found Mini. Two boys had been frozen while arguing over a comic book. A girl playing basketball had jumped for the hoop and stayed caught in the air, fingers still gripping the ball.

Beside Aru, Mini let out a cry.

"My neighbors! Are they okay? Did you know that if you don't have water for twelve hours, you could *die*? What —"

"The frozen do not suffer now," said Hanuman. "But they will if the Sleeper is not stopped by the new moon."

Aru's throat tightened. All those people . . . people she had never met. They would be hurt because of *this,* because of *her.*

"The Sleeper is right on our heels," said Boo somberly. "Looking where we last were."

"*Looking* is too quiet a word for what he's doing. He's *hunting,*" said Urvashi.

Shivers ran down Aru's spine. But something didn't make sense. If the Sleeper was looking for them, then why hadn't he just stayed in the museum when Aru had lit the lamp?

He was definitely looking for them (she

refused to think *hunting* — she was a girl, not a rabbit), but he was planning, too. At least, that's what she'd do if she were a demon. If your enemies were out to get you, you had to keep them guessing. It was like playing chess. You had to make the least predictable move. And to get to your goal — the king — you had to remove the defenses first.

"Has anything else happened?" Aru asked.

Urvashi's lip curled in disgust. "Anything other than the world gradually freezing, you mean?" she mocked.

But Hanuman understood. His tail snapped upright. "The vehicles . . ." he said slowly. "The vehicles of the gods and goddesses have gone missing."

Aru knew from her mother's stories that when Hanuman said *vehicles,* he wasn't talking about cars or bicycles. He was referring to the special mounts that the deities used. Ganesh, the elephant-headed god of new beginnings, rode a mouse. (*Must be a really muscular mouse,* Aru always thought.) The goddess of luck, Lakshmi, rode an owl. Indra, the king of the gods, rode a majestic seven-headed horse.

"The Sleeper intends to slow down the heavens, too," said Urvashi, her eyes widening. "He means to chop our legs from beneath us. . . . But if he has truly awakened, then why are the agents of the heavens . . . *them*?" She flailed a hand at Aru and Mini.

Mini tightened her hold on her backpack. But she wasn't glaring like Aru. Her eyes were shining, as if she were about to cry.

"Because . . . because we're Pandavas," Aru said, forcing her voice not to shake. "And it's your job or —"

"Dharma," whispered Boo. "It's their sacred duty to help the Pandavas fight the Sleeper one last time."

Fight? One last time? This was all news to Aru. Even the Guardians' faces turned stiff at his words.

"Right. That," said Aru. "So, you have to help us."

"Oh, really?" said Urvashi. Her voice turned devastatingly calm. "If you're Pandavas, then prove it."

Hanuman stood up on his throne. "We have never forced anyone to undergo the Claiming before they were ready. The Pandavas were always trained, at least!" He stared down at Aru and Mini. "They're only children."

"According to the rules," said Urvashi, smiling cruelly, "it must be unanimously agreed by the Guardians in residence that we believe they are semidivine. *I* do not believe. And if they're *only* children, they shouldn't bother."

Aru was about to speak, but someone else got there first.

"We'll prove it," said Mini.

Her hands were clenched into fists beside her. Aru felt a strange burst of pride in the surprisingly brave Mini. But Boo did not seem enthusiastic. He fluttered to his former throne, his face as pinched and solemn as a pigeon could look.

"Let the Claiming commence!" called Urvashi.

The Court of the Sky zoomed back into the shadows. And where the circle of thrones had once surrounded them, now something else did: five gigantic statues. If they weren't already in the sky, Aru might have guessed that the statues' heads would have scraped the clouds.

Aru's heart pounded, her previous burst of confidence gone. "You keep saying 'claiming,' but what are we claiming, exactly?"

"Like insurance? Deductions?" pressed Mini. She shrugged off Aru's bewildered expression. "What? My mom's a tax attorney."

"*You* are not claiming anything," said Boo. "It is the gods that will do the *claiming.*

Each of the Pandava brothers had a different divine father. You are about to find out who yours is."

From her mom's stories, Aru knew that there were five main brothers. The first three — Yudhistira, Arjuna, and Bhima — were the sons of the god of death, the god of the heavens, and the god of the wind, respectively. The twin Pandavas — Nakula and Sahadeva — were born by the blessing of the Ashvins, the twin gods of medicine and sunset. And there was one more: Karna, the secret Pandava, the son of the sun god.

Aru wasn't sure why they were all called brothers when they didn't even have the same mom, but maybe it went back to what Boo had talked about — that they didn't have to be blood-related to be siblings. There was a shared divinity-ness in their souls that was just as good as blood.

Or something like that.

"Wait. So, like, they're just going to reach out from the heavens, weigh us, and say *Yup, that seems like mine?*" demanded Aru.

"What about documentation?" shrieked Mini, her voice hitching with panic. "Is this like a conversation, or are there needles involved, like in a paternity test?"

If Boo knew the answers, he had zero interest in sharing. Ignoring their questions, he walked toward one of the giant statues.

"*Pranama* as I say the gods' names," he said.

Pranama was when you touched the feet of your elders. Aru had to do that when she went to the temple and ran into the priest or someone much, much older and well respected.

"I always have to do that when my mom's parents visit," whispered Mini. "My grandfather has really hairy feet. . . ."

"What about your dad's parents?" asked Aru.

"They're Filipino. My *lola* only likes her feet touched if I'm giving her a foot rub."

"Shh!" said Boo.

"How will we know if one of the gods is claiming us?" Aru asked.

"Simple. They'll choose to keep you alive."

"WHAT?" cried Mini and Aru at the same time.

The walls of ribbon-lights started flickering.

"Don't worry," said Boo airily. "I've only been wrong about someone being a Pandava once."

"So that means that person —"

"Watch out!" screamed Mini, pushing Aru.

The ribbon-lights slowly changed into a

91

bunch of tiny bright spots, like stars. But then they came closer, and Aru saw that they weren't stars at all.

They were *arrow tips.*

And they were heading straight for them.

EIGHT:
WHO'S YOUR DADDY?

Aru watched *a lot* of movies. Probably more than was good for her. Not that she cared. According to movies, right about now was when she should be seeing her life flash before her eyes while a bunch of people tearfully screamed, *Stay with us! Don't follow the light!*

The arrows grew bigger the closer they got. They cut through the air, and the sound they made was halfway between a wince and a whistle.

Aru's gaze darted across the empty sky. Forget the rules from a movie. She'd follow anything — even a suspiciously bright light at the end of a tunnel — if it meant getting out of here.

But then the rain of arrows stopped short. It was as if someone had just hit PAUSE.

"Don't worry," said Boo. "The arrows won't *actually* hit until you've paid your respects to the five father gods of the Mahabharata."

Aru and Mini were crouched and huddled together. Both of them were staring up at the quivering arrows hovering just a couple of feet over their heads. Maybe it was her imagination, but the arrows seemed really annoyed that they had to wait a bit before they got to launch themselves at Aru and Mini.

"Um, great?" said Aru.

"Dharma Raja, we acknowledge you," said Boo in a deep voice.

The statue of the Dharma Raja, Lord of Justice and Death, loomed above them. He was as gray as ash. Two sharp tusks curled from under his lip. In one hand he held his *danda* stick, the rod used for punishing souls in the afterlife. In the other, he held the noose he used to rope the souls of the dead. Aru's breath quickened as she remembered which Pandava was his son: Yudhistira. He was the oldest Pandava brother, and was known for being noble and just and wise.

Aru wasn't sure she wanted the Dharma Raja to be her dad. Being known for being the wisest and most just? *Way* too much pressure.

"Pranama!" hissed Boo.

Mini and Aru rushed forward and touched his feet.

"Lord Indra," said Boo.

The statue of Indra, king of the heavens, was next. His skin was the color of a thunderstorm. In his hand, he held the weapon Vajra, the thunderbolt. There was no way Aru could be the daughter of Indra. His Pandava son was Arjuna the Triumphant. Out of all the Pandava brothers, Arjuna was the most famous. He had the most adventures, and was known for his incredible skill with the bow and arrow. If being wise and just was pressure, imagine being considered the greatest hero out of the entire story.

No thank you, thought Aru.

"Lord Vayu."

Huh, thought Aru. *That wouldn't be so bad.*

Vayu, Lord of the Winds, stirred a slight breeze. He was dark-skinned and looked like the handsome star of a Bollywood film. He held a spinning flag that heralded the directions. His Pandava son was Bhima the Strong. Bhima was known for having a ridiculously large appetite, being superstrong, and also having a temper. All of which Aru thought she could deal with.

"The Ashvins, Nasatya and Dasra."

Two statues with the heads of horses glowed. They were the gods of sunrise and sunset, and medicine. Their Pandava sons were also twins. Nakula the Beautiful and Sahadeva the Wise.

Definitely would not mind being known for beauty, thought Aru. She still had some misgivings about the whole wisdom thing.

Mini and Aru paid their respects to each. When the final pranama was done, the two of them stood back-to-back within the circle of gods. Above her, Aru heard the impatient hissing of the arrows. They were trembling, not like a leaf that's about to fall from a branch, but like some sort of rabid beast that's legitimately *trembling* with excitement over tearing you apart. Too late, Aru remembered Boo's "reassurance" that the arrows wouldn't actually hit them until they had finished their pranama.

They'd definitely finished.

A sharp sound cut the air, as if someone had dropped a handful of sewing needles. An arrow landed near Aru's foot. Mini screamed.

A few more arrows pelted the ground. Not all at once. No, that would be too easy.

It was as if someone was tempting the gods: *Either of these kids striking your fancy? Wanna save one? Here, I'll give you a second to think.*

Aru threw up her hands, trying to see

through the lace of her fingers.

"Move!" screamed Mini, attempting to shove Aru out of the circle of statues.

Aru teetered backward. When she looked at where she'd been standing, she saw a handful of arrows stuck in the air.

"Stay calm!" shouted Boo.

"Who can stay calm when arrows are being shot at them?!" she screamed.

"A god!" said Boo.

"But we're not gods!" said Mini.

"Ah. Good point!"

Mini hefted her backpack and scuttled closer to Aru. "We have to hide," she hissed.

But what was the point of that? The arrows would find them regardless. Aru peered up at the statues and their cold, impassive faces. *Don't they care?* Aru tried to pry off one of the statue's toes to hurl it back at the arrows. Not that that would do anything, but at least it would *feel* useful. But the stone didn't yield.

More arrows landed in front of her. One was an inch from her pinkie. Another whispered past her ear. Now the arrows looked like a colony of bats.

"This is it," moaned Mini, holding up her backpack. She pressed herself tightly against Vayu's stone legs.

Aru braced herself.

The arrow points were spinning toward her, blowing wind against her face.

Aru flung out her hand, eyes pinched closed. "STOP!"

The whistling wind went silent. Aru blinked open. Her hand was still extended. For a moment she wondered whether *she* had stopped the arrows herself. But then she saw what was protecting her: a net. It crackled and shimmered as if its mesh were made out of . . . out of bolts of lightning.

Her feet weren't touching the ground anymore. She was floating, haloed by light. At that moment she had the most absurd desire to do two things:

1. Sing the "Circle of Life" song from
   The Lion King.
2. Throw up.

Being dangled by an unseen force? Yep, no thanks. But then she looked around and realized the arrows had vanished. Also, the statues had changed positions. Before, she had been leaning against the god of the winds. But now it was Indra, the god of thunder, who looked down at her. His face was still made of stone. But his expression had changed from indifferent to . . . amused. As if he had just realized who Aru was.

His daughter.

She, Aru Shah, was the daughter of Indra, king of the heavens.

NINE:
THE THREE KEYS

Many Hindus don't eat beef. Just like how some of Aru's Jewish and Muslim classmates didn't eat pork. Every time it was hamburger day at school, she would have to get the overly chewy portobello mushroom thing that looked (and probably tasted) like dinosaur hide. Her classmates would look at her pityingly.

"That sucks. Hamburgers are the *best*," someone would say. "You're missing out."

Aru disagreed. Pizza was the best. Besides, how could she be missing out on something she'd never had?

Maybe it was like that with fathers. She and her mom were just fine by themselves, thanks for asking.

Then again, a father is not a hamburger. A hamburger was something you could choose not to have. . . .

Aru had never had a choice when it came to not having a dad.

When she thought about it for too long, she got furious. How could her dad have left them? Aru considered herself fairly awesome. (Granted, she was a little biased.) And her mom . . . her mom was beautiful and brilliant and elegant. But she was also sad. Maybe if her dad was around, her mom would be happier. The fact that someone had dared to make her mom miserable only made Aru angrier.

But now that she was staring at the truth, she felt, well, struck by lightning. Which just seemed ironic now. She'd never had a hint that Indra could be her dad . . . or had she?

Aru had always loved thunderstorms. Sometimes when she had nightmares, a thunder and lightning storm would rise up out of nowhere, illuminating the sky like a lullaby created just for her.

Was that because of *Indra*?

But if Indra was her dad, that made Aru a reincarnation of *Arjuna*. The greatest warrior. She wasn't anything like him.

Arjuna was good and honorable and perfect. Almost, Aru thought, to the point of excess. Her mother had once told her a story about how Arjuna was so honorable that he agreed to a twelve-year exile in the forest just to keep his word.

Like lots of ancient rulers, the kings of

India had more than one wife. But it was a lot more unusual for a wife to have more than one husband. And yet that was the case in the tale of Draupadi, the virtuous and beautiful princess who married all five Pandava brothers. She spent a year as the wife of each. That made more sense to Aru than the alternative.

Imagine walking in your front door, calling out, *Honey, are you home?* and hearing:

Yes, dear!

Yes, dear!

Yes, dear!

Yes, dear!

Yes, dear!

But it was a rule among the five brothers that you couldn't barge in on Draupadi's privacy when she was with her husband-of-the-year. One day, Arjuna was called to fight off a bunch of demons. He had to answer the call, because that's what heroes do. The only problem was, he'd left his special bow and arrow in the dining room where Princess Draupadi was eating with one of his brothers. The penalty for barging in on their privacy was exile. Rather than let innocent people get hurt by demons, Arjuna chose to break the rule.

And that's why he had to go into the forest for twelve years.

Aru hated that story. The exile was completely unnecessary. His brother and Draupadi even forgave Arjuna when he explained that he just had to get his bow and arrow. And why did he even go *into* the dining room? He could've just knocked on the door and shouted, *Bro, I left my bow and arrow. Could you hand 'em to me?* It'd be like asking a friend to pass you some toilet paper under the stall if you're in a pinch.

But Arjuna didn't do that. Supposedly, this was a good thing. To Aru, it was just a bad use of time.

Aru stared up at the statue. She might not be anything like Arjuna, but maybe having the king of the heavens as your dad wasn't a bad thing when you've accidentally triggered the end of the world. . . .

Around her, the net of lightning vanished. In its place floated a golden orb no bigger than a Ping-Pong ball. Curious, she plucked it out of the air and turned it over in her hands. *The heck is this?* But it was right about then she heard Mini let out a sob.

Aru turned to see Mini sitting on a cloud, clutching her backpack to her chest. The statue of the Dharma Raja had moved and now loomed above her. The danda stick had been thrown from his hand, shattering the arrows headed toward Mini.

"Death?" she whispered. "I'm the Daughter of *Death*?"

In all honesty, Aru thought that sounded pretty cool. Imagine walking into a party and announcing, *I AM THE DAUGHTER OF DEATH*. You would almost certainly be guaranteed the first slice of cake. Plus, that would be the only appropriate time to use the brattiest phrase ever: *Wait till my father hears about this.*

But Mini's eyes welled with tears. "This ruins everything! I thought I'd be the daughter of one of the Ashvin twins! The daughter of the god of medicine! What medical school is going to accept me if I'm the Daughter of *Death*?" She rocked back and forth, crying.

A shadow cut across Aru. She looked up to see Boo circling them. There was something strange about his shadow, though . . . It didn't look like the kind of shadow cast by a pigeon. It was . . . *massive.*

Boo flew to Aru's shoulder. He glanced at her, then at Mini. Then he did it again.

Boo was not subtle about his hint: *Go forth and comfort!*

Sighing, Aru walked over slowly. She crouched at Mini's side and placed a hand on her shoulder.

"What?" Mini sniffled.

Aru thought about what she normally did to cheer herself up. She'd try to change the situation in her head. Look at it differently.

"It's not so bad," said Aru. "In the stories, Yudhistira was the son of the Dharma Raja and no one ran away from him. Everyone went to him for advice because he was really wise and just and all that. He was a really good king, too. . . . And maybe, as a doctor, you'll be even *better* because you're the Daughter of Death. Maybe you'll be able to tell faster when things are going wrong? Because you'll be able to *sense* death! Like a dog!"

Mini's head lifted.

Aru went on. "Think about it: you'll be able to *save* so many more people. You'll be the *best* doctor."

Mini sniffed again. "You think so?" *Maybe?*

"Definitely," said Aru. "It's all about what you do with what you have. Right, Boo?"

Boo huffed.

"See? Boo thinks so, too. And he'd never lie! He's, like, our sworn guardian and all that. He wouldn't try to steer you wrong."

At this, something in Boo's expression retreated. He hung his head a little. "True," he said softly.

Mini stood up. She flashed a little smile.

Without warning, she flung her arms around Aru and squeezed her tight, managing to catch a little of Boo's wing. He squawked. She squeezed tighter. "Thank you," she said.

Aru stood extremely still. She'd never been thanked, let along *hugged,* after telling a lie. But maybe she hadn't lied at all. Maybe it wasn't lying as much as it was applying some imagination. Looking at something from a different angle. That wasn't such a bad thing. And maybe this kind of thinking could actually help her make friends, instead of lose them?

Aru hugged her back.

Thunder boomed in the sky. Aru and Mini jumped apart. The statues of the Pandavas' soul fathers disappeared and the Court of the Sky rematerialized. Urvashi and Hanuman were perched at the edge of their thrones, their eyes wide.

"So it is true, then," said Urvashi, her voice soft with awe. "They're really . . . I mean . . . it is truly *them.*"

"The Pandavas have been awakened to do battle once more," said Hanuman, rubbing his chin.

"Not all of them," said Urvashi, staring at Aru and Mini. "Only the reincarnated souls of Arjuna and Yudhistira."

"For now," said Hanuman darkly. "If the

Sleeper isn't stopped, the rest will wake up, too."

Aru glanced beneath her feet, where the world was nothing more than a blur of trees and rivers. Somewhere out there were other people with Pandava souls. What were they doing? Were they frozen? Did they have some idea of who they really were, like Mini? Or were they like her . . . completely clueless?

"The others will only awaken as needed. With increasing darkness comes answering light," said Boo. "Even in chaos, the world will seek balance."

"Is this the part where you say *Do or do not, there is no try*?" asked Aru.

Boo scowled.

"If the Sleeper is going to try and wake up the Lord of Destruction, he'll need the celestial weapons," said Hanuman. "Do you know what that means, Pandavas?"

"We should break all the weapons so the Sleeper can't use them?" Aru responded at the same time that Mini said, "We have to get them before he does?"

"Or that," said Aru.

Hanuman regarded them somberly. "The Daughter of Death speaks true."

It took a moment for Aru to remember that *Daughter of Death* meant Mini. So what would that make her? *Daughter of Thunder,* Aru noted grumpily, sounded like a fancy name for a horse.

"Before I tell you of your quest, show me what gifts the gods have given you," said Urvashi. "Gods willing, they will ease the pain of your journey."

Gifts? Then Aru remembered the golden ball that had appeared when Indra's lightning net vanished. She drew it out of her pajama pocket. "You mean this?"

Urvashi's lip curled in distaste.

Mini rummaged in her backpack and pulled out a small purple compact. "This showed up when" — she choked on the words *Dharma Raja* — "claimed me."

"A plaything . . . and a mirror . . ." observed Urvashi. She turned to Hanuman. "Didn't heroes use to get fine steeds? Or battle armor? Swords, even?"

Was Aru overreacting, or was that a definite look of concern on Hanuman's face?

"Lord Indra and the Dharma Raja are . . . enigmatic," he said.

Mini frowned. "What's that mean?"

"I think it means they've got flaky skin," said Aru.

"You're thinking of *eczema.*"

"It means," said Hanuman loudly, "that your fathers are mysterious, but always for a reason. These gifts from them are intended to help you in your quest."

Aru felt ridiculous. What good was a ball against a demon? That was like trying to stop an avalanche with a spoon.

"There's your proof," said Urvashi. "Perhaps it means the gods do not wish the world to be saved."

"Or," squawked Boo, "it could mean that this time we need a different kind of hero."

"Heroine," corrected Mini under her breath.

Heroes. Heroines. Was that really what Aru was? Or was she just someone who made an epic mistake and had to do something epic to fix it?

Urvashi had a faraway look in her eye. Her mouth was pressed into a tight line. But a moment later, her shoulders dropped and she lifted her chin. "Very well. Come closer, children, to hear your quest."

Aru and Mini shuffled forward. The air kept them aloft. Wind rushed up and wrapped around them, and Aru shivered.

This no longer felt like a fun roller coaster. The moment she'd seen that sparkling net cast by the god Indra, her heart had turned heavy. In theory, a quest sounded awesome. But in reality, a whole lot of lives hung in the balance.

Maybe that's why superheroes wore capes. Maybe they weren't actually capes at all, but safety blankets, like the one Aru kept at the bottom of her bed and pulled up under her chin before she went to sleep. Maybe superheroes just tied their blankies around their necks so they'd have a little bit of comfort wherever they went. Because honestly? Saving the world was scary. No harm admitting that. (And she could have done with her blankie right about then.)

Urvashi leaned out of her throne. "The Sleeper needs the celestial weapons to free the Lord of Destruction. You must awaken the weapons before he does. To do so, you must go to the Kingdom of Death. Within the Kingdom of Death lies the Pool of the Past. Look inside the pool, and you will discover how the Sleeper can be vanquished once and for all."

"Scary kingdom, sleepy weapons, weird pool, got it. Okay, let's get this over with," said Aru. "So where's the door to the kingdom? Is there an entrance here? Or maybe —"

"Normally, you get to the Kingdom of Death by dying," said Urvashi.

Aru and Mini exchanged nervous glances.

"Eeny, meeny —" started Mini.

At the same moment, Aru shouted, "Nose

goes!" She smacked her nose.

Mini turned pale. "Oh no . . ."

"Children," said Urvashi, holding up her palm. "There is a way to open up the Door of Death without dying. You'll need three keys. But they are hidden, and need to be found. The first key is a sprig of youth. The second key is a bite of adulthood. And the third key is a sip of old age."

Aru stared at Urvashi. "Okay, so, which aisle of Home Depot do we go to?"

Mini laughed, but it was a panicked *I-am-definitely-gonna-die* kind of laugh.

"This map will help you," said Urvashi. "Merely touch the symbol of the key, and you will be transported somewhere close to it. But from there, it is up to you to find and claim the real key."

Urvashi opened her hands. Aru hadn't noticed until now that images covered Urvashi's skin from the tips of her fingers all the way up to her elbows. It was *mehndi,* a design made from the powdered leaves of the henna plant. They were temporary tattoos that women wore during celebrations like weddings and festivals. But this design was unlike anything Aru had ever seen.

For one thing, it was *moving.*

On Urvashi's wrist, a branch sprouted blossoms. "The sprig of youth."

A book opened and closed on the side of her hand. "The bite of adulthood."

A wave of water washed across her fingers. "The sip of old age."

But the very center of her palm was blank.

"You have nine days until the new moon, Pandavas. Less than that, perhaps, for time runs differently here than in the mortal realms," said Urvashi. "Stop the Sleeper from stealing the celestial weapons, find out how he may be defeated from the Pool of the Past, and then you will receive Pandava training from the entire Council." She paused to toss her hair over her shoulder. "Myself included. People would *kill* for the chance to be in my presence. In fact, they have." She smiled. "Succeed, and your disgraced guardian can even rejoin the Council."

Boo shuffled from foot to foot on Aru's shoulder. "They'll succeed, I know it," he said. "They have *me* to guide them, after all, and I was illustrious."

"Was," said Urvashi. Ignoring Boo, she grabbed Aru's hands. Then Mini's. When Aru looked down, the same mehndi map was covering her own skin. "There," she said. "Your map. Fight well."

For the first time, Urvashi's smile turned warm. But there was something sad about it. She folded her legs beneath her and tucked her hands into her lap. She looked so vibrant and beautiful that it was hard to believe she'd been present in all the ancient stories. Aru knew that Urvashi had not only trained heroes . . . she'd *loved* them. She'd even married one, and had kids with him. But they were mortal. She must have out-lived them.

"So young," Urvashi murmured. "It is not right."

And with that, she disappeared.

Hanuman looked between Aru and Mini. "The daughter of Lord Indra and the daughter of the Dharma Raja? Daunting indeed. Before you leave the Court of the Sky, there is something I'd like to tell you."

Daunting?

That seemed like a good thing? At least, she hoped so. Last year, everyone in home-room took the *Divergent* quiz on Buzzfeed, and she got "Dauntless" as her faction, which apparently meant she was brave and courageous. So . . . yay?

And if Hanuman — *the* Hanuman — thought they were daunting, maybe it wasn't so bad. But then she looked down at her hand with the three symbols of the absurd keys (how, exactly, does one take a *sip* of old age?) and her stomach turned. Nope, still bad.

Hanuman opened his paws. A small sun hovered above his palm. It burned so bright that Aru wished she had sunglasses.

"When I was young, I mistook the sun for a fruit. Got in a *lot* of trouble for that," he said, sounding more pleased with himself than guilt-ridden. "I clashed with a planet, and threw off a scheduled eclipse. Your father, Indra, was so mad that he used his famous lightning bolt to strike me down from the sky. It hit me in the side of the face, which is how I earned the name Hanuman, or 'prominent jaw.' " He stroked it, smiling at the memory.

"I used to play pranks on the priests, too. So they cursed me," he went on. "It was a tiny curse. The kind designed for mischievous immortal children."

"They punished you with a curse?" asked Mini.

"Just for being a kid?" added Aru.

That didn't seem very fair.

"They said I would never remember how strong and powerful I am until someone reminded me," said Hanuman. "Sometimes I wonder if it is a curse that we are all under at some point or another."

The small sun in his palms vanished. He patted their heads lightly. With a final nod at Boo, the monkey demigod disappeared. Now it was just the three of them and an expanse of empty sky.

"Come along, Pandavas," said Boo. "The map will guide us to the location of the first key. From there, it's up to you."

Aru touched the image of the first key, the blossoming twig on her wrist. She felt a tug in her stomach. Her breath caught.

One blink later, the three of them stood in the parking lot of a strip mall. Where were they? It didn't look like Atlanta. Snow frosted the bare branches of the few spindly trees. Only a couple of cars and loading vans were parked there. A shopgirl dropped her cigarette when she saw them. But if she thought it strange that two people and a pigeon had materialized out of nowhere, she didn't say anything.

Aru felt a rush of relief. If the shopgirl was still moving, it meant that the Sleeper hadn't caught on to their path. Yet.

"Oh no!" said Mini.

"What's wrong?" asked Aru.

Mini held up her hand. At the center of her palm, there was a symbol:

"It's the number of days you have left until the new moon," said Boo grimly.

"It is?" asked Aru, looking at her own palm sideways. "That's a weird-looking nine."

"It's in the Sanskrit language," said Boo.

Mini peered at her hand. *"Ashta,"* she said slowly. "The number eight."

Goose bumps fluttered down Aru's arm. They'd already lost a day!

"How do you *know* that?" she asked, feeling a little jealous.

"I taught myself how to count to ten in fifteen languages!" said Mini proudly.

"Sounds like a waste of time."

Even Boo nodded.

Mini glared at both of them. "Well, it's pretty useful right this minute, seeing as how we now know we only have eight days left until the world freezes over and Time stops."

Aru straightened her shoulders. A cold wind tangled in her hair. She felt that sticky sense of being *watched.* "Boo . . . what happens if the Sleeper finds us before we find the weapons?"

Boo pecked at the sidewalk. "Oh. Well. He kills you."

Mini whimpered.

Note to self, thought Aru. *Never go on a quest again.*

TEN:
A TRIP TO THE BEAUTY SALON

It took Mini a full five minutes before she could say another word. "Kill . . . us?" she squeaked.

"He's a demon, Mini," said Aru. "What do you think he's going to do? Sit you down for tea?"

Boo hopped along the sidewalk, gathered a pebble in his beak, flew up, and dropped it on Mini's head.

"Ow!"

"Good! You felt pain. Relish it, girl child. That's how you know you're not dead," said Boo. "Not yet, anyway. And you" — he glowered at Aru — "careful with that sharp tongue."

Aru rolled her eyes. She'd only been pointing out the obvious.

"Can't he just find his own way into the Kingdom of Death?" asked Aru. "Why does he have to follow us around?"

This demon sounded lazy.

"He cannot see what you can," said Boo.

"What if he tries to attack us in the meantime?" asked Mini. "We don't have anything to defend ourselves with."

That wasn't exactly true. They each had a gift. Aru opened her hand where the golden Ping-Pong ball sat. It didn't look like it would do anything remarkable. She threw it onto the ground. Instantly, it bounced back into her hand. Aru frowned. She threw it farther. Still it came back. Then she tossed it across the street, where it rolled straight into the gutter.

A blink later, it was in her hand.

"Okay, that's a little cooler, but still useless in a fight against a demon."

"Give thanks anyway," scolded Boo.

"Thanks, Universe," said Aru. "Even if I die, at least I can be buried with this ball attached to my hand."

"Not buried," said Mini. "Wouldn't you be cremated? I guess that depends on if you want to follow Hindu burial practices. . . ."

"Not helping, Mini."

"You never know what might turn out to be handy when you need it most," said Boo.

It looked like he was going to say something else, but then Mini squeaked.

"Whoa!" she said, staring at the compact she'd gotten from the Dharma Raja.

Envy flared through Aru. Did Mini's gift actually do something magical? Why didn't hers?

"What's it showing you?" she asked.

"A zit!" said Mini, pushing her nose to one side.

"What? That's it?"

"It means I'm growing up!"

"Or it means bad hygiene?" teased Aru.

"Or that," said Mini. She looked far less excited when she closed the compact.

"So we have a mirror and a glowing ball," said Aru.

"Yes," said Boo.

"To fight monsters."

"Yes."

Honestly, what was the *point* of being a demigod if this was all they got? The shiny weapons were half the appeal anyway! And where was her majestic steed? She'd feel a lot better if she at least had a cape.

"Perhaps you will not need any additional weapons to get all three keys," said Boo.

"And if we do?" asked Mini.

Boo's feathers shivered. "If you do, then I must take you to the Night Bazaar."

Night Bazaar? That sounds awesome, thought Aru.

"Assuming we survive getting the first key," said Mini.

That thought was less awesome.

Mini looked around at their surroundings. "If this is where Urvashi's mehndi map led us, then the first key should be somewhere around here. . . . But why would anyone hide a key to the Kingdom of Death in a strip mall?"

The three of them looked around the parking lot. There was a Chinese takeout place and a dry-cleaning store. Also a Starbucks that was missing some letters in its sign, so it read: STA B S.

Aru's gaze fell on a sign that was a little brighter than the rest:

BEAUTY SALON
YOU'LL BE SO HOT,
YOU'LL BURST INTO FLAMES!

The longer Aru looked at the sign, the brighter the mehndi version of the first key glowed. Beside her, Mini wiggled her fingers.

"Is your map glowing brighter? Maybe it works like a homing device . . ." said Mini, poking at the "sprig of youth" design on her wrist.

"Only one way to find out," said Aru. "We have to go inside."

Mini gulped loudly, but nodded, and they

121

made their way to the salon.

Light rippled around the edges of the storefront. It looked like a year-round Halloween store, with a few stray ghost decorations on the window and a rotting pumpkin by the entrance. Masks of screaming women hung from the roof. Their elongated faces and gaping mouths reminded Aru of that Edvard Munch painting her Art teacher had once shown the class.

"This place feels *off,*" said Mini, pressing closer to Aru. "And do you smell that?"

She did. A sharp, acrid scent, like overheated rubber or charred leaves. She wrinkled her nose and covered her face with her sleeve. "It smells like something was burned," said Aru. "Or . . . some*one.*"

Mini made little goggles with her hands and pressed her face against the door. "I can't see anything," she whispered.

The door was a dark mirror. Aru wondered if it was a two-way one that let people on the other side see you while you only saw your reflection. Aru had learned about those the hard way. Two weeks ago she had looked in the mirrored door to the teacher's lounge to see if there was something up her nose. A teacher had coughed quietly on the other side, and said, "Dear, you're free of boogers. Trust me. I can see quite clearly."

Aru had been mortified.

But now she didn't feel mortified. She felt a strange twinge of cold run up and down her spine. The air crackled and popped like logs in a bonfire. The hairs at the back of her neck lifted.

A light shone from her pajama pants pocket. The Ping-Pong ball was glowing.

Engraved on the door was: MADAME BEE ASURA, HEAD STYLIST.

Aru knew that name. But why?

"Boo, when we open the door, you can't act like, well, yourself," said Aru.

"And what is that supposed to mean?" retorted Boo.

"You've got to act like a pigeon! Or you'll blow our cover."

"You want me to stay *outside*?"

"I'll prop the door open," said Mini. She pulled a piece of biscotto from her backpack, crumbled it up, and threw it on the ground. "Here ya go, birdie!"

"I. Do. Not. Eat. Off. The. Ground."

That bitter taste of smoke filled Aru's nostrils. "I. Do. Not. Care," she whispered back. "Now stay here and be a good pigeon while we investigate."

A bell jingled as Aru opened the door.

The girls slipped inside. Mini left the door slightly ajar, so Aru could see one beady pigeon eye peering through the crack behind them.

The room was a bright lapis blue. Aru touched the wall gently and found it cold and hard. It was made of *gems*. Panels of mirrors formed the ceiling and floor. Big, comfy salon chairs lined the walls. But instead of a mirror in front of each chair, there was a portrait. Each one was of a beautiful woman. And yet . . . they didn't look very happy. . . .

Because they were frozen in the middle of screaming. Just like the masks on the roof.

The line of salon chairs seemed endless. There had to be as many as seventy pictures of screaming women.

"Nope. Nope. Nope," said Mini. "This doesn't look right."

"How can I help you girls?"

From the end of the room, Aru saw a lovely woman walking toward them. Urvashi had been beautiful in the way a rose was beautiful. The mind was already trained to find it exquisite.

But this woman was beautiful in the way that a bolt of lightning shattering the sky was beautiful. Almost scary. Definitely striking.

She was slim and tall, with shiny black hair that was piled in soft curls on the top of her head. When she smiled, Aru saw a crescent of sharp teeth behind her red lipstick.

"Did you come here for a haircut?"

"No?" said Mini.

Aru elbowed her in the ribs and said, "We didn't mean to, but we could get one?"

Aru wanted to spend more time with the stunning woman. Just being around her made her feel entranced. She had an overwhelming desire to please this person.

"No way," said Mini firmly, reaching for Aru's arm.

"What's wrong with you?" muttered Aru, yanking her arm away. The woman just wanted to cut their hair. Plus, she was so . . . pretty. "We need to look around anyway."

"Business *has* been a little slow," said the woman. Now she was standing right in front of them. "I'm Madame Bee. What are your names, lovely girls?"

"Mini . . ." said Mini, her voice getting squeaky. She wasn't looking at the woman. Her eyes were on the wall.

"Aru."

"Pretty names," crooned Madame Bee. "Usually I only cut older women's hair. Their beauty is a little more, well, *potent*." She grinned. "It has steeped longer, like tea, and therefore it lasts longer. Here, have a seat." She ushered them to two of the empty salon chairs.

"I'll only be a moment," said Madame Bee. "Just need to get some supplies from the back." Before she left, she smiled. It made Aru feel like she'd eaten a stack of waffles: rather warm and syrupy . . . and sleepy.

"Look!" hissed Mini. She grabbed Aru's face and turned it toward the wall.

The woman in the nearest portrait was still screaming. But there was something else: her eyes . . . they were moving. Following Mini and Aru. Another cold twinge coursed through Aru, waking her up.

"She trapped these women, Aru," whispered Mini. "We've got to get out of here!"

Aru slid out of her chair. Mini was right.

But there was another problem.

"The first key has to be here," said Aru. She held up her hand, where the design glowed brighter and brighter. "We have to find the sprig of youth before we leave!"

The girls scanned the room. It was pristine. With the mirrors on the ceiling and floor, they should have been able to find it easily. But they didn't see anything that looked like the mehndi design.

"It's got to be around here somewhere . . ." said Mini.

"Why couldn't the gods have given us more useful gifts?" grumbled Aru. She couldn't call Indra "Dad." It was too weird.

Mini took out her compact. When she opened it, a strange thing happened.

In the small mirror, Aru saw an alternate version of the room they were standing in. The walls were studded not with gemstones but with bone fragments. Instead of a polished floor, they stood on packed dirt. And when Mini angled the compact to reflect the portraits of screaming women, the paintings revealed something very different: skulls.

"The compact sees through enchantments," said Mini, in awe.

A sound made them jump.

They both looked up to see Madame Bee coming toward them, carrying a small tray that held two miniature jars. "Had to find small vessels for your ashes," she said, grinning.

Aru and Mini glanced at the compact. Where there had been a beautiful woman, now they saw Madame Bee for what she really was:

An *asura*.

A demon.

Her hair wasn't lovely black locks, but coils of fire. Her teeth weren't teeth at all, but *tusks* that curled up and out from thin black lips. Her skin wasn't a dusky shade of amber, but a pale and sickly white.

And there was something at the top of her head. A fancy blue hair clip?

No, a twig with tiny blue blossoms. Minus the color, it was identical to the design on their mehndi maps.

It was the sprig of youth.

The first key to the Kingdom of Death.

Eleven:
Ashes, Ashes, We
All Fall Down

"What are you doing out of your chairs, children?" asked Madame Bee.

Mini gulped loudly. The compact closed with a sharp *snap.*

"Taking in the scenery," said Aru quickly. "It's really pretty. Like you."

Madame Bee beamed her widest smile. She raised an eyebrow and flipped her hair over one shoulder. "I've collected beauty for years, so of course I'm beautiful," she said. "Now sit down, why don't you? Who should I cut first?"

"Uh . . . don't you mean whose *hair* should you cut first?"

Madame Bee tilted her head. Whatever light had been in the room dripped off the walls. Velvet shadows slid forward like snakes.

"No."

She tossed her tray to the ground and lunged. Aru only just managed to dodge out of the way, dragging Mini with her.

"Oh, come now, don't you know it's rude to play with food?" asked Madame Bee. "I don't like being rude. Just stay still."

Mini and Aru ran. Aru skidded on the floor, nearly crashing into a chair. She righted herself and her legs pumped beneath her. But no matter how hard she tried to get to the door, it seemed to loom farther and farther away.

Aru glanced up to the mirrors on the ceiling. Where was the asura? Her reflection didn't show in the mirrors. *Maybe she disappeared,* thought Aru for one bright moment.

But then a cold feeling spread through Aru.

A voice right behind her tickled her neck.

"Come closer, darling child. I'm running low on beauty. You don't have much, but it'll be good for a bite or two," said Madame Bee.

Aru jumped and spun around, but Madame Bee disappeared with a *pop* and reappeared on another side of the room.

"No use in hiding!" she sang.

With every word, she disappeared and then reappeared closer and closer.

"Psst!" hissed Mini.

Madame Bee was still cackling and spinning around in circles, or whatever it was asuras did whenever they were gloating. There, shoved up against one wall, was a giant table covered with postcards, hairbrushes, and bottles upon bottles of hair spray. Mini peered out from under it, and Aru scrambled after her. The asura just laughed, strolling toward them as if she had all the time in the world.

"Boo, help!" shouted Aru.

But if the pigeon could hear her, he didn't come.

"Don't think I don't know exactly who you are," crooned the asura, "little Pandavalings! It was very considerate of you to come all this way just so I can take your beauty. There's no use calling for your little feathered friend. He cannot enter my world. Just like you cannot leave it."

"Oh gods, what do we do?" whispered Mini, drawing her knees to her chest. "How are my parents going to identify my body if I'm only ashes? All I have are dental records and —"

"Mini! The compact!" hissed Aru.

Maybe there's a reason Madame Bee surrounds herself with false mirrors, thought Aru. All that talk of beauty had given Aru an idea. She fumbled for the bright Ping-Pong ball in her pant leg.

131

Suddenly, Madame Bee crouched down. Her face appeared upside down. "Peeka-boo!" she sang, her ghastly smile stretching wide.

Aru faced the demon, ignoring the goose bumps crawling down her spine. "I lied," she said. "You're not that pretty. See?"

Mini turned the compact mirror toward the asura. The demon's face turned even paler. Her hair crackled and snapped like she'd been electrified by the sight of her own ugliness.

"Nooooo!" the asura screamed. "That's not me! That's not me!" She writhed on the floor.

Aru and Mini scuttled backward. The golden Ping-Pong ball warmed Aru's pocket. She drew it out and squinted. It glowed like a mini-sun.

"I'll get you!" screeched the asura.

Aru threw the ball straight at her face —

"Not if you can't see us!" shouted Aru.

The ball's light blinded Madame Bee, and she fell back. "My eyes!" she howled.

A rosy golden glow filled the salon, and Aru had a strange vision of someone gathering up the first light of dawn in hundreds of buckets.

"Cursed heavenly light," growled the asura.

Huh, thought Aru. *So* that's *what's in the ball. . . .*

Maybe it wasn't so useless after all.

Aru raised her hand and the ball zoomed into her palm. Mini was still holding up her compact and when she saw the ball, she gasped. In Mini's other hand, an identical golden orb appeared.

"What the — ?" started Aru.

Mini closed her fingers around the ball. It vanished.

It was an illusion.

"How did you do that?" asked Aru.

"I . . . I don't know," said Mini, confused. "I just looked at the golden ball and *thought* about it, and then one appeared? But it wasn't real!"

"Where aaaaare you, Pandavas?" sang the asura.

Both girls backed away slowly.

The asura was crawling, turning her head from side to side, scanning the room. Aru's heart rate kicked up a notch. The demon's eyesight was returning!

"Now what?" asked Mini breathlessly. "How are we going to steal the you-know-what?"

Something was nagging at Aru. Where was that persistent smell of smoke coming from? Where was the asura burning things?

133

"Show me the room again in your compact," said Aru.

Mini turned the mirror toward them.

There was one detail Aru hadn't noticed before.

The unenchanted view of the room hadn't changed, but Aru's eyes snagged on a detail: handprints here and there. Handprints of *ash*. Maybe that smoky smell was coming from Madame Bee herself? Something clicked inside Aru. Everything started to make sense. Even the name of the salon: *Bee Asura*. B. Asura.

Aru lowered her voice to a whisper: "I know who she is. She's Brahmasura! The asura who could touch anyone and turn them to ash!"

"How is that comforting?" hissed Mini.

"Because we know how to defeat her."

"We do?"

"We do," said Aru, this time more firmly. "Keep the mirror in your hand. I think it doesn't just *show* what's an illusion; it can also *make* them."

"Like it made the ball," said Mini, catching on.

Just then, Brahmasura scuttled closer. "That was not very nice, children," she crooned. "Don't you know demons find it extraordinarily rude to be smacked in the

134

face with heavenly light? It . . . reveals things."

Right before their eyes, Brahmasura's skin began to wrinkle and sag. Teeth fell out between her shrinking lips. Her nose lengthened to a snout and a tusk grew on either side.

Aru almost gagged.

The asura's head whipped in their direction. She licked her lips. "There you are," she said in her soft, lilting voice. She crawled forward. "So you see the truth about me, don't you? Well, that's all right. I've always thought that women can see through illusions best."

Mini's fingers closed tighter over the compact mirror. She was shaking. Aru grabbed her free hand.

"Poor little Pandavalings." Brahmasura laughed. "And you thought you could be heroes!"

At this, Mini's eyes narrowed. "It's actually *heroines*," she said. "We're *girls*."

Madame Bee laughed. She crawled faster now, like some horrible scuttling mutant spider.

"Wait!" Aru shouted. "I wouldn't hurt us if I were you," she went on breathlessly. "After all, you've lost something, don't you want it back?"

She nodded to Mini. Sweat shone on Mini's forehead. She reached into her jacket pocket and pulled out a twig with bright blue flowers. She leaned out as far as she could. The asura's teeth showed. Mini didn't flinch as she waved it in Brahma-sura's face.

Madame Bee saw it and let out a shriek. "Where did you get that?"

"We stole it," said Aru. "You dropped it when you hit your head on the table."

Mini stepped back slowly. On one of the salon tables there was a blow-dryer. Mini snatched it quietly, gesturing wildly with one hand. *"Can't hold on much longer,"* she mouthed. Her fingertips were turning white from the effort of keeping up the illusion of the sprig of youth.

Just one more second, thought Aru.

Lightly, the asura felt around her own head, careful to avoid touching it with her deadly hand. When the backs of her fingers brushed the true sprig of youth, she sneered.

"You foolish little liars," said Madame Bee. "The Sleeper has been torn from his shackles. The rest of us may feast without fear. Did you really think you could —"

"Now, Mini!" shouted Aru.

Mini turned on the blow-dryer. Brahma-sura screamed as hot air gusted into her face. Her long, greasy hair whipped around, and the demon swatted at it, trying to brush it back without touching it. Mini squeezed her eyes shut, ran forward, and hammered the blow-dryer on top of the asura's hand.

The demon's palm landed with a loud *thunk* on her own scalp. A horrible shriek ripped through the air. Flames burst around Brahmasura's hand.

Aru yanked Mini out of the way.

Immediately, the smell of something burning filled the place. Brightness flooded the room, and Aru covered her face. Her ears rang with the sound of Madame Bee's screams.

When Aru could finally look, her eyes flew to Mini, who was on her hands and knees, searching the floor. Finally she sat up, beaming triumphantly.

"It blew off." She proudly displayed something in her hand: the shining blue sprig of youth. The real one.

Next to her, still pluming with smoke, was a pile of the demon's ashes.

TWELVE:
BRING ON THE NEXT DEMON!
WAIT, MAYBE NOT . . .

Mini held the sprig of youth at arm's length.

"Mini, why are you holding it like that?"

"It's clearly a biohazard! What if it's contaminated?" asked Mini. "It's been in a demon's *hair* for who knows how long. How'd she even get it there if everything she touches turns to ash?"

Aru thought of the hair products and jars in the salon. "I think she could only burn living things with her touch."

"You don't think the sprig is a living thing?"

"It's a key to the Kingdom of Death," said Aru. "You can't kill death."

"Hmm." Now Mini looked even more suspicious of the sprig. "What if holding it does something to me? Like make me young forever?"

"How's that a bad thing?" Aru wouldn't mind never getting wrinkles. As a forever-kid, she'd get to go to the front of the line all the time. And she could always get the kid discount at the ice cream place.

"Look at me!" said Mini. "I'd be stuck forever at four feet! That's . . . that's scary."

Aru pulled a crumpled tissue from her pocket. "If you're worried about that, then use this so you don't have to touch the sprig of youth for too long."

Mini eyed the tissue warily. "Is that used?"

Yep.

"Of course not."

"Then why are you carrying it in your pocket?"

Aru lifted her chin. "British royalty always carry crumpled tissues with them. They call them handkerchiefs."

"I'm pretty sure —"

"Four feet forever?" asked Aru, dangling the tissue.

Sighing, Mini took the tissue and wrapped it around the branch. They cast one more glance at the ashes of Brahmasura as they walked to the door.

"First demon slaying!" said Aru, holding up her hand for a high five.

Mini recoiled.

"You really don't want to touch other people's hands. That's the fastest way to get a cold. Or the flu. And if you're not vaccinated, you'll die."

"Yeah, but you might not stay dead. I thought Brahmasura was killed a long time ago."

"Maybe the souls of demons get to be reincarnated? Like us."

That was not a comforting thought. Aru lowered her hand. (Nothing is more awkward than an unreciprocated high five . . . especially when too much time has gone by and you can't pretend that you were just stretching.)

Seeing Aru's disappointment, Mini offered another suggestion. "How about an elbow bump instead? It's hygienic *and* fun!"

Aru frowned. "You sound like one of those posters in the doctor's office."

"I like those posters. . . . They're informative. And colorful."

Aru laughed. "All right, fine."

The girls bumped elbows.

As soon as they stepped out the door, Aru was slammed with a sense of *wrongness*. Before they had entered Madame Bee's salon, the weather outside had been a little breezy and chilly. Now there was no wind at all, and the temperature felt downright icy. It had been afternoon when they arrived, but now it was nearing nighttime. The sky was the color of a bruise. Aru glanced across the parking lot to where a stunted tree had lost almost all of its leaves. One leaf was slowly spiraling to the ground. A little too slowly.

From above, the flap of wings made Aru rear back and shout, "Stay back, Sleeper, I'm armed and dangerous!"

But then the winged thing turned out to be Boo. "Reckless!" he scolded. "Don't go about shouting his name!"

He descended on them, muttering, pecking their hair, and peering into their ears. "What took you so long?" he demanded.

"Excuse *you,* but we are *thinking* warriors," said Aru, smoothing her mangled pajamas with as much dignity as she could muster. "We had to plan. We had to analyze the situation. We had to —"

"Scream, almost die, beat back a demon with a blow-dryer," finished Mini.

"Here is where you stop regaling me with tales of your ineptitude and surprise me?" asked Boo hopefully.

Mini waved the sprig of youth. "One key down, two to go!" she said. "Next up: bite of adulthood."

Aru wanted to grin, but her eyes kept going back to the tree in the parking lot. Her thin pajamas weren't doing much good keeping out the cold.

"I'm sure it was sheer luck that saved

you," huffed Boo, ruffling his feathers.

Aru would've argued back, but she realized something. Boo *cared.*

"You like us!" Aru teased. "You were concerned!"

"Hmpf," snorted Boo. "If you'd died, that would've been a black mark on my reputation, so yes, at some base level, I was . . . worried."

Aru's flash of triumph disappeared with his next words.

"And I have even more reason to worry. Did the asura recognize you?"

Aru shuddered, remembering how Brahmasura had crooned *Pandavalings. . . .*

Mini nodded.

"That's not good. Not good at all," said Boo, anxiously pecking at the ground. "The Sleeper is trying to find allies. Show me the map of the second key."

Mini held up her hand so that the book with flapping pages showed on the side.

"It's in the Night Bazaar," said Boo thoughtfully. "We *just* might be able to convince those arrogant Seasons to give you some armor."

"The Seasons?" repeated Mini.

Boo ignored her question and continued talking to himself. "This was far too close. It's even worse than I thought if the Sleeper spoke to Brahmasura."

"If he knew her, why didn't the Sleeper just take the first key from Brahmasura?" asked Aru.

"He cannot see the keys, and Brahmasura never knew what the sprig really was. She probably just thought it was a magical bauble that kept her beautiful."

"Let me get this straight," said Mini. "The Sleeper can't see the keys, but he knows that *we* can. . . . Which means he could be after us *right now. . . .*"

That icy feeling Aru had wasn't just autumn turning sneakily into winter. . . . It was *him.*

In the parking lot, she saw the same shop-girl who had been smoking before. Now she was hunched over her phone, staring, her mouth caught in a frown.

She was frozen.

"Um, Mini? Boo?"

"What?" snapped Boo. "We need to come up with a plan in case he finds you!"

"I — I think he already did."

Aru watched in horror as a black line broke the sky, as if someone had unzipped twilight to show nighttime lurking just beneath its skin.

"We have to get out of here!" she screamed.

Mini shoved the sprig of youth into her backpack and grabbed Boo out of the air.

"Remember how to access the Otherworld!" hissed Boo. "Reach for the light, look but not look, and touch the second —"

But the rest of his words were drowned out as a gust of wind blew them backward. Aru would've slammed against the salon door if Mini hadn't caught her arm.

Together, they touched the second key symbol on the side of their hands. The wind howled. Aru could feel that familiar strand of light just out of sight, but something else caught her attention.

A dark shape started emerging from the concrete of the parking lot, a massive form of twisted ink and ice. And with it came laughter. The hairs on the back of Aru's neck rose. She *knew* that laugh. It was the same one she'd heard when she lit the lamp. A slick of ice spread from the places the Sleeper had stepped, crusting everything in his wake.

A powerful ache went through Aru. Every frozen thing — leaf, rock, and human — reminded her of one person: *Mom.* Hanuman had assured her that her mother wasn't in any pain. But how much longer would it stay that way? On the center of Aru's palm, the number eight was already beginning to change form. . . . She was running out of time.

And now the Sleeper had found them.

"Aru!" shouted Mini. "Hurry!"

Mini was a couple feet away from her and standing half in, half out of a cut of light. She extended her hand, and Aru raced to grab it. Her fingers brushed Mini's, and that familiar *pull* of the Otherworld tugged at Aru.

But then it snapped.

Something had caught her. She couldn't step forward.

"Come on, Aru!" screeched Boo.

Aru heaved. Something was *squeezing* her. She gasped and choked. Darkness squiggled at the corners of her vision. A black snake tail encircled her waist. She was trapped.

"I — I can't," she spat out.

Mini tugged her arm, trying to pull her into the portal.

As Aru heaved and strained, she heard a voice at her ear:

Just like your mother, aren't you, Aru? Slippery and deceitful —

Wings flapped against her face.

"Get off! Off! Off!" shouted Boo. He pecked violently at the Sleeper's coils until they shuddered, loosening just enough to let Aru grab the golden ball from her pocket. It was now a dull gold, not blindingly shining like it had been against Brahmasura.

"DO SOMETHING!" she roared at the orb, all her panic focused like a laser. She imagined it lighting up, becoming a sword, turning into a snake made of light, *anything* that would get her out of here. . . .

Light exploded, and the snake coils fell away from her.

Aru leaped for the portal. The Sleeper's angry screams chased her as she fell through. Finally, she landed on her butt (which hurt way more than it should have, because she didn't have a lot of built-in cushioning) in the middle of a forest.

Through the still-open seam, a man's arm reached out, swiping left and right as his hand grabbed for them.

Mini started beating the hand with the sprig of youth and shouting, "I" — *smack* — "do" — *smack* — "not" — *smack* — "like" — *smack* — "you!"

This didn't sound like very fierce smack talk to Aru, but considering that it was coming from Mini, it was about as violent as it would get.

With a final *smack,* the arm reared back. Boo flew through the gap of the portal, pecking at the line of light as if he were zipping it back up. After a final flash, the portal — and the hand — disappeared completely. When Aru opened her palm, the ball returned.

Boo fluttered to the ground, his wings drooping in exhaustion.

Aru scooped him up and hugged him. "Thank you," she said.

"No touchie!" huffed Boo. But he didn't move away from her.

"That was the Sleeper, right?" asked Aru.

There was no mistaking that voice, or that laugh. Guilt needled her. *She* had let him out into the world.

"He knew where we were," said Mini, clutching her backpack. "And now he knows where the second key is!"

Boo fluttered away from Aru. "No. He doesn't. I changed the portal location at the last minute to hide our whereabouts."

They were surrounded by wilderness. Aru didn't see a single other person. Wherever Boo had taken them was not in the same time zone as the salon, because it was still daytime. Not that there was much sunlight. Overhead, solemn oak trees drank up most of it, so that little was left to illuminate the cocoa-dark forest floor.

"You are safe, but not for long," said Boo.

"The Sleeper will be watching for any signs of magic. We need additional protection to get you to the Night Bazaar, where the second key lies."

"Protection? Like travel insurance?" asked Mini.

"What is *that*?" asked Boo. "You know what? Forget I asked."

"We could ask the gods for some help?" suggested Aru. "They weren't just going to leave us with a ball and a mirror, right?"

Aru felt silly for hoping their soul dads would care more, but it didn't stop her from looking at the sky, wondering if she might see a message spelled out in lightning. Just for her.

"I told you, they will not meddle in human affairs."

"What about demigod affairs?" asked Aru.

"*No* meddling. It is their rule."

"So who *is* going to help us?"

Boo seemed lost in thought for several moments. He circled the ground, then tottered over to a small anthill beside a log. He stared at it.

"I think I might know someone who would be very interested in meeting you . . ." he said slowly. "Now if I could only find him. Hmm. Ah, wait! There! See that?"

He was pointing at the dirt. Aru and Mini

exchanged nervous looks. Mini made a little swirling sign of *He's lost it* next to her head.

Boo glared at them. "No. *Look.*"

Aru moved closer and saw a slender line of ants leading away from the log and over a pile of leaves.

"We must follow the ants," said Boo.

"Yup," said Aru to Mini. "He's lost it."

"We follow the ants, because all ants go back to Valmiki."

"Valmiki? He's *alive*?" asked Mini, shocked. "But he was alive thousands of years ago!"

"So were you," said Boo curtly.

"Who's Valmiki?" asked Aru. The name sounded familiar, but she couldn't quite place it.

"The sage of learning," said Mini. "He's the one who wrote the Ramayana!"

Aside from the Mahabharata, the Ramayana was the other ancient epic poem that lots of Indians knew. It told the story of Rama, one of the reincarnations of the god Vishnu, who fought a ten-headed demon to rescue his wife. Aru's mother had collected some art depicting Rama's adventures, and now Aru recalled an image of a sage sitting on an anthill. She also recalled something else about him:

"Wasn't Valmiki a murderer?"

"Well, he started out as one," said Mini.

"Even if you murder only once, you're *still* a murderer. . . ."

"He changed," said Boo. "For many years, Valmiki sat and chanted the word *mara,* which means *kill.* But his chant changed over time and became *Rama,* another name of the god —"

"And then a bunch of ants swarmed around him, and that's how he got his name!" chimed in Mini. "In Sanskrit, it means *born of an anthill.*"

Aru wasn't sure that people could really change. On many occasions her mother had promised that things would be different. Sometimes she kept her word for as long as six days. For those days Aru would be walked to school, fed a non-bland dinner, and even spoken to about something other than her mother's newest museum acquisition.

But things always went back to normal in the end.

Still, having that mom was better than having a frozen mom. Aru swallowed her urge to cry. What were they doing here? They needed to get those celestial weapons, and soon!

"People *can* change," added Boo. His eyes looked very knowing in that moment, as if he'd read her mind. It didn't escape Aru that Boo sounded a little defensive.

"Okay, if you say so. But why do we have to meet this guy?" asked Aru.

"Valmiki's very wise," said Boo. "He's gathered all kinds of *mantras,* sacred words that will help you. But, be warned, he's still awful. . . ."

"Why?" asked Aru, shocked. "Because he was a murderer?"

"Worse," said Boo. "He's a . . ." His voice dropped. "A *writer.*" He shook his head in disgust.

Boo and Mini started marching forward (well, Mini marched while Boo rode on her shoulder), following the trail of ants. The ground was dark, and finding the insects was like trying to pick pepper off a black cloth.

"I can't see the ants anymore," Mini said.

"Use your phone light," said Aru.

"Can't," said Mini. "It died before you guys even came to get me. Don't you have one?"

Aru grumbled. "No. Mom won't let me have one until next year."

"*I* can see perfectly well," said Boo, picking his way carefully through the grass. This was probably the one time a pigeon sidekick was useful.

151

Ahead were several skinny trees. Between them stood a tannish boulder that Aru was quite certain hadn't been there when they were farther away. Boo walked up to the thing and pecked it twice.

"Valmiki! We are in need of your assistance!"

Was it Aru's imagination, or did the boulder shift a bit?

"Oh, come out of there. . . ."

Aru looked a little closer. What had seemed like a boulder was actually a giant anthill. She shook each of her feet, shivering a little. What if the ants were crawling on her right now?

The insects on the hill began to move quickly back and forth, forming lines that eventually spelled out words:

UNLESS YOUR LIFE YOU WANT TO
    CURSE
THE TIME IS NIGH TO SPEAK IN VERSE

Thirteen:
The Hipster in the Anthill

"Oh no," said Boo.

"What is it?" asked Aru.

"I hate poems that rhyme."

The ants rearranged themselves into a new message from Valmiki:

IF THAT IS TRUE
THEN I HATE YOU

"Poets are so dramatic," said Boo.

"O lord of learning," said Mini timidly, "we are yearning for your protection, so to speak. If you talk to us, we will be very . . . meek. We have a magic key, you see, and even if you hate Boo, I hope you don't hate . . . me. We really don't want to die. This is not a lie. Help us, please. So that we can get the other keys."

Aru's eyebrows shot up her forehead. She would never have been able to come up with a rhyme. It would have taken too much time.

The anthill paused, pondering.

YOUR RHYMES LEAVE MUCH TO BE
  DESIRED,
BUT PERHAPS I KNOW WHAT IS
  REQUIRED

Cracks started showing in the anthill. Gradually, it fractured like thin ice on a pond, and a head emerged. One bright brown eye peered at them. Another blinked open. Then the anthill split in half to reveal an elderly gentleman sitting cross-legged on the ground. His gray-streaked black hair was in a topknot, and he wore a pair of tinted glasses and sported a trim beard. His shirt said: I'M NOT A HIPSTER. He reached for a mason jar that appeared out of thin air. The orangish drink caught the light.

"I would offer you some turmeric tea, but you disturbed me at my apogee. I am trying to write a book, you know. Something about fifty pages or so. But I can't think of how to start the tale. . . . Perhaps with people on a forest trail?"

"Or you could be super annoying and have it start with them waking up," suggested Aru.

Mini frowned at her.

"We need some protection," Aru went on. "It's urgent, and —"

"You must convey it in rhyme, or I won't give you my time," said Valmiki mildly.

Out of nowhere, a typewriter materialized. He began to type furiously. Aru thought it best not to point out that there was no paper in it. Was it just for show? It seemed strange to announce *Look at me, I'm writing!* but then again, writers were quite strange.

"Be more like your sister!" scolded Boo.

Aru had a feeling this would not be the last time she heard that phrase. She pinched Boo's beak shut, much to his annoyance.

To be honest, she was more impressed than envious when it came to Mini's knack for rhyming. The only way *she* could've helped was if Valmiki liked beatnik poetry. They'd just studied that unit in English class, so Aru could snap her fingers in rhythm and start shouting about neon fruit supermarkets, but she didn't think that would be helpful here.

"We got the sprig of youth from a demon," said Mini. "But now we need armor from the —" Mini paused to look at Boo.

"Seasons," he mouthed.

"Seasons?"

Valmiki raised an eyebrow, as if to say

You're stretching the definition of rhyme, but then, you are *on an urgent deadline.* . . .

Mini hurried on. "Boo said you could protect us from evil; we hope he wasn't being . . . deceitful?"

Valmiki leaned back against the anthill and stroked his beard slowly. There are two ways to stroke one's beard. There is the villanous *I-am-devastating-but-also-fond-of-my-beard-texture* caress, and then there is the pondering *does-this-beard-make-me-look-devastating* rub. Valmiki's was the latter.

"To learn the right thing to say, there is a price you must pay."

Mini opened up her backpack and held it out. "I have no cash, as you can see," said Mini. "Perhaps Aru could pay the fee?"

Aru patted her pockets. "I've got nothing," she said, before remembering it was supposed to be a rhyme and adding, "too. How 'bout taking Boo?"

"I'm not for sale!"

Aru sighed. "Another fail . . ."

Hey, that rhymed!

"I don't want anything you have to sell; I want the stories you could help me tell." Valmiki leaned over his typewriter and tented his fingers. "This is a new age of epics, you see," said the sage-poet. "And I have two Pandavas before me! We have all the

156

legends and poems of yore, but it's time we offered readers some more. Promise to give me one day of your life, and I will grant you the gift of less strife."

So Valmiki wanted to write their biographies? Yes, please! That sounded . . . amazing. Aru was already brainstorming titles for hers:

The Legend of Aru
The Chronicles of Aru
The —

"Aru?" asked Mini. "On this man's terms can you agree? There is little downside that I can see."

Oh, right. The Chronicles of Aru *and* Mini.

"Wait!" said Boo. "Don't give your life rights away for free! The day has to be mundane, Valmiki. And *day* is a mortal's twenty-four hours. Comply, or else you'll face the gods' powers."

Aru hadn't even thought of that. This was officially the second time she was happy to have a pigeon guardian.

Valmiki shrugged, but he looked a little disgruntled. "You cannot rush a writer's art!"

"And here you thought you were so smart," said Boo smugly.

Good thing Boo answered, because the only thing Aru could think of that rhymed with *art* was *fart,* and that's not a word you want to throw around when you're talking to a legendary sage-poet.

"So, my friends, tell me: Do we have a deal?" asked Valmiki. "A nod is a sufficient way to seal. I will come and claim my payment one day. Until then, Pandavas, go forth and slay."

Aru grinned, nodding so fast she thought her head might fall off. Mini, as usual, was more thoughtful. She watched Valmiki for a long while before finally nodding.

Valmiki smiled. "This rhyme won't save your life, which is a light, but it will surely hide you both from sight. Say it once; be sure not to miss a beat, or you will risk becoming monster meat. Now repeat after me, little heroes, for I'd rather you not become zeroes. . . ."

Mini and Aru leaned closer.

"Don't look, don't see, there's no such thing as me," said Valmiki.

The words wound through Aru, powerful enough that she imagined she could see them floating around her.

Before they could thank Valmiki, he sank back into the anthill and it closed up around him.

"Now that you have the mantra," said Boo, "let's try again to reach the second key's location. The Sleeper shouldn't be able to find you this time."

Shouldn't, but not *won't.*

Aru steeled herself, and she and Mini spoke the words aloud. "Don't look, don't see, there's no such thing as me."

Up to now, Aru had never given much thought to how a word or sentence might taste. Sometimes when she said something mean, there was a bitter aftertaste. But when she spoke Valmiki's mantra, she *felt* magic on her tongue, like fizzing Pop Rocks candy.

The last thing Aru saw before she touched the second key symbol on her mehndi map were some new words on the boulder. The poetry ants had spelled out what looked to be the very bad first draft of an epic poem (then again, all first drafts are miserable):

IT WAS A DARK AND STORMY NIGHT
WHEN GIRLS WITH PIGEON DID TAKE
   FLIGHT
TO STOP THE SLEEPER IN HIS QUEST
   TO
WAKE LORD SHIVA FROM HIS REST

FOURTEEN:
A TRIP TO THE GROCERY STORE

Something touched Aru as she was flung through the Otherworld. Claws scraping lightly against her. Aru didn't feel safe. She had the prickly-neck sensation that someone was watching her. She looked down and saw something that nearly froze her blood:

The end coil of a thick black tail that was studded with stars.

It slithered over her feet. All the while she murmured, "Don't look, don't see, there's no such thing as me."

The whole thing lasted maybe a minute. All the while, Aru heard the Sleeper's voice in her head. *Just like your mother. Slippery and deceitful.*

How could the Sleeper possibly have known her mom? Did that mean Mini's mom was a hero, too? Not for the first (or last) time, Aru wondered why all this had been kept from her. How come Mini got to know and she didn't?

Light broke over her. Aru looked around to see that she was standing in another parking lot. Mini and Boo were there, too. She couldn't tell what city they were in, but it was a little warmer than the last place. Here, autumn gilded the world. The sky was bright, and the clouds seemed closer, as if they were weighed down by unspent rain.

"Why do we always end up in parking lots?" asked Mini.

"Better than in the middle of a road," said Boo.

They were standing in front of a Costco. Bright red grocery carts were lined up next to bales of hay. The trees burned scarlet and saffron, so vivid they looked as if someone had covered each leaf with gold foil.

Aru's palm itched. She glanced at her hand. The number eight had disappeared, replaced by a new, shining mark:

$$\xi$$

"What the heck does *that* mean?" asked Aru. "Please tell me the universe feels bad for us, and it's Sanskrit for *Treat yourself to a demonless day* and not the number three, which it kinda looks like."

Mini examined Aru's hand. "It's not the

number three."

"Yay!"

"It's the number six."

"WHAT?"

"*Sás.* Six," read Mini. She frowned and turned to Boo. "But yesterday, our maps said we had eight days left! What happened?"

Boo shook out his wings. "Traveling through the Otherworld requires a cost. Time does not always adhere to mortal standards."

"But that means . . . that means I've been awake for seventy-two hours," squeaked Mini. "I should be dead! Am I dead?"

Aru pinched her.

"Ow!"

"Nope. Alive and kickin'."

Mini rubbed her arm and glared.

"You're Pandavas," said Boo. "You need less sleep and food than mortals. But occasionally you do need something to keep your strength up. We'll get some snacks inside."

"Inside the Costco?" asked Aru.

Not that she had a problem with this. On the contrary, an industrial-size box of Oreos was *just* what she needed.

"That's not an ordinary Costco," said Boo proudly. "For Otherworld folks, it becomes a different store depending on who you are and what you need. For *us,* it will be the Night Bazaar. Inside, we'll find the Seasons and ask them to design you some weaponry. After that, we'll look for the second key."

Aru dearly hoped the second key would be located next to an industrial-size box of Oreos. But all thoughts of Oreos quickly vanished with Mini's next words.

"I'll go anywhere as long as we don't run into the Sleeper again. Did you see him when we left Valmiki?" she asked. "He was *right* next to me! I could've sworn he wanted something. He even *touched* me!" She shuddered. "At least I think it was him? It was just a giant snake tail. But it felt like him?"

"Did the Sleeper say anything to you?" asked Aru.

Mini frowned. "No. How 'bout to you?"

Aru stilled. "Earlier. The last time we tried to get to . . . wherever this is. He spoke in my mind and compared me to my mom. Called me deceitful like her. It was so weird."

Boo looked as if he was trying to make himself smaller on top of Mini's head.

"Do you know anything about this, Boo?" asked Aru.

"Me? No. Not a thing!" he squawked.

"Come along!"

"If he figured out where we were last time, and he can find us when we're traveling between places, he can probably do it again, even if we have the mantra to cover our tracks," said Mini. "What do we do if the Sleeper catches up to us?"

"Run faster than the other person," said Boo. And with that, he flew off toward the entrance to Costco.

Aru was about to make a joke to Mini, but she had turned on her heel and was jogging into the jungle of parked cars and abandoned shopping carts.

"Hey! Mini! There you are!" shouted Aru.

Aru had circled Costco Parking Lot Section A twice before she saw her. Mini was curled up on the hood of a minivan that boasted MY CHILD IS AN HONORS STUDENT.

When Aru walked up to her, Mini didn't turn her head. She just kept tracing the Sanskrit symbol on her left palm.

"You're going to leave me behind, aren't you?" asked Mini softly.

"What? Why do you think that?"

"I'm not as good as you are at . . . at this. . . . I wasn't even supposed to be going on any quests or anything! The first time

164

my mom ever took me to the Otherworld, I threw up. The threshold guardians didn't even let me past."

"That's better than me," said Aru. "My mom never even took me to the Otherworld. At least your mom told you about all this stuff."

"She had to," sniffed Mini. "She's a *panchakanya.*"

"What's that?" asked Aru. She could break down what the words meant, but it didn't help her understand.

Panch. Five.

Kanya. Woman.

"It's the sisterhood Mom's always talking about. Five women who are reincarnations of legendary queens from the ancient stories. These days their job is to raise and protect us."

"So my mom is part of this . . . sisterhood?" asked Aru.

"I guess," said Mini a little rudely.

Aru knew why Mini's tone had changed. They had started off talking about Mini's feelings, and now they were back to talking about Aru. But Aru couldn't help herself. There was so much she didn't know . . . and so much she *wanted* to know.

"Do you know who the other women are? Do they talk on the phone? Have you met

165

the other Pandavas? Are they all girls our age?"

Mini shook her head. "Sorry." Then her eyes narrowed. "Why? Do you wish you had a different Pandava with you, instead of me?"

"I'm not saying that. . . ."

"You're not *not* saying that," said Mini. "But it's fine. I'm used to it. Second choice for everything. I'm always getting left behind."

"Is this about what Boo said? That the slowest one of us is going to get caught by the Sleeper?"

She nodded, sniffling.

"Boo was just being Boo. He's a pigeon."

As if being a pigeon explained a lot of nasty behavior. But in Boo's case, the observation rang true.

"I just . . . don't want to be left behind." Her eyes welled with tears. "It happens to me all the time, and I hate it."

"Did you get chased by a monster with someone else?"

Mini laughed, but because she was crying, it sounded like a wet hiccup. Aru scooted away a little. The last thing she wanted on her was snot. She was already covered in monster ashes.

"No," said Mini when she had finished

snort-laugh-hiccupping. "You don't know what it's like. You're probably popular at school. I bet you're good at everything. . . . You've never even been to the Otherworld before and you fought Brahmasura better than me. I bet at school you don't get called the Tattletale. And you've probably never shown up at a birthday party to find no one is there because they put the wrong date on your invitation. . . . People wouldn't avoid you."

Aru tried not to wince. She had to admit that being a tattletale was the *worst* thing you could be at school. No one would tell you anything.

"Have you ever done anything you regretted?" asked Mini.

Aru didn't meet her eyes. She could have told the truth about a lot of things. That she wasn't popular. That she *did* know how it felt to be on the outside. That her best talent wasn't defeating monsters . . . it was pretending.

For a moment, Aru even wanted to tell her the truth about what happened with the lamp. How it hadn't been an accident at all, but something she'd done on purpose just to impress people who probably weren't worth impressing anyway, but she couldn't.

It felt nice to be considered *more* than

what she was for a change.

So she asked a different question. "If you could go back in time and un-tattletale on someone . . . would you?"

Mini looked up. "No. Dennis Connor was about to cut Matilda's hair."

"So? Why stick your nose into it?"

That kind of thing happened at school all the time. Aru just let it be. It wasn't her business. Or her fight.

Mini sighed. "Matilda had to leave school last year because she got sick, and when she got chemo, she went bald. Her hair has only just started to grow back. If Dennis had cut it, she would've been really sad."

"See?" said Aru. "You did a good thing. Plus, Dennis has *two* first names. He was asking to get in trouble."

Mini laughed.

"So you're not a tattletale . . . you're just honorable. Like a knight! Knights always rescue people."

Mini raised her palm. The sás symbol still looked like a backward three. "What about when knights aren't strong enough?"

"Even when they fail, they're still knights," said Aru. "Now come on. Boo said this was a special kind of Otherworldly Costco, and I want to see if their toilet paper floats. Maybe they have special Otherworld-Costco

168

things like bulk bags of wishes or dragon teeth or something. We can pick some up as soon as we get that second key. What is it, again? A bite of adulthood?"

This seemed to perk up Mini. She nodded.

"Still have the first key?" asked Aru.

Mini patted her backpack. "Right here, still wrapped in your Kleenex."

"Handkerchief."

"Uh-huh."

"Let's go, Sir Mini."

Like at every Costco Aru had been to, lots of customers were walking in and out. But here the people changed as soon as they crossed the threshold. For example, one woman pushing a cart toward the entrance looked like any woman you'd see on the street. Sensible shoes. Sensible hair. Sensible outfit.

The minute she stepped over the mat that said WELCOME TO COSTCO, she was suddenly covered in *golden* feathers. Like a giant bird! And her feathers were edged in flames. Little embers sparked and burned, falling onto the pavement and sputtering like a blown-out candle.

Another family was getting their receipt checked at the door before exiting. On the other side of the mat, they looked like humans from the waist up, but from the waist down they were snakes. The moment they crossed the mat, they were all human.

The snake boy winked at Mini.

She walked into a telephone pole.

"You are the *Daughter of Death,*" hissed Aru. "You don't walk into a telephone pole because of a boy."

"I didn't! I tripped. It wasn't because . . . you know. It's not because he did the thing with his mouth where it went up and his teeth showed."

"You mean when he smiled?"

"Yeah," said Mini, rubbing furiously at her bright red cheeks. "That."

Boo glared at them from the top of a grocery cart. "What took you so long? I almost started aging."

"You don't age?" asked Aru.

"If you do, you can use the sprig of youth," offered Mini. "Not sure how it works, though. Do we just hit you with it?"

Boo flew to Aru's shoulder and then poked his head out from underneath her hair. "You shall do *no* such thing, fiendish girl!"

"I was only offering to help," said Mini, crossing her arms.

"Well, stop offering before you get one of us killed," said Boo. "Now, before you go into the Costco, remember that it won't become the Night Bazaar until you stop looking so hard."

Aru blinked. "What does that mean?"

"It means go to the frozen food aisle, and start counting all the breakfast items. That should be enough to make your mind detach itself from reality and drift off. Or you could do algebra. Or read James Joyce's *Finnegans Wake*. That's my go-to."

"That sounds dangerous . . ." started Mini, but with one glare from Aru, she took a deep breath. "But I am the Daughter of Death, and so that sounds . . . like something I should like?"

Aru grinned.

The moment they walked inside, Aru was hit with that musty, industrial smell of supermarket. Why was everything made of concrete here? And it was so cold. . . .

Even if it was the middle of summer and so blazing hot outside that the road was melting, supermarkets were always freezing. Aru wished she'd brought a sweatshirt with her.

On her shoulder, Boo had made a strange nest for himself out of her hair and was now peering out of the hair-turned-shawl like an angry grandmother. "Not that way! That leads to the electronics. Too many bright, shiny things."

There were tons of people walking around them. Moms and dads and kids with those weird sneakers that had wheels on the bottom. There were all *kinds* of people, too — white, black, Hispanic, Asian, tall, short, fat, skinny. Not all appeared human, either. Some of them were feathered or furred, fanged or feline.

Aru's eyes widened. "Are they all . . . like *us*?"

"Dense as bricks?" offered Boo.

"No, like —"

"Scrawny heroes?" Boo guessed again.

"Ugh!"

"I don't know what an *ugh* is, but probably not," said Boo smugly. "But if you are asking whether they all have a connection to an Otherworld . . . Yes."

"Like ours?"

"Like *theirs,*" said Boo. "Whatever *their* version of the Otherworld happens to be. But let's not get into the question of metaphysics. Many things can coexist. Several gods can live in one universe. It's like fingers on a hand. They're all different, but still part of a hand."

They passed a display of potted trees. Apple trees with glistening fruit the color of pearls. Pear trees with fruit that looked like hammered gold. There was even a giant Christmas tree, sparkling with the flames of a hundred candles nestled on its branches.

Aru watched as a redheaded girl reached for the Christmas tree. The girl giggled and, right in front of Aru, stepped *into* the tree. The tree gave a contented little shake. But no sooner had she settled into the tree than a tall woman with long strawberry blond hair started knocking on the trunk.

"Come out of there, now!" she said. She had an accent. Irish? "I swear on the Dagda, I'll —"

The woman yanked on one of the pine branches, pulling it like an ear, and hoisted the girl out of the tree. The girl looked very unhappy.

"Every. Time," said the woman, who appeared to be the girl's mother. "This is why you're not allowed in parks. Maeve, my goodness, when your father learns that you . . ."

But Aru couldn't hear the rest of the scolding, because the two of them turned and hurried away down an aisle marked LAUNDRY SUPPLIES.

"All these . . . Otherworldly people . . . come *here*? To a *Costco*?" asked Mini.

Boo winked. "Who says it looks like a Costco to them? Who says they are even in the United States? The world has many faces, children. It's only showing you one at a time. Now hurry. Time will move even faster here, and you still need armor and the second key."

"And a snack?" added Aru hopefully.

"Yes, fine, one snack."

FIFTEEN:
WHY ARE ALL ENCHANTED THINGS SO RUDE?

The three of them stopped at the wide aisle of frozen foods and started taking inventory: black bean soup, lunch rolls, pizzas, bagels, pizza bagels, tripe, codfish, catfish, I-can't-believe-it's-not-fish fish. Gross. Aru waited for her perception to change, for magic to prickle on the outside of her vision like television static. But she didn't feel any different, and her hopes of seeing any magical toilet paper were quickly fading.

"So this is where every Otherworldly person does their shopping?" asked Mini.

"And weapons perusing, apparently," said Aru.

Not to mention key-to-the-Kingdom-of-Death browsing.

In all of Aru's previous grocery shopping, she'd never once picked up a gallon of milk and then wandered over to an aisle labeled SHARP DEADLY THINGS. (Unfortunately.)

"The Night Bazaar has had to adapt,

change form, and account for things like families moving to new countries and imaginations evolving," explained Boo.

"So what did it used to look —" Aru started.

"Just read the items," said Boo, irritated.

Mini yawned. "Fine . . . more pizza rolls . . . why do there need to be so many different brands of pizza rolls? Peanut butter sandwiches. Frozen salmon." She stopped. "Did you know you can get E. coli from salmon? It can kill you."

Aru, who was shivering from all the refrigeration, scowled. "Anything and everything can kill you, Mini! You don't need to point it out all the time."

Mini straightened her shoulders. "My mother always says that knowledge is power. I'm just trying to make us more powerful."

"And my mother says that ignorance is bliss," said Aru under her breath.

Muttering the words made her pause, though. Ignorance hadn't been bliss. Not even close. Bliss meant happiness, but here Aru was, not knowing who she was, where she was, or what she was supposed to do next. Had her mother said that because she had chosen to keep Aru in the dark?

Maybe her mom had done it to protect her. She did that a lot, even though Aru never understood until days (or even months) later. Like the time her mom had tearfully apologized when no one showed up at Aru's birthday party during third grade. She confessed that she'd accidentally thrown away all the invitations. They spent the day at the movies and had breakfast for dinner instead (which was awesome), but Aru had been furious. It wasn't until a year later that Aru learned the truth from a classmate. None of the invited kids had wanted to come, so her mom had lied to protect Aru's feelings.

Aru thought back to Mini's story about showing up to a birthday party on the wrong date. Mini had no idea how much they had in common. . . .

Mini started to drone on again about the aisle's offerings. "Frozen waffles, frozen pancakes, frozen stars, frozen wings, frozen —"

"Wait a sec . . ." started Aru.

Mini's eyes became unfocused. "Frozen prophecies, frozen orreries, frozen gold, frozen lead —"

Aru looked around, trying to see signs of magic. Slowly, her vision changed. The supermarket faded. The cement floor transformed to packed earth. The fluorescent ceiling lights stopped flickering.

Her bones felt heavy. She grew sleepy.

And then . . . then it was like dozing off in class. One moment of perfect, heavy-lidded happiness.

That was ruined by the sound of a bell.

Except it wasn't a bell; it was a loud squawking sound that came from overhead. The warehouse ceiling was gone, and a bird soared in the sky above them. Its wide wings were the color of evening turning into night-time. Half of the sky was sunlit; half of it was moonlit.

"Whoa," breathed Mini.

It looked as if someone had taken an ancient marketplace and squashed it to-gether with a modern grocery store. Beyond a pane of glass, aisles stretched far ahead in every direction. From what Aru could see, they held a combination of shelves, displays, small shops, and tents. One shop sold strange bolts of silk whose patterns looked like spun moonbeams and ribbons of rush-ing water. Next to it was an Apple Store.

There were still metal grocery carts, but they were . . . *alive.* The metal grilles curved up and down like mouths, and an extra set of handles slanted like eyebrows. When someone came near them, tiny spikes of metal rolled up and down the grocery cart like bristling fur. They seemed a bit feral. A

178

couple of them growled. One woman with a snake tail cursed loudly as she wrestled with her cart. Finally, when she took hold of its bright red bar with both hands, it gave in and allowed itself to be steered by the triumphant *naga* woman.

Three glowing signs hovered in the distance, but Aru couldn't read what they said. When she started walking toward them, she felt a sharp nip on her ear.

"Stay in line!" said Boo.

Only then did Aru realize they were in a long line in front of the entrance to the Night Bazaar, which glimmered on the other side of a pane of glass.

"This is absurd," said the naga in front of her. The snake woman turned to her husband, her cobra hood flaring. "I'm going to miss my haircut appointment. It took me *months* to book."

Her husband sighed. As he did, a forked tongue flicked out of his mouth. He rubbed the back of his head and sank lower into the bronze coils of his tail.

"It's a different world, *jaani,*" he said. "Less safe. Less secure. Plus, there's rumors that none of the gods can find their vehicles —"

Mini pulled on Aru's sleeve. "Did you hear that?"

"Obviously, Mini. I'm standing right here."

Mini blushed. "Do you think they know about the Sl—"

Before she could finish, Boo pecked her hand. The warning on his face was clear: *Don't say his name.*

"The You-Know-Who?" she whispered.

"He's not Voldemort!"

"Well, I don't know what else to call him!"

Aru knew better than to mention the Sleeper in the Night Bazaar. It would probably be the equivalent of shouting *Fire!* in a theater. Everyone here was clearly on guard. A frantic kind of energy was coming off the crowd, as if they were all waiting for something to go terribly wrong. Aru even caught a couple of muffled conversations:

"— the world is simply stopping. Whole groups of people and neighborhoods just utterly *frozen*! But the pattern makes no sense! Some place in the southeastern United States, another in a strip mall in the Midwest?"

"I'm sure there's a good reason —"

"The mortals are befuddled. . . ."

Aru tried to shrink. If anyone looked at her, would they see her guilt? All she'd done was light a lamp that everyone thought was *going* to get lit anyway (just maybe not so soon . . .). It felt almost cartoonish, like someone throwing a tiny snowball at a mountain and causing an avalanche.

The line moved quickly. Within minutes, the three of them were standing before a muscular man with the head of a bull. Aru recognized this type of Otherworld person from the paintings in the museum. He was a *raksha.* Aru almost panicked. But not all demons were bad. It was one of the things she liked best when her mother told her the stories: villains could be heroic, and heroes could do evil. *Makes you wonder who the villains really are,* her mother used to say. *Everyone has a bit of good and bad in them.*

The raksha regarded them with bored black eyes. "Empty your pockets, please. Take off anything remotely enchanted and place it in the bins at your left."

A couple of crystal baskets floated to the left of them. On the right was a conveyer belt that looked like it was made from molten gold. Straight ahead curved a sparkling archway that reminded Aru of the body scanners at airports.

"If you happen to be carrying a miniature universe, please place it in one of the baskets on the right. If it is unregistered, a Devourer of Worlds will eliminate it. If you would like to make a complaint, don't bother. And if you are a cursed being or under an enchanted form, please notify me prior to stepping through security."

Mini was the first to go through. She placed the compact in one of the glass baskets. She was about to walk through when the raksha raised a hand.

"Backpack," he said.

Mini handed it over. She was sweating and pale-faced. "Whatever's in there isn't mine," she said. "It's my brother's."

"That's what they all say," the raksha said, sifting through the contents.

He shook it upside down over the counter. Out spilled a sleeve of Oreos (Aru felt an indignant flare of *YOU-HAD-THOSE-THE-WHOLE-TIME?* feelings), a first-aid kit, a roll of gauze, a bunch of Boy Scout key chains (which made Aru raise her eyebrow), and the wrapped sprig of youth. The raksha scanned them with his eyes as he listened to someone talking in his earpiece. Then he pressed a small button on the lapel of his jacket and muttered, "Copy that. No sign of the godly mounts." He swiped the contents back into Mini's backpack and handed it to her. "Next."

Boo fluttered to his shoulder and whispered in his ear. The raksha's eyes widened for a moment.

182

"Sorry to hear that, mate. That's some rough luck. You may proceed."

Boo harrumphed and soared through the gate.

Next was Aru. She put the golden Ping-Pong ball in the basket and stepped forward, only to have the raksha stick out his hand.

"Shoes off as per Otherworld Transportation Security Guidelines."

She grumbled, took off her shoes, and placed them in a bin. She stepped forward, only to have the raksha stop her. *Again.*

"Miss, are those your feet?"

"Are you serious?"

"Does this job look like something that encourages humor?"

Aru considered this. "No."

"Then yes, I'm inquiring as to whether those are, in fact, your feet. You will notice on the board to your left that any removable body parts, yours or otherwise, must be registered as per Otherworld Transportation Security Guidelines."

"Dude, these are my feet. It's not like I'm hiding cloven hooves."

"Why did you specify cloven hooves?"

"It's just a joke! That's what we say in Georgia when we don't like someone! And then we add *Bless your heart* after!"

The raksha spoke into his lapel again.

"Yup. Copy. Potentially small, unregistered demon." Then, after listening to his earpiece: "Nope. Unthreatening." He looked at her. "You may pass."

Aru felt insulted. *I can* totally *be threatening*! But now was definitely not the time. She stepped through and glared at the raksha until he handed back her ball.

"Welcome to the Night Bazaar," he said. "On behalf of the gods and storytellers around the world, we hope you leave with your life intact and your imagination brimming."

Now that she'd stepped through the archway opening, the Night Bazaar truly unfolded around her. The half-torn sky of day and night glistened. And the *smells.* Aru wanted to roll around in them forever. It smelled like popcorn dripping with butter, cookie-dough ice cream, and fresh-spun cotton candy. She made her way to Mini and Boo, her head whipping back and forth so fast trying to see everything — the trees that weren't made of bark at all, but *glass;* the stores that seemed to literally chase after clientele — that she almost tripped.

"It's something else," said Mini, grinning. "And it smells *so* good. Like a book! Or vanilla!"

Aru was about to ask if Mini's nose was

working right, but Mini kept talking.

"Only my brother has seen this place, but I don't think he remembers it."

"Your brother? Why?"

Mini's face turned as red as a tomato. "They thought he was the Pandava brother . . . not me."

"When did they find out it was actually you?"

Mini turned even redder, now looking like a tomato's mutant cousin.

"Last week?" she said, squeaking on the word *week*. "Pandavas are supposed to sense danger and sometimes even react to it before they have full control of their abilities. Every time my brother did something that we thought was a miracle, I guess it was actually me doing it, because I was nearby and got scared, too. Last week, our car skidded into a ditch on the side of the road on the way to my brother's track meet. I must've freaked out or something, because I . . . I lifted the whole car."

"You *what*? I wanna do that!"

Mini looked horrified. "Really?"

"Mini, you lifted a car, when you're so small that I don't think you even register on —"

"Okay, okay. Geez, I get it." She sounded annoyed, but Aru could see the small smile

185

lifting up the corners of her mouth.

As impressed as Aru was, she also felt bad. Mini hadn't been lying when she said the backpack wasn't hers. It was meant to be her brother's, when he went off on his quest.

Now Aru understood why Mini was so hesitant about everything. Not once had Mini been taught to think that maybe *she* was supposed to be the hero.

"Imagine what your family will say when they wake up and realize you saved the world!" said Aru.

Mini beamed.

Boo fluttered to Aru's shoulder. "Come along. We need to find the Court of the Seasons. I know it's in here somewhere . . ." he said.

"And the second key, right?" said Mini.

Aru glanced at the mehndi design on the side of her hand. The symbol for the second key was a book. But there were no bookstalls in sight.

"You move so slowly," scolded Boo. "And your posture has gotten worse. I don't know how such things are possible."

"You're so grumpy," said Mini. "Maybe your blood sugar is low." She fished around in her backpack. "Here, have an Oreo."

"I don't want an —"

But Mini broke the cookie into small

pieces and shoved a bite into his beak. Boo looked outraged for about five seconds before he finally swallowed it.

"What ambrosia is this?" He smacked his beak. "Gimme more."

"Say please."

"No."

Mini fed him part of an Oreo anyway.

As they made their way into the bazaar, Aru could finally read the three huge signs pointing down the three main paths through the market:

THINGS YOU WANT
THINGS YOU NEED
THINGS YOU DON'T WANT TO NEED

"Well, we *need* to get our armor and the second key . . . so the second sign?" Aru guessed.

Boo nodded, and off they went. Around them family clusters streamed toward the three paths. The signs floated above the ground, completely unsupported and shaped like giant ribbons with hanging tassels. The round, scalloped ends of the tassels reminded Aru of cat paws.

As Aru, Mini, and Boo got closer to THINGS YOU NEED, the sign started moving. It skirted around the edges of a shop that sold laptops and computer wiring. They jumped and lunged at the sign, trying to catch it. But the sign kept scooting out of reach. It was dodging them.

"Hey! We're not playing!" shouted Aru.

But the sign wouldn't listen. It moved behind a pack of empty grocery carts. The carts swiveled on their wheels in unison, like a herd of antelope. The sign sneezed and the grocery carts scattered off in a huff.

"Why is it making this so difficult?" grumbled Mini. She had almost walked into a family of tortoise-shelled beings.

Boo flapped his wings. "You can't just ask for things you need. You have to chase them down! Make yourself known as a worthy recipient! I'll distract it. Then it's up to you two."

Boo strutted back and forth in front of the sign, as though he didn't care about it. The sign gradually lowered itself to the ground. It reminded Aru of the way a cat oozes down from a couch, curious to investigate. Boo walked faster and turned a corner.

The sign bent around to see where he had gone . . . and Boo jumped out at it.

"GOTCHA!" he shouted.

The sign whirled. It arched like a Halloween cat. When it had its back to Aru and

Mini, they crept forward. Aru slunk behind a palm tree, which hissed, "You have no *manners,* child!" Mini brought out her compact mirror and pulled out an illusion of a candy.

"Heeeeere, sign!" she cooed, waving it around. "Come here, sign! Come here!"

The second the sign turned, Aru ran up and caught it by one of its dangling tassels. Instantly, the sign went limp. It puddled onto the floor, forming a circle. The circle telescoped into a tunnel. Amethyst steps spiraled down into the dark. Boo perched on Aru's head and looked down the shaft.

"Ladies first."

Sixteen:
That Was *So* Last Season

No way was Aru going down those stairs first. And Mini looked like she was about to faint.

"Age before beauty," said Aru, grinning at Boo.

Sherrilyn, her babysitter, liked to say that line whenever the food trucks came to the museum and she wanted to order before Aru. Aru didn't mind, though. At least it meant someone thought she was pretty. With a pang, Aru realized she hadn't thought about Sherrilyn since the second she lit the lamp. She hoped she was okay.

Boo grumbled, but he didn't argue. Instead, he flew into the darkness complaining about the "privilege of youth." "In my day, we treated our elders with respect!" he huffed.

Aru and Mini walked down the steps. For the first time, Aru felt . . . hopeful. She wasn't sure why. It wasn't like she'd done anything heroic beyond trying to save herself.

But she had two companions on her side, and so far, aside from lighting the lamp, she hadn't made anything worse. Was she a heroine if all she did was fix a mistake she made? Or was it heroic because she was willing to fix it in the first place?

Aru wasn't sure what to expect ahead. The category THINGS YOU NEED seemed to cover a wide range of possibilities. For example, she *needed* water, sleep, food, and air.

At the bottom of the staircase, wind rushed past her. But it felt like three different things one after the other. At first, it was a gust of hot desert air that left her throat parched. Then it became the kind of sticky, humid air that felt like summer in the South. Her pajama top clung to her back, damp with sweat. In the next second, frost spangled across her skin and Aru shuddered with cold.

Beside her, Mini inhaled sharply.

Aru looked up, her eyes widening. Here there were no shopping aisles, just forest.

Aru and Mini stood in the center, Boo circling overhead. Around them, the forest was divided into six pieces, like a pie. In one section, frost sleeved the tree branches and icicles dangled like ornaments. In the next, a heavy downpour of rain made the trunks difficult to see. The third section was a riot of blossoms, the rich earth bursting with flowers and perfume. The fourth section was bright and dry, sunlight dappling the leaves. In the fifth, the leaves had turned scarlet and gold. The sixth section was a rich dark green.

"Where are we?" asked Mini.

"It's like we're stuck in all the seasons," said Aru, her voice soft with awe.

"We are," said Boo. "We're in the Court of the *Ritus*. The Six Seasons. Be on guard. They're brilliant, but *horrible*."

Aru's heart raced. "Why? Do they eat people?"

"Worse," said Boo, his feathers ruffling. "They're *artists*."

"I thought there were only four seasons?" asked Mini.

"Four?" repeated a voice from somewhere in the trees. "How boring! How bourgeois!"

"I don't know about that," said another voice, this time behind Aru. "I could make summer *endless*. Imagine that. An installation of infinite *fire*."

"People would burn up," said the first voice.

"Good! I don't like people anyway."

Figures from two different seasons made their way toward Aru, Mini, and Boo. A pale-skinned man with frosted hair and silver eyes sauntered forward first. He wore a shiny blazer and pants that looked as if they were made of glass. When he came closer, Aru saw that it wasn't glass, but *ice*. Fortunately, it wasn't see-through, but white.

"I'm Winter," he said coldly. "I'm underwhelmed by your acquaintance."

"Summer," said the other, extending a warm hand.

As Summer turned, the light seemed to change the spirit's facial features from feminine to masculine and back again.

Aru's confusion must have showed, because Summer shrugged and said, "Hotness doesn't belong to any one gender." The spirit winked before flipping their bright gold hair over one shoulder. Summer wore a tunic of flames. Their skin was the color of a smoldering ember, red-veined with fire.

"Why are you here?" Winter asked the girls. "Did that wretched sign bring you? Because we're not in the mood to design anything. Especially not for random people who haven't made an appointment. Besides, the inspiration to create just isn't there, is it?"

"It certainly is not." Summer sighed. "We only make dresses for the most fabulous of beings."

They glanced at Aru and Mini, making it clear that they did not consider the girls remotely *fabulous.*

"You're . . . tailors?" asked Mini.

"Did *that* just call us *tailors*?" asked Winter, aghast. Winter bent down to Mini's height. "My little sartorially challenged slip of a girl, we are *ateliers.* We dress the world itself. I embroider the earth with ice and frost, the most delicate silk in the world."

"I make the earth the hottest thing out there," said Summer with a blazing smile.

From the rainy section of the forest, a third figure appeared: a gray-skinned woman whose hair clung damply to her face. She looked soaked to the bone, and delighted about it.

"I am Monsoon. I make the world elegant with a dress of water."

A fourth walked up. Vines crawled over her skin. There were flowers in her hair. Her mouth was a rose.

"I'm Spring. I dress the earth in jewels," she said haughtily. "Show me a ruby darker than my roses. Show me a sapphire brighter than my skies. Impossible. Our other two siblings, Autumn and Pre-winter, would join, but they are in the outside world, attending to a number of designing needs. All celebrities need an entourage." She looked down her nose at the three of them. "But *you* wouldn't understand that."

"Do you always travel in pairs whenever you go into the world?" asked Mini.

"I will ignore the fact that you addressed me directly and will now face the empty space next to you to answer your question," said Spring.

Aru thought this was a bit much and wanted to roll her eyes, but she controlled the impulse.

"Of course!" said Summer, looking pointedly at the air next to Mini. "One for the incoming season, one for the outgoing. It's important to keep up with the times. Don't you know anything about fashion?"

Aru looked down at the Spider-Man pajamas she was still wearing.

"Apparently not," said Summer drily.

"What do you children want, anyway?" asked Spring, breezily.

"Well, we were hoping you could tell us?" Mini turned redder with each word. "Because, um, we were led here, and um —"

"Um-um-um," mocked Summer. "You were *led* here? By a pea-brained foul-looking fowl? I'd believe that."

195

"Puns!" said Winter, clapping his hands. "How devastating. How delightful. Chic cruelty never goes out of style."

"Watch yourself," warned Boo.

"Or what? You'll poop on us?" asked Monsoon.

The four Seasons started laughing. Aru felt as though someone had grabbed her heart in a tight fist. It was the same acidic feeling she got when she was called out for not arriving to a school in a fancy black car. This was just like Arielle and Poppy taunting and jeering, making her think she was small.

But they were wrong. She was Aru Shah. Daughter of Indra. And yeah, maybe she had made an epic mistake, but that didn't make *her* any less epic.

Most important: she had a plan.

They needed additional armor to reach the Kingdom of Death safely. Some extra weapons wouldn't hurt, either. That's why the sign had led them to the Court of the Seasons. And she wasn't leaving without what she needed.

Aru grabbed Mini's hand. Then she squared her shoulders and tossed her hair. "Come on, Mini and Boo," she said. "I'm sure we can find better."

Mini shot her a questioning look. Boo

cocked his head.

"They're not good enough," Aru said, glaring at the Seasons.

Aru started marching through the forest. The Court of the Seasons was the size of a football field, but she could see an EXIT sign glowing in the distance. Even without looking back, she could sense the shocked gazes of the Seasons. She would've bet all her pocket money that no one had ever walked away from them.

"Aru, what're you doing?" hissed Mini. "We need their help!"

"Yeah, but they don't know that," said Aru. "Bring out your compact. Conjure us some big sunglasses. And ugly hats. Things celebrities would wear."

"I hope you know what you're doing," huffed Boo. "I don't like groveling any more than you do, but this is no time to be proud."

"Oh, I know what I'm doing."

Aru knew because she'd dealt with it every day in school, that flare of not knowing where you belonged. That craving to be seen and go unnoticed at the same time.

Mini handed her a hat and sunglasses before jamming on her own pair. Even Boo got a pair of bird shades.

"These are ridiculous," he snapped.

197

"We're Pandavas," said Aru, loudly enough for the Otherworldly spirits to hear. "We can do better than the Seasons."

Leaves crackled behind her.

"Did you say . . . *Pandavas*?"

Mini slowed down as if she was about to turn, but Aru yanked her arm. "Let's not waste our breath," she said.

"Excuse me," said Summer, stepping in front of them. Their voice, which had been blistering before, had turned warm and languid. "Maybe there's been some mistake. Pandavas, you say? As in actual Pandavas?"

"Obviously," said Aru, lowering her sunglasses and speaking to the air next to Summer's face. "I thought you were designers. Aren't you supposed to be able to tell the difference between real and fake things? We're as real as it gets."

Monsoon stepped beside Summer and glared at her sibling. "*I* knew the whole time. Rain is cleansing, after all. It reveals the truth."

"Liar!" shouted Spring, marching over to them.

"*I* spoke to them first," said Winter. "I suspected right away."

"How can we help you?" asked Summer.

"Well," Mini started, "we need armor, or weapons —" Aru nudged her.

198

"You can't help us," said Aru, waving her hand. "Could you please move? Your shadow is touching mine."

"Oh, I am so sorry," said Monsoon apologetically. "I didn't mean to."

"Whatever," said Aru.

"We can make armor and protection! I make the best!" exclaimed Winter.

"Hmm . . ." said Aru. She drew out the silence just a beat longer. "Prove it."

Winter, Summer, Spring, and Monsoon nodded as one.

"And if my friend here" — Aru jerked her chin in Mini's direction, who merely adjusted her sunglasses — "approves, then I'll accept your measly and puny offerings."

Winter nodded enthusiastically. He opened his hands, and a cloak of delicate ice unraveled before Aru. With a twist of his wrist, it became a diamond bracelet. He presented it to Mini in a black velvet box. "Throw this on anything, and it will freeze an enemy in their tracks. Plus, it's an excellent accessory. Perfectly understated. Very elegant. Timeless."

"I have something better!" announced Spring. "You may be Pandavas, but you are children still." Aru narrowed her eyes, and Spring hastily added, "I don't mean that in an offensive way, of course!"

Spring spread her vine-covered arms, and a cube knitted from a thousand flowers floated in front of her. She snapped her fingers, and the cube transformed into a fancy bakery box. She opened it to reveal two little squares each covered in pink icing with a flower on top. Petit fours!

"Bites of rest and rejuvenation," she said proudly. "That is what I am known for, after all. From winter's slumber I create life anew. One bite and you will feel as if you have had several days of rest. Your stomach will be full, and you'll have no bodily aches and pains. It's good for your skin, too. Please do me the honor of eating one, Pandavas."

Curious, Aru took one of the cakes and popped the whole thing in her mouth. Instantly, her feet stopped hurting. She felt as if she'd just woken up from the best nap ever and still had a whole lot of afternoon left before dinner. It tasted delicate and floral, like one of those expensive rose-flavored cakes her mom brought back from her Paris trips. *Way* better than an Oreo. Mini ate hers, too, and a moment later looked like she was glowing.

"Well?" asked Spring expectantly.

"They're . . . edible," said Aru, taking the bakery box. "They will do."

Monsoon cast a waterfall in front of them,

then whispered a few words that shrank the waterfall into a gray pendant. Monsoon presented it to Aru.

"This is my gift to you, Pandava. Just as water can go anywhere and reach anything, this pendant, when thrown, will be able to hit any target, no matter how far away. But be warned: regret will always follow. It is the price of aiming true. For sometimes, when we take the deadliest aim, we are nothing if not reckless."

Aru didn't think it was fair that only her magical item came with strings attached, but it wasn't like she was in a position to refuse it. The necklace floated from Monsoon's hands and gently encircled Aru's neck. It was cold and a little damp against her skin.

Summer bowed before Mini. "Pandava, please accept our offering as well," they said.

The air shimmered. Thin flames erupted from the ground. They spiraled into coils and then braided themselves, forming the prettiest headband Aru had ever seen. It looked like it was made of beaten gold, complete with delicate roses and a glittering butterfly whose wings reminded Aru of stained glass.

"My season is one of lazy heat and forgetfulness ripening under a burning sun," said

Summer theatrically. "Forget can be a powerful tool for distracting an adversary. It can leave them feeling scorched and barren. Whoever wears this will forget something important."

"But, um, can —" Mini stammered as she stared yearningly at the headband.

"A Pandava may wear it without fear."

Mini nodded slowly, and Aru thought she could see a neon sign flashing above Mini's head that said MINE! IT'S ALL MINE! MWA-HAHAHA.

The headband was nice and all, but Aru wouldn't be caught dead wearing one. Headbands made her chin-length hair fan out weirdly around her face so that she ended up looking like a frilled-neck lizard.

By now, they had arrived at the end of the Court of the Seasons. Boo was staring at Aru, stunned. Mini kept touching her new headband and grinning.

Aru patted her necklace. "These things will do," she said rudely. "If we find them to our liking, we will —"

"Recommend you to everyone we know," finished Mini, smiling, before she realized she wasn't supposed to smile. "But only if we like them. Which we might not."

"Oh, thank you!" said Winter. "Can we, perhaps, get a selfie . . . you know, for the

Instagram?"

Do it for the Insta! Also known as the rally-ing cry of half of Aru's classmates.

"I hope they haven't changed the algo-rithm. *Again*. My likes are plummeting," moaned Spring.

"Sorry," said Aru. "No photos."

Winter's shoulders drooped. "Of course, of course. Thank you for accepting our gifts. You're most kind."

"Most generous," said Spring.

"Most lovely," said Summer.

"Most . . . clever," said Monsoon.

Out of the four of them, only Monsoon held Aru's eye for a moment longer than necessary. But when she smiled, it was with approval, not suspicion.

Aru waved her hand like a pageant queen — rotating it slowly at the wrist — before the three of them ducked through the large gateway marked EXIT. The moment they crossed the threshold, the entrance to the Court of the Seasons closed up behind them. They were left standing in a tunnel covered in vines. A crowd of people shuttled back and forth around them. On their right, an exasperated winged woman screamed into her phone and then incinerated it in her fist. At the end of the tunnel, a herd of wild grocery carts ambled past.

Boo ushered them to the side of the tunnel. A mechanical golden insect whirred to life above them, opening its stained-glass wings and hovering so they were lit as if standing under a Tiffany lamp.

"That was *awesome,* Aru!" squealed Mini. She held out her elbow and Aru bumped it, grinning.

Aru felt a little better, and it wasn't just because of those Spring cakes. At least now she knew that if they had to see that starry-tailed monster anytime soon, they weren't totally unprepared.

Boo fluttered to Mini's shoulder. "Well, that's not how the legendary Arjuna would have done it."

"I'm not Arjuna," said Aru, lifting her chin. "I'm Aru."

Boo puffed out his chest. "I know."

SEVENTEEN:
THE LIBRARY OF *A–Z*

The tunnel led to a massive cavern that opened out into a grand library.

"Books! Just what we need!" said Mini. Her eyes might as well have been heart emojis. "When my mom told me stories about the Night Bazaar, this was the place I wanted to see most. All the books are enchanted. They cover *everything* and *everyone.*"

"Great?" said Aru.

She liked libraries. She liked going to the audiobooks section and listening. And she liked pranking people by waiting until they pulled out a book, only to see her making strange faces in the empty space on the shelf.

But this library made her feel uncertain. She had that prickly cold feeling that had followed her in the parking lot right after they'd gotten the first key. Aru slipped her hand around the golden ball in her pocket.

It was warm to the touch, but thankfully not hot the way it had been when the Sleeper had shown up before.

"So the bite-of-adulthood key is somewhere in here . . ." said Aru. Was she mistaken, or was the book design on her hand glowing?

"Then by all means, meander slowly and ponderously until my feathers molt," said Boo.

"I'm looking!" said Aru defensively.

Easier said than done. The library was the size of a village. Shiny black stone formed the ceiling. Large windows cut into the walls looked out onto unusual settings. Through the first, Aru could see the depths of the ocean. A stingray glided past. Through the second Aru could see the leaves of a dense jungle. The third window peered out over the skyline of New York City.

Hundreds of shelves loomed before them. Aru watched, eyes wide, as the books hopped and fluttered around. Some of them even fought one another. A giant encyclopedia marked *A–F* squawked at a dictionary. And a book entitled *What to Expect When You're Reincarnated from a Cockroach* arched its spine and hissed at a bookmark.

"Maybe this place is organized like a regular library?" suggested Mini. She looked like she was in heaven, surrounded by all the books. "*Adulthood* starts with the letter *A*, so let's see if the shelves are alphabetical."

"What if adulthood isn't a book?" asked Aru. "Maybe it's hidden in something. A book isn't a key."

"Neither is a sprig. I think a book would make sense," said Mini quietly. "They're keys to lots of stuff."

When Aru stopped to think about it, she had to admit this was true. She may not have liked the books she'd had to read for school, but she'd loved the stories her mom had read aloud to her. Those tales had unlocked things that ordinary metal keys never could. A particularly good book had a way of opening new spaces in one's mind. It even invited you to come back later and rummage through what you'd learned.

"What do you think, Boo?" asked Aru.

He didn't respond. He was circling the ceiling. There was an agitated, restless quality to his movements. He moved jaggedly back and forth, as if he were trying to suss out something.

"Seriously, Boo? Do you have to stretch out your wings now? Must've been so tiring just sitting on our shoulders the whole time."

Shaking her head, Aru wandered over to the first aisle. Mini had already pulled out two stools, stacked them one on top of the other, and climbed up to read the book spines. A few volumes leaned out, inspecting Mini as closely as she was inspecting them.

"I can't quite see the titles at the top," muttered Mini. "Can you ask Boo to come help?"

"He's busy pecking at the ceiling or something," said Aru. "But I'll try. Boo?"

He was still flying in an agitated manner. Beneath him, his shadow sprawled over the books. It didn't seem like an ordinary pigeon's shadow. This shadow had wings the size of small boats and tail feathers that looked like trailing ribbons.

Aru turned to look at the tunnel entrance and saw that all the people who had once been in the library had disappeared. They were alone.

Aru frowned, looking upward for Boo again.

The ceiling had changed. It seemed to be moving. . . . The colors were swirling and melding. Aru realized that what she'd thought was polished marble was not stone at all, but *skin.*

She'd been wrong about something else,

208

too: they were definitely not alone.

Boo soared back to them, squawking, "RUN! It's him!"

Mini tumbled down from the two stools.

They took off, racing toward the tunnel, but the opening had disappeared. Behind them, someone started chuckling softly.

"Always so eager to run from your problems, aren't you?" asked a silky voice. "Well, you're just children. I suppose that's to be expected."

Aru turned slowly, expecting to see the snakelike Sleeper slithering toward her. But as it turned out, the Sleeper could take many forms. Before her eyes, the skin from the ceiling dripped down, coalescing into the shape of a man.

He no longer had a star-studded snake tail, but his hair was the same inky shade of night, and it looked as if there were stars caught in his hair. In the form of a man, he was tall and thin. He looked . . . hungry. His cheekbones stuck out. He wore a black *sherwani* jacket over dark jeans, and an empty birdcage swung from his hand. Aru frowned. Why would he carry something like that? Then she looked up at his eyes. They were strange. One was blue, and the other was brown.

She felt like she knew him from somewhere. How was that possible?

"Hello, daughter of Indra and daughter of Dharma Raja," he said. "Remember me? It's been a while. . . . A couple millennia. And then some."

His voice took her back to the moment she lit the lamp.

Aru, Aru, Aru, what have you done?

"I apologize for not stopping to chat after you let me out of that drafty diya, Aru," said the Sleeper, "but I had business to attend to. Things to gather." He grinned, revealing unnervingly sharp teeth. "But it seems I went to all that trouble for nothing. This won't be much of a fight."

"We don't even want to —" Aru started.

He slammed his foot against the ground, and the earth rattled. Books fell off the shelves and scattered around them. One of them, entitled *Afloat,* flapped its endpapers, drifted to the ceiling, and refused to move despite *Artful Guile* trying to tempt it back down with a bookmark.

"Don't even *think* about interrupting me," he said. "I've waited for ages. Eons." He glared at Aru. "Ever since *your mother* locked me into that miserable lamp."

"My . . . my mother?"

"Who else would smile as she slid the knife into my chest?" the Sleeper chided.

"And you're just like her, aren't you? A liar. I saw you when you lit the lamp. Anything to impress your friends, right? What a coward you are, Aru Shah."

"My mother is *not* a liar!" shouted Aru.

"You don't even know her," sneered the Sleeper.

Aru didn't want to listen. But she felt a twist in her gut. All those times she had waited for her mother, the dinner she'd made going cold on the table. All those doors that had been closed in her face. All the questions that had been shushed. It was a different kind of pain when the hurt came not from a lie, but the truth. Her mother had hidden an entire world from her.

She really *didn't* know her mom at all.

The Sleeper gestured to Mini with a fake frown on his face, but he kept his gaze on Aru. "And what's this? Your little sister here didn't know that you summoned me? That you are the reason her whole family is in danger? That *you* are the cause of all this, and not poor old me?"

Aru risked a glance at Mini. Her eyebrows were drawn together. Aru may have freed the Sleeper, but she hadn't done it on purpose. Would Mini ever believe her now? Aru couldn't get the words out — they were clogged by guilt.

211

"I — I can explain, Mini," she said. "Later."

Mini's face hardened, but she nodded. There was no point hashing it out now, right before certain death.

The Sleeper's eyes narrowed. He dropped the birdcage beside him. It wasn't empty after all. Small clay figurines in the shape of horses and tigers rattled together as they hit the floor.

"Give me the sprig of youth," he said.

Aru and Mini started inching backward. Aru was aware of Boo flying in frantic circles above them, as if trying to signal something. She risked a glance up. Boo dipped, landing on a book with a silver spine. It was too far away for Aru to read, but she knew what it said: *Adulthood.*

The second key was right over their heads. If they could just distract the Sleeper, they could get it. Mini caught Aru's eye and nodded once. Apparently they'd had the same thought. Which would've been really cool if Mini didn't also look as though she'd like to strangle Aru at the first chance.

They wedged themselves between the stacks of *A*-shelves.

"How'd you find us?" asked Aru.

"Rakshas are very talkative," he said, smiling. "Two little girls entering the Night

212

Bazaar with enchanted objects bearing the marks of Lord Indra and the Dharma Raja? How curious."

"What kinda name is Sleeper?" asked Aru. "Are you just really good at napping?"

He frowned. Out of the corner of her eye, she saw Mini touch her diamond bracelet.

"Or is it like a metaphor?" pushed Aru, proud that she'd remembered the word from last week's English class. "Maybe a bad nickname from middle school, when you fell asleep on a test and all the ink got on your face?"

"Enough!" he thundered. "Where's the second key? You know what it is, don't you?"

Mini slid her backpack to the floor, nudging it closer to Aru. When Mini turned around, Aru saw that she had managed to tuck the sprig of youth into the back of her jeans.

Aru felt as if she'd tapped into a wavelength that belonged only to her and Mini. They moved in sync, their thoughts aligned.

"If you want the key, catch it!" shouted Aru.

She picked up the backpack and threw it into the air. The Sleeper lunged after it, while Mini tore off her bracelet. With a flick of her wrist, it expanded, flashing and shimmering. Cold flooded the air. Frost seeped

213

out, lacing the floor.

Mini tossed the Cloak of Winter over the Sleeper.

"I've got him! You go grab the you-know-what," Mini called to Aru.

Mini wrestled with the cloak, her feet skidding across the floor. Underneath, the Sleeper froze. But he wouldn't stay frozen solid for long. Already, cracks were forming in the ice and his eyes were rolling furiously. Mini pushed him and he fell over on his side, knocking into the birdcage on the floor. It rolled down one of the library aisles.

"Over here!" shouted Boo from atop the books.

Aru really wished she could fly. But since she couldn't, she lost a couple of moments grabbing the stools, restacking them, and climbing to the top shelf. She was out of breath by the time she spotted the book.

It stood apart from the other volumes. Aloof and — if books could act that way — a little judgmental of its neighbors. Its title glowed in silver foil on the spine: *Adulthood.* Boo hopped onto her head and pecked at her hair, urging her to take it.

Aru glanced at the other titles next to it. *Adulation* was singing. Pink hearts kept oozing from its pages. *Adullamite* hopped away, running toward the *B* titles, which flapped their pages to welcome it.

A bite of adulthood . . . What was she supposed to do? Grab the book and actually sink her teeth into it?

She glanced at Mini, who was trying to keep the cloak tied over the frozen Sleeper. But he was beginning to move. Shards of ice flew off him. Mini met Aru's eyes and hollered, "Do it!"

Boo soared down to help Mini, leaving Aru on the shelf.

"What are you waiting for, Aru?" demanded Mini.

"Ew, ew, ew!" said Aru. She squeezed her eyes shut, grabbed the book, and bit into it.

It squealed.

She hadn't given much thought as to what a book might taste like. But *Adulthood* had a strange flavor. Sweet and bitter at the same time, like candied orange peel. It reminded Aru of walking to school on a cold February morning, when the sun was bright but distant and everything was a little too stark.

She spat the bite of *Adulthood* into her palm. The wet wad of paper transformed into a glowing silver coin. Aru shoved it in her pocket, then ran her tongue along her teeth, hating that she couldn't quite rid herself of the taste.

"I got it —" she started, but her victory was short-lived.

The Sleeper had thrown off the cloak. Now it lay dull and limp on the floor, slowly melting.

"You are testing my patience —" he hissed.

"You slept in a lamp for a hundred years and that's the best you could come up with?" shouted back Aru. "What a cliché. All you're missing is the villain mustache."

She was trying to keep his attention on her while Mini fumbled for another magical item from the Seasons. But it wasn't Mini who launched herself at him next. It was *Boo.*

"Those!" he snapped. "Are!" He pecked at the Sleeper's eyes. "My!" He pooped. "HEROINES!"

Aru clambered down from the stools and snatched the backpack off the ground. Mini was trying to shake the Cloak of Winter back into something that would tame the Sleeper, but it stayed lifeless.

Boo let out a loud, pained squawk. The Sleeper had caught him in one hand. With the other hand, he wiped the bird poop off his head. He peered more closely at Boo. He didn't yell or scream. Instead . . . he *laughed.*

"What has happened to you, old friend?"

Eighteen:
A Strange Case

Friend? Aru almost dropped the backpack.

"You are much changed since you were the king of Subala."

"Boo, what's he talking about?" asked Mini.

The Sleeper smiled. "*Boo?* That's what they call you? Has all that guilt made you soft?"

Something clicked in Aru's head. Subala wasn't Boo's name, but the name of his *kingdom.* She remembered Urvashi's laugh. . . . *If they really are Pandavas, then the irony that* you *are the one who has been chosen to help them delights me.*

"I get it," said the Sleeper mockingly. "Boo is short for Subala." He turned to the girls, his eyebrows knitted in that *oh-I'm-so-sorry-for-you-NOT* way that only truly awful people can pull off. "His name isn't Subala. It's *Shakhuni.* I suppose you could call him Shocky. In which case I imagine this might

218

be a *shocker*."

He *chuckled* at his own joke. Which is another thing that only truly awful people do (grandparents, dads, and that one well-meaning but weird uncle are exceptions).

Shakhuni. Aru's heart went cold. She knew that name from the stories. It was the name of the deceiver. The sorcerer who led the eldest Pandava brother astray in a cursed game of dice, where he was forced to gamble away his entire kingdom. Shakhuni started the great Kurekshetra war. His revenge consumed his own kingdom.

He was one of the Pandavas' greatest enemies.

And she . . . She had let him sit on her shoulder. Mini had fed him an Oreo. They'd *cared* for him.

"Your quarrel is not with them," Boo said to the Sleeper.

"My, you have become quite the addled one," said the Sleeper. "You're telling me you have actually been tasked to help the Pandavas? What is this, your penance for committing so horrible a sin?"

"No," said Boo, and this time he looked at Aru and Mini. "It is not my penance. It is my *honor*."

Aru felt a flush of pride in the same instant that she felt a stab of misgiving. Nice

219

words, but why should she believe them? Poppy and Arielle had been nice to her up until the moment when they weren't.

"You *have* gone soft," said the Sleeper, frowning.

"I've grown stronger. In a way that, perhaps, you can no longer understand. People change. You used to believe that most of all," said Boo. "Or have you forgotten?"

"People don't change. They just grow weaker," said the Sleeper. His voice was as icy as the Cloak of Winter. "For the sake of old times, I will give you one chance. Join me. Help my cause. I will make us gods, and end this age."

This is it. Aru waited for Boo to betray them. She braced herself to feel a rush of hurt, but Boo didn't hesitate. His voice was loud and strong when he said, "No."

Aru's heart squeezed.

The Sleeper growled and threw Boo across the room. The pigeon hit a shelf with a loud *smack* and slumped to the floor. Mini and Aru screamed, but the moment they tried to run toward him, a wall of air forced them back. Aru braced herself, her hand flying to the pendant that Monsoon had given her. She wanted to throw it at him, but all it could do was *aim* right. Making sure a rock hit the Sleeper on his nose wouldn't do much good if he could just shake his head and keep going. She needed something bigger or more powerful.

The Sleeper prowled toward them. As Aru was scanning the collection for a giant book to hit him with (the biggest one, *Atlas,* growled at her from the lowest shelf), Mini let out a scream. She tore off her headband and threw it like a Frisbee at the Sleeper. It caught on his ear.

For one moment, his eyes went all black. But then he recovered, and the headband vanished.

"That was your best effort?" he asked, laughing. "A headband? I'm trembling with fear. Now, let's be honest. I could kill you easily. Two little girls. No training, no valor. Do you really think you can get the celestial weapons?"

Aru felt her face turning red. Indra had claimed her as *his* daughter. Maybe she'd been light-headed from standing up in the clouds when it happened, but she'd seen (at least she *thought* she'd seen) the statue of Indra smile at her. As if he was . . . pleased.

Remembering that gave her the courage to say, "We were chosen by the gods."

Then again, what was with the golden ball? Aru didn't have any experience with dads, but she was pretty sure giving your

221

kid a glowing Ping-Pong ball to fight demons was like getting pocket fuzz and spare
change instead of an allowance.

The Sleeper scoffed, "The gods would
never trust you to do anything. Just look at
you."

The more he talked, the angrier Aru
became. She wasn't going to back down.
They had something the Sleeper didn't.

"Threaten us all you want, but you need
us to get those keys, don't you?" asked Aru.
"You can't see them. You don't even know
what they *are.*"

The Sleeper grew quiet and stroked his
chin thoughtfully. Finally he said, "You're
right."

Aru couldn't believe it. Had she talked
him down?

The Sleeper raised his hand, curling his
fingers. Boo zoomed into his palm. The bird
wasn't moving.

"I do need you," he said. "I would've
taken the key you have now, but it may lead
you to the other two. And it doesn't matter
that I can't see them, because *you* are going
to deliver all three to me by the new moon."

He squeezed Boo, and Mini began to
whimper.

The Sleeper turned toward her. "I know
so much about you now. From listening to

your heartbeats," he said with mock sweetness. "Your father wears a cross beneath his shirt and an *agimat* necklace passed down from his family in the Philippines. Your brother hides a photo of his soccer teammate beneath his pillow, and when you found it, he swore you to secrecy. Your mother's hair smells like sandalwood."

Mini's face turned white.

Then the Sleeper faced Aru. Something flashed in his eyes. "And you. Well. You and I might as well be family."

"What are you *talking* about?" Aru blurted. "You're crazy! I —"

He cut her off with a look. "Summon me just before the new moon, or I will do more than just freeze your loved ones."

"Never!" said Aru. "We'll fight if we have to, and —"

"Tsk-tsk," said the Sleeper. "Before you even think about fighting me, know that I am gathering my own friends." He gave them a cruel smile. "And trust me, you won't like meeting them."

He disappeared, taking Boo with him.

For a whole minute, Aru and Mini didn't budge. Aru felt like she was spinning even though she was standing still.

Too many things were zipping through her

head. Boo had fought for them just now. But once he had been the Pandavas' enemy. Was that why he was being forced to help them in this life, in the form of a pigeon, no less? And then there was the fact that the Sleeper knew her mom — and Mini's family. How was that possible?

Around them, the books began to run about, desperate to restore some order. Their pages ruffled like birds settling back down to sleep. Without the Sleeper covering it, the ceiling now looked like open sky. Bruised purple storm clouds drifted across it. Aru scowled. It didn't make sense for the magic around them to look so beautiful when she felt so . . . *ugly.*

What was the point in even trying to get to the Kingdom of Death without Boo? The Sleeper was right. She had caused all this. And she had failed everyone.

"Why?" croaked Mini.

She didn't have to say the rest.

Why had Aru lied about the lamp? Why had Boo hidden his past? Why was *any* of this happening to them?

Aru was tired. Tired of lying. Tired of imagining the world as it could be and not as it was. She was tired of making herself bigger and better in her own head when it was clear that she never would or could be in her real life.

She pulled the coin that she'd gotten from *Adulthood* out of her pocket. It had faded to dull silver.

Aru couldn't meet Mini's gaze. "I knew a little of what would happen if I lit the lamp — my mom had told me, but I didn't really believe her — and I lit it anyway. What the Sleeper said was true: I did it to impress some classmates that I thought I wanted as friends."

Mini's shoulders shook. "My family is in danger because of you," she said. She didn't cry or yell. And that made it so much worse. "You lied about everything, didn't you? Were you just laughing at me the whole time?"

Aru looked her in the eyes now. "What? No! Of course not —"

"Why should I believe you?" Mini cut in. "You said you thought I was brave. And that it wasn't a bad thing to be the Daughter of Death." She stared at Aru as if she could see straight through her. "You even told me that you wouldn't leave me behind."

"Mini, I meant all of that."

"I don't care what you say, because you're a liar, Aru Shah." Mini snatched the bite of *Adulthood* from Aru.

"Hey! What are you doing?"

"What's it look like I'm doing?" said Mini. She put the coin in her backpack along with the sprig of youth. "I'm finishing this. I have to try to save my family."

"But you need me," said Aru. She had that hot, stuffed-inside-a-sausage feeling that always happened before she cried. She didn't want to cry.

"Maybe," said Mini sadly. "But I just don't trust you."

Mini pressed the image of the last key on her hand, the wave of water shimmering across her fingers.

"Mini, wait —"

She stepped through a cut of light. Aru tried to grab her hand, but only found air. Mini had disappeared.

Aru was left standing by herself. The books around her tittered and gossiped. There was no place left for her here in the Otherworld. The Sleeper didn't even think they were enough of a threat to bother with killing them. She should have felt grateful, but she just felt invisible. Useless. On top of that, Boo was hurt, and Aru had earned and lost a sister in a matter of days.

At the thought of days, Aru slowly turned over her hand. She felt like she was being handed back a quiz that she'd *definitely* failed and was doing her best to turn over the paper as slowly as possible.

8

What the heck was that?

Whatever number it was, it definitely wasn't the number six. Mini would know what it meant. But Mini wasn't here.

Aru was running out of days, and if ever there was a time to cry, it was now.

But she couldn't. She was too tired. And *angry.*

She paced. There was no way she could go back to the museum. What would she do, sit under the elephant and wait for the world to end? And yet she couldn't follow Mini, either. Mini didn't want her help. Aru had nothing to offer. Her only natural gift was lying.

That wasn't a very heroic quality.

Aru was nearly at the end of the library's row *A* when a strange book caught her eye. It was small and bright green. It bounced up and down when she got close. The title was simple: *Aru.*

Curious, she reached for it and opened the front cover. There she was. There was a picture of her at school. And there was another picture of her waiting at home for her mom. She rifled through the pages, her heart racing. There was even an illustration of her and Mini at Madame Bee's beauty salon. Aru was in the middle of talking. In the next painting, Aru was looking down triumphantly in the Court of the Seasons.

She tried to flip to the end, but the pages were glued together. Mini had said something about the library of the Night Bazaar, that this place held the stories of everything and everyone. Including her. Maybe it meant that her story wasn't finished just yet. She had deceived both Madame Bee and the Seasons . . . but her lies hadn't been *bad.* They had led to something good. She'd talked herself and Mini out of trouble, and gotten them new weapons. Maybe . . . maybe her gift wasn't lying. Maybe her gift was imagination.

Imagination was neither good nor bad. It was a little bit of both. Just like her.

Was Arjuna at all like this? Did he ever lie or worry that he was more bad than good? The legends made him sound perfect. But maybe if he'd grown up the way she did, he would've made mistakes, too. It was hard to judge, based on a story, what he might really have been like. If she were writing about herself, she wouldn't put in the bad parts, only the good. *Tales are slippery,* her mother

228

had often said. *The truth of a story depends on who is telling it.*

If that *Aru* book was to be believed, it meant that her story wasn't finished yet.

Aru glanced at her palm. Whatever that Sanskrit number was, it looked too fancy to be a one. She was sure there was still some time left. She closed her hand into a fist.

Forget the Sleeper. I'm going to fix this.

Aru shut the book. Part of her wanted to take it with her, but she stopped herself. It reminded her of the time she'd passed a cemetery that had an apple tree. The fruit looked like jewels, and Aru had wanted to pluck one. But she had the weirdest sensation you weren't supposed to take them, let alone eat them. That was how she felt about the book. Aru ran her finger along its green spine and felt an answering trace down her back. Then she forced herself to put it back on the shelf.

As Aru rounded the corner, something bright caught her eye.

It was the birdcage. The one the Sleeper had carried.

She remembered now: it had rolled away from him. It had come to rest in the *B* aisle. The shelves were noisy, and it smelled like vanilla here. *Baby,* a small blue book, was wailing, while *Backhand* and *Backward* took turns smacking each other with their covers.

Aru knelt and picked up the birdcage. It seemed odd that the Sleeper had taken the bird, but not the cage. Rattling around inside were a few small clay figurines, each no longer than her pinky. She reached in and pulled out a goat, a crocodile, a pigeon, a snake, an owl, and a peacock. There was even a seven-headed horse. And a tiger with its mouth still open in a roar.

As she arranged the animals in a line on the floor, she frowned. Didn't the goddess Durga ride a tiger? And she could have sworn that the god of war rode a peacock. . . .

Why would the Sleeper be carrying this with him?

Aru traced the manes of the seven-headed horse. Indra, her father, rode an animal like this. Except it wasn't made of clay (duh). In the stories, the creature was said to shine brighter than the moon. Aru pulled the glowing ball from her pocket so she could see the figurines better.

The moment the light of Indra fell upon the clay, the entire chamber began to quake. Aru dropped the horse.

Had it really been made of clay, it would have exploded into shards.

But it didn't.

On the contrary, it began to *grow*. And not just the horse, but *all* the animals.

Aru scuttled backward. The ball in her hand glowed so bright she couldn't make out the books anymore. Light burst around her.

The hubbub of the *B* section faded and was replaced by new sounds: the rustling of wings; the clop of hooves on the floor; the chuffing of a tiger. Even the hiss of a snake.

Aru blinked, her eyes adjusting.

Standing before her were the stolen mounts of the gods. So *that's* what the Sleeper was carrying the whole time. How could he leave it behind — ?

Oh, thought Aru.

The magical headband from Summer that Mini had thrown at him. *Whoever wears this will forget something important.* Welp. It had definitely worked. As soon as they were out of his sight, the Sleeper had forgotten all about the precious mounts.

There was a beautiful burnished orange tiger. A stately peacock that trailed jewels. A stunningly white owl. But the creature that stole her breath was none other than the seven-headed horse. It trotted toward Aru, all of its heads lowering at once.

"Thank you, daughter of Indra," said the

231

horse, speaking from all seven of its mouths in seven melodious voices. "You have freed us from imprisonment."

One by one, the mounts walked forward. The tiger nuzzled her hand. The peacock nipped her fingers affectionately. The owl lowered its head.

"Merely call for us, and we will come to your aid, Pandava," said the owl.

They took off, leaping and flying and trotting into the air, until only the horse was left.

"You have somewhere to be, don't you?" asked the horse.

Aru looked down at the waves on her knuckles and nodded. The third key — the sip of old age — was still out there.

"I shall take you," said the horse. "None can move faster than I, for I move at the speed of thought."

Aru had never ridden a horse. Unless you counted sitting on a rainbow-colored unicorn while revolving on a carousel and yelling *Giddyup!* (Which definitely shouldn't count.) A step stool magically appeared on the left side of the horse. Aru clambered atop it, shoving the ball back into her pocket. She swung her legs over the horse's broad back.

"Are you ready, daughter of Indra?" it asked.

"Nope," said Aru. She took a deep breath. "But let's go anyway."

NINETEEN:
I REALLY . . . REALLY . . .
WOULDN'T DO THAT

There are many ways to make an entrance. Aru, who had watched way too many movies, staunchly believed your three best options were:

1. You could show up like Aragorn in the last Lord of the Rings movie and raise your sword while a bunch of ghosts spilled out behind you.
2. You could show up like John Mc-Clane in every Die Hard movie, screaming "YIPPEE-KI-YAY!" while waving a machine gun.

Or . . .

3. You could show up like an actor in every Bollywood movie, with an invisible wind blowing through your hair and everyone suddenly dancing around you.

234

But after today, she was going to have to change that list. Because honestly? Riding in on a seven-headed horse beat *all* those options.

They burst through the Night Bazaar to a flurry of gasps. Shopping carts squealed and scattered. Tents leaped out of the way, tassels wrapping around them like someone hugging themselves after a bad fright. A raksha who had just purchased a snack from a street vendor dropped his food. A smaller raksha cackled, swooped down, and ate it.

They crossed through worlds that had cities filled with monsters, and (she was almost certain) worlds where monsters made cities. She saw a giant scaly creature squish a mountain with its thumb, muttering, "Make a mountain out of a molehill, you say? Ha! How about making a mountain *into* a molehill! That's far more interesting. Yes, yes."

They charged through a cloud bank. On the other side, there was nothing but a vast expanse of ocean. But it was unlike any ocean Aru had ever seen. It was not blue or gray or even greenish. It was as white as milk. A small stone island stuck out of the middle like a lump of oatmeal in a cereal bowl.

"That was once the pedestal from which

the Ocean of Milk was churned," said the horse.

Just like that, Aru knew where she was. In the museum's panorama back home, there was an illustration of the Ocean of Milk. Long ago, a powerful sage cursed the gods, causing them to lose their immortality. Weakened and in trouble, they churned the ocean to get the nectar of immortality. When they started churning, poison burst into the air. The gods asked Shiva — the Lord of Destruction — to get rid of it. He drank it down, and the poison turned his throat blue.

Aru always liked lying down in the panorama theater where it was cold and dark and silent, watching the stories of the gods and goddesses rotate around her. Which is how she knew that there had been a battle long ago over the nectar of immortality. The gods had not churned the ocean by themselves — they had needed the help of the asuras, the demons. But when the ocean finally gave up the secret of immortality, the gods tricked the asuras and took all the nectar for themselves.

Aru shuddered. She wondered how long a demon could hold a grudge. They might not be able to live eternally like the gods, but they could be reincarnated from one life to the next. Forever and ever . . .

The seven-headed horse began to descend. It slowed to a moderate clip once they reached the island's shore. Past the sand dunes yawned the entrance of a large tunnel.

Aru thought it would look old and creepy inside, but it turned out to be just an abandoned office space. Marble cubicles had been cut into either side of the tunnel. They were all unoccupied. Some contained corkboards pinned with photographs. A headset, like the kind a telemarketer might use (except these were made of gold and studded with diamonds) had been left behind on each desk. Every so often, she saw a vending machine. But they didn't offer candy or chips. Instead they had things like "seven hours of sleep," "a good daydream," "a *very* good daydream" (with, Aru noticed, a strange winking face beside it), "a shot of eloquence," and a miniature antibacterial hand sanitizer.

Posters, covered with a thin layer of dust, still adorned the tunnels. A gleaming city of gold was featured on one of them. Scrawled across it were the words:

COME VISIT THE CITY OF LANKA!
THE PREMIER DESTINATION OF

DREAMS AND NIGHTMARES!
SERVICE: GOLD!
FOOD: GOLD!
ENTERTAINMENT: NOT GORY, BUT
DEFINITELY HAS MOMENTS OF GORE!

Another poster advertised an underwater city with a very attractive naga model, who was winking and baring shiny fangs:

THE CITY OF SNAKES!
COME FOR THE SCENERY, STAY FOR
THE SLITHERING BEAUTIES!

But wherever Aru looked, there was no sign of Mini.

"This is the tourism headquarters of the Otherworld," explained the horse. "But it's currently closed. Nobody will disturb you while you're here."

One part of the tunnel was boarded up. A large sign proclaimed NO TOUCHING! and CAUTION: UNDER RENOVATION. A bitter smell wafted between the planks of wood hammered over the opening.

But there was enough space under the boards that someone the size of Mini (but not necessarily mini-size) might be able to squeeze through to the other side.

It was here that the horse stopped. "This

is where I leave you, daughter of Indra." It knelt so she could dismount.

"Thanks for the lift," said Aru. Her legs felt wobbly when she slid off.

"Call on us when you have need."

Hmm . . . What constituted *need*? Because she'd really love to show up to school on a seven-headed horse. All those sleek black cars would probably explode on the spot. The horse seemed to guess at what she was thinking, because it whinnied.

"*Urgent* need," it clarified.

"Wait. What's your name?"

"Uchchaihshravas," it replied.

"Uchcha . . . Um, maybe I could just whistle?"

The horse huffed.

"So that's a no on the whistling," said Aru.

"Declare your name to the sky. We shall hear and answer."

The horse bowed its seven heads, then took off the way it came. Aru didn't stay to watch it disappear. She crawled under the planks, covering her nose with her hand. This place *stank*. Mini would probably be concerned that the whole room was full of toxic fumes.

She found herself in a narrow alley. When it opened into a cave, Aru knew where the strange smell was coming from. . . .

In the center of the space stood a cauldron the size of a claw-footed bathtub. But the cauldron wasn't made of iron or steel . . . it was made of *vapors.* It was transparent enough that Aru could see blue liquid sloshing angrily inside it. Trying to contain a liquid with only vapors seemed like a really bad idea . . . and judging from the way the whole thing kept quivering, it looked like it was ready to burst at any moment.

But there was also something solid inside, about the size of her shoe, floating on top of the blue liquid. The mehndi design on her fingers pulsed gently. Was that shoe the third key?

If so, how was she supposed to get it out?

Just behind the cauldron crouched a huge statue of Shiva, the Lord of Destruction. He bent over the cauldron, his mouth wide open, as if shocked by its contents. Aru couldn't see the rest of the statue. It disappeared behind the ledge on which the cauldron bubbled.

"Aru?" called a familiar voice.

There, standing off to the side with a notebook in her hand and a pen in the other, was Mini.

The two of them regarded each other warily. Aru wasn't sure what to say. She had already apologized. But it never hurt to say

240

I'm sorry again. And the truth was that Aru hadn't come here just to save her own skin. She had come because Mini was her friend. Plus, she'd made a promise not to leave her behind. She might fib a little, but she never broke her promises.

"Mini, I'm sorry —" she started.

At the very same time, Mini said, "I may have overreacted."

"Ack! You go first!" they both said. Again at the same time.

Now they glared.

"Nose goes!" declared Aru, quickly smacking her nose. (Did it hurt a bit? Yes. Would she do it again to avoid having to discuss her feelings first? One hundred percent yes.)

Mini, who had not reached for her nose, grumbled. "Fine!" she said. "All I was going to say was that maybe I shouldn't have left you like that. I hate when people do that to me. And I know you didn't meant to hurt anyone when you lit the —"

"Apology accepted!" said Aru, feeling immensely relieved. "Now —"

"I just want you to know that . . . that I understand how you feel," continued Mini. "My parents, they, well, I love them. And they love me. My family is great. Honestly. But they didn't think I'd be a Pandava. They thought it was a mistake. I guess it just

241

meant a lot that *you* believed . . . in me. And I get that maybe you felt like that, too — like an impostor — and probably that's why you lit the lamp."

Aru didn't say anything for a moment. She wasn't mad or embarrassed. She was grateful. She'd found someone she could breathe easier around, and it hurt. In a good way.

"I do believe in you, Mini," she said. "I think you're really smart. Definitely a bit on the neurotic side, but totally smart. And brave, too."

She meant it. With all her heart. Maybe Mini could see that, because she smiled and stuck out her elbow. Aru bumped it and she knew they were good.

"Did you see that thing floating in the cauldron?" asked Aru.

"Yup. I'm guessing it's the third key, but I don't know how to get it out. Do we have to *sip* from the cauldron?"

Sip from that bubbling vat of gross blue liquid?

"Ew . . ." said Aru. "Well, I already bit a book, so if anyone's going to be sipping whatever *that* is, it's not me."

"*That* is *poison.* Specifically, *halahala* poison."

"Okay, definitely not drinking it."

"It's the same poison that was released

242

when the gods churned the Ocean of Milk. It will kill us. Please tell me you read the sign." She pointed to a poster off to the side.

Aru skimmed it briefly. Once she read LIKELIHOOD OF DISMEMBERMENT, she stopped.

"Nope."

"According to the warnings, if you touch the cauldron, the whole thing will explode," said Mini. "It happens once a year, kinda like a volcano, which is why this place is blocked off. We'd both *die.*"

Then Aru had an idea. "Maybe I can call in a favor."

She told Mini about the cage full of godly mounts. When she was finished, Mini looked impressed and even a little envious.

"A seven-headed horse?" she asked. "Can you imagine all of its neural pathways? That would be fascinating to study!"

"*Focus,* Mini!"

"Okay, okay. Well, you can't even call in that favor. The rules specify that no animals may drain the poison. Apparently, it can turn them into huge monsters that eat everything around them."

"*Ughhhhh.*"

"Details, details," said Mini, chewing her pencil. "There's gotta be a trick to this."

"What about creating an illusion with your

mirror?" asked Aru.

"Not possible."

Mini drew out the compact. It shimmered, but it wouldn't conjure anything. And Aru's Ping-Pong ball didn't offer any clues, either. It wasn't even glowing.

"It's like a magical dead zone," said Mini. "I don't even think our gifts from the Seasons will work. I couldn't get the bakery box from Spring to open, and the only stuff around here is rocks and the big ole fire."

Huh?

Mini pointed upward and Aru's mouth fell open. A giant chandelier of fire hung from the ceiling. The flames twisted, and embers sparked but didn't fall to the ground. It looked weirdly shiny, as if the whole thing were encased in glass like a chemistry vial full of blue and gold flames.

"I feel like the fire and the poison are connected somehow," said Mini, chewing on the pencil. "If we touch either of them, they'll explode. But at least nothing will get past the entrance."

"Wait. If the fire and poison can't get out of this room, why has the entire tourism office been evacuated?"

"The smell. Also, they have designated vacation days. At least, that's what the sign says," said Mini. "This is the weirdest tourist spot."

Aru shrugged. Considering that the last place her class went to on a field trip was a museum of lunch boxes, a poison volcano sounded way cooler. And the Otherworld apparently thought so, too. A brightly painted wooden panel stood next to the cauldron, awaiting the next photo op. Visitors could stick their faces through a cutout hole (allowances had been made for horns, cobra hoods, and multiple heads) and pretend they'd drunk the poison. On the bottom there was a bucket for donations along with a small sign: THANKS FOR SUPPORTING YOUR LOCAL HAUNTING!

Aru circled the cauldron. "So . . . short of trying to drink this thing and definitely dying, there's no way?"

"I didn't say that. I just said we can't approach it like anyone who's had *any* experience with magic. A magical person would try to trick their way into emptying the cauldron."

Mini's gaze had turned intense. She looked at the cauldron, then back at her notebook, then back at the cauldron. "It's a liquid."

Aru thought it would be uncharitable to say *DUH,* so she just nodded.

"If you heat liquid, it can turn into a gas.

Some of the poisonous liquid in the caldron has become the poisonous vapors that are *holding* the liquid."

Aru's head hurt. Was this really the time and place for a chemistry lesson?

"That's the trick," said Mini, talking to herself. "They don't *want* us to think with magic. We've got to think about it like any ordinary person would. . . . I've got a plan."

Mini seemed so shocked by the idea that she could have a plan that it ended up sounding more like *I've got a plan?*

"Awesome!" said Aru. "What's it involve?"

"We've got to break it," she said, her whole face brightening. "And not with magic."

"Wait. Say what now?"

Mini reached for a small pebble on the ground.

"Um, Mini . . . ?"

And then she hurled it straight at the gigantic cauldron full of poison, hollering, "For science!!!"

Twenty:
Welp, She Did It

If Aru had been politely indifferent to science before, now she straight up hated it. She watched as the pebble soared from Mini's hand. It was a valiant throw. Nice arc. Very dramatic.

But the pebble fell short and dropped about a hairbreadth away from the cauldron. Aru breathed a sigh of relief. They were safe.

But then the infernal pebble did what pebbles can't help but do:

It rolled.

Then tapped the cauldron.

"Maybe that wasn't too strong of a —" Aru stopped as the cauldron began to quiver more violently. Its vapor sides began to swirl. "Nope. I take it back. We're dead."

"We're not dead," said Mini. "I just wanted to stir up the liquid a little. We've got to hit the fire next."

"Spewing poison isn't enough for you?" demanded Aru. "You have to add fire to it?"

"The way this room has been designed, the heat from the fire above has turned some of the poison liquid into a gas," reasoned Mini. "If we bring down *all* of the fire, it should vaporize *all* of the poison and leave behind only the third key!"

The vapor shell of the cauldron began to split. The cave ceiling trembled, and bits of black rock flaked down. The chandelier of fire swung back and forth.

"Gather as many rocks as you can and start throwing them at the fire," said Mini.

"What if they hit the cauldron by mistake? We'll —"

"You said you believed in me!" shouted Mini. "So believe me!"

Aru clenched her jaw. "All right," she said.

She gathered up rocks, and together the two of them started pelting the fire. A cracking sound rolled through the cave. Aru looked up — her guess had been right! The fire *had* been encased in something. And whatever it was that had been protecting them from the flames was beginning to break.

Fire tumbled down in long, flaming ribbons. In a moment, it would meet the poisonous vapor and liquid of the cauldron.

"Run!" shouted Mini. "To the entrance!"

Aru ran just as blue plumes of poison

spiraled into the air. She gagged. The smell was *awful.* Her toe had barely crossed the threshold when she heard a *boom* behind her. The cauldron exploded. Out of the corner of her eye, Aru saw a giant wave of rising poison liquid.

A burst of heat and light threw her and Mini onto their backs. Aru blinked and looked up to see a wall of flames towering above them, blocking the cave entrance. The wave hit the threshold of the entrance . . . and stopped. Aru heard sizzling and steaming. But the poison had disappeared! The magical flames had formed some kind of fence, and must've cooked up all the liquid.

Mini walked to her side, out of breath, but her face shining. "See? Enough heat, and time, will turn a liquid into a gas."

"That was *incredible,*" said Aru. "How'd you think of that?"

Mini just beamed.

Aru couldn't help recalling what Lord Hanuman had said before they'd left the Court of the Sky. About how sometimes you needed someone to remind you of how powerful you were — then you would surprise even yourself.

All the flames in the room had burned out. Mini tiptoed carefully toward the center of the cave. Where the cauldron had been, there was a scorch mark on the ground. A tiny bit of the poison had found shelter from the fire in a new place: the statue of Shiva who had once crouched openmouthed behind it. Now his throat glowed bright blue.

Also on the ground stood a small turquoise goblet. Aru wondered whether that was the shoelike thing that had been floating in the cauldron. A silver liquid filled the cup. Mini picked it up gingerly.

"The third key," she said. "A sip of old age."

Aru reached for it, grimacing. She tried to dump out the liquid, but it didn't budge. Magic was often a stickler for rules. *Rude.*

"It should be your turn," Aru said. "But let me guess: I have to sip this because you saved our butts back there?"

"Yup," said Mini.

Aru gagged just looking at it. "What if it's poison? It came from a poisonous cauldron, after all. . . ."

Mini shrugged. "Then maybe I could save you with one of Spring's petit fours."

Aru was still doubtful. "What if I swallow the key?"

"I wouldn't recommend doing that. When I was three, I ate my mom's engagement ring, and they gave me a bunch of bananas, and they had to —"

"NEVER MIND! I DON'T WANT TO KNOW."

"Drink up or I'll finish the story!"

"You are *evil.*"

Mini crossed her arms over her chest. "I believe in fairness."

Aru took the *tiniest* of sips, the kind she occasionally took from her mom's Sunday glass of wine just to see why people fussed over the stuff. She always ending up spitting out the foul-tasting liquid. But old age didn't taste . . . bad. It reminded Aru of her birthday last year. Her mom had taken them to a fancy Italian restaurant. Aru had eaten so much that she'd fallen asleep in the car. Her mom had picked her up (Aru remembered because she kept pretending to be asleep) and carried her to bed. The sip of old age was like that — a happy kind of fullness.

A weight pressed down on her tongue. Startled, she spat it out and found a small white key. It was made of bone. *NOPE.*

"AHHHH!" screamed Aru. She started to scrape her tongue. Then she realized she hadn't washed her hands since Brahmasura became a pile of ashes. Aru spat on the ground.

"The third key!" said Mini excitedly.

251

"Cool! It's a bone! I wonder if it was like a phalanx, or maybe a —"

Aru glared at her, and Mini quickly changed the subject.

"We did it!" said Mini. "We've got *all* three keys to get inside the Kingdom of Death."

Despite being thoroughly grossed out, Aru smiled. They'd really done it. And what made it even better was that Mini wasn't standing quite so timidly anymore. With the glow of the poison in Shiva's mouth behind her, it almost looked like she had a halo.

"Ready?" asked Aru.

Mini nodded.

Aru's palms had started to sweat. Her hair felt pulled too tight. Part of her was wondering whether she should make a last-minute bathroom run, because there was no telling whether the Underworld had public restrooms. But maybe that was just nerves.

The girls laid down the three keys in a row: the sprig of youth, the coin from the bite of *Adulthood* (now shiny again), and the bone key.

Aru wasn't sure what was supposed to happen next. But that didn't matter, because the keys knew what to do. At once, they melted and ran together, forming a puddle of light. Aru held her breath as the puddle rose, growing higher and higher until it was about the height of the seven-headed horse that had carried her across the Ocean of Milk.

In the darkness of the cave, a door took shape.

The door to the Kingdom of Death.

TWENTY-ONE:
THE DOOR AND THE DOGS

The door to the Kingdom of Death was wrought of bone and leaf and light.

Mini raised her hand to touch it. Then she shook her head. "I thought I'd feel . . . differently," she said.

"About what?" asked Aru.

"About the door and where it was going."

"It's going to the Kingdom of Death. That's all."

"Yes, but this is the door to my —" Mini stopped and stuttered. "I mean, I guess he really isn't my . . . my . . ."

"Dad?"

Mini flinched. "Yeah. That. But I don't know him. And he doesn't know me. I mean, I guess it doesn't matter. Boo and my parents said he's my soul dad, not my home dad, but I guess I hoped he'd do something other than give me a mirror, you know?"

No. She didn't know. Aru knew it was a

little mean, but she didn't feel that bad for Mini. Aru was in the same boat, and she didn't have a home dad to comfort her. Yeah, Indra might have made her soul, but where was her real father? He could still be out there . . . somewhere. And whoever he was, he hadn't wanted her.

She pushed down that surge of envy. It wasn't Mini's fault.

"What're you going to do if you meet the Dharma Raja?"

"I'll just thank him for letting me exist, I guess? I dunno. It's weird." Mini took a deep breath. "Okay, I'm ready now."

Aru reached for the doorknob, but it shocked her hand. She pulled back, stung. "I think you should do it."

"Me? Why?"

"Because you're the Daughter of Death. It's like going into your house."

"What if it shocks me, too?"

Aru shrugged. "Maybe say your name first?"

Mini looked doubtful, but she squared her shoulders. "My name is Yamini Kapoor-Mercado-Lopez, and this is . . ." She turned to Aru and hissed, "I don't know your last name!"

Aru was tempted to say that her name was Bond. James Bond.

"Aru Shah."

"No middle name?"

She shrugged again. "If I have one, no one ever told me what it was."

Mini nodded, apparently satisfied, then continued talking to the door. "Aru Shah. We are entering the Kingdom of Death because we have been sent on a quest to awaken the celestial weapons so that, uh, so that Time doesn't end and also to find out how to stop this really awful demon by looking for answers in the Pool of the . . . Last?"

"Pool of the *Past*," whispered Aru.

"Pool of the Past!" finished Mini. "Please and thank you."

The door didn't budge. Then again, Mini hadn't pushed it.

"Why aren't you even trying to open it?" demanded Aru.

"It's not polite to force things."

With that, the door gave way with a sigh and a groan.

From the side, the door to the Kingdom of Death was as slim as a closed laptop. And yet, the moment Mini stepped inside, she disappeared. It was as if she had stepped into a slice in the air.

After a few seconds, Mini poked her head out. "Are you coming or not?"

Aru's stomach turned. She couldn't remember any stories about the Halls of the Dead. But just the idea of them was enough to scare her. She kept imagining faceless ghosts behind the door. Fires that never went out. A sky devoid of stars.

And then she imagined her mom's face frozen in horror, her hair falling around her. She remembered Boo lying limp in the Sleeper's hand. Those images made her move.

"It's an *adventure*?" she said, trying to rally herself.

Aru's hand drifted to the pants pocket where she kept the Ping-Pong ball. It was warm and reassuring. "It's fine. This is fine. Everything is fine," she muttered to herself.

She placed her foot across the threshold.

A frigid wind picked up the hairs on the nape of her neck. On the breeze, she could hear the final words of people who had died: *No, not yet!* And *Please make sure someone remembers to feed Snowball.* And *I hope someone clears my Internet browser.*

But mostly, Aru heard love.

Tell my family I love them.

Tell my wife I love her.

Tell my children I love them.

Tell Snowball I love her.

Aru felt a sharp twist in her heart. Had she told her mother she loved her before she left the museum with Boo?

There was no going back now. The moment she stepped into the Kingdom of Death, the door disappeared. She was left in a tunnel so black she couldn't tell what she was walking on. Was it darkness itself? There were no walls, no sky or sea, no beginning or end. Just blackness.

"My mom used to tell me that death is like a parking lot," whispered Mini. She sounded close, and like she was trying to reassure herself. "You stay there for just a bit and then go somewhere else."

"Again with the parking lots?" Aru joked shakily.

She breathed a little easier when she remembered that, in Hinduism, death wasn't a place where you were stuck forever. It was where you waited to be reincarnated. Your soul could live hundreds — maybe even *thousands* — of lives before you got out of the loop of life and death by achieving enlightenment.

A dog woofed in the distance.

"Why so serious?" asked a deep voice.

"Serious, or Sirius?" said a different voice, this one high-pitched. "We know that dog, don't we? Howls at the stars? Chases the sun?"

"You ruin everything! I practiced that

258

opening for a whole year!" grumbled the first voice. Now it wasn't so deep.

"Well, how was I supposed to know?" said the second.

"*The Dark Knight* is my favorite movie, remember? You should listen to me. I'm Ek, after all! You're only Do."

"Just because you were born first doesn't make you more important," said Do.

"Yes, it does," said Ek.

"No, it doesn't!"

Ek? Do? Aru knew those words. They were the names of numbers in Hindi, the most commonly spoken language in India. *Ek* and *Do* meant *one* and *two.* They sounded like *ick* and *dough.*

Aru's mother had grown up speaking Gujarati, a language from the state of Gujarat. Aru didn't speak either Gujarati or Hindi. All she knew were a few words, including some curses. (Which she hadn't even known were bad words until the time she'd stubbed her toe in front of the priest at temple and just let loose. Her mother had not been amused.) When her hand tightened on the golden ball, it turned into a dim flashlight.

Four sets of eyes peered at Aru and Mini. In the glow of the ball, Aru could make out the shapes of two giant dogs.

Ek and Do each had two rows of eyes, and

short brindled fur. When they walked forward to sniff the girls, their coats rippled and shimmered. Aru wondered whether they were soft.

Mini had pulled up the collar of her shirt and was pressing it over her nose. *"Ermarregictodaws."*

"What?"

She surfaced from the cloth. "I'm allergic to dogs."

"Of course you are," said Aru.

"Are you dead?" asked Ek, the dog with the high-pitched voice.

"I don't think so?" replied Mini.

At the same time, Aru said, "Of course not!"

"Well, you can't come in if you're not dead," said Ek. "Those are the rules."

"You don't understand —" started Aru.

"Ah, but we do!" said Ek. "You have two choices. You can die on your own, or we can help by killing you!"

Do wagged his tail. "I love helping! Helping is fun."

TWENTY-TWO: WHO'S A GOOD BOY?

"Nope!" said Aru. "No thanks! We'll find another way in —"

"I'm not going anywhere!" said Mini.

Ek yawned as if he'd heard this before. His teeth were really sharp. Why did they need to be that sharp? And was that . . . *blood* on his fangs?

"You don't have to go anywhere to die, little one," said Ek.

"That's not what I meant. I'm not going anywhere, because . . . because this is *my* kingdom?" said Mini. Her voice went up at the end. "I am the daughter of the Dharma Raja, and I demand entrance —"

"And I'm the daughter of Lord Indra!" butted in Aru.

Mini glared at her.

"Celebrities! Oh! Welcome, welcome!" said Do. "Could I get your autograph? We could do it before or after the whole killing-you thing. Whichever is most convenient."

"Who cares if they're celebrities? Death is the greatest leveler of them all! They are not the first. Nor the last. We've carried the souls of queens and murderers and infernal Yogalates instructors between our teeth," said Ek proudly to the girls. "Even the Pandava brothers had to die. Even *gods* reincarnated in mortal bodies have to die."

"That's true," said Do agreeably.

"It's just a body!" said Ek, staring down his nose at them. "Leave them behind! Then we'll let you through."

"You can get new ones!" said Do.

Aru saw the telltale signs of Mini's confidence waning: glasses off-kilter, lip tucked between her teeth.

"Um," said Mini.

Ek's teeth gleamed whiter. "We'll make it quick."

"I don't really feel like rending someone apart," mourned Do, even as his fur turned more bristly and his fangs elongated. "Why don't we go out to the cremation grounds instead and bury bone shards? Or we can play Catch the Beheaded Thing! I've always liked that game."

Ek growled. "Not now, Do! This is our job! Our dharma! Our duty!"

"Ha. Duty. *Doo-tee.*"

"Do, now is not the time —"

"It's never the time, Ek! Yesterday you said we could play catch. Did we? No!"

Aru nudged Mini. Just beyond the two dogs, a thin sliver of light appeared. Maybe that was the *true* door to the Kingdom of Death and this was just the stuffy front hall. In which case, the reason it was opening now was probably because it sensed that someone was about to be dead. Aru gulped. If they could just get past these guardians, they could get into the kingdom.

Not that Aru was particularly excited about entering.

Something seemed to call to her from beyond that door. Something she already knew she did not like. Something that taunted. It reminded her of the Sleeper's voice in her ear.

But still, anything was better than being torn apart.

"Wait till my father hears about this!" bellowed Mini. "I mean, my godly father. Not the human one. My human one would be mad too, but —"

"Mini," Aru interrupted. "You're not supposed to explain yourself after you say 'Wait till my father hears about this.' "

"The girl is a brat," hissed Ek.

"I thought she seemed nice," said Do. His ears flattened against his skull.

"I can't believe they're not listening to me . . ." said Mini, shocked.

"Maybe it's because you sounded like a brat?" suggested Aru.

Ek, who had grown to the size of a respectable town house, laughed. It was not a friendly laugh. "It certainly didn't help."

"Aru . . ." said Mini, her voice squeaking.

Aru had little experience with Door of Death dogs. But she did have experience with regular dogs. Last summer, she had taken Mrs. Hutton's poodle (P. Doggy) on a walk and almost lost her arm when he spotted a cat.

"Compact," whispered Aru, not taking her eyes off the two dogs. And then, in an even softer voice, she said, "Cat."

"How shall we choose which one to eat first?" asked Ek. "Perhaps in a game of heads or tails?"

"Heads!" said Do.

"Are you flipping a coin?" asked Aru.

If she could distract them, maybe they wouldn't see what Mini was conjuring with her compact.

"We're not flipping coins!" said Do, excited. "We're deciding which one of us gets to go after which parts of you!"

"But we don't have tails," said Aru.

Do looked at her for a moment longer, as

if just realizing that she did not, in fact, possess a tail.

"Oh, that's true. . . ." Do looked to Ek. "Can we still eat them if they don't have tails?"

"I meant 'tails' in a *metaphorical* sense," said Ek.

"What's that mean?"

"Metaphorical means symbolic, Do. Honestly, it's like you never paid attention in class! A metaphor is a word representing something else. They don't have *tails* per se, but they have a top and a bottom. So the head is the top and —"

"What's the opposite of metaphorical?"

"Literal!"

"But then —"

While the two of them bickered, Aru and Mini put their heads together. (Metaphorically *and* literally.) Purple smoke emerged from the compact Mini was clutching. The smoke took a shape and began to grow a tail and a head. (Literally.)

"Ready?" asked Aru.

"Ready," said Mini. She stayed hunched over the smoke.

"Hey! Ek and Do!" shouted Aru.

She looked at the glowing orb in her hand. She rolled it between her palms, wishing it weren't so tiny. As she thought about it, it actually changed. It grew to the size of a tennis ball.

Do cocked his head. One fat pink tongue lolled out the side of his mouth.

"No!" growled Ek. "It's a trap!"

"IT'S A BALL!"

Aru threw the ball as hard as she could. Do bounded off after it.

Ek stayed put. "If you think that a ball —"

Mini let go of her enchantment. A sleek purple cat leaped out of her arms and away into the darkness. Ek's eyes turned huge. His tail started wagging, and the darkness began to vibrate around them. The crack of light just behind him widened.

"WOOOOOOO!!!" he shouted, taking off after the cat.

"Good boy!" said Aru.

Mini and Aru took off toward the slender doorway of light. As Aru's pumping legs churned the darkness beneath her, the only thing on her mind was this:

Maybe she should ask her mother about getting a cat instead of a dog.

Twenty-Three:
Soul Index

With the dogs' howling cut off behind them, Aru and Mini went from utter darkness to blinding light. Aru squinted around, trying to get her bearings.

When her eyes finally adjusted, she saw that they were standing in a line. One glance around immediately told her they'd come to the right place. These people were definitely *not* alive.

One person was on fire. He yawned and went back to poking at the inside of a toaster with a fork with a very sheepish expression on his face. Then there was a very sunburned-looking couple in hiking gear sporting some nasty bruises and scratches. And beside Aru, moving quickly and calmly, was a bald girl in a hospital gown clutching a silk rabbit. Everyone was packed tightly together, and the crowd kept growing. Before her, she could just make out the letters of a hanging office sign that said:

KARMA & SINS
Est. at the first hiccup of time
Please, no solicitors
(As of the 15th century, indulgences are
no longer permitted. Nice try.)

There was a lot of murmuring around them.

"I can't understand what anyone is saying," said Mini.

Aru caught fragments of words. It didn't sound like English. "Mini, do you speak any Hindi?"

"I can ask for money and say I'm hungry?" said Mini.

"Wow. So useful."

"It *was* useful!" said Mini. "When I went to India and had to meet all my mom's relatives, those were the only two phrases I needed."

"They never taught you more?"

"Nope," said Mini. "My parents didn't want me and my brother to get confused in school, so they only spoke English. And my lola got mad when my mom tried to teach me Hindi, because my name was already Indian and she thought my mom was trying to make me forget I was Filipina too, and it became this huge fight at home. I don't remember it, because I was little. My mom tells it one way, my lola tells it another. Ugh." She took a deep breath, and then brightened. "I do know some curse words in Tagalog, though! They're really awful, like this one —"

But before Aru could hear what Mini was going to say, a large speaker materialized in the air, shouting, "NEXT!"

Beside them, a tall pale man wandered forward. A glint of shrapnel stuck out of his leg.

"*Gel eht ni yretra gib,*" he said pleasantly. "*Nodrap!*"

"Quick, Mini, ask for money in Hindi and see what happens!"

"Um, Aru, I don't think he's speaking Hindi."

"Maybe he's speaking Russian? Sounds like Russian . . ." Aru looked up at the man. "Comrade?"

The man just smiled the kind of uneasy smile one uses when one is utterly confused. Mini got out her compact, and Aru caught on right away. If it could see through enchantments, maybe it could see through languages, too. Mini flipped it open. The mirror was now a tiny screen where the man's words scrolled in blue and were translated into English underneath.

"He's speaking backward!" said Mini. She held up the compact to show the words in small, green print:

BIG ARTERY IN THE LEG. PARDON!

"Why would the dead speak backward?" asked Aru.

Mini tilted the compact from one side to the other, as if she were trying to catch and read all the things that the dead spoke around them.

"Maybe because they can't go forward in life anymore?"

The man frowned. *"Daed kool t'nod uoy?"*

The compact read YOU DON'T LOOK DEAD.

Aru typed out a response, and then pronounced it haltingly. *"Sknaht! Snimativ eht s'ti."* Thanks! It's the vitamins.

"NEXT!" boomed the speakers.

They shuffled forward once more. The neon sign for KARMA & SINS glowed. Up front, the people in line were doing all kinds of things. Some of them were crossing themselves. Others were crawling forward on their hands and knees, murmuring under their breaths.

Beside Aru, Mini stood rigid. "How can you even look at that?" she asked, her voice hushed. She sounded as if she was about to cry.

"Look at what? It's just a sign, like something outside a lawyer's office," said Aru. "Why? What do you see?"

Mini's eyes widened. She turned her head away. "Right. I see that, too."

Mini didn't know how to lie, but she didn't sound entirely truthful. Aru suspected she was seeing more than just the sign for KARMA & SINS. Whatever it was, Mini didn't like it.

The line ahead of them slowly dwindled. Now Aru and Mini stood near the front.

"Do you think the Kingdom of Death looks the same to everyone?" asked Aru.

"I doubt it," said Mini. "Maybe it's like that Costco. We're all seeing something different."

"Huh. Where's the hippo that chomps on people?"

"Pretty sure that's Egyptian mythology, Aru."

"Oh."

Aru wished that she had a better idea of what to expect when they went through the next door.

All she knew was that the celestial weap-

271

ons were housed somewhere inside this place. But where? And where were they going to find the Pool of the Past? What if she mistook it for a different pool that was ten times worse? Like the Pool That Looks Like the Past but Is Actually Eternal Torture.

So far, the Kingdom of Death was just standing in an absurdly long line. Like at an all-you-can-eat buffet, or at the DMV, where her mother sometimes dragged her, and the workers looked equal parts smug and furious.

The door in front of them opened. *"Evom!"* shouted a grumpy old woman behind them. She was carrying an orange tabby cat in her arms.

Mini held up the compact for Aru to see: MOVE.

Aru spelled out the right response in her head and then shouted it as they walked through the door: *"Edur!"*

Inside the room, a kind-eyed man with a bulbous nose sat at a desk. He reminded Aru a little bit of her school principal at Augustus Day. Mr. Cobb sometimes subbed for their Social Studies teacher, and he always managed to slip in a story about the Vietnam War, even when their class unit was on ancient civilizations.

The man stared at them. On his desk,

272

seven miniature versions of himself ran back and forth carrying pens and stacks of paper. They argued among themselves.

"Report, please," said the man. "You should have received one upon expiration."

Mini inhaled sharply. "Dad?"

The seven miniature men stopped running and stared at Mini.

He was unfazed. "You don't have my nose, so I don't think so . . ." he said. "Plus, I think one of my wives would have told me. But there is an ultimate test." He coughed loudly. "Yesterday, I bought eggs at a human grocery store. The cashier asked me if I wanted them in a separate bag. I told her, 'No! Leave them in their shells!' "

Mini blinked. Aru felt a rush of pity for this man's children.

The man sniffed. "Nothing? Not even a smile? Well, then, that settles it. All my offspring have my nose and sense of humor." He chuckled. "I must say, though, that's a rather clever ploy to get out of death, claiming to be my child." He turned to one of his tiny selves. "Write that one down for my memoir!" Then he turned back to Aru and Mini. "Now, how about those records?"

"We don't have any," said Aru.

"Of course you do. You're dead, aren't you?"

"Well, about that —" said Mini. She was waving her hand, ready to explain their strange situation, when the compact fell from her palm and landed on the desk with a loud *thunk.*

The man leaned over to take a look. All seven miniature versions of him dropped what they were holding and raced to the compact.

Aru scanned the table and saw a small brass plaque that read: CHITRIGUPTA. There was also a mug that read: FOURTEEN WORLDS' BEST DAD. Behind him were bookcases and file cabinets and mountains upon mountains of paperwork. It took a moment for Aru to remember Chitrigupta from the stories. He was the one who kept a record of everything a soul had ever done, both good and bad. This was why *karma* mattered. Her mom used to say, *Chitrigupta will see and write down everything.*

Aru wasn't sure she believed in karma. *What goes around comes around* sounded suspiciously convenient to her. But the one time she'd said *Karma isn't real,* she'd walked outside and a bird had pooped on her head. So who knew?

"Where did you get the mirror, child?"

274

asked Chitrigupta.

Most adults would have gone straight to accusing a kid of stealing. But not Chitrigupta. Aru liked that.

"It was given to me during the Claiming."

"The *claiming* . . . Wait. *The* Claiming?" Chitrigupta's eyes widened. "I don't think there's been a Claiming since . . ." He rose from his chair. "Bring up the records!"

The room spun into chaos. Aru and Mini stepped back as the seven miniature versions of Chitrigupta jumped onto him and disappeared. He slumped back into his chair, and his eyes glazed over. Then they flashed and crackled, and words streamed across his gaze.

When the text finished scrolling, he leaned forward again. Tears shone in his eyes. "Never been a girl before," he said, looking between Mini and Aru. "How unusual . . ."

Aru braced herself, waiting to hear the usual lines that they couldn't possibly be heroes, or that they were too weak, too young, or too . . . *girly.*

"And how refreshing!" he said. His shirt changed to say: THIS IS WHAT A FEMINIST LOOKS LIKE. "Upend the patriarchy! R-E-S-P-E-C-T! Et cetera, et cetera. And you got past Ek and Do, too. Well done, well done."

Mini brightened. "So can you help us? We need to wake up the celestial weapons and then we have to go to the Pool of the Past to find out how to stop the Sleeper from ending Time forever."

"Oh, that does sound dire," said Chitrigupta. He reached for his mug and sipped from it. "Sadly, I'm not allowed to help. Not even the Dharma Raja could help you, little ones."

Mini turned red. "Does he . . . does he know we're here?" she asked.

"Undoubtedly."

"Doesn't he want to . . . I dunno . . . meet me?"

At this, Chitrigupta's face softened. "Oh, child, I'm sure he does. But the truth is, he will eventually meet you one way or another. Your soul is what matters — *it* is the immortal thing, not the body. The gods no longer get involved with mortal affairs."

"Can't you make an exception?" asked Aru.

"If I could, do you not think I would have helped the heroes who came before you? Bright, shining things they were. Like living stars. I can only do for you what I did for them."

"And that is . . . ?"

Chitrigupta sighed. He spread out his

hands. Two ivory-colored tokens — flat squares with screens, like tiny iPhones — appeared on the table. "I wish there were more, but you two simply haven't *lived* long enough."

Aru picked up one of the tokens. She saw little images of herself flashing on its surface. In one she was holding open the door for a young woman carrying a stack of books. In another, she was washing the dishes in the apartment. In the next, she was pulling a blanket over her sleeping mother.

"What are these?" asked Mini.

"Good karma," said Chitrigupta. "They should allow you to get past at least some of the things buried within these halls. You see, there are many rooms in the Kingdom of Death. Many places you may enter but not exit. All I can tell you is that you must follow the signs and find your own way. The celestial weapons are kept near the Pool of Reincarnation. Right next to the Pool of Reincarnation is where you will find the Pool of the Past."

"There's only one way to get to them?" asked Aru. She was thinking about the handy trick Boo had shown them, where all they had to do to go somewhere was reach for a place with intention.

Thinking about Boo made her heart

tighten. Was he okay? She hoped he was somewhere safe, blissfully asleep. Deep down, however, she feared that wasn't the case. . . .

"Oh, I don't know about that. There are hundreds of ways. Some paved, some pebbled, some pockmarked."

One of Chitrigupta's miniature selves hopped onto his shoulder, climbed onto his face, and scratched his nose while he spoke. Aru tried not to let her eyebrows soar up her forehead.

"Even I do not know what you will find in the Halls of Death," said Chitrigupta. "Things and places move through death differently than humans do. Things that were once real are now mere stories in this kingdom. Forgotten things endure their own death, for they are never reincarnated into something new."

Forgotten things?

Aru wanted to believe this meant they would find objects like deflated basketballs, mismatched socks, or bobby pins. Or that pen you could have sworn you put into the pocket of your backpack but wasn't there when you went to look for it. But she knew that was wishful thinking.

Mini was looking beyond both of them to the door behind Chitrigupta. It was made of polished onyx.

"When was the last Claiming?" asked Mini.

"Just before World War II."

"That can't be right . . ." Aru said. "Boo mentioned something about the last Pandava brother being a yoga teacher or something."

"Oh, *him,*" said Chitrigupta. He rolled his eyes. "Couldn't get that man to leave all the other dead people alone! He kept insisting on leading everyone through breathing exercises. Made some people want to die all over again, which is saying something. He was a *latent* Pandava. His divine powers were hidden, even to him, and there were no calamities that forced his inner godhood to awaken. Sometimes you don't even know how special you might be. Sometimes it takes moments of horror or happiness to, if you will, unleash that knowledge."

"So the last ones, in World War II . . . did they make it through the Kingdom of Death and get to the celestial weapons?"

Chitrigupta sighed and leaned back in his chair. Even though he looked like a young man, there was something very old and tired in his eyes. His smile was sad when he said, "We had a war, didn't we?"

Twenty-Four:
Dare, Disturb, Deign

Chitrigupta refused to send them off without any food.

"I think I might be your uncle," he said, whizzing about the office. "Or, at the very least, we all share some divine something or other. I do hope you make it back! I never even had a chance to regale you with my stories or essays. Did I tell you about that time I interviewed a snail? You wouldn't believe how fast he could talk. Downright speedy."

From a file drawer, he brought out a box of cookies. He opened it and offered one to Mini, who sniffed it.

"Why does this smell like . . . books?"

"Ah, they're wisdom cookies! I've made these from scratch before. The secret is to allow the books to hit room temperature before mixing them. Cold writing doesn't sit well in the mind."

"Uh, sure?"

"Save it for later," said Chitrigupta, pluck-ing the cookie from Mini's hand and return-ing it to the box. His outfit had changed again. Now he was wearing an apron that said DO NOT KISS THE COOK. YOU HAVE GERMS. "And don't eat them all at once. That might leave you feeling a little queasy. Or empty."

"Thanks, Uncle!" said Mini.

"And you don't want to get dehydrated or —"

"You could die!" said Mini and Chitrigupta at the same time.

They looked at each other with an expres-sion that so clearly said *We must be related!* that Aru wanted to knock her forehead against the door. Repeatedly.

"Yeah, thanks, Uncle," said Aru.

Chitrigupta patted both of them on the head, and handed them two small thimble-fuls of a bright orange liquid. It looked like a captured flame.

So much for not being dehydrated. This couldn't even be called a full sip. But Aru swallowed it dutifully.

A warm glow spread through her bones. Her throat no longer felt dusty. Between the sip of whatever this was, and one of the fancy Spring petit fours from the Court of the Seasons, Aru felt clearheaded and sharp-eyed.

"The dead have a tendency to leave us parched and tired. Watered-down *soma* always does the trick."

"*Soma?*" repeated Mini. "As in the drink of the gods?"

"Yes, which is why it needs to be watered down. Undiluted, it can be deadly. Even to demigods."

"Too bad it can't make us immortal," said Aru. "Then we'd definitely get through the Halls of Death alive."

Chitrigupta eyed her shrewdly. "You must be the daughter of Indra."

Aru raised her eyebrows. "What makes you say that?"

"Did you know that Indra's Pandava son, Arjuna, was one of the greatest warriors who ever lived?"

Defensiveness prickled through Aru. "Just because Arjuna was an amazing warrior and we have the same soul doesn't actually mean that I'm a great warrior, too, you know."

"Aru!" hissed Mini.

"Sorry," she bit out.

But she wasn't, and she was sure Chitrigupta knew. He didn't get mad, though. Instead, he smiled.

"What made Arjuna great wasn't his strength or his valor, but the way he chose to see the world around him. He looked around, questioned, and doubted. You, too, are perceptive, Aru Shah. What you do with those perceptions is up to you."

The hairs on Aru's arm lifted. For a moment, she thought of the giant library in the Night Bazaar, and the book with her name on it. Maybe her imagination wasn't just something that would keep landing her in trouble. Maybe it could actually help her save people.

Chitrigupta looked away from her and clapped twice. "All right, then, off you go!"

Mini and Aru reached for the door at the same time that Chitrigupta called out, "Wait!"

"Whaaaaat?" asked Aru.

It wasn't that she was particularly anxious to embark on a journey of near-certain doom, but there was always "just one more thing!" when it came to Indian aunties and uncles. She experienced this whenever her mother dragged her to parties. The relatives would start saying good-bye in the living room, then spend another hour saying good-bye at the door. It was inevitably how they spent half the visit.

If they didn't leave *now,* they were probably *never* going to leave.

"Just this," said Chitrigupta. He held out his hand. A slim ballpoint pen lay in his palm.

"What does it do?" asked Mini.

"What do you think it does?" asked Chitrigupta. "It's a pen! It writes!"

"Oh. Thanks?" said Mini.

"Don't mention it. I cannot help you in defeating the Sleeper, but perhaps this will come in handy at some point. Wherever you are and whatever you write on, I will get the message. And if it is within my means . . . I will answer."

With a final farewell, they were off.

The moment the door closed behind them, all of Aru's old fears raced back to her.

"I like him," said Mini.

"Of course you do! You guys are practically the same person."

The Halls of Death unfurled like a maze before them and actually *grew.* Colors gathered and stretched into passageways. The signs cropped up shortly after that:

TO DARE
TO DISTURB
TO DEIGN

An arrow was attached to each sign.

DARE pointed right and down a blue corridor.

DISTURB pointed left and down a red corridor.

DEIGN pointed up and into nothing.

Beneath them, the floor was polished marble, and the ceiling was a strange twisting river of names that, Aru imagined, belonged to the dead.

"Red pill or blue pill?" said Aru, in her best imitation of Morpheus.

"What pill? It's a red road or blue road, Aru."

"I know that! I'm quoting *The Matrix*!"

Mini blinked. "But a matrix has nothing to do with color. In mathematics, a matrix is a rectangular array of —"

Aru groaned. "Mini, you're *killing* me. Don't you ever watch old movies?" She shook her head and pointed ahead. "Which way should we go? Why don't they have signs that say *Weapons of Mass Celestial Destruction,* and then *Everything Else Is Actually a Trap*? That would be helpful."

Mini laughed. "What if we went with *dare*?"

"Why?"

"Because it's like . . . we're *daring* to save Time?"

"Are we, though? Or are we just panicking around and trying to save what we like?"

And the people we love, thought Aru with a pang.

"That doesn't sound very heroic . . ." said Mini.

"What about *disturb*?" asked Aru. "Like, we're *disturbing* the natural order of things?"

"I don't think that's right," said Mini. "That makes it seem like we're doing something wrong, and we're not."

"Fine. What does *deign* mean?"

"I'll look it up," said Mini, and she dug in her backpack.

Aru thought she was going to use her compact, but instead she brought out a *Merriam-Webster Pocket Dictionary.*

"Seriously?" asked Aru. "Of all the things you thought to pack on a quest, you brought a *pocket dictionary*?"

"So what? I like being prepared," said Mini. "What did you pack?"

"I didn't pack anything," said Aru. "Who has time to pack when you're told the world is going to end —"

Mini shushed her. " *'Deign,'* "she said. "It means 'to do something that one considers beneath one's dignity.' "

"None of those options makes sense," said Aru. "What if we just try walking in a different direction? Like in between the signs?"

So they tried. But their feet met a wall of air. Something prevented them from taking a single step that was not in a specific direction. The only place they couldn't access was DEIGN, because the sign pointed *up,* and there weren't stairs or anything.

"Chitrigupta could have told us which way to go," grumbled Aru. "We're practically family. He said so himself."

"But then we wouldn't —"

"Yes, I know. Character-building blah-blah, and the world wouldn't be saved. That's way too much pressure. Are our brains even fully developed? We shouldn't be allowed to make these decisions —"

"Aru! That's it!" said Mini.

"Okay, now I'm worried. None of what I said was good."

"We're not smart enough," said Mini.

"Yay?"

"But we can change that," she said.

Out of her backpack, she pulled out the box of wisdom cookies.

"Book cookies?" asked Aru, grimacing. "All right, fine. Gimme."

Mini looked inside the box, then checked her backpack again. "There's only one in here."

The girls stared at each other for a moment. Mini's fingers reflexively curled over the cookie. Aru could tell how much it meant to her friend.

"It's yours," said Aru. "You've got the same soul as Yudhistira, and he was always known for being the wisest of all the brothers. That cookie has your name all over it. Plus, I don't need more wisdom. I'd explode."

Mini flushed. "Thanks, Aru."

"How long does the wisdom last?"

"I think only for the duration of the decision making," said Mini.

"How do you know that?"

"Because it says so on the back of the box."

Sure enough, the duration of the wisdom cookies was listed alongside the nutritional facts.

"Ooh!" said Mini. "It has my entire daily serving of potassium and zinc!"

"Hooray."

Mini took a bite of the cookie.

"What's it taste like?" asked Aru.

"Kinda smoky? And cold. Like snow. I think it's supposed to taste like my favorite book."

"What's your favorite book?"

Mini bit into the second half of the cookie. "*The Golden Compass.*"

"Never read it."

"Really?" asked Mini, shocked. "I'll loan you my copy when we get home."

Home. A home that was full of books Aru had never cracked open because her mother always read to her. Aru had trouble remembering things she read herself, but if she *heard* something, she'd never forget it. Maybe that's why her mom had told her so many stories. Her mom might have left her in the dark about being a Pandava, but at least hearing the stories about them had prepared Aru somewhat. *Mom,* thought Aru, *I promise I'll thank you as soon as I get home.*

"Oh no," said Mini.

"What? What is it?"

Mini held up her palm to show the symbol there:

$$\text{?}$$

"Another doomsday squiggle?" asked Aru. "Okay, well, it looks like a two, which would be *really* bad news, but maybe it means four?"

"It means two."

"*Nooooooooo!* Betrayal!"

Only two days left? And the entirety of the Kingdom of Death left unexplored?

Mini ate the rest of the wisdom cookie.

"Feel any wiser?" asked Aru anxiously.

"No?"

"What about warmer? Or bloated? Like you're full of hot air?"

But Mini wasn't paying attention. She was staring at the three signs.

"Deign," she whispered. "That's the answer."

"Why?"

"It's kinda like a riddle," said Mini. "The word *deign* means *to look down on.* The arrow pointing up is a trap, because the whole point is that we have to look at what's beneath us. It's like when you have to make a choice you don't want to make and you feel like you're reluctant to do it."

"Whoa," said Aru. "You got all that from a cookie? Sure there isn't any left?"

She grabbed the box from Mini and shook it. Nope. Not even a crumb. Mini stuck out her tongue.

At the edge of the DEIGN sign, a hole formed in the marble floor.

"Why is it only opening now?" asked Aru.

"Probably because we're looking down and not up?"

Both girls peered down the hole. Something glittered far below. A strange fragrance wafted up. It smelled uncannily like Aru's

290

apartment in the museum: musty fabric, chai, lavender candles, and old books.

Mini frowned. "Let's go in alphabetically," she said.

"No way! My name starts with A. It's *your* kingdom, sorta; *you* go first —"

"*I'm* the one who made sure we could get even this far."

"Only because *I* let you eat the cookie!"

"Chitrigupta gave it to *me* —"

Aru took a deep breath and settled this the only fair and logical way she could imagine.

"NOSE GOES!" she screamed, smacking her face.

Mini, who must have anticipated Aru being sneaky, immediately smacked her face, too. Except she moved so fast that her glasses flew off her head and fell. Down the hole.

"Ughhhhh," said Mini. "You're the worst, Aru."

And with that, she jumped in after them.

TWENTY-FIVE:
WHAT MEETS THE EYE
(AND WHAT DOESN'T)

The descent wasn't bad. It was like a long waterslide, without the water. It dumped them out in a forest.

But something was off about this place.

Granted, Aru didn't have much experience with forests. Once, her mother had taken her to San Francisco. At first it had seemed like it was going to be a boring trip, because they spent the whole morning with the curator of the Asian Art Museum. But after lunch, her mother had taken her to Muir Woods. Walking through it was like a delicious dream. It had smelled like peppermint. The sunlight was soft and feathered, hardly skimming the forest floor because the trees were so thick and tall.

But this place, tucked inside a pocket of the Kingdom of Death, didn't have that foresty feel. Aru sniffed the air. There was no perfume of green and wriggling alive-ness. No smell of woodsmoke or still ponds.

It didn't have a smell at all.

Mini toed the ground. "This doesn't feel like dirt."

Aru bent to check it out. She ran her fingers over the floor. It was *silk*.

She walked to one of the trees, planning to snap off a branch and inspect it, but instead walked straight *through* it.

"It's not real!" exclaimed Mini. She jumped through another one of the trees. "This is amazing!"

A small puddle of water caught the light.

"What is this going to be, a trampoline?" Mini laughed, jumping into it. But the second she did, the liquid stuck to her legs. And then it *pulled*. With every blink, Mini was vanishing beneath the —

"QUICKSAAAAAND!" screamed Mini. She started struggling.

"Stop!" shouted Aru. "Haven't you seen any movies? Thrashing around is, like, the fastest way to die!"

"Quicksandquicksandquicksand," moaned Mini. "I don't want to go this way. My body will be preserved forever like those bog mummies! I'll become a Wikipedia page!"

"You're not gonna die, Mini. Just stop screaming and let me think for a minute!"

She was going to reach for a branch to pull out Mini, but the branches weren't really there. Aru ran through a couple of the trees. Maybe there was an actual tree lurking in the midst? But there wasn't.

"Aru!" screamed Mini. By now, she was up to her neck. Any farther, and she wouldn't even be able to scream. Her arms waved wildly in the air.

"I'm coming!" said Aru, running back.

But Aru tripped. She braced herself for a fall, but of course, the silky ground was soft. She landed with a light *thump.* When she looked down, her hands were clutching folds of the "dirt."

"That's it," whispered Aru.

She lifted some silk off the ground. It came up in a dark, slender rope. Aru dragged it over to Mini, who, by now, was buried up to her chin.

Mini grabbed hold of the rope, but the quicksand yanked her under.

"No!" cried Aru.

She pulled the rope as hard as she could. Under ordinary circumstances, she might not have been able to do it. Under ordinary circumstances, Aru probably would have slipped into the quicksand herself and both of them would have become dismal Wikipedia pages.

But worry for a friend can make ordinary circumstances extraordinary. In that moment, all Aru knew was that Mini was her first true friend in a long time . . . and she would not — *could* not — lose her.

Mini gasped as Aru heaved her onto the silky ground.

Aru was shocked. *She did it.* She saved her. Even though she'd faced down a demon and tricked the seasons, this was the first time she felt like she'd done something magical.

Mini spluttered and coughed. "There was a *shark* down there." She shuddered, then gathered a handful of silk and started toweling off her hair. "A *shark*! And you know what it said to me? It said, 'Is it true your sharks don't talk?' I didn't have a chance to answer, because you pulled me out so quickly."

"What kind of thank-you is that?"

"Why should I say thank you?" asked Mini. "I knew you could do it."

I knew you could do it.

Aru bit back a grin. "Fine. Next time I'll let you drown a bit longer."

"No!" squeaked Mini. "Drowning is number three on my Top Ten Ways I Don't Want to Die list."

"Who makes a list of *that*?"

Mini primly straightened her shirt. "I find that organizing scary information actually makes me less scared."

Once Mini had finished toweling off, they looked at the path ahead of them. The road that wound through the forest was the same color as the DEIGN sign.

"Do you think it goes to another hall?" asked Aru.

"Maybe? I wish we had a map again," Mini said, squinting as she studied her hand.

Ever since they had arrived in the Kingdom of Death, the mehndi had grown lighter and lighter, as they did naturally, because they were not permanent. But now all that remained of the fantastical designs were faint waves on their fingers and the dark Sanskrit numbers on their palms.

The forest arced over them. In this place there was even a sky. But given how topsy-turvy everything was, Aru wondered whether it was a sea. Maybe here the moon really was made of cheese.

"Does this place feel familiar to you?" asked Mini. She rubbed her arms as if she had goose bumps.

"No?"

Aru would have remembered a place that looked like this. But she couldn't deny the smell that she had caught right before they'd jumped into DEIGN. It was the smell of . . . home.

She was still thinking about this when she experienced a very rude awakening. Every tree they had seen so far had been intangible, so Aru had walked straight through them. She was passing through one of the trunks, not really minding where she was going, when she smacked her nose. *Hard.*

"What the — ?" she muttered, glaring.

She had run into the side of a cliff. A rocky black wall glistening with water. No, it was a *hard* waterfall. She reached out to touch it carefully. It seemed like actual water, cold and cascading through her fingers. But the minute she tried to put her hand through it, it pushed back. As firm as stone.

"Yet another illusion," said Aru. "Except this one's got substance to it."

Beside her, Mini paled. "Aru, that's it! I think I know where we are!"

Mini closed her eyes and put her hand on the waterfall. She groped around, and then her hand abruptly stopped moving. She must have found what she was looking for, because her eyes opened suddenly. Behind the waterfall, Aru heard the faintest unclasping sound. Like a key sliding into a lock.

The next instant, the waterfall swung open.

It hadn't been a waterfall at all, but a secret door.

"Just like in the stories about the Palace of Illusions," breathed Mini.

"Is this your wisdom cookie speaking, or you?"

"Me," said Mini, frowning. "I only remember the story because of the carnival my mom took me and my brother to. She brought it up when we went to the place with all the weird mirrors —"

"You mean the fun house?"

"Right, that. She told me the Pandavas had lived in a place like that. A famous demon king, who was also a really great architect, made it for them."

Aru remembered hearing that story. In exchange for their sparing his life, the demon king Mayasura agreed to build the Pandava brothers the most beautiful palace the world had ever seen. It came with illusions that befuddled the mind and heightened the senses. They were so convincing that when an enemy prince (who was also the Pandavas' cousin) came to visit, he fell through a floor tile that was actually water, and he nearly broke his foot jumping into a pool that turned out to be cleverly polished sapphires.

"What if this is the original palace?" asked

Mini. "Maybe that's how I knew how to open the door?"

"So what if it is? It's not like we'll remember anything about it from our former lives. It's just a house, no big deal. And I doubt it's the real Palace of Illusions. What would it be doing here, anyway? We didn't reside in the Kingdom of Death. . . ."

Mini frowned. "Uncle Chitrigupta said we'd find all kinds of things here, including forgotten things. Maybe when people forgot about the palace, it moved to the forest?"

"It's a house! Not a person," said Aru.

But Mini didn't look so convinced. The path led to the waterfall door, and there were no other routes around it. "We have to go through the palace, don't we?" she asked, her voice barely above a whisper. "I really don't want to. I couldn't even get through the Haunted Mansion in Disney World. My dad had to take me out."

"Well, if we have to go through it, it's going to be fine. It's a palace. It might be a bit weird inside, but we've seen a lot of weird stuff on this trip! Like a magical-door crocodile, and Door of Death dogs, and I don't even want to think about what else. You can get past a couple of stones, some statues, and some optical illusions. Trust me."

Mini took a deep breath. "Fine, if you say so."

"Plus, think about it this way: if there are any enchantments inside, you have the magical compact. Just swing it around and look at things out of the corner of your eye."

Mini nodded, threw back her shoulders, and pushed open the door.

Aru walked in after her. The stone door closed behind them, cutting off the sound of the waterfall and leaving a deep silence. Was this how everyone had once entered the palace of the Pandavas? For a moment, Aru wondered about the life she had apparently lived thousands of years ago. How many times had her former self run into the hard waterfall? Or maybe Arjuna had never hit his head on anything. It didn't make any sense how they could share the same soul and be completely different.

Beneath her feet, dust caked the palace floor. She caught the sheen of lapis lazuli tiles that must have been brilliant in their day. Now they were cracked. The air had that unstirred quality of an abandoned house.

Or a mausoleum.

"I bet it was really pretty once," said Mini.

Aru grimaced as she looked around her. Some dust — at least she hoped it was dust and not pulverized skeletons or something equally gross — fell onto her shoulder from the crumbling ceilings. "Yeah . . . *once.*"

"Huh. What's this?" asked Mini.

She touched a cobwebbed torch on the wall. Aru wondered if this was going to be one of those Indiana Jones moments and now the floor was going to open up beneath them.

Instead, the torch glowed.

"Mini, 'what's this' is *never* a good question in a movie —"

But she didn't get a chance to finish. Around them, the air began to crackle. The shadowy palace halls brightened as torches flickered to life along all the walls.

And then the sound of cantering hooves thundered through the palace. For one sparkling moment, Aru wondered whether Indra's seven-headed horse was coming to save them and get them out of here. Instead, a herd of horses charged toward them. If a herd of horses were charging at her in any other situation, Aru would have turned and run. But these horses weren't like any she'd ever seen.

For one thing, they were made of rose petals. Their eyes were bloodred blossoms, and their floral manes were the luminous pink of dawn. When they opened their mouths to neigh, Aru saw that their teeth were tightly furled white buds.

But when they got about a foot away from Aru, they *burst.* Petals rained down. In their wake, she could smell wildflowers and fresh rain. It would have been pleasant if it hadn't been for the walls shaking soon after, and the deep, dark sound echoing around them:

"WHO DARES DISTURB THE PEACE OF THIS HOME?"

Twenty-Six:
My Home, Not Yours!
No Touchie!

"Technically, it's *our* home," said Aru.

"Maybe we shouldn't —" started Mini.

Suddenly both of them were slammed, *hard,* against a wall by an unseen wind.

"*Your* home?" repeated the voice.

It took a moment for Aru to realize that it wasn't some dude skulking in the shadows who was talking, but the palace itself. It shook with laughter. More dust (or pulverized skeletons, Aru was beginning to think was more likely) fell down on them. Hundreds of lights flashed on the walls. It looked a little like a movie theater coming to life. Except here, the broken tiles began to arrange themselves. They rolled across the floor until they formed a smile. Two bright braziers sparked alive, slanting into eyes.

"I do not think so," said the palace. "This was once the seat of the Pandava brothers and their wife, Draupadi. You mere pinches of mortality are nothing compared to them.

You cannot possess *me*!"

All the torches in the palace guttered at once. It was hard to remember that this was the Palace of Illusions and not of, say, nightmares.

Aru took Mini's hand and tried to reassure her. "Whatever happens, it's not real."

"I think you should leave, little pinches," said the palace.

The ceiling quaked. Wind blew in their faces. The ground beneath them glowed strangely, as if they were standing over an aquarium. An illusion flickered to life on the ground, showing a rocky cliff that dropped off into the sea.

"It's not real, it's not real," whispered Aru under her breath.

A gigantic shark swam up right under her feet. It grinned and looked like it was saying, *Come on in, the water's great!* Aru squeezed her eyes shut and gripped Mini's hand even harder.

"We're — we're not going *anywhere*!" called out Mini. She had to draw in great big gulps of air to get the words out.

"Don't you recognize *us*?" shouted Aru. It was easier to be brave (or fake bravery) with her eyes closed. At least that way she didn't have to see the shark. She was pretty sure it was tying a napkin around its neck, clapping its fins, and saying, *Dinner, dinner, dinner!*

"We are the Pandavas!" said Mini. "We've got the souls of Yudhistira and Arjuna!"

"What?! Don't say that! It sounds like we've kidnapped them!"

"I mean . . ." shouted Mini. "We're the daughters of the Dharma Raja and Lord Indra!"

The wind stopped roaring. The fires sputtered to smoldering embers. When Aru opened her eyes, the floor was just that: a floor.

"You lie," hissed the palace.

The actual words came from every direction. She even saw letters bubbling up like blisters on her skin: *L-I-A-R.* She winced, but the red marks vanished. Just another illusion.

"When the Pandavas left," said the palace, "they bade farewell to all except the one thing that had given them shelter and watched over them as they slept. Was my beauty not enough to tempt them to stay? My illusions were forged of the same stuff that made up their dreams. I was their dream home. Literally. But still they left. So why should I believe they would come back?"

The palace smelled sour. As if it was sulking.

Aru didn't think it was possible to sympathize with a palace, and yet she did. Before now she had never thought about how a house must feel when its family stuck a FOR SALE sign on the lawn and then packed up and left. If the palace could be sad, did that mean her apartment missed her? Now she really wanted to run to the museum and hug a pillar.

"I'm . . . I'm so sorry you felt left behind," said Mini carefully. "Maybe they — I mean, we left you a note? But I promise we're not lying about who we are. You see, we've got urgent business and need to get through the other side of the palace."

"Why?" it asked.

The ceiling caved inward. When Aru squinted, it looked a bit like a frowny face. And then it blazed red.

Maybe not a frowny face. Maybe more of a fury face.

"Because we need to save the world," said Aru. "If there's no world, what's going to happen to you?"

A wall of fire sprang up in front of Aru.

"You're horrifyingly rude!" said the palace. "Is this what I have missed out on during all these millennia in the depths of

Death's kingdom? Well, then, I'm not sorry. Not a whit."

"Please," said Mini. "Just let us through. This was the only way in from the forest."

"Ah, I miss my true forest," said the palace fondly. "I am hewn from its trees. Sand from those puddles sealed my cracks. My woods once wriggled with deplorable things. When the Pandavas decided to build their home, the creatures were banished. The great architect king Mayasura's life was spared in exchange for building them a palace the likes of which no one had ever seen: *me.*"

The wall of fire disappeared, revealing a most magnificent hall. Tall living statues studded with jewels paced back and forth. One of them had a glass belly that housed a miniature library.

"The eldest Pandava liked to read," the palace recalled wistfully. "But he had trouble choosing a room to read in. So I made sure his bed could float anywhere and books could be brought to him."

The walls were covered with thinly beaten gold, and the floor was a marvel of mirrors and sapphire pools.

"The youngest liked to admire himself, so I made sure there were plenty of places where he might catch glimpses of his beauty."

A lush garden dripped from the ceiling, eclipsing the previous illusion. Glass vials and sheaves of parchment dotted a worktable.

"The second youngest liked the sciences, so I made sure there was always an abundance of living things to study."

A stadium unfurled in front of them. It contained spinning wheels, moving targets, and racetracks that curved from the floor to the ceiling.

"The second eldest liked to test his strength, so I made sure he had challenging arenas."

The next image showed a mishmash of all the items from the previous illusions.

"The third eldest liked a little of everything, so I made sure nothing escaped his interest."

The final image was a room full of soft light.

"And wise and beautiful Draupadi, wife to the five brothers — what she wanted most of all was peace. I tried to grant her wish, but the closest I could muster was light."

The images faded.

"How fitting that I am called the Palace of Illusions when all I have left are memories. Perhaps memories are the grandest illusion of all," said the palace quietly. And then, in a voice even softer and smaller: "In my memories, they seemed so happy with me."

Pity twisted through Aru. But it was quickly erased when the twin braziers flickered back to life.

"And now you wish to spoil those memories, too? Taunt me with the idea that the Pandavas have returned?"

"We didn't mean to hurt your feelings," said Mini. Her eyes shone.

"Not *returned* so much as been *reincarnated,*" said Aru. "There's a difference. I didn't even remember that we had a house! Honest."

The house shivered.

"You," it started sniffling, "are saying that I'm not worth *remembering*?"

"No!" Aru winced. "Not at all!"

Mini scowled at Aru and bent down to rub one of the tiles like you would a dog's belly. "No, no," she said soothingly. "What she means is, we don't really have much of a memory about our past lives! We didn't even know we were Pandavas until, like, last week."

"I have never let anyone past these halls that was not a Pandava, or a guest of a Pandava."

More dust fell on Aru. Yup. It was definitely pulverized bone. She tried not to gag.

A scroll of parchment unraveled from the ceiling. Thousands upon thousands of names were written on it. The ink dripped down the paper before puddling on the floor.

"Ah, so sorry, but you're not on the list," said the palace. There was a malicious tinge to its voice now. "So I suppose you'll just have to prove that you really are Pandavas."

Once more, the house shook. The walls flashed with different colors. No longer was Aru staring at the ruins of a palace. Now she was in the middle of a forest.

But it wasn't real. The illusion — as she had to keep reminding herself — felt so real that the grass even prickled beneath her feet. Fireflies drifted drowsily through the evening air. The jungle had that smell of overripe fruit that had fallen and gone uneaten.

"Whoa," she breathed, turning to Mini.

But Mini wasn't there.

"Hey! Where — ?" Aru spun around wildly. She was all alone. Around her, the forest began to laugh. Leaves fell down on her slowly. Cruelly. Each leaf that touched her skin left a tiny wound the size of a paper cut.

"I told you that if you wanted to get through me, you'd have to prove yourself a Pandava," murmured the forest that was not a forest but a palace. "Arjuna was the greatest hero who ever lived."

Aru thought that was a rather sweeping statement to make. *The greatest?* Really?

In front of her, a bow and arrow appeared on the ground.

Oh no.

She didn't even know how to use a bow. Did you string it? Notch it? Aru cursed.

She should have paid more attention when she was watching Lord of the Rings last week. Maybe if she'd looked at how Legolas used a bow instead of, you know, just looking at Legolas, she would've been a little bit more prepared.

"Are you truly a Pandava brother, or are you just a liar?"

"What do you want me to do with this?" Aru said, gesturing at the bow.

"Simple, little pinch of mortality: If you aim true, you'll escape this illusion. If you don't, well, you'll die. Don't worry, we can make this whole ordeal go much more quickly. Watch."

As he spoke, the fireflies began to grow

brighter. Heat filled the air. Aru's eyes widened.

The fireflies were made of actual fire.

Twenty-Seven:
. . . And Then Came the Horde of Godzilla-Size Fireflies

Silence settled over the forest.

"Mini!" screamed Aru.

Was this illusion different from the others? Was it a physical thing, or something living in her mind? Aru squeezed her eyes shut, then opened them quickly. Nothing. She thought the illusion would be like a creepy glitchy thing, as if one moment she'd see the illusion and the other moment she'd see the reality.

"Mini?" Aru called again.

On the ground, the bow and arrow taunted her.

"Hey, palace!" she called. "If you let me out, I'll wash your windows!"

Still no reply.

"Fine, roll around in filth for all I care!"

Something burned her toe. "OW!"

It was one of the fireflies.

At first, the fireflies had simply floated through the darkness, heating the air. But then they'd begun to *land* on the boulders and the branches of the giant forest. Now it looked like a golden net had been stretched over the forest, but it was eerily *still.*

The smell of something charred hit her. A burnt circle appeared right next to her toe.

"Oh no," said Aru softly.

Whatever the fireflies touched, they kindled.

At her back, she heard crackling, the sound of brush catching fire. Smoke plumed into the air. The fireflies reflected off the shiny forest leaves, looking like possessed Christmas lights.

Aru swiped the bow and arrow from the ground and took off running.

The fireflies followed close behind. A flame nearly scorched her ear.

Aru dove behind a rock and peeked out. The forest was on fire. Literally. Metaphorically. All the –allys.

She fumbled with the bow and arrow. They were abnormally heavy and awkward. The arrow alone must have weighed as much as her backpack on a Monday before Christmas break.

"There —" she grunted, "is — no — way — this — is — going — to — work —"

Finally, she slid the arrow into place. *This shouldn't be difficult.* Katniss and Legolas made it look easy enough. She plucked at the heavy string. It cut her fingers.

"Owowow!" she wailed, dropping the bow and arrow.

What did the palace mean? *If you aim true, you'll escape.* Aim at *what*? She looked around, scanning the tops of the forest trees and the branches underneath. But there was no target.

How could she possibly be like Arjuna? She couldn't even pull a bowstring, let alone do one of his famous feats, like shoot an arrow through the eye of a fish just by *looking at its reflection.* Even the Ping-Pong ball in her pocket was of no help in this situation.

"Exit . . . If I were an exit, where would I hide?"

She was beginning to feel uncomfortably warm. Was that a swarm of insects coming her way? Or was it just her imagination? Aru snuck a second glance from her hiding spot behind the rock.

Nope. It was definitely not her imagination.

The fireflies had converged into what looked like one great big glowing bug. It pulsed with fire. With one flap of its wings, three trees turned to smoking ash.

Aru uttered a word that, at school, would

have gotten her thrown into detention for a week.

The firefly-nightmare-monstrosity flew closer. Aru bolted from the rock and sped into the deep thicket of trees. The shadows of a thousand fires loomed in front of her. Heat glowed on her back, and still Aru ran.

She flew past a valley of boulders and stumpy trees and found a stream flowing from the mouth of a cave. Aru jumped into the water and winced. This was the problem with creeks. They looked so inviting, but beneath the water, the ground was always sharp and slick. Jagged rocks punctured the bottoms of her feet as she waded toward the cave.

Once she got there, Aru plopped down on the cold, wet floor of the cave to catch her breath. She could still hear the *bzzz bzzz* of insect wings nearby.

"How awful is my life that I'm hoping for a giant fiery toad to come and eat the giant fiery fly?" she muttered.

She examined the soles of her feet. For an illusion, this was sickeningly realistic. Her physical condition — cut-up skin and a heart trying to break free of her ribs — didn't feel fake. And even if all of this *was* fake, not even her fake self wanted to be the victim of a giant fake bug.

If Mini were here, she could make an enchantment of a giant shoe and squash the nightmare creature. Once again Aru found herself missing Boo big-time. He'd know what to do. At the very least, his constant stream of insults would help distract her.

FOCUS, Shah!

Aru tugged her hair. *Think, think, think.* But brains are uncooperative. At that moment, the only thing running through her head was the tagline of a commercial for acne cream: *Don't pop and poke! Try Dr. Polk's!*

"*Pop and poke,*" she sang in an off-key, slightly panicked voice.

She reached beside her for the arrow.

Her hand hit cold stone.

Arrow . . .

She turned, scanning the cave floor. But there was nothing around her but wet rocks.

The memory flashed painfully in her head: she had left the arrow behind when she fled the burning forest.

Around her, the cave began to warm up. Steam wafted off the creek. A cloud of fireflies appeared at the mouth of the cave. The heat became harsher, the light brighter. Aru clawed at her throat. It was getting harder to breathe.

Aru had no arrow. No athletic prowess.

No hope.

She started nervously scratching at her neck and felt something cold there. The monsoon pendant! Monsoon had said it would hit any target. But what exactly was she supposed to aim *at*?

If you aim true, you'll escape this illusion.

But how could she escape an illusion when it didn't exist?

"It's not like I can escape my head!" she said, tugging her hair.

Wait. That wasn't entirely true, was it? She *had* escaped her own head. Lots of times.

Aru thought back to every time she'd woken up from a bad dream. She would bolt upright, shot straight out of a nightmare just by remembering what it was: a nightmare.

All of her nightmares were the same. She dreamed about coming home and finding the apartment empty, cleaned out. Her mother hadn't even bothered to leave a note saying good-bye. Aru had that nightmare whenever her mom left for business trips. But even when her nightmares seemed so real — down to the scratchy carpet of their apartment that would always be caked with dust — they were nothing more than flimsy images shot through with fear. That was the real thing: the *feeling.* Everything else was . . .

A lie.

The flames licked closer. Light and heat splashed across her face.

She closed her eyes and let go of Monsoon's pendant. She could feel in her bones that pretending like this whole thing was real wasn't the right thing to do. This time, no acne commercial flickered through her thoughts. Instead, she recalled the story of Arjuna and the fish's eye.

In the tale, the archery teacher of the Pandavas had tied a wooden fish to a tree branch. He instructed the brothers to shoot an arrow at the fish's eye. But they could only aim by looking at the reflection of the wooden fish in the water below them.

The teacher asked Yudhistira, the oldest brother, what he saw in the reflection. He said, *The sky, the tree, the fish.* The teacher told him not to shoot. He asked Bhima, the second oldest brother, what he saw. He said, *The branch of the tree, the fish.* The teacher asked him not to shoot.

And then the teacher asked Arjuna what he saw. He said, *The eye of the fish.*

Only he was allowed to shoot.

It was a tale about focusing, about peeling away distractions one by one until all that was left was the target. The eye of the fish.

The flames touched Aru's feet. She grimaced, but didn't move. She closed her eyes.

The bow and arrow were only distractions.

The real way out . . . had always been in her mind.

She pictured Mini and the museum, her mother and the memories. She pictured Boo's feathery chest puffed out in pride. She pictured the red, blinking light of Burton Prater's phone. She pictured freedom.

It wasn't an all-of-a-sudden thing. She wasn't yanked from one place to the next. She didn't open her eyes and see a new world where there had been an old one. Instead, she felt something like a latch unclasping inside her.

People are a lot like magical pockets. They're far bigger on the inside than they appear to be on the outside. And it was that way with Aru. She found a place deep within her that had been hidden until now. It was a place of silence that seemed deafening. It was a feeling of narrowness turned vast, as if she could hide small worlds within her. This was what escape was: discovering a part of herself that no one else could find.

Aru reached. She imagined a door to the Otherworld with a tether of light wrapped around its handle. She grabbed on to that tether . . .

And pulled.

In that moment, she could no longer feel the flames. She could no longer hear the buzzing of cruel insect wings. She heard only her heartbeat pounding against the silence. She saw only her dreams of freedom turning bright and wild, like a rainbow glimpsed through a prism.

And in that moment, she escaped.

TWENTY-EIGHT:
THE PALACE'S STORY

When Aru opened her eyes, she was standing once more in the decrepit palace hall.

Mini was a couple feet away from her, furiously arguing with . . . with herself? *Two Minis?* One of them was getting increasingly red in the face and hunching her shoulders. The other pushed her glasses up her nose and kept talking. *Her!* Aru would've bet money that version was the real Mini. Aru tried to run forward, but she was kept back by some kind of invisible barrier.

"Hey!" called Aru, pounding her fists against the air. "Mini!"

But the Minis kept right on arguing. The real one said, "And so it stands to reason that the fastest thing in the world is not a person or a creature, but a thought!"

The other Mini let out a horrible groan, as if she'd just gotten attacked by a headache, and vanished.

The remaining Mini braced her hands on

her knees and took a deep breath. The invisible barrier must have disappeared, too, because Mini finally noticed Aru. A grin stretched wide across her face.

"You're alive!"

"So are you!" shouted Aru, running toward her.

But no sooner were they next to each other than the palace roared to life. Torches flamed on. Even the roof pulled itself up, like someone adjusting his suspenders.

The two of them braced themselves. Aru wrapped her hand around the glowing ball in her pocket. Mini gripped her compact.

The palace shuddered.

"Only Yudhistira would've been able to out-reason himself through wisdom," it said.

Aru dropped her voice to a whisper. "*Seriously?* Your task was to annoy yourself?"

Mini scowled.

"And only Arjuna," continued the palace, "would've had the vision and perception to escape the mind's own fear. Which means it's you! It really *is* you. . . ."

"Duh!" said Aru. "We told you that when we got —"

But the moment Aru started speaking, the ceiling split above their heads. Rain gushed in from the cracks in the roof. The whole palace rolled.

"I —"

The beams creaked.

"— thought —"

The foundation whined.

"— you —"

The roof caved in.

"— forgot —"

The floor tiles beneath them split.

"— about —"

The walls peeled back.

"— me."

The rain was a waterfall now. There was nothing for Aru and Mini to do except clutch each other as the palace broke apart around them. When the crying (and rain) finally stopped, the walls pulled themselves back together. The roof dried its shingles and stitched itself whole again. The foundation rolled one last time, as if heaving a sigh.

The palace had a right to be upset. They had forgotten all about it. But was that really their fault?

"I missed you," said the palace. "For three hundred years after you left, I kept the floors polished and the ceilings free of dust. I kept the larders full, and I watered the plants. But you never returned. Did I do something wrong?"

"No, of course not!" said Mini. She looked as though she wanted to drop to her knees and embrace the entire palace as if it were a sad giant dog.

"We're not really the people we once were," tried Aru. "We don't even remember anything about that life. Otherwise . . . otherwise we would have visited."

Moments later, the floors started to gleam. The fire in the torches turned from harsh to warm. Paintings that had been hidden behind layers of skeleton dust glowed with color.

"And yet you must leave again?" asked the palace.

There was a plaintive note to its voice. Like a pet who really didn't want you to go and was convinced that if she were on her best behavior you might change your mind.

"We don't have a choice," said Mini. "You know that."

Trickles of silver liquid ran down the walls. "I know," said the palace. "This time, I won't forget to polish the floors —"

"Don't go to the trouble," started Mini.

Aru jumped in. "Yes! Please do that, thank you," she said. "And make sure you do a good job."

Aru knew better than anyone that the worst part about being left behind was the wait. Whenever her mom left on business trips, Aru always cleaned the apartment from top to bottom. Sometimes, she even went to the farmers market so that there would be bright apples on the table instead of thick gray books like *Representations of the Feminine in Ancient Hindu Sculpture*. Every time her mom came home, Aru would stand off to the side, chest puffed out like a blue jay, waiting for her to notice. Sometimes she did, and sometimes she didn't. Not knowing how her mom would react was what made Aru do it all over again the next time. And so she understood how the house must have felt.

"Excellent!" shouted the palace.

All at once, chandeliers dropped from the ceiling. Crystal bowls of light pink ice cream floated into Mini's and Aru's hands.

"Please . . ." coaxed the house. "Just a bite. You can eat and walk at the same time. I'll make sure you don't trip. Or would you rather skate? You liked to do that once upon a time."

The ground beneath them turned to ice, and their sandals were replaced with pretty metal shoes with blades on the bottom.

Aru took a bite of the ice cream. It melted on her tongue and left behind the delicate flavor of rose.

"I'm not very good at skating," said Aru. "Can we travel any way we want?"

"It is limited only by your imagination," said the palace.

One step later, they were zooming through the halls.

Aru grinned. Imagine having a home like this. . . . A home that knew what you wanted and leaped to answer. A home that grew carousels made of bits of stars and petals, and let her gallop on a horse made of dandelion fluff while she balanced a bowl of ice cream in one hand. A home with a floating bed, and books that knew when to flip the pages, so you didn't have to get up from your pillow or move your hand. . . .

But this wasn't home.

Her home was small and littered with books she didn't understand. The apartment had cracks in the walls and old plumbing. There was always straw on the floor from the wooden crates the statues were shipped in.

Her home had her mother.

The palace, as always, could read her thoughts. It sighed again. "You must be on your way, and what kind of home would I be if I pampered you and kept you back?"

Mini blushed. She had been bicycling through the air, ice cream in her hand and a book floating in front of her face. "You're right," she said. She wiped her mouth and set aside the rest of the ice cream.

Aru finished hers so quickly, she got brain freeze. The palace enchanted a hand towel to wrap around her head. *"Mfanks,"* she mumbled, hoping that the palace understood she was trying to say *Thanks.*

Unexplored rooms hovered around them, promising rich histories and secrets. Aru caught a glimpse of a chamber full of glass birds. A serpent slithered out of a hole in a wall, its scales fashioned of rivers and seas. Down a long hallway, Aru saw the skyline of a distant city. Part of her longed to explore, but she knew she couldn't. Even without looking at her hand, Aru could feel the number on her palm as if it were searing her skin. They had *two* days left. They couldn't waste time.

The dandelion horse, recognizing her unspoken wish, set her down gently.

Within moments they were at the rear exit of the palace.

"Here we are," said the palace mournfully. "I'm sorry about the, you know, death threats, trials, and such. . . . I do hope you can forgive me. I didn't realize that it was . . . you. . . ."

"We forgive you," said Mini.

"I would have done the same if I were a palace," added Aru graciously.

The palace beamed. Silver lights burst from the ceiling and drifted down like glittering confetti.

"I have a present for you as you continue on your journey," said the palace shyly.

"What is it?"

"Just a trifle," it said. "Something you might keep in your pocket and remember me by, should you not be able to visit me again."

Aru and Mini held out their hands. In the center of their palms appeared a little blue tile shaped like a five-pointed star.

"This is a piece of home," said the palace. "It will provide you with rest and shelter when you are in need. Granted, it cannot create an arena or training grounds like I can . . . but it can give you the part of me that matters most: protection."

Aru curled her fingers around the tile, grinning. "Thank you, palace. It's perfect!"

"I hope we won't need to use it, but I'm glad we have it all the same," said Mini.

More silver confetti rained in a happy shower from the ceiling. "Glad to be of service," said the palace. "That is all I ever wanted."

"Palace, what lies beyond this kingdom?" asked Mini. "We need to get to the hall where they keep the celestial weapons."

"Ah! You need . . . a map!" said the palace excitedly.

"But maybe not one of those big road maps, though," said Aru. "More like a pamphlet? Something small?" She had trouble reading maps. And she had even more trouble folding them up when she was done. *Follow the lines!* her mom used to scold. (But there were *so many* lines.)

"Ah, yes, of course! How efficient you are, my princess, how noble and precise are your manners!" creaked the palace. "Alas, I have failed you once more." The walls cried silver rivulets again. "I have no pamphlet and cannot procure you such a thing, because I do not know what that is. However, I *can* tell you that what lies beyond is a place of sadness. For, you see, it is the Bridge of Forgetting. Only there might you find what you are seeking with the weapons. There is a reason why I have not disappeared: I am not yet forgotten. But I reside in the Kingdom of Death because I am not considered 'true.' I am myth. One day, perhaps, I too will cross the Bridge of Forgetting like so many other stories before me."

Aru braced herself for more tears and rain, but the palace seemed oddly at peace with this statement.

"It is better, perhaps, to be thought of as

a fiction than to be discarded from memory completely. If it is not too much to ask, would you think of me fondly every now and again?" The torches sputtered. "It makes a difference to me to know that every now and again I am remembered."

Aru and Mini promised. Aru didn't know how to embrace a palace, so she did the next best thing. She planted a kiss on her palm and pressed it to the wall. The palace shuddered happily. Mini did the same.

"Good-bye, good-bye, Pandavas! Do great things! Make good choices!" said the palace. The door swung shut. "And if you must forget me, at least do it with a smile."

Twenty-Nine: The Bridge of Forgetting

Once they had closed the door to the Palace of Illusions, a winding road stretched out before them. The sky was black, but it wasn't nighttime. It was the flat darkness of a room with the lights off. Here, in the middle of myth and the Bridge of Forgetting, the landscape was different. Statues were half sunken into the earth. Tall white trees blocked their view of what lay ahead.

"I'm starving," Aru moaned. "I shouldn't have eaten that ice cream so fast. Do you have any more Oreos?"

"Nope. I gave the last one to Boo." At the mention of their pigeon friend, Mini sighed and wiped at her eyes. "Do you think he's okay?"

Aru wasn't sure. The last time they'd seen him, he'd been knocked unconscious. That automatically said *not okay.*

"Even if he isn't okay right now," she told Mini, "we're going to rescue him, and then he'll definitely be okay."

"I hope so."

Two minutes later, Aru's stomach grumbling had gone from a smattering of sound to giant, growling *there's-a-monster-in-my-belly-and-it-wants-to-eat-you* noises. She pulled out the glowing ball and poked it. Was it edible?

"Borborygmi," said Mini.

"*Bor-bor* what? Who's a pygmy?"

"Your stomach sounds . . . they're called borborygmi."

"Did you get that from the wisdom cookie?"

"Nope. Medical textbook."

"Mini, *why* were you reading a medical textbook . . . ?"

"I like to." She shrugged. "Bodies are so cool! Did you know that more than half of us is made of water?"

"Yippee," said Aru. "Are we there yet?"

"How am I supposed to know?"

"Well, you're the one who ate the wisdom cookie."

"*Like I said,*" said Mini, clearly annoyed, "it only makes you wise until the thing you're asking wisdom for is done."

"Technically, we're not done. We're still questing, or whatever, through this place. Honestly, what's the point of making us go through all this? Don't the gods *want* the world to be saved quickly? This journey is more useless than a unicorn's horn."

Mini looked highly affronted. "What do you mean, *useless*? It wouldn't be a unicorn without a horn. That's what the word means! *Uni,* for *one.* And then *corn* for, you know, *horn. One-horned.*"

"Yeah, but they're supposed to be all peaceful and nice. Why would a unicorn need a horn? What's it *do* with it?"

Mini turned red. "I dunno. For shooting off magic and stuff."

"Or they use it to maul things."

"That's horrible, Aru! They're unicorns. They're perfect."

"Maybe that's just what they *want* you to think."

She, personally, did not trust anything that had a built-in weapon and claimed not to use it. *Yeah, right.*

"It's so cold all of a sudden," said Mini.

She was right. The temperature had dropped. Well, not dropped so much as fallen off a cliff and tumbled straight down.

Aru's long-suffering Spider-Man pajamas did little to protect her. The wind blew through the cloth, chilling her skin. "Imagine having to live in a place like this," she said through chattering teeth. "You'd have to pick your nose all the time just so that your boogers wouldn't freeze into icicles and stab the inside of your nose."

"Gross!"

The air felt tight. Not that stifled, staleness of the palace. It reminded Aru of how sometimes in winter it hurt to breathe because the air had become overly sharp and thin.

"Aru, look, it's snowing!"

Aru craned her neck and saw blue-bellied clouds drifting above them. In slow spirals, white flurries fell to the ground.

A single white flake landed on her palm. It looked like a snowflake, down to the delicate lacework of ice. But it didn't *feel* like snow. Even though it was cold.

It felt like a pinch.

Beside her, Mini winced.

The snow, or whatever it was, was beginning to fall harder. Now the flakes were hitting the ground. They didn't melt.

As Aru watched the snow, she spotted a tall tree with hundreds of tiny mirrors for bark. Something slipped behind the trunk. A figure — pale and slim, with a cloud of frosted hair. But when she blinked, she couldn't remember what she had seen.

"Aru!" called Mini.

She didn't respond. Not because she

hadn't heard, but because she hadn't realized Mini was talking to her.

For a second, she had forgotten that Aru was her name.

Panicking, Aru tried to rub the snowflakes off her arm and shake them out of her hair. Something about it was making her lose track of things she should remember. It wasn't like snow at all. It was like salt thrown on a slug. Slowly dissolving what you were.

"Is it such a bad thing, children, to forget?" asked a voice from somewhere in front of them. "If you never remember, you never grow old. Innocence keeps you ageless and blameless. People are rarely punished for deeds they cannot recall."

Aru looked up. The snowflakes now hung suspended in the air, a thousand white droplets. A man parted the droplets as if they were a giant beaded curtain. He was beautiful.

Not movie-star handsome, which was something else; this was a distant, unearthly beauty. The way you could watch a thunderstorm brewing across the ocean and find it lovely.

The man was tall and dark-skinned, his hair a shock of silver. His eyes were like blue chips of ice. His jacket and pants were an unnaturally bright shade of white.

"I'm sorry, did you say something?" Mini asked him. "If you did, I . . . I can't remember . . . ."

"Ah, forgive me," said the man. He laughed.

He waved his hand, and the snowy particles lifted off the girls' skin and hair. Bits of knowledge thudded back into Aru's head.

Only now did she remember her favorite color (green), her favorite dessert (tiramisu), and her name. How could she have forgotten those things? Aru found that very scary, because it meant she wouldn't know when something had been stolen from her.

"My name is Shukra. I am the guardian of the Bridge of Forgetting. It is rare that I talk to living beings. You see, I do not venture often beyond my bridge."

Aru couldn't remember a single story about him, but that made sense, given who he was. And no wonder he never left. Imagine how rough that would be at parties. *"Who are you, again?" "I'm Shukra! Don't you remember?" "Right, right . . . So, who are you?"*

As Shukra walked toward them, Aru noticed that there were five mirrors floating around him. One over his head, one below his feet, one on his right, and one on his left. Another floated at chest level, high enough that he would only need to tilt his chin down to see his reflection.

Was this normal for beautiful people? In Madame Bee's salon, the whole place had been covered in reflective surfaces. Aru wondered whether mirrors just conveniently flocked to pretty people like sheep.

Behind Shukra, the land dropped off into a cliff. The snow — or whatever it was — clung to the outline of an invisible bridge. If Aru and Mini could cross that, they'd be well on their way to the place where the celestial weapons were kept.

"I've already forgotten my manners once," said Shukra silkily. "I would be remiss to do so twice. Pray, what are your names, children? Your full names, please."

Aru felt a tickle at the back of her throat. As if her name was trying to escape. She didn't want to say it, but it was like she couldn't help herself.

"Yamini," said Mini.

"Arundhati," said Aru.

It was weird to utter it aloud. She only heard her full name once a year, when teachers called roll on the first day and stumbled over the pronunciation. Aroondottie? Arun-dutty? Arah-hattie? *Aru,* she would say. *Just Aru.* Usually, one of her classmates would howl in the background, pretending to be a wolf calling to the night: *Arooooooooo!* (In first grade, Aru had tried to go along with it by leaping out of her chair and barking. She'd been sent home.)

"Lovely names. They will be beautiful ornaments for my bridge," said Shukra, examining his fingernails.

"So can we go across?" asked Aru.

"Of course." He smiled. He may have been handsome, but his teeth were terrifying. They were black, crooked, and filed to points. "But to those who wish to cross the Bridge of Forgetting, I always offer a choice. And I will offer the same to you. First, will you hear my tale, daughters of the gods?"

"How did you know we were the daughters of gods?" Mini asked.

"You reek of it," said Shukra, not unkindly.

Aru discreetly sniffed her armpits. Still good. She mentally high-fived herself.

"The scent of godhood does not lurk in the pits of humans," hissed Shukra.

"Oh."

"The scent of godhood lies in the burdens that hover above you. Pungent and powerful stenches they are," he said. "Each of you has a past, present, and future that was robbed from you. I, too, was robbed. Hear my tale. Then you can decide if you still wish to cross the Bridge of Forgetting."

Two chairs made of ice swiveled out of the ground and Shukra gestured for them to sit down. Aru didn't really want to, but the chair didn't care. Every time she stepped away, it slid a little closer, finally tripping her so she fell into the seat. The chair was so cold it burned her skin. Beside her, Mini's teeth chattered.

Shukra eyed himself in one of his five mirrors. "Do you know why I'm cursed to be forgotten?" he asked.

"Run-in with a bad demon?" guessed Aru.

Mini glared at her.

"If only it were that simple," said Shukra.

Aru really wanted to kick the chair and get out of here. Shukra seemed even more dangerous than the dogs that had guarded the entrance to the Kingdom of Death. There was something too . . . *quiet* about him. As if he knew he'd already won and was just taking his time.

"I killed the one person who could stand to look at me."

Stand to look at him? Uh, it wasn't like he was hard on the eyes.

"My wife," said Shukra. "She loved me, and so I killed her."

THIRTY

The Tale of Shukra

It was said that, when I was born, the sun was so revolted it went into hiding for a full month. Scars riddled my skin. My smile was gruesome. But though I was ugly, I was a good king. Beloved, even. What I could not perfect in my body, I tried to perfect in my mind.

For many years, I was ashamed to show myself to my subjects. I chose to rule from the shadows. But I could not wed in darkness. When my bride first looked upon me, her smile never wavered. She held her palm to my cheek and said, "Our love is what will make us beautiful."

And so it did.

The changes in my appearance were small. So small that at first I did not recognize them, for I was not used to gazing at myself in the mirror.

341

Four years passed, and by then her love had made me more handsome. And my wife? She was resplendent. The moon stayed out longer just to gaze upon her. The sun lingered to witness her grace. I no longer had the kind of ugly face that incited horror or pity, but now I was made unremarkable by my passing good looks.

I wanted more. I started noting the changes in my appearance each day. My wife assured me that, as our love grew, so would our beauty. For her, beauty went hand in hand with joy.

I grew impatient.

I installed mirrors everywhere, even in the floors. I made checklists by which I might daily appraise my altering visage. I was continually discarding my clothes and trying new outfits. I neglected my people.

I began to shun my wife. Every time I saw her, I was filled with fury. Why should she grow more beautiful than I? She, who had so much beauty to begin with.

One day I confronted her. "Do you still love me?" I asked.

She did not meet my gaze. "How can I love someone I no longer know? You have changed, my king. I would have loved you until Time itself had ended. Perhaps I still could, if you would only —"

But I did not hear beyond her first words.

I do not remember doing what I did.

It was only when the red had cleared from my eyes that I saw her corpse. I tried to tear at my skin. To burn every trace of her love — my ill-gotten beauty — from my body. But it was too late. I could not escape her love, so freely given, even in her final moments.

I smashed every mirror. Broke every window. Drained every pond.

And yet I could not escape the truth of what I had been given, and what I had lost.

When Shukra finished speaking, tears ran down his cheeks.

"Now I live surrounded by the memory of my mistakes," he said, gesturing at the mirrors that accompanied him. "Without these, the snow would steal my memories, as it does for all who visit here."

"I'm sorry," said Mini softly.

Aru said nothing. Part of her did pity him, but the other part was disgusted. He'd killed someone who loved him, someone who had given him a special gift. He was selfish.

Shukra brought his hands closer together. "It is time for you to make your choice. Should you not succeed in crossing the bridge, you will fall into one of the fires of hell and be forced into the next life."

343

"You mean . . . we'll die?" asked Mini.

"Oh yes," said Shukra, waving his hand as if Mini had asked something as casual as *Do you have chocolate ice cream?*

"How do we succeed?" asked Aru.

"To cross the Bridge of Forgetting, you must pay the toll."

"And that is . . . ?" asked Aru.

"You must sacrifice a part of yourself: your memories. Give them to me and leave lighter. As you can see, only the outline of the bridge is visible. Your memories are needed to form the rest of the bridge."

"Our *memories*?" repeated Mini. "Why would you want that?"

"So I will not be alone."

"*All* of them?" asked Mini. "Can I just give you all the bad ones? Last week, my backpack strap got caught in an escalator and —"

"All of them," interrupted Shukra.

"Why do you even bother staying here?" asked Aru. "Why not just go on to the next life? You could be free of all —"

"*Free?*" Shukra laughed. "Where is the freedom, little ones, in moving on to the next life?" he asked. "Do you not know that these things chase you past the doors of death? The ills of one life will affect you in the next."

There it was. Karma. That idea Aru just couldn't wrap her head around. *What goes around comes around and all that maybe-nonsense.* Aru thought it seemed like a scaredy-cat thing to do: decide not to move on just because it was bound to be hard. To her it didn't make much sense for him to stay here. All alone forever.

She stood up. Mini had a more difficult time. Her chair seemed to have grown fond of her and kept trying to twine around her legs.

"Do we get our memories back once we cross the bridge?" asked Aru.

"No."

Aru's hands formed twin fists at her side. "Then you're not getting any memories from me."

"Or — Ouch, get off!" said Mini, finally freeing herself from the chair. It made a soft whining sound. "Me neither!"

"That is a pity," said Shukra. "For you could have always made new ones."

He glanced at each of the mirrors that pressed close to him. They weren't supposed to remind him of beauty at all, realized Aru. They were supposed to remind him of pain. *Loss.* And he had no choice but to see it every single day.

"If you insist, I will let you die. Go ahead

345

and try to cross," he said. "You will fail."

They scooted past Shukra and were soon standing at the edge of the cliff. They could still see the outline of the bridge ahead, but a foot away from their feet there was nothing but a steep drop. No platform, no step, no anything. Was the bridge invisible? Was it even solid?

"The bridge will build itself," said Shukra. He hadn't moved from his spot. "The question is, can you cross it quickly enough? Judging by your ages, I doubt you'll make it farther than a few steps. You have had fewer memories than most."

The memory-stealing snow — which had been suspended in the air — began to fall again. This time, when the snow landed on Aru, it stung. Because it was taking. With every flake, another memory was ripped from her.

There! Gone in a flash, the memory of her eighth birthday, when her mother . . . her mother did something.

Something she could no longer recall.

"I offered you help," said Shukra. "A life of weightlessness, free of pain. But you rejected my proposition."

The bridge was slowly cobbled together with the girls' stolen memories. Aru lost the taste of chocolate. It was one of her most favorite things in the world, and yet she couldn't for the life of her remember how it tasted, or even how you spelled . . . spelled what? What had she been thinking about?

Beside her, Mini was tugging at her hair. "Stop this!" she cried.

Aru reached for the golden ball. But why she did, she wasn't sure. It's not as if it had ever done much more than glow. It wasn't like Mini's compact that could see through illusions or make some of its own. And now she couldn't even remember where she'd gotten the ball in the first place.

"You cannot escape pain in life," said Shukra. "For that I am sorry. I wanted to grant you a different ending, to let you leave without pain."

The snowfall grew faster and heavier. Aru could barely see through it. She turned to look at Shukra and she noticed something. The snow was landing everywhere except on him.

Her eyes narrowed. Something about Shukra's mirrors must be protecting him.

At that moment, a snowflake stamped her arm. Once, Atlanta had gotten two inches of snow, so, naturally, the city had gone into a panic and shut down. Her mother's flight out had been cancelled, and they'd spent the whole day inside, snuggled together on the couch. They'd eaten ramen while watching a Bollywood film where everyone got fake-slapped at least once, and —

The beloved memory vanished.

Aru could feel the hole it left behind in her heart. And even though she couldn't remember it now, she wanted to weep. Those memories were *everything*. They were what she held close when she had to spend a night without her mother at home. They were what she returned to whenever she was scared.

She couldn't lose them.

She needed to loosen Shukra's control of the memory-stealing snow. . . .

"The snow is hungry," said Shukra. "It will feed."

He turned his back to them, walking farther and farther away, as if he couldn't bear to see what would happen next.

But Aru had a plan —

Mini grabbed her around the wrist. "No, Aru." Her eyes were wide, and Aru knew that Mini had guessed what she was going to do. "There has to be some other way."

"If we don't break his mirrors, we won't remember anything, Mini."

"It's not right! He has those mirrors because he feels bad —"

"He killed his wife. Why should I feel

sorry for him?"

"Aru, he's . . . he's in pain. If we take from him, then we're no better —"

"Fine. *I'll* take from him, so that *we* can survive."

Aru didn't wait for Mini to answer. She had to act now.

Around her neck, the gray pendant from Monsoon was cold and wet. Even as she reached for it, she remembered Monsoon's words.

But be warned: regret will always follow. It is the price of aiming true. For sometimes, when we take the deadliest aim, we are nothing if not reckless.

Aru didn't hesitate. She threw. Mini turned away as if she couldn't witness this.

The stone struck the mirror in front of Shukra's chest. He shuddered, clutching his heart. "Irsa?" he called. He stumbled forward, clawing at the air as if he'd suddenly gone blind.

The pendant bounced, shattering the mirror above him. Then it broke the third and the fourth.

Shukra fell to his knees. The snow seemed to notice him then. It stopped falling on Aru and Mini, perhaps drawn by how much more potent his memories were.

"No!" he screamed. "Please! They are all I

have left of her!"

But the snow showed no mercy. Aru couldn't watch.

"The bridge . . ." said Mini softly.

When Aru turned around, she saw that the bridge was being built, more quickly now. Each moment stolen from Shukra's life was fashioning a sturdy step over the ravine.

Aru and Mini leaped across it, Shukra's screams and cries chasing them all the way. No snow followed them. When they reached the other side, Aru turned to see Shukra looking lost. Snow frosted his skin.

"You are merely a child, and children are sometimes the cruelest of all. You have taken everything from me. For that, I curse you, daughter of Indra," said Shukra. He held out his hand. "My curse is that, in the moment when it matters most, you, too, shall forget."

With that, Shukra disappeared. Where he had once stood, now there were just two footprints gradually filling with snow.

THIRTY-ONE:
THIS PLACE SMELLS FUNKY

Aru was no stranger to curses.

It's just that she was usually the giver and not the receiver.

In the sixth grade, Aru had cursed Carol Yang. It was during a week when Aru had been suffering from a cold. Jordan Smith had used up all the tissues giving himself pretend boobs, which was not nearly as funny as he'd thought it would be, and it was the *worst* for Aru, who'd *really* needed to blow her nose. The teacher wouldn't excuse her to go to the bathroom. So Aru had been left with that horrible, tickly feeling of a drippy nose, and she'd had no other choice. . . .

Carol Yang had shouted, "Gross! Aru Shah just used her sleeve to wipe her nose!"

Everyone had started laughing. For the rest of the day, Carol had thrown balled-up toilet paper at the back of her head.

After school, Aru had gone home and cut

out a picture of old-looking text from one of the museum's pamphlets. She'd burned the edges of the photo with the stove flame to make it look even more antique.

The next day, right before homeroom, Aru had gone up to Carol and held the paper in her face. "I *curse* you, Carol Yang! From this day forth, you'll always have a runny nose. Every time you look in the mirror and think you don't have a booger, one is going to appear, and everyone will see it except you." And then Aru had hissed, *"Kachori! Bajri no rotlo! Methi nu shaak! Undhiyu!"*

In actuality, those words weren't a curse at all. They were just the names of various Gujarati dishes. But Carol Yang did not know that.

Neither did their homeroom teacher, who had walked in to find Carol holding a tissue to her nose and crying. Aru had been sent home with a note from the principal: *Please tell your daughter to refrain from cursing her classmates.*

Ever since, Aru hadn't had a high opinion of curses. She'd thought they would function like gifts (It's the *thought* that counts!), but both of those things were lies. Thoughts weren't powerful enough by themselves, and the curse hadn't worked.

But this time . . . This time was all wrong.

Behind them, the Bridge of Forgetting looked like a crescent of ivory. Every memory that had forged it had been stolen from Shukra.

She thought she heard the Sleeper's voice. *Oh, Aru, Aru, Aru. What have you done?*

But it wasn't the Sleeper. It was Mini. She touched Aru's wrist lightly. "What'd you do, Aru?"

"I saved us." Her voice wobbled. "I got us across the bridge so that we could get the weapons and save the world."

This was true.

And true things were supposed to feel . . . clean. Unquestionably good. But she didn't feel good. Shukra had given up his lifeform, and a curse had followed Aru over the bridge.

She was allegedly a hero. Was this how heroes felt, knotted up with doubt?

Mini's face softened. "It's okay. When this is over, we'll get the curse removed. I bet they've got places for that in the Night Bazaar. Or we can ask Boo?"

At least Mini was optimistic. Aru forced herself to smile. She tried to push the curse from her thoughts. "Yeah! That's it! Good idea, Mini. People do that with tattoos all the time. There's a girl at my school whose sister got a butterfly put on her lower back during spring break, and her parents took her out of school for a week to get it zapped off."

Mini wrinkled her nose. "Why would anyone want a butterfly *permanently* on their skin? Butterflies are creepy. Their tongues are weird. And did you know that if tattoo needles are contaminated and not properly sterilized you can get hepatitis?"

"And let me guess. . . . You die?"

"Well, you can get treated," said Mini. "But you *could* die."

Aru rolled her eyes. "C'mon. We must be getting close."

Chitrigupta had said that the celestial weapons were past the bridge, but there was nothing in sight except a giant cave.

The cave was so tall, it seemed less like a cave and more like a ravine through a mountain range. Pale stalactites dripped down from the ceiling, jagged and sharp, and crowded so tightly that they reminded her of teeth.

And then there was the *smell*.

Aru almost gagged.

It was worse than that time she had forgotten the groceries in the backseat of her mom's Honda. The whole car had smelled so bad, her mom had been forced to leave the windows open all weekend. This place smelled like . . . rotting.

She stepped on something that crunched. Aru looked down to see a slender fish spine stuck to her shoe. She peeled it off and flung it into the cave. It landed with an echoing *splat.*

"This floor is weird," said Mini.

It was firm, but springy. Like a mattress. And it wasn't gray or brown, like the floor of most caves, but a cherry red so deep it glinted black.

"It smells awful in here," said Aru.

She held her shirt over her nose and mouth as they walked. Almost everything she had seen that had anything to do with the gods and goddesses was lavish and beautiful. But this place looked like a prison. The walls were a wet shade of pink. Every now and again, a gust of hot wind brought the stench of rotting fish.

"Maybe the weapons are rotting?"

"They can't rot! They're celestial."

"How do you know?" demanded Mini. "Are you an expert in all things celestial?"

Aru was going to answer, but she tripped and stumbled. A slender, shining silver thread stretched across the ravine, and the moment she touched it, it triggered something deep in the large cave. Neon words now dangled from the stalactite:

Astra meant *weapon.*

Specifically ones that had supernatural abilities.

Aru's pulse raced. She knew she wasn't supposed to be excited about needing a highly magical and highly powerful weapon (because that just meant your enemy was also highly magical and highly powerful), but she still wanted to *see* it. She would've wanted to take a selfie with it if her mom hadn't refused to buy her a phone. . . .

"Why wouldn't the gods keep their weapons with them?" Mini asked. "What if they got stolen or something?"

Aru looked around this dark place. Above them, the stalactites cast a light so stingy that Aru couldn't see much of what lay ahead. "Maybe they figured they were safe here?"

"But there's no protection!" Mini said archly. "It's just a smelly cave. That makes no sense."

"Maybe the smell is what's protecting it?"

"Hmm . . . maybe you're right. Definitely smells like demon repellent."

Aru frowned. For a room that was supposed to be full of celestial weapons . . . it was decidedly *empty* of weapons.

"Hey, there's something on the floor," said Mini. She crouched, pressing her palm to the ground. "Ugh. It's wet. More of that weird smelly water stuff." And then Mini was quiet for a minute. "Aru?"

Aru heard Mini, but didn't turn. The ball turned warm in her pocket, but she didn't take it out. She was distracted by the dangling words. Before, they had spelled out:

THE CHAMBER OF THE ASTRAS

But now the words had elongated and changed. She stepped closer to read it.

ANSWERS HIDE IN PLAIN SIGHT. THINGS AREN'T AS THEY SEEM. THERE'S POWER TO FIND HERE AND KNOWLEDGE TO GLEAN. BUT TIME WAITS FOR NO MAN, AND TIME HAS NO EARS. IF YOU DON'T MOVE QUICKLY, YOU'LL MEET ALL YOUR FEARS.

"Did you see this sign?" demanded Aru. "It talks about men, but what about women? Rude."

Mini ignored her. "Aru, this moisture isn't some weird humidity."

"So?"

"So I think that it's —"

357

Another hot gust of air blew at them. Deep within the cave, she heard a bellowing sound. Like a gigantic pipe organ breaking apart.

Or . . . lungs drawing in air.

The ground trembled. Above them, the stalactites began to grow larger. Aru squinted. Not larger. *Closer.*

"Those aren't stalactites," said Mini.

Aru had a sneaking suspicion she already knew what Mini was going to say.

They were *teeth.*

And whatever beast they had stumbled into was beginning to close its mouth.

THIRTY-TWO:
#1 ON MINI'S TOP TEN WAYS
I DON'T WANT TO DIE LIST:
DEATH BY HALITOSIS

Aru had lost count of how many times she'd thought *We're going to die.*

Granted, they'd always managed to wriggle their way out of dying before. But that didn't make the thought any less terrifying. Thankfully, by now the two of them had had so much practice that they didn't scream and cry like the last couple of times. This time they only screamed.

Beneath them, the tongue (*gross*) began to shake and quiver. Several stalactites — *nope,* thought Aru, *giant teeth* — crashed and fell, swallowing up the entrance.

"There has to be another exit!" shouted Aru. "Try using the ball?"

Aru drew it out of her pocket and threw it on the ground, but nothing happened. Then again, nothing *ever* happened with her stupid ball.

Mini opened and closed her compact. "My mirror isn't working either! It's just showing my face —" She frowned. "Is that another zit? Aru, do you see anything — ?"

"Focus, Mini! Maybe we can prop its jaws open or something?"

"With what? We don't have anything big enough. Besides, look." Mini pulled back her sleeve and bent her arm.

"What the heck are you doing?"

"Flexing my muscles!"

"I don't see anything?"

"Exactly!" said Mini, tugging her hair. She started pacing. "Okay, we're in a body. Most likely — given the fish breath — it's some kind of giant demonic whale. So. Let's think about anatomy and stuff."

"Cool, I'll just pull out my pocket anatomy book! Oh, wait! I don't *have* one!"

"Do whales have uvulas?"

"How am I supposed to know if it's a girl whale?"

"It's the dangly punching-bag–looking thing in the back of your throat," said Mini. "It makes you gag. If we could throw something at the whale's, then it would have to throw us up!"

That was not a bad idea. Except it had a giant flaw. "You want to ride out on whale vomit?"

"I just want to ride *out.*"

"Good point."

The girls raced toward the back of the throat. Here, the stench was even worse. Aru's chin-length hair stuck to her face. Her shirt was soaked through with wet whale breath.

The neon sign flashed in the dark, suspended by back teeth that seemed to be growing longer by the second. Maybe *that* was where the uvula thing was. But when they got there, Aru couldn't see anything that looked like a punching bag. Instead, the tongue sloped down into the whale's throat. Aru could hear water sloshing angrily below. Worse, it was *rising.*

"There's no uvula!" said Aru.

Mini groaned. "*Finding Nemo* was a lie!"

"Wait. You made a life-and-death choice based on *Finding Nemo*?"

"Well, uh.. ."

"MINI!"

"I was just trying to help!"

"And I'm just trying not to push you down this throat right now!"

The teeth pressed a little closer. At first, Aru had only seen rows upon rows of pale, crowded teeth. Now she saw something else. Something that glinted.

The heck are those? Behind-the-teeth braces?

Wait. *Weapons!*

This was where the *devas* had hidden them. Aru could now make out long swords, axes, maces, and arrows with strung bows, all jutting from the tangle of teeth.

"The weapons," breathed Aru. "We have to find the right ones for us! That's how we get out."

"I don't want to kill the whale. . . ."

"We're not going to kill the whale," said Aru. "We're just going to poke it a bit, so that it keeps its mouth open long enough for us to escape."

Mini didn't look convinced. "How do we know which ones are the right weapons for us?"

Aru started sprinting back toward the front of the whale's mouth. "Whichever ones we can grab fastest!"

If Mini rolled her eyes or said something snarky, Aru didn't notice. She measured the distance to the giant weapons above them. Maybe if she jumped, she could reach one of them. A sword with an emerald hilt glittered temptingly.

The whale's jaws continued to close. Aru had no idea whether the sword was the right choice. She'd thought she'd find something based on her divine parent, but she didn't see anything like Lord Indra's thunderbolt in this collection. So a sword it was. . . .

"Mini, give me a lift?"

"We're never gonna get out of here," moaned Mini.

Aru struggled for balance as she climbed up, but she refused to believe they weren't getting out of here. They hadn't gotten this far just to be killed by whale halitosis. That would be so embarrassing on a Wikipedia page.

Mini layered her palms, boosting Aru higher.

Aru reached for the hilt of the sword hanging above her. "Just . . . a little farther —"

A gust of hot air knocked her to the ground. Or tongue. Whatever it was.

Aru scrambled to her feet, but she kept getting thrown off-balance. The rotting wind turned fiercer.

"Aru!" called Mini behind her.

Aru spun around to see Mini trying to hold on to the floor. But the whale's lungs were too strong. Her legs kicked out behind her, lifting into the air.

"It's trying to *inhale* us!"

"Hold on!" called Aru. She crawled to-ward Mini, but it was like crawling over ice. Her palms slipped, causing her elbows to jam into the tongue-floor. The whale's breath sucked at her. "I'm coming," she croaked.

There was no way they were going to get those weapons. She knew it now. Behind her, the light shrank.

"I don't think I can hold on any longer!"

"Don't think, then!" shouted Aru. "Just *do.* I believe in you, Mini."

"There were so many things I wanted to do!" moaned Mini. "I never even got to shave my legs."

"*That*'s your life's biggest regret?"

Aru braved a glance at the sign. The neon riddle flashed and flickered. ANSWERS HIDE IN PLAIN SIGHT. Well, Aru was looking around (as *plainly* as she could) and there was nothing to help them. Nothing at all.

Mini was straining in the wind. Her backpack was now flying behind her. Her knuckles had turned white. One of her hands lost its grip. "I'm sorry," she said.

Their eyes met.

Aru watched as her sister was flung back against the dark throat. *Sister.* Not just Mini. Now that she had thought it, she couldn't unthink it. It had gone from idea to truth.

She had a sister. A sister she had to protect.

Aru didn't waste any more time thinking. She just reacted. She reached for the ball in

364

the pocket of her pants. In her palm, it glowed a little brighter, like a creature waking from a long nap. She let the ball loose.

Above her, the teeth descended. She could feel the hilt of the sword sinking into her shoulder blade. Aru could just see the outline of Mini, suspended in a moment of falling.

Aru imagined a fishing line. Something that could fly out, and reel back in —

Light haloed in front of her. It unfurled from the ball, unspooling in the air like loopy cursive letters. The tethers of light stretched around Mini, gathering her up and yanking her out of the creature's throat.

Aru whooped happily. The golden ball zoomed back into her hand. Only this time it wasn't a golden ball at all. It was a lightning bolt.

The sheer size of it was enough to prop open the creature's jaws, which she immediately started to do.

Before she could finish, Mini came running toward her, screaming. And not in a happy *YOU-SAVED-MY-LIFE-WE'RE-FRIENDS-4EVA* way. It was more like a *GET-OUT-WHILE-YOU-STILL-CAN* kind of scream. Which didn't make any sense. Aru had just saved her life. . . .

That's when Aru felt it:

The barest scrape of teeth along her scalp. But she couldn't move! Aru tried to jump out of the way, when a violet light burst around her, hardening into an enormous sphere. The whale's teeth glanced off the sphere.

Before her, triumphant in a sphere of her own, stood Mini. In her hand was the danda of the Dharma Raja, a staff that was as tall as she was and braided with purple light. The whale's teeth pressed down on the sphere, causing faint lines to spider across it, but the protective device held, and finally the jaws relaxed. Light filled the cavernous space, and the two spheres dissolved.

In the back, the neon riddle flashed. ANSWERS IN PLAIN SIGHT. That had been true after all. The glowing ball had been Vajra, the lightning bolt of Indra, the whole time. And Mini's compact hadn't been a compact at all, but the danda stick of the Dharma Raja. It had just been waiting for a reason to show up. Which made Aru think of the words Urvashi had said so long ago when they had visited the Court of the Sky: *You must awaken the weapons . . . go to the Kingdom of Death.* Their trying to save one another had activated the weapons. Maybe what they'd done had proven to the weapons that they were worthy of wielding them in the first place.

"You're welcome," said Mini breathlessly.

It took Aru — who was still staring at the lightning bolt in her hand — a full minute to realize what Mini had said.

"Um, excuse you," she said, crossing her arms. "*You're* welcome. I saved you first."

"Yeah, but I saved you *right* after that. It was basically at the same time. How about we'll both be welcome?"

"Fine, we'll both be welcome. But who's going to say thank you first? I think that —"

"NOSE GOES!" shouted Mini, promptly thwacking her face.

She had her there. Aru grinned, feeling strangely proud of Mini. She offered her elbow. Mini bumped it.

"Thanks."

"Not *Thanks, sis*?" asked Mini.

"Mini, no one says *sis*. Like, ever."

"We could bring it back! Make it retro-cool."

"There's nothing retro-cool about *sis.*"

"Fine. What about *sister from another mister*?" asked Mini.

"No."

"What about . . . ?"

This continued for far too long.

Thirty-Three:
I'll Be a Cow
in My Next Life

Lightning bolts are much heavier than they look.

After Vajra had revealed its true form, it seemed reluctant to revert to the size of the ball. Aru had finally solved the problem by imagining Vajra as flip-flops to be worn on her feet *after* they'd walked on that goopy whale tongue. The weapon had shuddered at the idea and obediently shrunk.

Mini, on the other hand, preferred to use the Death Danda (or "Dee Dee," as she had nicknamed it) as a walking stick, and was currently acting as though she were twelve hundred years old instead of twelve.

"I think I'm predisposed to having joint problems," she said. "And you only get two knees. I mean, I guess I *could* replace them, but it won't be the same, and getting surgery isn't something you should do lightly. Tons of things could go wrong. You could even die."

Once they were safely out of the creature's mouth, they followed the stone path that wound around the cave that wasn't a cave at all but a gigantic whale thing.

When Aru looked up, the top of the creature was concealed by clouds. Strange protrusions that Aru had thought were just rocks now looked a lot more like fins covered in sharp barnacles. Streams of water ran down the sides, like someone was continually pouring liquid over the monster.

"It's a *timingala,* by the way," said Mini, following her gaze. "At least, I think it is."

"Never heard of those."

"They're basically giant whale sharks out of the stories."

"I thought whale sharks were supposed to be friendly. And not have teeth!" said Aru. "That was the rudest one ever. It basically tried to kill us with halitosis."

"It was just doing its job! Besides, it was a *celestial guard* whale shark," Mini pointed out. "And it had all those weapons stuck in its mouth, poor thing. Imagine if you had to spend the rest of your life with sharp popcorn stuck in your teeth. Just thinking about it makes me want to floss more than twice a day."

"You floss twice a day?"

"Of course," said Mini. "Don't you?"

"Um."

"Aru . . . Do you even floss?"

Aru considered herself extremely lucky if she remembered to *brush* her teeth at night, much less floss. Sometimes, when she was running late for school, she'd just eat toothpaste. In fact, she wasn't even sure they *had* floss in the house.

"Of course I do." *When I've got something stuck in my teeth.*

Mini was skeptical. "If you don't floss, that can lead to tooth decay. And if that happens, the tooth decay can spread into your sinuses, and then get behind your eyes, and then enter your brain, and then —"

"Mini, if you say *You die,* I will *actually* die just because you keep saying it."

"You're my sister. It's my familial duty to make sure that you survive."

Aru tried not to smile. *You're my sister.* She wasn't sure she'd ever get tired of hearing that.

"I'm doing fine so far. And I've got all my teeth. Death: zero. Aru: um, at least four."

Mini just shook her head and kept walking. Everyone knew that the only way out of the Kingdom of Death was to enter a new life. Which meant that the only exit lay through the Pool of Reincarnation. But they didn't have to be reincarnated, or so

370

Chitrigupta had said. So that meant there *must* be another way out of the Kingdom of Death. At least, she hoped so.

Aru wanted nothing more than to get out of the Kingdom of Death. First of all, it stank. Second of all, she was starving. Third of all, she wouldn't even be able to brag about going there. *Final destination* was not as impressive as a *destination vacation.* It was just flat-out terrifying.

But she had to admit that part of her was excited to see the Pool of Reincarnation.

How did the Kingdom of Death decide what people got to be next? Was there some kind of checklist? *You met the minimum number of good deeds, so you get to avoid premature balding in your next life.* Or *Enjoy being a cockroach! On the upside, at least you'll survive a nuclear disaster.*

Yet that would have to wait.

Because there was another pool they had to visit first: the Pool of the Past. This was the only place where they could finally learn how to defeat the Sleeper.

Aru and Mini walked around the bend, only to end up in a hall of windows.

Thousands upon thousands of windows looked out onto worlds that Aru had never considered real. Lands where there were palaces of snow and palaces of sand. Places

371

where sea creatures with rows of eyes blinked back at them from the other side of the glass. It made sense that every place should have a connection to death. Death had some claim everywhere. Death was in the wind coaxing a flower to blossom. Death hid in the wing of the bird folding itself to sleep. Death was in every breath she inhaled.

Aru had never given much thought to death before now. No one she knew had died. She'd never had to mourn anyone.

She assumed she'd be full of sadness on the day that happened. But walking through the Kingdom of Death, she felt a drowsy sort of peacefulness, like balancing on the border of sleeping and waking.

In the distance, Aru heard the sound of machinery. Wheels gnashed and ground. Around them, the atmosphere had changed. The walls had that iridescent quality of polished oyster shells. Stalactites made of paper spiraled down from the ceiling.

"These must be Chitrigupta's archives," said Mini. She reached for one of the papers and read aloud: " 'On May seventeenth, Ronald Taylor jumped into the Arctic Ocean yelling "Sea unicorn!" and he startled a narwhal. He did not apologize.' "

"So . . . these are just accounts of what people do every day?"

The papers spun slowly.

"I guess so?" said Mini. "I think we might be getting closer to the pools. He'd only keep all of his records here if they needed to consult them when they remake people's bodies and all that."

"I wonder what happens if you scare a narwhal. Maybe karma gives you a gigantic zit in the middle of your forehead and you get called an ugly unicorn for a month."

Mini's eyes widened. "Wait, I have a zit on the side of my nose — does that mean I did something to deserve it?"

"Did you?"

Mini frowned and was opening her mouth to say something when new ground loomed up ahead. The floor beneath them changed from rigid stone to something wet and slick, surrounding . . .

Pools of water.

Some were the size of rain puddles. Others were the size of ponds. There were at least fifty of them, spread out in concentric circles.

Large incense burners floated silently above each one. The walls hadn't changed, though, so the shining water looked like a bunch of pearls hidden in an oyster. Beyond the Chamber of Pools, Aru spotted the dim light of an exit. She didn't hear any voices.

It didn't seem like anyone else was around.

This place smelled weird. It smelled like . . . longing. Like an ice cream cone you were really excited about eating, but after one lick, it fell onto the sidewalk.

Unlike in the forest or the Otherworld Costco — or even the whale shark — there weren't any signs here. Nothing indicated which pool was for what. Or who. Aru rubbed her neck, grimacing. This wasn't going to be easy.

Mini carefully stepped between two of the pools. "Go slow," she said. "It's slippery. What would happen if we fell in?"

Aru shrugged. "Maybe we'd get instantly reincarnated?"

"What if we came back as animals?"

"Then I get dibs on being a horse."

"Enjoy that."

"I like horses . . . ."

"I'd want to come back as a cow," said Mini loftily. "Then I'd be worshipped."

"Yeah, if you lived in India . . . Otherwise you'd just be a hamburger."

The smile dropped off Mini's face. "I hadn't thought of that."

Aru was just about to say *Mooooooo* when her foot slipped.

Water skidded beneath her heel. Her arms pinwheeled. Seconds later, she was flat on the ground, her nose an inch away from a face in the water.

Not hers.

Her mother's.

Thirty-Four:
The Pool of the Past

Secrets are curious things. They are flimsy and easily broken. For this reason, they prefer to remain hidden.

A fact, on the other hand, is strong and powerful. It's proven. Unlike a secret, it's out there for everyone to see and know. And that can make it more terrifying than even the deepest, darkest secret.

In the pool, Aru saw a secret break and become a fact.

Secret: The Sleeper *did* know her mother.

Fact: He didn't just *know* her.

For instance, Aru "knew" their mail carrier. He always acted like he understood her, just because he had changed his name to Krishna Blue at the age of seventeen. He was always listening to slightly eerie Indian music in his earbuds, and he was constantly telling her that her "aura wasn't vibrant enough" and she should drink more tea. She also "knew" P. Doggy, the poodle she walked during the summer. He liked to steal her sneakers and bury peanut butter sandwiches. But that wasn't the way the Sleeper knew her mom.

When Aru looked into the pool, she saw a memory of her mother — a much younger version — walking hand in hand with the Sleeper. They were strolling along the banks of a river, laughing. And occasionally stopping to . . . kiss.

The Sleeper hadn't just known her mother . . . he'd *loved* her. And she had loved him. In the memory, her mom was actually laughing and smiling, way more than she ever had with Aru. She tried not to be offended, but it was hard not to be. Who was this version of her mom? Aru leaned hungrily into the water, the tip of her nose almost grazing the surface.

The images changed . . . revealing her mom standing at the doorstop of a house Aru had never seen. There was her mother, Dr. Krithika Shah, thrumming her stomach. Aru was used to seeing her dressed like a shabby professor, in a blazer with scuffed elbows and a worn skirt with the hem coming undone. In this vision, she was wearing a black velvet salwar kameez. Her hair was done up in fanciful curls, and she wore a brilliant tiara.

The door opened, and an older man looked shocked at the sight of her.

"Krithika," he breathed. "You're early for the Diwali celebrations, my child. The other sisters are inside waiting for you." When she didn't step inside, his eyes went to her midsection. "Has it . . . has it happened?"

"Yes," she said. Her voice sounded cold and wooden.

It took Aru an extra moment to guess what was in her mother's womb.

Her.

"He's not who you said he was," she said, through tears. "And I can't let this happen. You know as well as I do that the moment the child comes of age, Suyodhana is destined to become . . . to become.. ."

"The Sleeper," finished the old man. "I know, daughter."

"There has to be some other way! He is aware of his own prophecy and believes he won't lose himself to it. She could have a father. We could be a family." Her voice broke on the last word. "He can change his fate. I know it."

"No one can change their fate."

"Then what would you have me do, Father?"

Aru gasped. That was her *grandfather*. According to her mother, he had died when

Aru was too young to remember him.

He shrugged. "You must choose. Your child, or your lover."

"I can't do that."

"You will," said her father. "You've already done your duty and stolen his heart. I assume he has told you the secret of how he might be defeated?"

Krithika looked away. "He told me out of trust. I would never betray it. I believe that the world could be different. I believe that our destinies aren't chains around our necks, but wings that give us flight."

Her father laughed gently. "Believe what you will. You're a young woman, Krithika. Young, lovely, and smart. All I ask is that you don't throw away your life."

At this, Krithika's eyes turned sharp. "Is it throwing away my life to do what I think is right?"

Her father stopped laughing. "If you insist on taking this path, you will jeopardize your family. You will defeat the purpose of the panchakanyas."

"I believe we have more of a purpose than just breeding," she whispered.

Her father's face puckered. "And you will never be allowed to set foot inside this home again."

At this, Aru's mother flinched, but she still

raised her chin. "It stopped being a home to me a long time ago."

"Then on your own head be it," said her father, slamming the door in her face.

The vision fast-forwarded. Her mother was wearing a hospital gown and cradling a baby: Aru. Slouched in a chair beside her was the Sleeper. He was wearing a T-shirt that said I'M A DAD! Across his lap lay a bouquet of flowers. Krithika watched him as he slept, looking between him and Aru.

Then she lifted her head toward the ceiling. "I love you both," she whispered. "One day I hope you'll understand that I'm doing what I must to free you. To free us all."

The setting changed to the museum. It wasn't as it looked now. The statues were different, except for the stone elephant, which had yet to be moved to the lobby. Everything was sparkling and new. A small sign on the door read: OPENING SOON TO THE PUBLIC! THE MUSEUM OF ANCIENT INDIAN ART AND CULTURE!

Krithika walked through the Hall of the Gods. White cloths covered all the statues, so it looked like a room filled with poorly dressed ghosts. In her hands, she carried something small and glowing. Tears streamed down her cheeks.

She stopped at the end of the hall, where

the diya awaited. "I'm sorry," she said. "So sorry. I never wanted this to happen. But know that I used your secrets not to destroy you, but to hold you. I bind you with my heart, the same heart that I gave to you willingly. I bind you with something that is not made of metal, wood, or stone. I bind you with something that is neither dry nor wet."

She dropped the glowing thing — little more than a wispy ribbon — and Aru realized that it was the Sleeper she had just trapped in the lamp. Light burst and haloed around the antique before quickly fading away.

"I was supposed to destroy you, but I couldn't. But I couldn't risk Aru's safety, either," Krithika went on. "I'll find an answer. I'll examine every ancient site, read every treatise. And I will find a way to free both you and Aru. I promise."

Mini yanked Aru and she drew back, sputtering and spitting. She sat up.

Mini clapped her on the back, hard. "Speak to me, Aru! If you're dead, tell me! Just talk!"

Aru thought she was going to hack out her ribs, but finally she was able to take a deep breath.

"I'm alive," she croaked.

"Oh, good," said Mini. "I was going to do CPR."

"You know how to do that?"

"Um, not really, but it looks pretty easy on TV."

"Glad I dodged that one," said Aru, laughing weakly.

She stared back at the pool. So much new information was racing through her head. Her mother had been the one to bind the Sleeper. And not because she hated him, but because she couldn't bring herself to kill him.

Did he know that?

Aru didn't think so, given that he'd called her mom a liar. Not that she blamed him. Being locked up with nothing and no one for eleven years had to be rough.

"Really, Mom?" she muttered. "You had to pick the demon dude?"

"I saw it all, too. The Sleeper was almost your home dad," said Mini, pretending to gag.

Aru blinked. She remembered what the Sleeper had said to her in the Library: *You and I might as well be family.*

"Why couldn't your mom have dated a nice doctor instead?"

"Why does it always have to be a doctor?"

"I dunno," said Mini, shrugging. "That's

what my mom always says: 'Go to school, study hard, then go to medical school, study even harder, and marry a nice doctor.' "

A minute of silence went by. For the first time in her life, Aru had nothing to say. What *could* she say after seeing those visions in the pool? It felt like her life had been completely readjusted.

Was this why she never saw her mom smile? Because she'd had to rebuild her whole life as if she were just some room in the Palace of Illusions? She'd done it not just for the Sleeper . . . but also for *her*?

Mini touched her shoulder. "You okay?"

"Not even a little bit."

Mini gasped. "You didn't even try to lie. Do you have a fever?" She smacked her hand against Aru's forehead.

"Ow!"

"Sorry," said Mini sheepishly. "My patient bedside manner needs some improvement. . . ."

"I'm not your patient!" snapped Aru, batting at Mini's hand. Then she sighed. "Sorry. I know this isn't your fault."

"It's okay, Aru. But what do we do now?" asked Mini. "Urvashi said that we'd get the answer about how to defeat the Sleeper from the Pool of the Past. . . ."

"And we did," said Aru. "But it's not

383

exactly helpful. You heard my mom. She said that she'd used his secrets to bind him, not *kill* him."

"Right, and she said he can't be killed by anything made of metal, wood, or stone. Or anything dry or wet. Your mom bound him with her heart, but I feel like she meant that more metaphorically than literally. I have no idea how she did that, do you?"

Aru's head was spinning. "Nope. And if we did know, what're we going to do with a bunch of hearts? Throw them at his head?"

"So what does that leave?"

"We could pelt him with slightly undercooked pasta?"

Mini rolled her eyes. "What about animals?" she asked.

"It has to be *us,*" said Aru. "That's what Urvashi said. Besides, he's a demon. Even if we found a hungry man-eating tiger, it would probably turn on us — the humans — before it turned on him."

"Maybe slightly undercooked pasta is the right call."

"I could use a pasta sword."

"Pasta mace."

"Pasta club."

"Pasta . . . pasta bow?"

"Weak."

"Pasta lightning bolt?" joked Mini.

"Wait," said Aru. *"The lightning bolt.* It's not dry or wet —"

"Or metal or stone or wood!"

Aru's grip around the ball form of Vajra became clawlike. When she blinked, she saw the Sleeper in the hospital room, wearing the I'M A DAD! T-shirt.

Her eyes burned. Her home dad hadn't left them at all . . . he'd just been locked away. In a lamp. By her mom. *This is so messed up,* thought Aru.

He'd *wanted* to be her home dad.

Aru's throat tightened, and tears pressed at her eyes. Then she forced herself to sit up straight. It didn't matter what he used to be like. The truth was that the Sleeper from the Night Bazaar was no longer the man from her mother's vision. Now he was cruel and cold. He was evil. He'd hurt Boo and threatened to kill their families *and* them if they didn't bring him all three keys. He wasn't her dad.

Aru tossed the ball form of Vajra in the air and caught it with one hand. "Let's do this."

But even as she said the words, a thread of misgiving wrapped around her rib cage and squeezed tight.

They stood up and began silently walking between the ponds, ducking the low-hanging incense burners. Aru knew, deep in her bones, that this was where the Kingdom of Death ended: on the brink of new life. The atmosphere felt like that of a crowd holding its breath with anticipation. The light on the pearly walls was ever-shifting, ever-changing; the colors never settled on one shade, always glimmering with new potential. Like life starting anew.

Aru took a deep breath. They had made it through the kingdom.

Now the question was: Could they get out?

Thirty-Five:
Can You Give Me Better
Hair on the Way Out?

It's challenging to shoulder all the stuff you get from the Kingdom of Death.

Dee Dee (Mini's Death Danda) kept popping out of its compact form and turning into a gigantic stick. Twice it almost put out Aru's eye. She was beginning to think the weapons had a sense of humor. At random times Aru's weapon, Vajra, liked to shift into lightning-bolt form and zip across the sky before turning into a ball and bouncing in front of her. Aru imagined it saying, *Throw me at a demon! Do it, do it, do it! I wanna play. Squirrel!*

"I'm not really even sure of all the stuff this thing can do," said Mini, shaking the danda.

Aru raised her eyebrow. That danda stick belonged to the god of death and justice. It had probably beat up its fair share of demons and also punished a bunch of souls. And now Mini was shaking it like a remote control that had stopped working.

"Maybe it's like a video game, and you get to access more powers and levels once you complete something?" Mini guessed.

"Well, we got one demon, shopped at a magic Costco, and made it through the Kingdom of Death. . . . What else does our video game magic want?"

"Maybe to defeat the real demon?"

"Oh, yeah, true."

Mini awkwardly cradled Dee Dee. "Aru, do you think these weapons are a sign that they like us?"

Aru didn't have to ask who *they* were. She meant their godly fathers.

"The danda is his most precious possession," reasoned Mini. "He wouldn't just give it to someone he didn't care about, right?"

"I'm sure he cares," said Aru. "Just, you know, in his own way? In the stories, the Dharma Raja took the form of a dog and kept Yudhistira company at the end of his life. Yudhistira refused to enter heaven without him. I think it was some kind of test? If your soul dad is willing to become a dog just to keep you company, that means they like you at least a little bit."

Mini grinned. "I like the way you think, Shah."

Aru dramatically flipped her hair over her shoulder, which was a bad idea, because it was still damp from whale spit and ended up smacking her in the eye. *Smooth.*

"Do you think it's the same for Lord Indra?" asked Mini.

Aru eyed Vajra, who was happily bouncing beside her in a way that reminded Aru of someone excitedly nodding. If her mom could care from a distance, why not her dad?

"I hope so," said Aru after a moment's pause. "My mom told me it was Indra who taught Arjuna how to use all the celestial weapons. He even tried to sabotage Arjuna's nemesis."

That reminded Aru of the mom at school who'd gotten banned from the library after tearing out certain pages in books just so her kid's rival classmate couldn't do his research. (The librarian had screamed, *Book murder!* And now all the parents were scared of her.) Indra probably would have approved of that kind of sabotage.

"And he gave you his famous lightning bolt," added Mini. "He must care."

The thought made Aru smile.

Once they were away from the Chamber of Pools, they turned the corner toward the violent sounds of machinery. A large archway was emblazoned with the sign:

This, Aru guessed, must be where souls were fitted for new bodies and new lives.

A spiderlike creature made of clockwork and gears scuttled by. It took one look at them and started screaming.

"BODIES!" it shouted. "Out-of-commission bodies running rampant!"

Another creature, this one shaped a bit like a small dragon with fuzzy wings that trailed on the ground, bustled past. It wasn't made out of clock parts; it was furred . . . brindled like those dogs that stood watch outside of the Kingdom of Death, and its eyes were a warm shade of gold and slitted at the pupil like a cat's.

"How'd you get in?" asked the furred thing. "Rogue souls are —"

"Rogue souls?" repeated Aru, delighted in spite of the weirdness surrounding them. "That's a great name for a band."

"Band?" said the clockwork creature. "Did you hear that, Wish? They're banding together! We're going to be overrun. Forced into that awful samsara cycle of lives! As punishment! This is what we get for thinking that scaly orange skin and fake hair could keep that former demon out of elected office. It's all *your* fault —"

"We're not banding together," said Mini. "We're just trying to exit. But, um, we want to stay in these bodies. Please?"

"Who are you?"

Aru grinned. This was the moment she had been waiting for *all* her life. In school, the teachers always asked instead: *What's your name?* Now, finally, she could say her *dream* response to *Who are you?*

"Your worst nightmare," she said in a deep Batman voice.

At the same exact time, Mini said, "We're the Pandavas," before adding, "Well, we've got their souls, at least. In us."

"Mini, you keep making it sound like we *ate* them —"

"Pandavas?" interrupted Wish.

The dragonlike creature and its companion reeled back in shock. Wish circled them, snuffling.

"That makes sense," said the clockwork creature. "Heroines usually are the Kingdom of Death's worst nightmares. They're always barging in, waving scraps of metal around, and demanding things. No manners whatsoever."

"Excuse you!" said Aru. "What about *heroes*? I bet they're just as bad as heroines."

"It's a compliment! Heroes rarely have the

391

guts to demand things. Usually they just sulk until a magical sidekick feels bad for them and does all the work while they get all the credit."

"So this is how reincarnation works?" asked Mini. "With machines and stuff?"

"No words in any language can pin down exactly how life and death function. The closest we can come is by explaining samsara. Are you familiar with the concept?" asked Wish.

"Kinda. It's like the life-and-death cycle," said Aru.

"It's far more complicated than that," said Wish. "As you live, your good deeds and bad deeds are extracted from karma. Along the way, the body is subjected to the wear and tear of time. But the soul sheds bodies, just as the body sheds clothes. There is a goal, of course, to leave all that behind, but sometimes it takes people many, many lifetimes."

"And who, exactly, are you?" asked Mini.

"Ah, we are the things that make a body what it is!" said Wish. "I am unspent wishes."

"Is that why you're covered in" — Mini peered more closely — "eyelashes?"

"Ah, yes! Sometimes, when people find a tiny lash on their cheek, they hold it tight, make a wish, and then blow it away. Those unspoken yearnings of the heart always find their way to me. They make my hand soft when I'm pouring a soul into a new form."

"And I am Time," said the clockwork creature, sinking into a graceful bow on its insect legs. "Like any part of Time, I am hard and unyielding, the heavy hand that shapes the vessel."

"*You're Time?*" asked Aru. "Like *the* Time?"

"We're supposed to be trying to save you!" said Mini. "You should probably go into hiding or something."

"What a quaint notion, child," said Time. "But I am just one part of Time. I am Past Time. You see, there are all kinds of Time running around. Future Time, who is invisible, and Present Time, who can't hold any one shape. Pacific Standard Time is currently swimming around near Malibu. And I think Eastern Standard Time is annoying stockbrokers on Wall Street. We're all quite wibbly-wobbly. If what you say is true, I am merely one part of what you must save."

Aru tried to sidestep them. "Well, umm, then we better get to it?"

It was impossible to see what lay beyond the two creatures. It seemed like a tunnel, but every time she looked away from it, she couldn't remember what she'd seen. It made Aru think she wasn't *supposed* to see it.

"Not so fast!" said Time. "Can't let you out without your giving us something! You must pay!"

"Pay?" repeated Mini. She patted her pockets. "I — I don't have anything."

Aru scowled. First, nobody had appreciated her Batman joke. Second, why did they have to keep paying for things? *They* were the ones going to all the trouble to save everyone else, after all! *Rude.* Her hands formed fists at her sides.

"Why should we give you anything, anyway?" she demanded. "You do realize we're doing all this to save *you.*"

Time rose up a little higher on its insect legs.

Oh.

Time could be a lot . . . *bigger* than she imagined. It just kept growing until it was the size of one of the pillars from the museum. She had to tilt her head up just to see its featureless face regarding her.

"Did I just detect a trace of impertinence?"

Mini stepped in front of her. "No! Not at all! That's just how she talks! She's got a medical condition. Um, Type One

394

Insufferable-ness. She can't help it."

Thanks, Mini. Thanks a lot.

"You must leave behind something of yours in order to get out," insisted Time.

The spider creature grew even taller. It was clicking its front legs together, steepling them like hands grown impatient from waiting.

"Sorry," said Wish, daintily licking one of its paws. "Rules are rules, although . . . good karma can let you out, if you have any."

"What, like good deeds?" asked Aru.

She took a careful step back, and Mini followed her example. Time was looming vast and terrifying before them. *Click, click, click* went its slender legs on the marble floor.

"Er, I take my neighbor's dog on walks?" started Aru.

"I floss my teeth twice a day!" said Mini.

"Prove it," said Time.

Mini hooked her fingers into her cheeks and pulled. "Rike zish?"

"Not good enough . . ." said Time.

Mini started laughing hysterically.

Can we fight *our way out of Death?* wondered Aru. Her hand slipped into her pocket, reaching for Vajra, but something else met her fingers. She fished it out:

An ivory-colored token.

The same one Chitrigupta had handed to her what felt like a lifetime ago. She turned it this way and that, watching the little good deeds she had done throughout her life shimmer on the surface.

"Wait!" shouted Aru, holding up the token. "We've got proof!"

Mini dug into her backpack and pulled out hers. "It'll show you I flossed. I swear!"

Wish padded forward, took the token between its teeth, and bit down on it. Then it did the same to Mini's. It turned to Time and said, "It rings true."

In one blink, Time shrank until it stood eye level with Aru. "You may go, then, daughters of the gods."

There was no way Aru was going to hang around another moment for a second invitation.

"Great!" said Mini with fake cheer. She pressed a bit closer to Aru.

"Yes! This was . . . such a treat." Aru edged past them. Wish and Time simply watched the two of them inch toward the exit. "See ya later!"

Time bowed its head.

"Inevitably."

People joked about the afterlife. They said things like *Don't follow the light!* But there was no heavenly glow here. Yet, somehow, it was still bright. It burned with something else, whiting out the setting around them.

All Aru remembered when she crossed the threshold was a curious sense of bemusement. As if she had done this before, and never quite wanted to, but submitted to it all the same. It was kind of like getting a shot: a necessary evil. And it was also a bit like a dream, because she couldn't recall much about the place they'd left behind. One moment it was there, and the next moment it was not.

With every step she took into that tunnel between life and death, sensation washed over her. Sensation that belonged to memories. She remembered impossible things, like being cradled and held close and told over and over by her mother that she was loved. She felt the pinch of her first loose tooth from so many years ago. She remembered how she had once broken her arm after swinging from the museum elephant's trunk and felt more surprise than pain. It hadn't occurred to her until that day that she could ever get hurt.

Aru blinked.

That single blink felt like hundreds of years and no time at all.

When Aru opened her eyes, she and Mini

were standing in the middle of a road. A couple of cars had been left running, doors still open, as if their drivers and passengers had fled in a hurry. A few feet away, Aru heard the cracklings of a television coming from inside a tollbooth.

Mini turned to her.

"At least it's not a parking lot?"

THIRTY-SIX:
THE TV STARTED IT

Aru flexed her hand and Vajra changed from a ball to a glowing circlet around her wrist. It looked *really* cool. Too bad she didn't know the first thing about what to do with it. Other than throw it at people, obviously.

Mini tried to turn the Death Danda into a staff, but it apparently didn't feel like it. "Come on!" she whined, banging it a couple times on the ground.

Aru wondered whether this was what great warriors of yore did: hit their weapons and hope they started working right.

They walked to the tollbooth. The television was on, but no one was inside. The whole road looked as if a bunch of people had gotten out of this place as quickly as they could without looking back. She glanced at the TV, which was blaring the news:

"Reports are coming in about an airborne virus sweeping through the Northeast.

Experts have been able to follow the trajectory from its point of origin somewhere in the Southeast, likely Georgia or Florida. Is there anything else you can tell us about the virus, Dr. Obafemi?"

A lovely woman with a tower of twisted braids smiled into the camera. "Well, Sean, at the moment we don't know how the disease is being spread. It seems to be jumping from place to place. There was an outbreak in Atlanta. Then it hit a strip mall area north of Houston. In Iowa, we think the epicenter was a supermarket. It's not acting like any virus we've seen before. Really, all we know is that the victims are unresponsive, as if sleeping while wide-awake. They are always found in a position as if the virus attacked quickly and caught them off guard —"

"Hence the name: the Frozen Syndrome!" The anchor laughed. "Too bad we can't just let it go, let it go. Am I right, Doctor?"

The doctor's tight smile could have cut glass. "Ha," she mustered weakly.

"Well, that's it for updates. Next, we'll go to weather with Melissa, and then Terry for 'Is Your Cat Obese?' Stay tuned —"

Aru muted the television. Taking a deep breath, she glanced at her palm. The Sanskrit number had changed. Now it looked squigglier but still, thought Aru, like the number two. At least, she hoped it was. She held up her hand to show Mini:

$$\text{Ϙ}$$

"Does this mean that we've got one and a half days left?"

Mini studied her own palm, then bit her lip.

Don't say it.

"One." Mini looked up. "This is our last day."

One last day.

Aru felt like someone had wrapped sharp wires around her heart. Her mom was depending on them. Boo was depending on them. *All these people,* she thought. She shuddered, remembering the word the doctor on TV had used: *victims.*

Mini seemed to know what she was thinking, because she placed her hand on Aru's shoulder.

"Remember what Lord Hanuman said? At least all these frozen people aren't in any pain."

Yet.

Aru hadn't forgotten what the Sleeper had threatened. She and Mini only had until the new moon (one day more . . .) before he would stop them from ever seeing their families again. And Boo would remain caged forever — if he was even alive.

But a few things the Sleeper hadn't expected had come true:

1. They'd found their way into the Kingdom of Death.
2. They'd awakened their weapons.

And most important:

3. They now knew how to defeat him.

Mini seemed to be thinking the same thing, because she sighed. "We're going to fight him, aren't we?"

She didn't say this as she might have before, with cowering and shrinking. She said it as if it were an unpleasant chore she was still going to honor. Like *Today I will take out the trash.* Another necessary evil.

Aru nodded.

"We know how to find him. He said that all we have to do is summon him with his name, but what about fighting?" Mini asked. "All we have are Vajra and Dee Dee, which I don't even know how to use. . . ."

Aru glanced at the desk where the television stood. The toll collector had a couple of knickknacks littered across the surface: a unicorn with its wings outstretched and a tiny clay bear. They gave Aru an idea.

"We're going to have help, Mini."

"You know, every time you say something like that, I keep expecting light to burst around your head," said Mini. "Or really dramatic music to start playing."

At that moment, the television decided it no longer wished to be mute. Mini flinched, and Dee Dee morphed from a compact into a staff just as a man dressed up as an Elvis impersonator sang, *"You ain't nothing but a bad mop, breaking all the time!"*

A woman jumped in front of the camera. "Looking for alternative cleaning supplies?"

Aru touched the TV with her bracelet. The screen sizzled and popped. And then the whole thing went up in flames.

"That wasn't the kind of music I had in mind," said Mini, clutching Dee Dee tightly.

Aru stepped out of the booth. The air was so cold that it hurt to breathe. She didn't know where they were, but she knew exactly where they were going.

"We're going to summon him," said Aru.

"To come *here*?" squeaked Mini. She coughed, then said in a deeper voice, "Here?"

"No," said Aru. She thought about what the Pandava warrior Arjuna would have done when facing a demon. He would have formed a plan . . . a military strategy. That's what he was best known for, after all: the way he chose to see the world around him. He would have tried to turn the war in his favor. And part of that meant picking the battleground. "We've got to go somewhere he's not going to like. A place that will throw him off guard or distract him long enough to give us a fighting chance." And then the right idea came to her: "The museum."

Mini nodded. "His old prison. He won't like it there. But how are we going to get there in time? I don't think we should use the Otherworld networks. Something really weird happened when I used it to get to that island in the middle of the Ocean of Milk."

"Valmiki's mantra didn't work?" asked Aru, frowning.

"It worked, but just barely. I don't think it was strong enough. We need as much help as we can get. And we know that *he* is getting his own army ready."

Aru remembered the Sleeper's last words: *Know that I am gathering my own friends. And trust me, you won't like meeting them.*

She shuddered. They needed more than

just protection. They needed soldiers of their own. And those desk figurines of the unicorn and bear had given her the answer.

Aru raised her arms to the sky. She wasn't actually sure that was what one was supposed to do when calling down celestial animals, but at least it looked good?

"Vehicles of the gods and goddesses!" Aru called loudly. Then she lost her train of thought, because she'd been too focused on making her voice sound really deep. "Uh . . . it's me, Aru? Remember that whole freeing-you thing? Could I get some help?"

"What if they don't come?" asked Mini. She started biting her nails. "What if they only send one of the super-tiny ones, like the mouse?"

"If the mouse can support an elephant-headed god, I think we're gonna be fine."

"Yeah, but —"

The sound of a stampede drowned out the rest of Mini's words. The sky split open. Translucent staircases staggered down from the clouds, ending right in front of Aru and Mini. Aru waited. *Is that it?* But then it was like an entire zoo had shaken itself loose from the heavens. A crocodile lumbered down the steps, followed by a peacock. A tiger roared as it bounded to the bottom of the stairs. Next came a ram and a three-headed elephant, a giant swan, and a graceful antelope.

Last but not least, the seven-headed horse galloped down the steps until it appeared before Aru. Its sable eyes did not immediately rest on her, but on the bracelet, Vajra. It gave a huff of approval. "A true daughter of Indra, indeed," it said.

A water buffalo trotted up to Mini. It took one look at the danda in her hand before lowering its head. Aru recognized the water buffalo as the mount of the Dharma Raja.

"This Pandava is mine," said the water buffalo.

"Oh, good!" said Mini. "I don't think I'm allergic to water buffalos."

"O great steeds," started Aru dramatically, but then she didn't know where to go from there. She just cut to the chase. "I need you to take us somewhere and, if you can, help us fight? Please?"

The horse nodded all seven of its heads. "We will pledge you one true battle. But when we are called back to our deities, we must go."

"They're welcome to come join in on the fight?" said Aru hopefully.

"Ah, but it is not their fight, daughters of Lord Indra and the Dharma Raja. They will help where they can, but that is all."

"I figured." Aru sighed. "Worth a shot."

The horse knelt. This time, it didn't take Aru half as long to clamber onto its back. Behind her, Mini was trying to balance the danda and hold on to the reins of the water buffalo at the same time.

"Declare your destination," said the horse.

Aru really wished she had a better rallying cry. But the truth would have to do.

"To the Museum of Ancient Indian Art and Culture!" shouted Aru, before quickly adding: "The one in Atlanta, please!"

With a clatter of hooves and paws and claws, the celestial mounts shot straight into the sky, carrying Aru and Mini with them.

Thirty-Seven:
Attack!

Mini asked if they could avoid going through the clouds, because she didn't want to catch a cold.

The mounts dutifully lowered themselves, speeding closer to the surfaces instead. Right now, they were racing across the Atlantic Ocean. The hooves of the seven-headed horse hardly skimmed the waves.

Beside Aru, Mini screeched. "Is that a shark?"

Aru only had a second to glance back and see the dorsal fin that had scraped Mini's ankle.

"Nope. Dolphin," said Aru.

It had definitely been a shark. Shark dorsal fins stood up straight, and dolphin fins were curved back. Aru had learned that from a movie. But Mini didn't need to know.

Once the waves were behind them, still and silent landscapes loomed ahead. Everything was frozen. As they got closer to

Atlanta, they rose higher into the air so that they wouldn't bump into buildings. Aru could make out the Atlanta skyline, like the Westin Peachtree Plaza and the Georgia-Pacific Tower. They flew toward the sunset, and Aru had never found her city more beautiful than in this late evening light, all gilded and glittering, with polished buildings so tall and sharp they might have served to pin the stars into place when night fell. Traffic was at a standstill. But Aru was used to that. After all, it was Atlanta.

Before long, they were standing at the entrance of the museum.

"Whoa," said Mini as she slid down from the back of the water buffalo. "This is where you live?"

Aru felt a weird burst of pride. This *was* where she lived. Now that she thought about it, she didn't want the private island or the mansion so big you could get lost in it. She didn't want to live anywhere else but here, with her mom. Her thawed, happy, and healthy mom.

One of the divine vehicles, the golden tiger with startlingly long claws, walked up to the door and pawed it. The entrance swung open, and all of them flooded inside.

Aru's heart pinched when she reached the Hall of the Gods. She was fully expecting to find what she saw there, but that didn't make it any easier. Her mother hadn't moved from her frozen spot. Her hair still fanned around her face. Her eyes remained wide with panic.

But even though she looked the same as before, Aru couldn't help but see her differently. She kept picturing the woman from the Pool of the Past, the woman who had given up so much just to keep Aru safe.

Aru ran up to her and threw her arms around her waist. She refused to cry, but she may have sniffled a couple times. She thought of what her mom had said to the Sleeper: *I'll find an answer. I'll examine every ancient site, read every treatise. And I will find a way to free both you and Aru. I promise.*

Every time her mom had left . . . it was because she loved her.

"I love you, too," Aru said.

And then she pulled away, wiping her nose on her sleeve.

"Do you want a tissue? Er, never mind . . ." said Mini.

The mounts stood around them, looking like a terrifying bunch. The lion bared its teeth. The tiger sharpened its claws on the stone elephant. *Rude!*

"We await your command, Pandava," said the horse.

Command? Aru stuffed her hands into her pockets. She took a deep breath. Like her, Arjuna had seen the world differently than most. If there was one thing that had survived all those reincarnation cycles, it was the imagination they shared. And now it was time to use it.

"Mini, can the Death Danda make an illusion that looks like a human being?"

Mini nodded. "I think so."

"Okay, good. Because we're going to do something a little strange. . . ."

Half an hour later, the only thing outside that proved not to be frozen was the sun. It had sunk completely. The museum was pitch-black except for the bits of light Aru had been able to convince Vajra to spit out. Now those lights hovered in the air.

The mounts were either pacing or playing. The crocodile was posing next to the stone makara, glancing at the statue and grinning as if to say *Hey guys! Look! Look! It's me!* And, as it turned out, all cats — even celestial ones — were highly intrigued by boxes. The tiger kept sticking its head in one of the wooden crates before awkwardly trying to cram its whole body into the space. Whenever it saw Aru looking, it would stop and lick its front paw self-consciously. Aru was grateful to it; earlier, the tiger had gently picked up her frozen mother in his mouth and placed her in her bedroom, so she was out of harm's way. Two mounts had gone into the Hall of the Gods solely to protect the frozen forms of Poppy, Arielle, and Burton.

For the umpteenth time that evening, Aru glanced at her palm, watching the symbol fade. . . .

"It's time to summon him," said Aru. "Ready?"

The mounts molded back into the shadows, disappearing completely. Just as Aru had planned.

Mini gripped the danda. "Ready."

Aru faced the closed museum doors and said loudly into the dark:

"Sleeper, we, the daughters of Lord Indra and the Dharma Raja, summon you!"

For emphasis, Mini hit the floor with the danda. A couple moments passed. Then a full minute. Mini's shoulders dropped.

"How are we going to know when he's here? Is there going to be a sign or something? Like maybe the earth will split down the middle and he'll pop up?"

"He's a demon, Mini, not a mole."

"What if we're wrong and we're stuck here waiting all night? There's got to be a sign, *something* —"

The door to the hall, which had been closed tightly, was flung open. It smacked into the wall. If this were a movie, there would have been a loud clap of thunder outside, too. But it was real life, and real life doesn't always sound like it should.

Aru thought the Sleeper would be standing in the doorway.

But it wasn't him. It was something far worse. A dozen or so demons with blood-spattered jaws peered through the entrance. The horns on top of their heads looked like they'd just been sharpened. They sniffed the air, licking their lips. The whole front wall of the hall fell down like a domino.

"There's your sign," said Aru.

She refused to let herself be scared. But her hands shook, and her mouth felt suddenly dry.

"I warned you," called a voice.

The Sleeper stepped through the crowd of demons.

He looked like a man, and also not like one. His eyes were no longer round and dark like in the vision from the Pool of the Past. Instead, they were slitted and gem-bright, like a cat's eyes gone narrow with fury. When he smiled, small tusks curled out from his bottom lip.

"Strange choice of location," sneered the

Sleeper. "Although perhaps predictable for a little girl who needs her mommy. If you thought coming back here would dissuade me, you were wrong."

A small birdcage swung from his hands. The pigeon inside began to shout and hop. Boo! He was okay!

"What are you two doing?" shouted Boo the moment he saw Aru and Mini. "Get out! Go!"

Mini locked her legs, swinging the Death Danda over her shoulder as if it were a baseball bat.

"Oh gods," moaned Boo. He flapped in his cage. "I can't look."

"Sleeper! We're not going to let you go through with this," warned Mini.

"I'm bored already," the Sleeper yawned.

Then he opened his hand. From his palm, a ribbon of black spilled out, snaking across the floor and seeping into the walls. It was the same horribly familiar starry black that had nearly strangled Aru. She tried to dodge it, but the enchanted muck yanked her back, flinging her and Mini to the wall so that they were like bugs trapped on flypaper. *Keep calm, Shah.* Aru had expected this. In fact, she'd banked on him acting like this.

"Don't you understand, little ones?" asked the Sleeper. "You're not worthy opponents for me. You would be far too easy to defeat. In fact, you're not worthy of noticing at all. You might think you're clever for freeing those vehicles, but I'll have them back in a cage in no time."

There it was. Those words. *Little ones. Not worthy.*

But Aru was beginning to think that, maybe, being overlooked or considered different wasn't always a bad thing. In social studies class, she had learned that it was a good thing for warriors to be left-handed. In ancient Rome, the gladiators who won the most were the ones who were left-handed. They had the element of surprise on their side, because people only defended themselves from a right-handed attack.

I hope you like surprises, thought Aru.

She and Mini had rehearsed what they would do. Now it was time to put it into action.

Mini held her gaze. Her face looked pale, but she was still smiling hopefully. Aru felt that strange humming buzz once more, the same thrum she'd experienced when they'd fought together in the library. They were connected to one another's thoughts when they were in combat.

The Sleeper hadn't bothered to tie up their hands. Why? Because he didn't think they could do anything that would harm him.

He stepped over the threshold of the front door. The demons spread out around him, taking up all the space in the museum lobby. Aru could feel an invisible wind stirring against the back of her neck. *Just a few steps farther,* she said silently. He stepped farther.

Aru gave the signal to Mini. Her sister nodded.

Mini opened her compact, and a bit of light seeped out. From there, an illusion of Aru's mother stepped out into the Hall of the Gods. She was still beautiful, Aru thought, as she stared at the vision. The Sleeper stopped walking. His face became pinched, haunted.

"I know the truth about you," said the illusion.

The Sleeper dropped the cage holding Boo, and the door opened. The pigeon flew out, rushing straight to Aru and Mini. He started pecking at the shadows that had them pinned to the wall. Aru pried herself loose.

"Krithika?" asked the Sleeper, his voice hoarse. "How . . . ? I thought —"

"I just want to talk," said the vision of her mother.

"Talk?" repeated the Sleeper. "After all this time, you just want to *talk*? That's simply not good enough."

He lunged forward.

And stepped right into the trap that Aru and Mini had laid.

The Sleeper hadn't noticed the small chalk circle she had drawn in the middle of floor. And walking into it didn't just mean that he was in the center of the room.

He was in the center of a circle of every single one of the celestial mounts.

The golden tiger prowled out of the wall, her muzzle wrinkled in a snarl. The peacock's feathers glittered menacingly. The water buffalo began to paw the ground.

The seven-headed horse turned to Aru.

The Sleeper had only a second to look startled, eyes wide and confused, before Aru shouted, "ATTACK!"

THIRTY-EIGHT:
ARU SHAH IS A LIAR

Aru used to think that the nature documentary she'd seen with two lions fighting each other would be the scariest thing she'd ever watch.

She'd been totally wrong.

The demons charged, trampling through the museum as they launched themselves at the heavenly mounts. Aru felt bad for the sign in the lobby that read PLEASE DO NOT TOUCH. Now it was lying on the floor, currently being crushed by a demon with the head of a wild boar.

The tiger flew at one of the rakshas who had the head of a stag. The peacock joined in, its tail sweeping the floor and cutting out the legs of an asura right next to it.

Boo fluttered to the top of Aru's head. "Nicely done," he said, impressed. "But a little lacking in terms of sophistication. An ambush is so bourgeois."

Aru ducked under the guest sign-in table

as someone's head (literally) flew past her. "Now is not the time!"

"Fair enough."

Mini crawled under the table with her. Everywhere they looked was chaos. Bits of pottery were flung across the room. Heads, too. A bear mount was foaming at the mouth. One of the horns of the celestial ram was bent at an uncomfortable-looking angle. Sweat gleamed on the body of the seven-headed horse. Aru scanned the lobby. Almost everyone was accounted for except one. . . .

The Sleeper.

Where had he gone? The moment the attack had started, he'd disappeared in a flood of demons and animals.

"Boo," hissed a voice behind her.

"Ugh, what do you want?" snapped Boo before squawking, "AHHHHH!!!"

Aru and Mini jumped, banging their heads on the underside of the table. Behind them, the Sleeper's face pushed out of the wall.

Goose bumps prickled down Aru's arm. The Sleeper could move *inside* the walls. She scrambled backward. Vajra was still in her hand, but although the weapon had been awakened, Aru couldn't do much with it except hit a couple of things. She'd tried to throw it, but Vajra wouldn't leave her hand. It just did what it wanted, like a giant cat.

Aru scuttled crablike from under the table. Her hand slipped and she banged her funny bone on the floor. "*Owwwww!* Not funny, not funny, not funny," she said, trying to shake the tinglies out of her arm.

Mini, who had not fallen, got out and up on her feet first. She swung Dee Dee around her head. A blast of violet light shot through the end of the stick, but the Sleeper, now fully emerged from the wall, merely batted the beam of light aside. The force of it pushed Mini back. Her arms pinwheeled, but just as she caught her balance, a raksha slammed into her.

"Mini!" called Aru.

Boo dove into the crowd, pecking the demon's eyes until the asura screeched and teetered backward. Aru glanced up. Dangling a short distance away was a giant, heavy, and *very* sharp chandelier. It had been handcrafted by a local glassblower and was her mom's favorite part of the lobby.

"You're a liar, Aru Shah," said the Sleeper, creeping toward her. "You lie to your friends, your family, but most of all yourself. If you think you've beaten me, you're wrong."

Aru moved back some more. Her palms felt slippery. One wrong move, and the Sleeper could end her on the spot.

"I'm not a liar," said Aru.

The Sleeper took another step forward. Aru let Vajra loose. For once, the lightning bolt did as she wanted. Light sparked from the end of it, slicing the column of the chandelier. She rolled out of the way just as the Sleeper glanced up.

"What the — ?" he started.

"I've just got a big imagination," she said, grinning.

The chandelier crashed down. The Sleeper barely got a scream out before a bunch of glass and crystal erupted around him.

"Sorry about the chandelier, Mom!" Aru whispered. She raced back toward Mini.

All around her sister lay the slumped-over forms of demons and rakshas.

"They're not dead, unfortunately," said Boo, landing on Aru's shoulder. "But they're out of commission for now. The problem is, this is only a fraction of the Sleeper's army."

"Where're the others?"

"Sleeping," said Boo in a *duh-why-do-you-think-he's-called-that-it's-not-like-he's-known-for-his-own-epic-napping-skills* tone.

The seven-headed horse shook its head. Blood and spit flew over the walls. "We cannot stay much longer, daughter of Indra, but you have fought . . ." The horse paused, struggling to find the right word.

"Bravely?" Aru guessed.

The horse heads snorted.

"Valiantly?" she suggested.

"Cunningly," it finally said.

Aru sighed with relief, bracing her hands on her knees. Now that the Sleeper was down, all she needed was to finish him off with Vajra.

She turned toward the wreckage of the chandelier, but a demon rushed at her. Boo acted quickly, and bird droppings rained across the demon's eyes and forehead.

"ARGH!" it shouted, spinning around before knocking itself unconscious by running headlong into the wall.

"If only I was in my former form," the pigeon moaned. "Ah, well. Annoyance is its own power."

Aru raised her arm and Vajra transformed into a whip. The lightning bolt was very heavy, like carrying three gallons of milk in one hand. But she was so close to having everything back to normal that strength rushed through her. She brought Vajra down with a sickening *crack,* and the demon flew back, slamming into the wall before evaporating into . . . demon dust? No, demon *gunk.* There was some sticky-looking residue on the paint. Nasty.

The chandelier shards twitched. Mini ran to Aru's side. Time for their final blow.

It should have been easy. Quick and painless.

But then a lot of unexpected things happened at once.

Around them, the room went from full to empty in the space of a second. The army of demons and rakshas — many of them now little more than melted lumps on the lobby floor of the museum — vanished in a puff of smoke. With a rush of wings and paws, the celestial mounts disappeared, called back to the deities they served. The last thing Aru heard was "Blessings upon the Pandavas."

The Sleeper rose from beneath the smashed chandelier. Pieces of glass scattered in a thousand directions. Aru squeezed her eyes shut, gripping Vajra tightly. Then she raised the lightning bolt over her head. Beside her, she could sense Mini's thoughts: *Now, Death Danda, move quickly!*

Unfortunately, the Sleeper moved faster. Black ribbons streamed from the tips of his fingers. They were aimed not at her, but at Mini and Boo.

The two of them slammed backward and

were pinned to the wall.

"Aru!" croaked Mini.

Aru raised the lightning bolt, but a ripple of instinct held her hand. It was as if Mini's thoughts alone had stopped her: *If you attack, he'll kill us.*

Aru paused, her lungs heaving from the weight of the lightning bolt and the decision put before her.

"Your move, Aru," said the Sleeper. He grinned. "You can destroy me, or protect them."

Aru stood still. There was nothing she could do. No right answer.

"The chandelier was a rather clever move," said the Sleeper, rubbing his jaw. "But not quite clever enough, I'm afraid. Here's some advice: let your family die, Arundhati. The love of one's family can be a powerful and horrifying thing. Why, just look at the stories of the Mahabharata. Consider Shakhuni — although you know him as 'Boo.' He felt his sister had been insulted when she was forced to marry a blind king, and for that he swore destruction on your ancestors. And he succeeded. That's just one example among many. You see, child? To act with your heart is a dangerous thing. Let them die."

"Let them go," croaked Aru.

424

"Oh, dear," said the Sleeper. "And here I thought you would have turned out to be so much more clever."

"I said, *let them go.*"

"Drop the lightning bolt, and I will."

Aru lowered her hand, hating herself.

The Sleeper flexed his wrists, and Mini and Boo slumped to the ground, unconscious.

But alive.

"You just reminded me of something, child," he said softly. "Mercy makes fools of us. I've had eleven years of torture to think about all the ways I was made a fool."

The Sleeper was next to her in an instant. "Rather fancy toy for a child," he hissed, snatching up Vajra.

Aru hoped it burned him. How could her mother have ever loved someone like this?

The young, hopeful Krithika had misjudged him. He couldn't help but be a demon after all.

The Sleeper grabbed her arm and dragged her across the museum lobby. "You made me into what I am now," he said. "You and your mother. All I wanted to do was end the tyranny of destiny. Can you understand that?" For the first time, his voice grew soft. "Do you realize how cruel it is to tell someone that their future is fixed? That they can do nothing but play out their life like a puppet? Do you see how even your gifts have enslaved you?"

Aru was only half listening. Panic had sharpened her thoughts. When her hand had knocked against her pajama pant leg, she had felt something in her pocket: a nub of tile from the Palace of Illusions. *It can give you the part of me that matters most: protection.*

"Your death will signal the end of not just a life, but an *era,*" said the Sleeper. His eyes were shining. "You and your siblings will no longer be damned to live life over and over again. I'm doing this *for you,* because your mother" — he sneered — "didn't have the *guts* to free you."

"Sorry," said Aru, yanking her arm from his grip. "I'm just not in the mood to die right now."

Her fingers dug out the little piece of home, and she threw it on the floor. A fierce gust of wind blew the Sleeper back. For one blissful blink of her eye, Aru could catch her breath. She felt the tile of home thud back into her pocket. The piece of home was tiny and so only bought her a second's worth of distraction. Still, it was enough.

The Sleeper had lost his grip on Vajra. Aru raised her hand, and the lightning bolt snapped into her palm. Now she held it out. She steeled herself. She *had* to do this.

The Sleeper lifted his arm, as if he was trying to block out the light. "Child, wait —" he said. "You don't know what you're doing."

Aru was twelve years old. Even she knew that half the time she didn't know what she was doing.

But this wasn't one of those times.

"You're cursed," said the Sleeper. "I'm only trying to help."

Cursed . . .

Before Aru could throw the lightning bolt, an image sprang before her:

In this vision, Aru was older. Taller. Across from her, on a night-soaked battlefield, stood four other girls . . . four other *sisters,* she realized. She wasn't even sure how she knew that, but it was undeniable. All five Pandava girls, together. All of them wielding weapons. Even Mini.

Mini was older, too. Her face was a fierce mask of hate.

Hate that was directed against . . . *her.*

"Don't you see?" said the Sleeper. "Fate never intended for you to be a hero."

THIRTY-NINE:
WHO'S THE LIAR NOW?

The image faded.

Aru couldn't shake it from her thoughts. She had done something so bad that her own sisters had turned against her. Why were they on a battlefield? What had happened?

"You think your partial divinity is a blessing," said the Sleeper. "It is a curse."

"You're lying," said Aru, but her grip on Vajra had slackened.

When she blinked, she saw them — *all* of them — turning against her. Rejecting her. *Abandoning* her.

Where were they going?

Why were they going?

Nausea jolted through Aru. She thought of every time she had rushed out of her bedroom and run to the window, only to see her mother leaving for the airport and Sherrilyn giving her a sad smile and offering to take her out for ice cream. She

428

thought of every day she had walked through school filled with dread, knowing that all it would take was one word, one *gesture* out of line and she'd lose it all: the friends, the popularity, the *belonging.*

The lights that Vajra had cast into the museum lobby had dimmed. Mini and Boo were still out cold. It was just Aru and the Sleeper.

"Kill me, and that is the future you will face," hissed the Sleeper. "You think *I'm* the enemy. Do you even know what that word means? What is an enemy? What is evil? You are far more like me than you realize, Aru Shah. Look inside yourself. If you hurt me, it will mean losing everyone you ever cared about."

In the stories, the Pandava brothers fought an epic battle against their own family. But they never turned on one another. In the vision the Sleeper showed her, Aru saw something else: her family turning against her.

Tears ran down Aru's cheeks. She didn't remember when she'd started crying. All she knew was that she wished the Sleeper would choke on his words.

But he kept talking.

"I pity you the most, little one," he said. "For you think you are the hero. Don't you realize the whole universe is laughing at you? That was never meant to be your destiny. You are like me: a hero draped in evil clothing. Join me. We can wage war on fate. We can break it together."

He walked toward her. She raised the lightning bolt a little higher. He stood still.

"Your mother pays no attention to you," he said. "Don't you think I've sensed it through the lamp? But if you're with me . . . I will never leave you, child. We can be a team: father and daughter."

Father and daughter.

Aru remembered her mother's face in the vision from the Pool of the Past. The way she had talked about the three of them being a family. She had shared her husband's idea of people defying their own destiny.

Her mom had lived with only half of her heart for eleven years.

Eleven years.

And only because she loved Aru that much.

"Kill me, and your sisters and family will grow to hate you," said the Sleeper. "You will never be a hero. You were never meant to be a hero."

Hero. That one word made Aru lift her chin. It made her think of Mini and Boo, her mom, and all the incredible things she

430

herself had done in just nine days. Breaking the lamp hadn't been heroic . . . but everything else? Fighting for the people she cared about and doing everything it took to fix her mistake? *That* was heroism.

Vajra became a spear in her hands.

"I already am. And it's not *hero,*" she said. "It's *heroine.*"

And with that, she let the lightning bolt fly.

The moment the bolt left her hands, doubt bit through Aru. All she could see was the image of her sisters lined up against her. All she could feel was the shame of being *hated,* and not knowing what she'd done to deserve it. A single dark thought wormed into her head: *What if the Sleeper was telling the truth?*

Her fingers tingled. The bolt cut through the air. One moment it was spinning straight at the Sleeper. She watched his eyes widen, his mouth open up for a scream. But the next instant, everything changed.

That tiny, needling doubt shifted everything. The lightning bolt stopped just short of hitting him, as if it had picked up the barest *whiff* of Aru's misgiving.

The Sleeper stared at the lightning bolt poised an inch from his heart. Then he glanced at Aru. He smiled.

"Oh Aru, Aru, Aru," he taunted. It was the same voice she had heard when she lit the lamp. *What have you done?*

"Vajra!" called Aru.

"One day, you'll see it my way, and I will welcome you, daughter."

"Strike him, Vajra!" shouted Aru.

But it didn't matter. When she looked up from the spear of lightning . . . the Sleeper had vanished.

FORTY:
FAILURE

Once, when Aru was really stressed about an exam, she didn't eat for a *whole* day. She was too busy trying to remember all the dates from her history textbook.

When the last bell rang, she stood up from her desk and got so dizzy that she fell right back down.

That had been a bad day.

But this day was worse.

Aru had thought that magic would make her powerful. It didn't. It just kind of kept things at bay. Like how anti-itch cream erased the pain of a bee sting but didn't repel the bee itself. Now that all the magic had drained out of the room, hunger and exhaustion rushed into her.

Aru sank to the floor. Vajra flew back to her hand. It was no longer a spear or a bolt of lightning but just an ordinary ball. The kind of harmless toy a kid would play with and a demon wouldn't look twice at.

Aru shuddered. What had just happened?

She kept staring at the spot on the floor where the Sleeper had disappeared. She'd had him in her sights, right there. She'd had the lightning bolt poised and *everything.* And yet somehow — even with everything lined up to help her — she'd *failed.* The Sleeper had let her live, not because he pitied her, but because he thought she'd actually *join* him.

Tears ran down her cheeks. After everything they'd been through, she had *failed.* Now her mom would be frozen forever, and —

A touch on her shoulder made her jump.

It was Mini, smiling weakly. There were a couple of cuts on her face, and one of her eyes looked a bit bruised. Boo fluttered down from Mini's hands and hovered in front of Aru.

Aru waited for him to yell at her. She wanted him to tell her all the things she'd done wrong, because that would be better than knowing that she'd done her best and still wasn't good enough. But Boo didn't yell. Instead, he tilted his head in that strange pigeon way of his and said something Aru had not expected:

"It is not failure to fail."

Aru started to cry. She understood what

Boo meant. Sometimes you could fall down and still win the race if you got up again, but that wasn't how she felt right now. Mini sat down next to her and put her arm around her shoulders.

Aru used to think that friends were there to share your food and keep your secrets and laugh at your jokes while you walked from one classroom to the next. Sometimes, though, the best kind of friend is the one who doesn't say anything but just sits beside you. It's enough.

Boo circled the museum. As he did, all the rubble and chaos sorted itself, the dust and debris jumping and wriggling. The front wall of the Hall of the Gods rose from the floor. Even the chandelier in the lobby gathered its crystal shards and took its place on the ceiling.

The front door to the museum had fallen into the street. Aru peeked out and heard familiar, beautiful sounds.

Cars honked. Tires screeched against the asphalt. People shouted to one another:

"Is there an eclipse? Why's it nighttime?"

"My car battery is dead!"

Aru couldn't believe it.

"See?" Mini said quietly from behind her. "We did something."

The girls stepped inside, and the front

door zoomed back into place. Aru leaned against it, completely worn-out. "What's happening?"

Boo flew down and landed in front of them. "Only if the Sleeper reached the Kingdom of Death by the new moon could his curse of frozen sleep become permanent."

"But I didn't defeat him . . ." said Aru.

"But the two of you managed to distract and delay him," said Boo kindly. "And you did it without *me*. Which is, frankly, mind-boggling."

"What about the Council of Guardians?" asked Mini. "Do you think what we did was enough to impress them?"

"Ugh. *Them*. Are they going to want to train us after I . . ." Aru paused, not wanting to say the word even though it hung over her head: *failed*. "At the last minute, I . . . I let him get away."

"It was that curse," said Mini gently. "Remember?"

On the Bridge of Forgetting, Shukra had told her that when it mattered most, she would forget. But had that really been the fulfillment of the curse? Aru couldn't remember — or perhaps she didn't *want* to remember — what she had felt the moment the Sleeper disappeared.

"Yeah," said Aru weakly.

"But even *with* the curse, you stopped him," said Mini.

Aru didn't point out that he'd stopped himself, and only because he thought she would join him. *Never in a* million *years.*

"And on top of that, we prevented the end of Time," said Mini. "What more do you want?"

Aru jolted upright. "My mom! I should —"

From the top of the staircase, Aru heard a door open and close, and then feet racing down the steps. Even without turning, she could feel her mother in the room. The burst of warmth. And the smell of her hair, which always reminded Aru of night-blooming jasmine.

When Aru spun around, her mother looked at her. *Only* her. Then she opened her arms, and Aru ran in for the hug of her life.

FORTY-ONE:
GOT ALL THAT?

Boo, Mini, and Aru were sitting in the kitchen. Behind them, Aru's mom was making hot cocoa and talking on the phone to Mini's parents. Every time she walked past Aru, she dropped a kiss on her head.

"Do you think they're awake yet?" asked Aru.

Poppy, Burton, and Arielle still hadn't woken up yet. According to Boo, their proximity to the lamp when it was lit meant that they were going to be stuck in place for just a little bit longer than everyone else.

"I'd give it another twenty minutes," said Boo. "Don't worry, they'll be fine and won't remember a thing. Now, as to the question of training, it is natural that the Council of Guardians will want to train you. You're the Pandavas, after all. And this fight is not done. The Sleeper will be adding to his army, and now we must do the same."

Mini scowled. "Training classes . . . on

top of *school*? Will that affect my normal extracurricular activities?"

"That's like saying, *Clean your room so you can do extra homework,*" added Aru.

"Ungrateful children!" harrumphed Boo. "It's an honor of the century! *Several* centuries, in fact!"

"But you'll be right there with us, won't you, Boo?"

At this, Boo bowed, his wings dragging on the floor. "It would be a privilege to train you, Pandavas," he said. He raised his head but did not look at them. "You will still accept my tutelage knowing who I once was?"

Aru and Mini exchanged glances. They didn't need to use their Pandava bond to know what the other was thinking. Aru thought about the version of the Sleeper she'd seen in her mom's secrets. The kind-eyed man who thought he'd never become evil. Then she recalled who Boo had been in the stories. Once, Shakhuni had been evil and bent on revenge. He'd gotten himself cursed. But maybe curses weren't all that terrible, because he'd saved their lives not only once, but *twice.* Maybe he wasn't all bad or even all good. He was just . . . human. In pigeon form.

"People change," said Aru.

It could have been her imagination, but

Boo's eyes looked particularly shiny, as if he were about to cry. He needled through his feathers with his beak. Nestled in all that boring gray was a single golden feather, which he extended to them.

"My troth," he said solemnly.

"Troth?" repeated Mini. "Gross! Isn't that what people do when they get married?"

"Ew!" said Boo.

"I'm a catch," gasped Aru when she was done laughing.

"It's a *troth*! Not a *betrothal*!" said Boo, looking thoroughly disgusted. "It's a promise — of trueness. Of loyalty. I hereby pledge my troth to serve the cause of the Pandavas."

Mini and Aru looked at each other. *What now?* Mini grabbed the Death Danda and tried to knight Boo, saying "Rise, Sir —" but Boo hissed and fluttered off to a different part of the museum.

Aru's face hurt from grinning. She gazed out of the window panel on the left side of the door. Even though it wasn't quite nighttime yet, the stars had begun to shoulder their way into the sky. Usually, she wasn't able to see them so clearly, because of all the city smog and light pollution. But tonight the stars seemed close and bright. Twinkling, almost. A flash of lightning spidered across the sky, followed by a powerful bang of thunder. Mini jumped, but to Aru it was like the sound of applause. And she knew Indra was watching out for her.

"Everything's going to be different now, isn't it?" asked Mini, staring out of the window panel on the right side. "And it isn't over. The Sleeper's going to come back one day."

"We'll be ready," said Aru fiercely.

I'll be ready, she thought.

An hour later, Mini hoisted her backpack onto her shoulders. In her hands, the Death Danda had shrunk to the size of a purple compact. She stuffed it into her pocket.

"Do you want me to come with you?" asked Aru's mom.

The stone elephant had once more knelt to the ground, lifted its trunk, and opened its mouth, offering Mini a way back home. The barest trace of magic stirred the air.

"No, that's okay," said Mini. "Thanks, Auntie."

Some people might find it strange that Mini was already calling her Auntie when they'd only just met (although Mini *did* know a lot about Aru's mom by now). But that's how the girls had been raised. Anyone who was a friend of your parents was automatically called "auntie" or "uncle.""

"Your mother and I will talk again soon," said Aru's mom. "It's . . . it's been some time."

"I know," said Mini. And then she turned bright red. "I mean, I don't *know* because I've, like, seen your deepest, darkest secrets or anything."

Boo, who had only recently been filled in on everything, squawked loudly. It very clearly meant *Shut up while you're still ahead.*

Mini threw her arms around Aru for one last hug. "See you soon," she said.

And with that, she climbed through the elephant door. Boo watched her go, shouting, "Don't forget to hydrate at home! Pandavas are *always* hydrated!"

Boo flew to the tip of the elephant's trunk to address Aru's mom. It's not exactly intimidating when a pigeon speaks to you from the ground. Then again, a pigeon talking at all doesn't conjure a portrait of solemn respectability.

"Krithika," he said gently. "Perhaps we should have a few words."

Aru's mother sighed. She pulled her arm away from Aru's shoulder, and Aru felt a rush of cold. Then she tilted Aru's face and smoothed the hair away from her forehead. She looked at Aru hungrily. As if she had never looked at her long enough.

"I know you have a lot of questions," she said to Aru. "I will answer them. All of them. But Boo is right, there are some things he and I need to discuss."

"Can Boo live with us?"

"I'm not some stray you found on the side of the road!" huffed the pigeon.

"I'll get you a nice cage?"

"I am not a pet!"

"I'll hug you and squeeze you, and name you George —"

"I am an *all-powerful sorcerer* —"

"And I'll get you the softest pillow."

Boo cocked his head. "Pillow, you say? Well, I *could* use a nap —"

Before her mother could object, Aru said, "Yay! Thanks, Mom!"

Then she ran into the Hall of the Gods. If her mom and the rest of the world had recovered, then surely by now . . .

Aru flipped on the light switch. There, huddled in a corner with the broken remnants of the lamp's glass case, stood Burton, Poppy, and Arielle. They were staring around the Hall of the Gods, utterly confused. They glanced at the smashed glass, then up at the window.

Arielle frowned. "I thought . . . I thought we got here in the afternoon?"

But all confusion disappeared when Poppy caught sight of Aru. "Knew it," she said gleefully. "What a liar! You couldn't even admit the truth, so you had to break the lamp? That's pathetic."

"I didn't lie," said Aru casually. "That lamp was totally cursed. I just got back from fighting an ancient demon in the lobby."

Burton held up his phone. The red light started blinking. It was recording. "Wanna say that again?" he asked smugly.

"Sure," said Aru, walking forward. "I lied. Sometimes I do that. I've got a big imagination. I try not to lie about important things, though. Here's the truth: I just saved your lives. I even walked through the Kingdom of Death to do it."

"Get help, Aru," said Arielle.

"Can't wait to show this to the whole school," said Burton.

"I can prove it," said Aru.

She felt in her pocket for the pen from Chitrigupta. She used it to write a message in the air. *Help me out of this, Uncle.*

Immediately, something sharp poked her in the pocket. She fished it out — a piece of paper that hadn't been there before. She scanned it quickly, fighting back a smile.

"Still recording?" asked Aru.

"Yup," said Burton.

The three of them snickered.

"Good," said Aru. She started reading: " 'On September twenty-eighth, Poppy Lopez went to Mrs. Garcia's office and told her that she thought she saw someone taking a baseball bat to her car. When Mrs. Garcia ran out of the room, Poppy pulled the pop quiz out of the file cabinet and snapped a picture with her phone. She got an A-plus on the quiz.' "

Poppy turned pale.

" 'On Tuesday, October second, Burton Prater ate his boogers, then handed Arielle a chocolate chip cookie that he had dropped on the ground. He did not wash his hands. Or the cookie.' " Aru looked up with a frown. "Seriously? Dude, that's gross. Pretty sure that's how you catch the plague."

Arielle looked like she was going to vomit. "Is that *for real*?"

" 'And yesterday, Arielle wore her mom's first engagement ring and lost it at recess. She told her mom that she saw the housekeeper holding it.' "

Arielle turned red.

Aru folded up the paper. Then she tapped the blinking red light of Burton's phone. "Got all that?"

"How — how — how . . . how did you —" stuttered Poppy.

"I've got friends all over the place," said Aru.

This was one of those times when she wished she were sitting in a big black leather armchair with a weird-looking cat and an unlit cigar. She wanted to swivel around and say, *Feelin' lucky?* Instead, she settled for a shrug. "Still want to show it to the school?"

Burton held up his phone, scrolled to the video, and deleted it.

As a show of good faith, Aru handed them the piece of paper. "Now we're even."

The three of them stared at her. Aru grinned.

"Let's get outta here," said Poppy.

"Have a nice weekend —" started Burton, but Poppy smacked him.

"You're such a suck-up."

When they left, there was a new note in her pocket:

Consider that the first and last time!
Naughty child.
PS: The palace sends its love
and says hello.

Aru smiled. "Hello, palace."

Maybe it was just her imagination, but she thought she felt the faintest bit of warmth coming from the tile of home in her pocket.

FORTY-TWO:
WORD VOMIT

When the end bell of sixth period rang, Aru could barely stop herself from jumping onto her desk. She wasn't the only one who was excited. It was the day when school got out for winter break.

Even though Atlanta was just cold instead of snowy, the whole world felt like almost-Christmas. Which was the best. Fairy lights and paper snowflakes covered the ceilings. The Christmas songs that had been playing since November hadn't started to drive her crazy yet, either. And in that day's chemistry class, their teacher had taught them how to make fake snow with baking soda and water, so most of the tables were covered with tiny snowmen.

Aru started to pack up her things. Her lab partner, Arielle, smiled at Aru, but it was a slightly wary *are-you-a-witch?* grin.

"So . . . where are you going for Christmas?" Arielle asked.

As usual, Aru lied. But this time, it had a far different purpose. "Nowhere," she said. "You?"

"Maldives," said Arielle. "We've got a timeshare on a private island."

"I hope you have fun."

Arielle looked a bit surprised at that. But then she smiled more genuinely. "Thanks. Um, by the way, my parents are throwing a New Year's party at the Fox Theatre downtown. I don't know if you got the invite already, but you and your mom are invited if you want."

"Thanks!" said Aru. This time she didn't lie. "But we've got family plans."

She'd never said the words *family plans* before, and she didn't think she'd ever get tired of saying it.

"Oh. Well, have fun."

"I'll try!" called Aru. "Have a good break!"

And with that, she slung her backpack over her shoulder and stepped into the cold. While most of her classmates were on their way to their private jets or chauffeurs, Aru was on her way to her training session in the Otherworld.

Every Monday, Wednesday, and Friday, for three hours, Aru and Mini learned war strategy from Hanuman, dancing and etiquette from Urvashi, and folklore from Boo.

They were supposed to get more teachers starting next week, and even join the other Otherworldly kids who were training (although none of them were the offspring of gods).

"Other kids? Like us?" Mini had asked.

"Yup," said Aru. "Maybe that snake boy from Costco will be there."

"I don't think he'd remember me. . . ."

"You walked into a telephone pole, Mini. I'd say that's pretty memorable."

Mini *thwacked* her on the head with Dee Dee.

But before they could join the other students, their parents had wanted to make sure they had mastered the basics and caught up. It was essentially, said Boo, "remedial classes for divine dunces." *Rude.*

Aru wasn't thrilled about having to take Dance, but as Urvashi had explained, "When Arjuna was cursed to lose his manhood for one year, he became a wonderful dance instructor, and it made him *that* much more graceful in combat. I should know — I'm the one who cursed him, after all."

"When are we going to get to the stabby stuff?" Aru had asked last Wednesday.

Vajra, who had decided to become a glowing pen instead of a lightning bolt for that day, burned brighter at her question.

Boo's gaze had narrowed. "One should not want to rush toward violence."

Today, as she walked home, she thought about the last message she'd received from Mini. Aru still didn't have a phone, so they couldn't text, but that's where the stone elephant came in handy. When she'd checked the elephant's mouth this morning, Mini's letter was simple:

How am I going to train today?
I'm 99% sure I've contracted bubonic plague. (I even saw a rat yesterday.)

Aru laughed, remembering it. But the laugh quickly died in her throat when she saw who was walking just a few feet in front of her on the sidewalk.

The new boy at school.

Aiden Acharya had enrolled just last week, which seemed really impractical, considering that winter break was just about to start. But according to the school's best gossip (Poppy), his family had been very convincing (read: they were superrich). He was having a pretty easy time adjusting at school, which made sense considering he looked like . . . *that*.

Until recently, Aru hadn't given much

thought to what made a boy good-looking. Just the basic standards of not sounding like a braying donkey and not smelling like a pair of cursed sneakers ruled out half the guys in her class. Aiden, on the other hand, had dimples and curly black hair. And he smelled nice. Not like soap or deodorant, but like clean laundry. Plus, his eyes were really dark and framed by even darker lashes.

She hadn't spoken to him yet. What would she say? All she knew was that he and his mom had moved into the large house right across from the museum. Yesterday, his mom and her mom had started talking on the street. Indian people did that all the time. (*Oh, you're Indian? Me too! How 'bout that?*)

Aiden had been standing with his mom. At one point, it looked like he had seen Aru watching them from the museum window. Aru had flashed her most attractive smile (she even sucked in her nose) before remembering that she was wearing a pair of metal horns. Boo had insisted that she wear them whenever she was at home. (*What if you need to wear a helmet while fighting demons? Your neck needs to be strong!*)

Aru had panicked, walked straight into the fridge, and fallen flat on her face. She'd then continued to lie on the kitchen floor for another hour.

She still wanted to strangle Boo.

Now Aru was squeezing her eyes shut in embarrassment over Aiden possibly having seen her in horns when she banged her nose into something. His backpack. She looked up. Aiden looked down. He was at least a foot taller than her. In the afternoon light, his skin looked golden.

"Hi," he said.

Aru opened her mouth. Closed it. *Come on, Aru. You walked through the Kingdom of Death. You can talk to a —*

He smiled. "Don't I know you?"

"I. . ." She choked.

Why did her voice suddenly seem so deep, out of *nowhere*? She sounded like the weatherman. She made a fist and hit her throat. Which only made her cough. *Say something!* But the only thing her brain could come up with was: *How* you *doin'*? *No!* thought Aru. *Definitely* do not *say that.* This was what she got for marathoning *Friends.* Aru smiled. And then she opened her mouth. "I know where you live!"

Aiden stared at her. She stared at him.

"You *what*?"

"I . . . um . . . demons. Good-bye."

She had never run home so fast in her life.

FORTY-THREE:
WHY, WHY, WHY?
STUPID WORDS

"You didn't . . ." said Mini.

This was the fifth time Mini had said this.

"Mini, if you say that again —"

A cackle from Urvashi made Aru shut up.

On Fridays, their first class was traditional dance (specifically, *bharatnatyam*) and etiquette with Urvashi. But Aru had arrived looking so shaken after her encounter with Aiden that Urvashi had demanded to know what happened.

When Aru had told her, Urvashi had laughed hard enough to cause a lightning storm. Several merchants from the Night Bazaar had come to complain that she'd ruined their stock of raincoats (actual coats that shed rain). But the minute Urvashi had smiled at them and cooed, "What's the problem again?" they'd forgotten what they were going to say, and they went away dreamy-eyed.

Now Urvashi had called in Hanuman and

Boo and forced Aru to tell the story again. Hanuman hadn't laughed, but his mouth had twitched. Boo was still trying to pull himself together.

"I remember Arjuna being a lot more . . ." started Urvashi.

"Suave?" offered Boo.

"Charming?" chimed Hanuman.

"Good-looking?" suggested Mini.

"Mini!" said Aru.

"Sorry," she said, blushing.

"You know, in my day, you could just swoop in and take the person you liked," said Boo. "It's far more efficient than talking."

"I'm pretty sure that's called kidnapping," said Mini.

"It was romantic."

"It's still kidnapping."

Hanuman clapped. "Come, Pandavas, it's time for strategy lessons."

Pandavas. The word still sounded strange in Aru's head, especially because she knew that it wasn't going to stop with just her and Mini. The Sleeper was still out there, and as the danger grew, more Pandavas would be required. She had even gotten a glimpse of them in her vision. All girls. . . . So where were they?

Sighing, Aru took off the bells around her

ankles and handed them to Urvashi.

Urvashi patted Aru's head. "Don't worry, my dear. When I'm done with you, you will fell men with a laugh."

Aru didn't want to *kill* the guy. Just maybe talk to him?

Why was everything the worst?

As Aru and Mini left Urvashi, the Night Bazaar dance studio closed up behind them. Urvashi refused to rent space anywhere, because *I have an image to maintain, and I'm not going to put my feet on a floor that's been stained by other people's shadows.* Which meant that, three times a week, the sky of the Night Bazaar opened up to allow Urvashi to descend in a celestial blue lotus as big as the museum. When the girls finished their lesson, the petals of the lotus closed over Urvashi and she floated back to the heavens.

Hanuman's lessons were a lot more . . . rugged.

"This way," said the monkey-faced demigod, bounding ahead of them.

Aru and Mini trudged dutifully after him. Hanuman liked to use the terrain of the Night Bazaar. Today, he took them around the orchard of Dream Fruit and beneath an archway of gleaming silver feathers.

"Those feathers come from *chakora,* or

moon birds," said Hanuman. "A feather plucked from a moon bird will glow brightly, but only for a moment. If you wait until the feather is shed naturally, it will forever bring you light."

Sure enough, the feathered archway never seemed to dim.

On the other side of it, the landscape was steep and more treacherous. They peered down into a deep canyon with a wide river rushing through it. Far below, on the opposite bank, a shiny crown hovered in the air.

"Pandavas!" called Hanuman over the roar of the river.

Mini turned white. Aru remembered that her sister had a horrible fear of heights. Not of spiders, though she wasn't wild about spiders, either . . .

"Imagine that it's your duty to retrieve the crown," said Hanuman. "How would you get to it?"

"Find another way?" offered Mini.

"Trick the other side into bringing it over here?" suggested Aru.

Hanuman frowned. "Always choose the simplest route! Aru, you have a tendency to choose . . . complication over simplification."

"Or maybe I just don't want to drown?"

Mini nodded vigorously.

"In my day, I built a bridge. I called on my friends to help. We gathered rocks and threw them into the ocean so I could get across," said Hanuman.

"I don't have any friends like that," said Aru.

"Hey!" said Mini.

"*Besides you,* I mean."

"What about changing shape?" asked Hanuman. "Always consider how you might *adapt* to your surroundings rather than forcing your surroundings to adapt to *you.*"

"But . . . we can't change shape?" said Mini.

"Use your tail!" said Hanuman. His tail curled over his shoulder.

"We don't have tails." She stuck out her butt so he could see.

"Oh," said Hanuman. His tail went limp.

At that moment, an alarm went off. Hanuman tensed. Before, he'd been the height and build of an average man. At the sound of the alarm, he shot up in size, snatching up Aru and Mini in the process so that they could stand on his open hands.

"I'm gonna throw up," said Mini, crouching on Hanuman's palm.

"Whoa," said Aru. It took her a moment to get her bearings, but she had an incredible view of the entire Night Bazaar. It looked like thousands of cities were attached to it. From here, Aru could see the entrance line, which stretched into a bank of clouds. At security, the bull-headed raksha had been replaced by a raksha with the shell of a tortoise. She could even spot the brilliant jewel that was the Court of the Seasons.

The alarm blared once more.

The sky changed from the split colors of daytime and nighttime. Now it was a uniform black.

"Something has been stolen," said Hanuman, sniffing the air. "You must go to your homes immediately. I'll send word by Monday."

"Wait, what's been stolen?" asked Aru. She craned her neck over the side of Hanuman's hand, as if she could catch sight of a runaway thief. She felt bad for whoever had lost whatever it was. But at least she wasn't the only one who'd had the Worst Day Ever.

"It's something even the gods fear," said Hanuman darkly.

It took only three steps for Hanuman to cross from one end of the Night Bazaar to the other. He let Aru and Mini down near the stone door carved with elephants. The door had been created just for them when their moms had decided it was high time

458

the girls started their training.

"Be safe," said Hanuman. He patted their heads with the tip of his pinky (which was still big enough to almost crush them) and then strode off in the other direction.

"At least we have some free time?" said Mini.

"Yeah," said Aru.

But at what cost?

FORTY-FOUR: WOOF

Mini was lying upside down on Aru's bed.

It was a Saturday, the day after the entire Night Bazaar had panicked about something being stolen. Aru had checked the stone elephant's mouth every hour, but there hadn't been any news from Hanuman yet.

Boo was acting particularly nervous. He was probably still mad because the neighbor's cat had snuck up on him and stolen two of his tail feathers. Aru had watched him chase the poor feline down the sidewalk, shouting, "I AM A MIGHTY KING! YOU HAVE INSULTED MY HONOR!" But even his "vengeance" (he nipped the cat's tail and hid her food bowl) hadn't been enough to calm him down.

"Are you coming over tonight? My dad is making *pancit*!" said Mini excitedly. "It's my favorite."

Aru wanted to, but it was the last night before her mom was leaving to go on another archaeological dig. They still hadn't talked about what had happened between her and Aru's dad. Sometimes Aru could feel her mom attempting to get the words out before her shoulders slumped. It meant a lot that at least she was trying. Aru still didn't like it when her mom went away, but now they both tried harder to enjoy the time that they did have together.

"I'll call every day, and you'll have Sherrilyn, too," her mom had promised. "But you have to understand that I'm doing this for you."

"I know," Aru had said.

And she'd meant it. Her mom was insistent that somewhere out there, just waiting to be found, was an ancient object that might help them defeat the Sleeper once and for all.

"How do you know he won't come after you?" Aru had asked.

"Trust me, *chuckloo*," her mother had said, sighing. "I'm the last person he wants to see."

Aru knew how important it was for her mother to continue searching. She understood now that her mom wasn't only securing artifacts for the museum, but also trying to secure their future. She was looking for answers . . . and a way to fix her mistakes.

Still, it was hard for Aru to go to Mini's house and see how she was fussed over and coddled and always tucked in at night. . . .

Love looked different to everyone.

Boo perched on Aru's feet. "Why aren't you reading poetry or practicing war strategies? You've got to be diligent with your training!" he said.

"Boo, it's Saturday."

"The Sleeper is gone, but not defeated. Who knows what kind of trouble he's getting up to?" Boo said. Mini poked him with the Death Danda, laughing when his feathers ruffled and he hooted like an angry owl. "Fiendish child!"

Boo preened himself, taking dramatic pauses to glare at them every now and then. "He's called the Sleeper for a reason. It could be a long time before you hear from him again, that is how well he hides. But you *will* hear from him again. Until then, other beings, darker and more dangerous than the ones you faced, will come out and try to test their strength."

"Killjoy," muttered Mini.

Aru rubbed her shoulder. It was still sore from their last training exercise. And she was pretty sure Hanuman had sprained her neck just by patting her head.

"Can I live? It's Saturday!" complained

Aru, frustrated.

"You won't if you don't take this seriously!"

"We *are* taking this seriously!" said Aru. "In the stories, the Pandava brothers partied half the time and fought the other half. I'm just keeping with tradition." She turned to Mini. "I can't come over today, but how about tomorrow? Should I bring Twizzlers or Twix bars?"

"Twizzlers," said Mini.

"Absolutely ungrateful —" started Boo.

This was his favorite speech. Aru almost had it memorized. *Ungrateful children! The gods would be ashamed to see that this is how you choose to apply yourselves!*

But just then, there was a howl outside the museum.

Mini bolted upright. "Did you hear that?"

The girls ran to the window. Boo fluttered after them. Since it was December, Aru had to rub some frost off the latch in order to open it. Aru leaned out, scanning the street.

On the sidewalk, a massive wolf paced restlessly. It was carrying something in its mouth: a heavy golden bow and arrow. No passersby on the sidewalk took any notice.

Aru had a bad feeling about that bow and arrow. It glowed with its own light, the way Dee Dee and Vajra did. Was it a celestial weapon?

"Um, hello?" called Mini. "Giant wolf!"

"Why are we the only ones that can see it?" asked Aru. "Should we go down?"

Vajra flew into her hand, shifting between knife and sword and arrow. Not that Aru could do anything with any of those weapons.

"What's it holding?" asked Mini.

Right before their eyes, the wolf changed shape. A blue light burst and crackled all around it. The next instant, it became a girl. She was taller than any guy in Aru's class, but still looked about twelve years old. She had hazel eyes, tan skin, and long brown hair. She clutched the bow.

"That's not good," said Mini.

The girl paused, sniffing the air. Was she smelling . . . *them*?

A noise must have startled her, because she twitched and turned into a blue bird. She picked up the bow in her beak and flew off.

Downstairs, the stone elephant began to blare its warning siren. It was the Otherworld's call signal. A call for help.

Aru had the sneaking suspicion that the stolen item everyone was looking for just might be a golden bow.

"How could no one else have seen that?"

demanded Mini.

Aru had no idea. But then she looked across the street and spotted someone standing in the window: Aiden. From his surprised expression, it was obvious he had observed the wolf-girl-bird, too.

But that didn't make any sense. Why would he be able to see something from the Otherworld? Aru frowned as she shut the window and pulled the drapes down.

"This should be entertaining," said Boo, chuckling.

"What's so funny?" asked Mini.

"Shouldn't we do something about her?" asked Aru. "Who was that?"

"That," said Boo, "was your sister."

Aru's eyebrows skated up her forehead. "WHAT?" she and Mini said at the same time.

"But she . . . she's a beast!" said Mini, shrinking.

"She's a *beast*," said Aru, admiringly.

"And she probably stole that!" said Mini. "She's a thief!"

"You know what they say," said Boo. "Can't choose your family."

Mini started knocking her head against the doorframe. "But we *just* finished a quest . . ." she moaned.

Aru looked beyond her, to the now empty

sidewalk and the near-wintry light. The world still smelled like almost-Christmas. There was a hint of frost in the air. But there was something else, too . . . a current of magic that Aru could feel singing through her veins.

Beside her, Mini had begun to tug at her hair. The Death Danda, as if it were matching her mood, hopped and danced, then turned from a purple compact into an imposing stick at the blink of an eye. As for Vajra, the lightning bolt had stayed silent. Waiting. Lately it had stopped assuming the form of a ball. It now preferred to take on the shape of a slim golden bracelet around her wrist.

Boo soared near the ceiling, gleefully shouting, "I told you so! This is why you need to do your homework! Evil strikes whenever it pleases!"

In spite of herself, Aru smiled.

She was Aru Shah.

A reincarnated Pandava. Daughter of the god of thunder.

She had her best friend at her side, a slightly deranged pigeon, and the Otherworld's knowledge to guide her. She could handle whatever came next.

"What are you thinking, Aru?" asked Mini.

Aru tapped Vajra at her wrist. The bracelet

turned into a gigantic bolt of lightning that stretched from the floor to ceiling.

"I'm thinking that we should start working on a battle cry."

"What about *AAAAAAHHHH-don't-kill-me*?" suggested Mini.

Aru frowned. Okay, maybe she wasn't 100 percent sure that they could handle whatever came next. But she was *kind of* sure.

Which was way better than last time.

GLOSSARY

Hiyo! I'd like to preface this glossary by saying that this is by no means exhaustive or attentive to the nuances of mythology. India is GINORMOUS, and these myths and legends vary from state to state. What you read here is merely a slice of what *I* understand from the stories *I* was told and the research *I* conducted. The wonderful thing about mythology is that its arms are wide enough to embrace many traditions from many regions. My hope is that this glossary gives you context for Aru and Mini's world, and perhaps nudges you to do some research of your own. ☺

Apsara (AHP-sah-rah) Apsaras are beautiful, heavenly dancers who entertain in the Court of the Heavens. They're often the wives of heavenly musicians. In Hindu myths, apsaras are usually sent on errands by Lord Indra to break the meditation of sages who are getting a little too powerful. It's pretty hard to keep meditating when a celestial nymph starts dancing in front of you. And if you scorn her affection (as Arjuna did in the Mahabharata), she might just curse you. Just sayin'.

Ashvins (Nasatya and Dasra) (OSH-vin, NUSS-uht-yuh, DUS-ruh) Twin horsemen gods who symbolize sunrise and sunset, and are considered the gods of medicine and healing. They're often depicted with the heads of horses. Thanks to the boon of Kunti (the mother of Arjuna, Yudhistira, Bhima, and Karna, who was blessed with the ability to call on any god to give her a son), the Ashvins became the fathers of Nakula and Sahadeva, the twin Pandavas, by King Pandu's second wife, Madri.

Astras (AHS-trahz) Supernatural weapons that are usually summoned into battle by a specific chant. There are all kinds of astras, like *Gada,* the mace of Lord Hanuman, which is like a giant hammer; or *Indraastra,* invoked by the god Indra, which brings a shower of arrows, much like Indra, the god of the weather, can summon "showers." Get it? Ha! Gods like irony. And violence.

Asura (AH-soo-rah) A sometimes good,

sometimes bad race of semidivine beings. They're most popularly known from the story about the churning of the ocean. You see, once upon a time the gods were not immortal. In order to attain the drink of immortality (*amrita*), they had to churn the Ocean of Milk. But . . . it's an ocean. So the gods needed help. And who did they call? You guessed it, the asuras. The asuras were promised a cut of the immortality. But the gods, obviously, did not want to share. Lord Vishnu, the supreme god, transformed into Mohini, an enchantress. Once the asuras and devas (divine ones) had churned the ocean, Mohini sneakily gave *all* the amrita to the devas. As one can imagine, the asuras were *not* happy.

Bharata (BAH-rah-tah) The Sanskrit name for the Indian subcontinent, named after the legendary emperor Bharata, who was an ancestor of the Pandavas.

Bharatnatyam (BAH-raht-naht-yum) An ancient, classical dance form that originated in South India. Yours truly studied bharatnatyam for ten years. (You can ask my kneecaps about it. . . . They're still angry with me.) Bharatnatyam is its own kind of storytelling. Oftentimes the choreography of the dance draws on episodes

471

from Hindu mythology. Bharatnatyam is frequently connected to Lord Shiva. One of Shiva's other names is Nataraja, which means "the Lord of Dance" and symbolizes dance as both a creative and destructive force.

Bollywood India's version of Hollywood. They produce tons of movies a year. You can always recognize a Bollywood movie, because somebody gets fake-slapped at least once, and every time a musical number starts, the setting changes *drastically*. (How did they start off dancing in the streets of India and end up in Switzerland by the end of the song?) One of Bollywood's most enduring celebrities is Shah Rukh Khan. (Yours truly did *not* have the most giant crush on him and keep his picture in her locker. . . . You have *no* proof, go away.)

Brahmasura (BRAH-mah-soo-rah) Once upon a time there was an asura who prayed long and hard to the god Shiva (Lord of Destruction, as you might recall). Shiva, pleased with the asura's austerities, granted him a boon, and this dude, real casually, BTW, asked for this: "ANYONE WHOSE HEAD I TOUCH WITH MY HAND GETS BURNED TO ASHES." I imagine their convo went like this:

Shiva: Why, though?

Brahmasura: ☺

Shiva: No, seriously, why? That's a horrible wish.

Brahmasura: ☺

Shiva: I . . . ugh. Okay. Fine. You will regret this! *shakes fist*

Brahmasura: ☺

Okay, so fast forward, and everyone hates Brahmasura and is scared of him, so Lord Vishnu has a solution. He changes form to Mohini, the beautiful enchantress. Brahmasura is like "OMG I love you," and Mohini's like "LOL, okay, let's dance first, and see if you can match me move for move," and Brahmasura is super excited and does the thing. Well, joke's on him, because when Mohini/Lord Vishnu puts her hand on her own head, Brahmasura imitates her. *BAM.* Turned into ashes. Let it be known to all ye mortals: don't underestimate what you might consider froufrou things, like dancing, because you might just end up a pile of ashes.

Chakora (CHUH-kor-uh) A mythical bird that is said to live off moonbeams. Imagine a really pretty chicken that shuns corn kernels in favor of moondust, which, to be honest, sounds way yummier anyway.

Chitrigupta (CHIT-rih-GOOP-tuh) The god

tasked with keeping records of each human's life. He's known for being very meticulous and is often credited with being the first person to start using letters. Before Chitrigupta arrived in the Underworld, the Dharma Raja (the god of the dead) kept getting overwhelmed with the number of people in his kingdom. Sometimes he'd get so confused, he'd send a good guy to hell and a bad dude to heaven. Whoops. That must've been awkward to explain. I wonder if they got freebies in the next life: *So sorry about that mix-up! Here! Enjoy a lifelong ten percent discount at any Pizza Hut of your choice.*

Danda (DAHN-duh) A giant punishing rod that is often considered the symbol of the Dharma Raja, the god of the dead.

Devas (DEH-vahz) The Sanskrit term for the race of gods.

Dharma (DAR-mah) Oof. This one is a doozy. The simplest way to explain *dharma* is that it means *duty.* (Sorry, I keep imagining the dog, Do, interjecting here with a barking laugh and shouting, *Doo-tee, doo-tee!*) But it's not duty as in *this is your job,* but as in *this is the cosmically right way to live.*

Dharma Raja (DAR-mah RAH-jah) The Lord of Death and Justice, and the father of the oldest Pandava brother, Yudhistira. His mount is a water buffalo.

Diya (DEE-yuh) An oil lamp used in parts of South Asia, usually made of brass and placed in temples. Clay diyas are color-fully painted and used during Diwali, the Hindu Festival of Lights.

Gandhari (GUN-dar-ree) The powerful queen of Hastinapura. When she married the sightless king, Dhritrashtra, she chose to wear a blindfold in order to share his blindness. Only *once* did she let her blindfold drop: to see Duryodhana, her eldest son (and an enemy of the Pandava brothers). Had he been naked at the time, her gaze would've made him invincible. But the dude was modest and left his underwear on, thereby remaining vulnerable. (Sounds a bit like the story of Achilles, doesn't it?)

Ganesh (guh-NESH) The elephant-headed god worshipped as the remover of obstacles and the god of luck and new beginnings. His *vahana* (divine vehicle) is a mouse. There are lots of explanations given for why Ganesh has the head of an elephant. The story my grandmother told me is that his mother, Parvati, made him out of clay while her husband, Shiva (Lord of Destruction), was away. As Parvati is getting their home ready for Shiva's return, she tells Ganesh not to let anyone through the door. (Guests can be a nuisance.) So Ganesh, being a good kid, says "Okay!" When Shiva strides up to the door, shouting, "Honeyyyy, I'm hooooome!" Ganesh and Shiva look at each other, frown, and at the same time say, "And just who do you think *you* are?" Keep in mind, this is the first time father and son are meeting. Angry that he's not being let into his own house, Shiva lops off Ganesh's head. Which I can only imagine was supremely awkward for the family. To avoid a big fight with Parvati, Shiva goes out and grabs an elephant's head, sticks it on his son's body, and *bam,* now it's fine.

Gunghroo (GOON-groo) Anklets made of small bells strung together, worn by Indian dancers.

Halahala (HAL-lah-HAL-lah) When the gods and the demons churned the Ocean of Milk to get the nectar of immortality, *lots* of other stuff came out of the ocean. Some things were really good! Like the seven-headed horse that Indra claimed as his vahana. One of the not so great things was halahala, the most vicious poison in the world. Shiva saved the lives of the gods

476

and demons by drinking the poison when it spewed out of the ocean, which is why his throat is blue and why one of his names is Nilakantha, meaning *the one with the blue throat.*

Hanuman (HUH-noo-mahn) One of the main figures in the Indian epic the Ramayana, who was known for his devotion to the god-king Rama and Rama's wife, Sita. Hanuman is the son of Vayu, the god of the wind, and Anjana, an apsara. He had lots of mischievous exploits as a kid, including mistaking the sun for a mango and trying to eat it. There are still temples and shrines dedicated to Hanuman, and he's often worshipped by wrestlers because of his incredible strength. He's the half brother of Bhima, the second-oldest Pandava brother.

Indra (IN-druh) The king of heaven, and the god of thunder and lightning. He is the father of Arjuna, the third-oldest Pandava brother. His main weapon is Vajra, a lightning bolt. He has two vahanas: Airavata, the white elephant who spins clouds, and Uchchaihshravas, the seven-headed white horse. I've got a pretty good guess what his favorite color is. . . .

Jaani (JAH-nee) A term of endearment that means *life* or *sweetheart.*

Karma (KAR-mah) A philosophy that your actions affect what happens to you next. Imagine there's one last piece of chocolate cake at a bakery. You've just bought it for your mom, but some dude steals it while you're putting your change into your pocket. As he runs out the door cackling *"Mwahaha, the chocolate is mine,"* he slips on a banana peel and the cake box soars out of his hand. It lands, *unharmed,* on the floor by your feet. You would shake your head, say, "That's *karma*!" and take the cake. For a musical rendition of karma, listen to Justin Timberlake's "What Goes Around . . . Comes Around."

Kurekshetra (KOO-rook-SHET-rah) Kurekshetra is now known as a city in the state of Haryana, India. In the Hindu epic poem the Mahabharata, Kurekshetra is a region where the Mahabharata War was fought. It gets its name from King Kuru, the ancestor of both the Pandavas and their mortal enemies/cousins, the Kauravas.

Lakshmi (LUCK-shmee) The Hindu goddess of wealth and good fortune, and the consort (wife) of Vishnu, one of the three major Hindu deities. Her vahanas are an owl and an elephant, and she's often depicted in art as seated in an open lotus

478

blossom.

Mahabharata (MAH-hah-BAR-ah-tah) One of two Sanskrit epic poems of ancient India (the other being the Ramayana). It is an important source of information about the development of Hinduism between 400 BCE and 200 CE and tells the story of the struggle between two groups of cousins, the Kauravas and the Pandavas.

Mahabharata War The war fought between the Pandavas and the Kauravas over the throne of Hastinapura. Lots of ancient kingdoms were torn apart as they picked which side to support.

Makara (MA-kar-ah) A mythical creature that's usually depicted as half crocodile and half fish. Makara statues are often seen at temple entrances, because makaras are the guardians of thresholds. Ganga, the river goddess, uses a makara as her vahana.

Mayasura (MAI-ah-SOO-rah) The demon king and architect who built the Pandavas' Palace of Illusions.

Mehndi (MEN-dee) A form of temporary body art made from the powdered dry leaves of the henna plant. The designs are intricate and usually worn on the hands and feet during special occasions like

Hindu weddings and festivals. It has a distinct smell when it dries, like licorice and chocolate. (I *love* the smell!)

Naga (nagini, pl.) (NAG-uh, NAH-gee-nee) A group of serpentine beings who are magical, and, depending on the region in India, considered divine. Among the most famous nagini is Vasuki, one of the king serpents who was used as a rope when the gods and asuras churned the Ocean of Milk to get the elixir of life. Another is Uloopi, a naga princess who fell in love with Arjuna, married him, and used a magical gem to save his life.

Pandava brothers (Arjuna, Yudhistira, Bhima, Nakula, and Sahadeva) (PAN-dah-vah, ar-JOO-nah, yoo-diss-TEE-ruh, BEE-muh, nuh-KOO-luh, saw-hah-DAY-vuh) Demigod warrior princes, and the heroes of the epic Mahabharata poem. Arjuna, Yudhistira, and Bhima were born to Queen Kunti, the first wife of King Pandu. Nakula and Sahadeva were born to Queen Madri, the second wife of King Pandu.

Pranama (PRAH-nuh-mah) A bow to touch the feet of a respected person, e.g., a teacher, grandparent, or other elder. It makes family reunions particularly treacherous, because your back ends up hurting from having to bend down so often.

Raksha (RUCK-shaw) Rakshas (sometimes called rakshasas) are mythological beings, like demigods, who are sometimes good and sometimes bad. They are powerful sorcerers, and can change shape to take on any form.

Rama (RAH-mah) The hero of the epic poem the Ramayana. He was the seventh incarnation of the god Vishnu.

Ramayana (RAH-mah-YAWN-uh) One of two great Sanskrit epic poems (the other being the Mahabharata), it describes how the god-king Rama, aided by his brother and the monkey-faced demigod Hanuman, rescue Rama's wife, Sita, from the ten-headed demon king, Ravana.

Ritus (RIH-tooz) Seasons. There are typically six seasons in the Indian calendar: Spring (Vasanta), Summer (Grishma), Monsoon (Varsha), Autumn (Sharada), Pre-winter (Hemanta), and Winter (Shishira).

Salwar kameez (SAL-vahr kah-MEEZ) A traditional Indian outfit, basically translating to *pants and shirt.* (A little disappointing, I know.) A salwar kameez can be fancy or basic, depending on the occasion. Usually, the fancier the garment, the itchier it is to wear.

Samsara (SAHM-sahr-uh) The cycle of

death and rebirth.

Sanskrit (SAHN-skrit) An ancient language of India. Many Hindu scriptures and epic poems are written in Sanskrit.

Sari (SAH-ree) A garment worn by women in South Asia that is created by a length of silk intricately draped and tied around the body. Attempting to put one on unassisted usually results in tears. And they are very difficult to dance in.

Shakhuni (SHAW-koo-nee) One of the antagonists of the Mahabharata. Shakhuni was the king of Subala, and the brother of the blind queen, Gandhari. He is best known for orchestrating the infamous game of dice between the Pandavas and the Kauravas that led to the Pandavas' twelve-year exile and, ultimately, the epic war.

Sherwani (share-VAH-nee) A knee-length coat worn by men in South Asia.

Shiva (SHEE-vuh) One of the three main gods in the Hindu pantheon, often associated with destruction. He is also known as the Lord of Cosmic Dance. His consort is Parvati.

Soma (SO-muh) The drink of the gods.

Uchchaihshravas (OOCH-chai-SHRAH-vahs) A seven-headed flying horse created during the churning of the milk ocean,

the king of horses, a vahana of Indra.
Forget dragons, I want one of these.

Urvashi (OOR-vah-shee) A famous apsara,
considered the most beautiful of all the
apsaras. Her name literally means *she who
can control the hearts of others.* Girl also
had a *temper.* In the Mahabharata, when
Arjuna was chilling in heaven with his
dad, Indra, Urvashi made it known that
she thought he was pretty cute. But Arjuna wasn't having it. Instead, he respect-
fully called her *Mother,* because Urvashi
had once been the wife of King Purura-
vas, an ancestor of the Pandavas. Scorned,
Urvashi cursed him to lose his manhood
for a year. (Rude!) In that year, Arjuna
posed as a eunuch, took the name Brihan-
nala, and taught song and dance to the
princess of the kingdom of Virata.

Valmiki (VAHL-mee-kee) The sage revered
as the writer of the Ramayana. He earned
the name Valmiki ("born of an anthill")
after performing severe religious penances
for several years. During that time, large
anthills formed near him. Not sure why.
Building a nest around a human dude
does not seem like a sound housing decision. Maybe they thought he was a boulder. Must've been quite a shock when Valmiki finally opened his eyes and stood up.

("Boulder, how could you? Betrayal!")

Vayu (VAH-yoo) The god of the wind and the father of Bhima, the second-oldest Pandava brother. Vayu is also the father of Hanuman, the monkey-faced demigod. His mount is a gazelle.

If you made it to the end of this glossary, you deserve a high five. Sadly, I'm a little wary of those. (As Mini would say, "Germs! PLAGUE!") How about an elbow-bump instead? Ready? Three . . . two . . . one . . .

ABOUT THE AUTHOR

Roshani Chokshi is the author of the instant *New York Times* best-selling novel *The Star-Touched Queen* and its companion, *A Crown of Wishes*. She studied fairy tales in college, and she has a pet luck dragon that looks suspiciously like a Great Pyrenees dog. *Aru Shah and the End of Time*, her middle grade debut, was inspired by the stories her grandmother told her, as well as Roshani's all-consuming love for *Sailor Moon*. She lives in Georgia and says "y'all," but she doesn't really have a Southern accent, alas. For more information, visit her website, www.roshanichokshi.com, or follow her on Twitter@Roshani_Chokshi.

Rick Riordan, dubbed "storyteller of the gods" by *Publishers Weekly*, is the author of five *New York Times* #1 best-selling series, including Percy Jackson and the Olympians, which brings Greek mythology to life for contemporary readers. Millions of fans across the globe have enjoyed his fast-paced and funny quest adventures. The goal of Rick Riordan Presents is to publish highly entertaining books by authors from under-represented cultures and backgrounds, to allow them to tell their own stories inspired by the mythology, folklore, and culture of their heritage. Rick's Twitter handle is @camphalfblood.